A TASTE OF ITALIAN SUNSHINE

LEONIE MACK

B

Boldwood

First published in Great Britain in 2023 by Boldwood Books Ltd.

Copyright © Leonie Mack, 2023

Cover Design: Alice Moore Design

Cover Photography: Shutterstock

A CIP catalogue record for this book is available from the British Library.

Paperback ISBN 978-1-80415-844-9

Large Print ISBN 978-1-80415-843-2

Hardback ISBN 978-1-80415-842-5

Ebook ISBN 978-1-80415-846-3

Kindle ISBN 978-1-80415-845-6

Audio CD ISBN 978-1-80415-838-8

MP3 CD ISBN 978-1-80415-837-1

Digital audio download ISBN 9978-1-80415-839-5

Boldwood Books Ltd
23 Bowerdean Street
London SW6 3TN
www.boldwoodbooks.com

To my reading and writing friends in Anita Faulkner's
Chick Lit and Prosecco group – this one's for you!

1

Jenn hopped down from the bus with a sigh of relief, murmuring, 'Grazie,' as the driver plonked her suitcase down after her. She was sticky with sweat and exhausted from her convoluted journey from London, but she'd arrived at last – if you could call it arriving, when she appeared to be in the middle of nowhere. The air smelled faintly of mould and wood smoke with an unfortunate hint of cow.

The bus had just passed through a hamlet called Combai, with stone houses and little shops. The leafy hills and terracotta roofs could have come straight out of a travel brochure, but Jenn knew the reality was never so idyllic. The town had been tiny, with no supermarket, and the shops weren't even open in the afternoon. The Italian countryside didn't look so romantic after the hours she'd spent waiting for buses that day.

Even more inconvenient was the location of Jenn's accommodation, near this godforsaken bus stop. Stood at the side of a road with no footpath, clutching her enormous suitcase as cars zoomed by so fast she was worried about being pulled into their slipstream, she'd take the stop-start traffic on Oxford Street any day.

I can't do this...

She wanted to be driving one of the speeding cars, rather than sitting on buses with whining air conditioning and too many curious fellow passengers. She wanted to be anywhere but here.

Her phone rang and she connected the call in a hurry when she saw her boss's name flash up – Filippo Baretti, MW, Brampton Hotel Group. When she'd started working for him five years before, she'd been impressed by the 'Master of Wine' distinction, and now she had her own: Jenn Park, MW. Except she didn't feel very masterful at that moment.

'Filippo, hi!'

'Everything all right, Jenn? I expected to hear from you by now.' His voice was rich and deep, with a hint of a swoon-worthy Italian accent.

'Everything's fine,' she lied. 'I, uh, had a hold-up at

the hire car company, but I'm almost at the agriturismo.' When her boss had suggested she stay at an 'agriturismo', an Italian farmhouse bed and breakfast, it had sounded fashionable, but she suspected her head had been turned by the charming Italian. She should have realised anything with a hint of agriculture in the name was going to be outside her comfort zone. The 'turismo' part made her think of *Gran Turismo* and reminded her of the unfortunate situation with her driver's licence.

'You booked somewhere in the vineyards like I suggested? An agriturismo might be a bit simple for your tastes, but good for your first buying trip on your own. Make sure you take photos. I'm planning to organise an event when the new wine list is ready. "Prosecco with Miss Park". What do you think?' He chuckled.

I think it's a disaster.

He continued without waiting for her to respond. 'Did you ever expect you'd be our resident prosecco expert? After what you said to Cooper?' He laughed again and, if Jenn hadn't already been so hot in the face, she would have blushed.

She was distracted by a rumble behind her and stepped up onto the grassy shoulder, yanking her poor suitcase after her as she picked her way along the uneven ground.

'Cooper didn't have a very good selection,' she defended herself weakly. 'I'm sure I'll find *some* prosecco that I actually like.' Except she knew she wouldn't, and it was only partly to do with the wine.

'Ha! You're a tough nut, Jenn. My best pupil – you and your nose. Call me back tomorrow after your appointment with the Elisir di Cartizze winery. I've heard good things about it, but I'm deferring to your opinion on this. And don't let them put you off. Solidarity between the wineries up there can be annoying when you only want the best. Don't forget you hold the power. Try to make friends, get invited to dinner. You know what I say?'

'Never shake hands in farewell if you're still sober,' she mumbled. God, if only Filippo knew what would happen if she actually took his advice. And making friends might be easy for him, but not for Jenn. 'I'll keep you updated. I'll be back when I've finally found a decent prosecco. Hopefully it won't take too long.'

'Take your time. We'll pencil in the tasting evening for October, so you've got weeks, if you need them.'

Weeks, in this place with fields and tractors instead of convenient shops and reliable public transport. She glanced behind her in annoyance to find that the tractor she'd heard a moment ago appeared to be trailing her. 'Erm, I have to go Filippo. I'm... driving and there's a... tractor.' After all these lies, she could almost see her grandmother shaking her fist at Jenn from beyond the grave.

'Country drivers!' her boss grumbled. 'Ciao, bella! Look after that magic nose!'

Jenn scrunched up said nose as she ended the call. 'Magic nose' wasn't quite the compliment she hoped to get from him and 'ciao, bella' was a throwaway line he used all the time.

A sudden moaning made her jump in alarm and she stumbled, expecting to see a rabid cow on the loose. But it wasn't a cow. It was a tractor horn. The driver pressed it again and the mooing groan sounded afresh. She stopped and stared.

The big wheels rolled to a stop a foot from her suitcase and Jenn shaded her eyes to squint at the driver. He was a young man with tight, ripped jeans, a long-sleeved plaid shirt, unbuttoned over a grimy white vest, and a chunky baseball cap. He gave her a smile, his eyes gleaming as though he'd made a hilarious joke, instead of just pressing the dying-cow horn of his muddy tractor. Clamped between his teeth was an actual stalk of wheat.

When he doffed his cap in greeting and extracted the wheat stalk to call out something that was entirely vowels, Jenn asked herself if the heat was getting to her.

'Non capisco,' she said, turning away and continuing her march down the hill. She'd learned a little Italian in preparation and 'I don't understand' was a helpful phrase she'd practised with the aim of discouraging small talk with strangers. He called something after her which she still didn't understand, but she kept walking, sincerely hoping she was going the right way.

'English?' he tried. A dull thud and the sound of footsteps followed.

Jenn gritted her teeth and stopped. She was about to get the Asian tourist treatment. She could smell *that* a mile away. It was a shame her usual response – breaking into the convincing South London accent she'd perfected at secondary school – wouldn't work here. She turned back with a withering look.

The look died on her face when she took in the sight of him without his farm vehicle. He was very tall and rangy, all arms and legs – and shoulders. His muddy work boots were enormous. He'd pulled his cap off and his face was unexpectedly pale under the mess of dark brown hair, showing up the day's stubble of beard. He wore two black studs in his lobes. What kind of farmer was this? He was... kind of cute.

'I... can take you somewhere?' There was a rough timbre to his voice that was appealing, as though he'd laughed too much already in his life. But was he suggesting that she ride on the roof of the tractor, or in the muddy trailer?

'No, thank you,' she said firmly.

'It's very hot.'

'You don't say,' she muttered, tugging her suitcase back onto the road. She stepped carefully around an enormous pothole, thankful she'd packed her heels in the case and worn her sensible court shoes – although even they were feeling less sensible by the minute on the uneven surface in the extreme heat.

'If you're certain...'

'I'm certain.'

The footsteps retreated and the tractor came to life again with an unhealthy splutter and a grinding squeak that reminded her of scrap metal wreckers. It crunched past, making her skip to avoid the spots of mud it spat in her direction. The farmer waved a big hand at her and gave her that grin once more as he bumped on by. Was he just being friendly, or was he laughing at her? Surely the sight of visitors in the region wasn't that unusual.

To her dismay, the tractor turned at the next corner, exactly as she did a moment later. The farmer's idle whistling reached her ears as the smell of oil assailed her nose. She tramped after him, wishing the machine wasn't so damn slow. He was drawing ahead of her, but at the pace of a regimental parade, with the coughing engine as the drums.

When the tractor turned again, into the street where her agriturismo was located, her stomach dipped. Oh, God, she might have to see him again, *talk* to him. She was already tying herself up in knots about all the forced social interactions with her hostess she'd have to navigate, without adding the pleasantries required to placate strange farmers with long arms and twinkling eyes.

The tractor turned up a steep driveway and came to a stop outside a dilapidated barn. Jenn would have to walk right past. Even worse, when she checked her phone, she saw her destination was just beyond that barn. Tractor man was apparently her neighbour.

Drawing herself up, she increased her pace, puffing as the road climbed and ignoring the drips of sweat that dribbled down when she peeled her silk blouse from her chest. She heard the tractor door opening and closing, but ignored the farmer, crossing her fingers and hoping he wouldn't flag her down again. Just beyond his barn, she caught sight of the farm – her home for this assignment – and breathed a sigh of relief. She might have to endure farm smells and small talk, but it was certainly beautiful.

The large farmhouse was full of rustic charm, made of cream stone with crumbling mortar, gleaming in the late afternoon sun. Roses rioted over the front door, blooming in red and orange. Small stone buildings with clay roofs clustered around a cracked concrete courtyard with a rickety wrought-iron table and chairs under a faded awning. A pair of tall pines loomed over the farm and every patch of land was green with life – herbs and vegetables and flowers.

Beside the farm rose a steep slope planted with rows of vines and at the top stood a faded wooden crucifix with a park bench at the base.

'It's beautiful, no? Best country in the world,' the farmer called out from behind her.

Jenn only noticed her jaw had dropped when she snapped it shut again. He ambled in her direction and then he said the last thing she expected.

'The perfect place to finally find a "decent prosecco". Are you Jenn Park?'

2

Jenn froze. She'd put her foot in it, it seemed.

'You're staying at the Agriturismo Evangelista?'

Jenn tried not to let her wariness show. Why did he want to know?

'I'm Tiziano, but you can call me Tits.' He grinned and gave her a wink.

Surely he hadn't just said 'tits'? It had sounded more like teats – not that it mattered. She wasn't calling him anything mammary.

'Uh,' was all she managed in response.

'Is everything okay? Are you sure I can't help?'

'I'm fine,' she insisted. 'I don't need help. I need water and air conditioning and somewhere quiet to sit down.'

His smile slipped as he nodded slowly. 'Ciò, we'll... I'll see you around,' he said.

She managed a tight smile and continued on her way, releasing a deep, agitated breath. So much for comfortable anonymity. She'd been in this little hamlet for less than half an hour and was already beating herself up for her inability to have a normal conversation. Jenn glanced back to see Tiziano shoving the stalk of wheat back between his teeth and ambling up the steep drive to his tractor. She forced her eyes away, trying not to obsess over what had gone wrong in that conversation and what on earth she'd say to him the next time she saw him. She would look forward rather than back. She was here to select wines and not to make friends with farmers. She'd be back home before she knew it, comfortable in her London flat, where no one drove a tractor or took any interest in her at all.

* * *

The farmhouse might have been rustic and beautiful, but her room wasn't at all like a hotel room. It was a guest bedroom in the family house. The bed was a single, made of chunky, dark wood and covered in a red-and-gold bedspread that could have been woven in the

Renaissance. The ceiling was all dark wood, with enormous beams that could hold up the earth. Perhaps the overuse of the words 'rustic' and 'peasant style' in the listing should have rung warning bells.

Her hostess Filomena was also ancient. Her lined and weathered hand clutched an aluminium cane as she shuffled around and it had taken her about twenty minutes to climb the stairs. At one stage, Jenn had entered the '112' emergency number into her phone, her thumb hovering over the call button, just in case.

'The camera is simple, but I hope... commode,' Filomena said as she showed her the open window with its wooden shutters, the green paint peeling. No air conditioning, then, but Jenn consoled herself with a glance at the ceiling fan.

'Uh, camera?' And what did she mean by commode? Jenn didn't see an en-suite bathroom.

Filomena gestured around the room. 'La camera.'

With a stifled sigh of relief, Jenn realised Filomena was mistranslating an Italian word. Hopefully commode was simply another miscommunication, although the jug of water on the vanity didn't bode well.

The greatest shock came when Jenn asked for the Wi-Fi password, pointing to her phone and making wavy gestures with her fingers to pantomime the internet when the word 'Wi-Fi' didn't seem to register.

Filomena shook her head firmly and said, 'Senza internet,' and Jenn's vision tunnelled a little in panic, mentally tallying exorbitant costs for taxis *and* roaming charges.

She fumbled for her phone, stifling a panicked groan at the little symbol in the top corner. She didn't even have 4G. She might have had a fine sense of smell, but she felt completely blind without a data signal. How would she get anything done?

'You eat here tonight? I cook,' Filomena asked, distracting Jenn from her dismay. She remembered the surprisingly low room rate and the fact that some of these rural places made their money by charging a fortune for food. She had a daily allowance she couldn't exceed, but she didn't have much choice and when she would have to hike back to the sleepy town – or hitchhike on a tractor, she thought with distaste.

'Yes, thank you. I'll eat here tonight. How much will it cost?'

'Ohhhhh, I cook. I don't know cost.' She mumbled a few more words and Jenn understood only her reluctance to answer the question. She hoped she wouldn't have to stay here too long. Family BnBs weren't designed for introverts and Jenn already dreaded the inevitable moment when Filomena started thinking she was rude.

The older woman clasped Jenn's hand and patted her wrist. 'Alle otto. In cucina.' At least Jenn understood that: eight o'clock in the kitchen.

'Grazie,' Jenn managed to respond as Filomena shuffled out again, mercifully closing the door behind her. Jenn slumped against the enormous farmhouse wardrobe, bumping the back of her head with a satisfying thump.

She glanced grimly around the room. She would make this work. With luck, the tip Filippo had given her about Elisir di Cartizze, an exclusive organic winery in Valdobbiadene, would pay off and she'd be home in a week – two, maximum. And no one back in London needed to know she'd landed in Backwater, Treviso province, with no internet and no driver's licence.

She plonked onto the bed, kicking off her buckled shoes. It was stifling in the room. The heat reminded her of every other vineyard she'd ever visited, including her ill-fated internships during her degree. South-facing was all well and good until it was August. She peeled off her silk top and studied it critically. She suspected the classic Jil Sander blouse would never be the same. She hauled herself upright again to switch on the ceiling fan and it whirred to life, bringing a few minutes of relief before it clicked off again with a snap. The ancient clock radio turned off, too.

Great. Maybe this house had been wired in the First World War. Jenn took a few deep, controlled breaths and tried not to picture how strange she would look trying to mime the word 'fan' to Filomena.

A slight breeze trickled towards her through the rickety door in the corner of the room and she padded across the floorboards to investigate. She found a postage-stamp balcony with a rusty wrought-iron railing, just big enough for the single bowed chair. Her phone rang as soon as it caught a whiff of signal.

'I tried calling five times.'

'Hello to you, too, Umma.' It was just like her mother. She didn't call for weeks at a time and then she tried five times and panicked when Jenn didn't answer. 'I was travelling, remember?' She stepped out onto the balcony.

'Ah, yes. Buying champagne. Somewhere in Tuscany.'

'It's not—' She couldn't complete the sentence, not when she'd lifted her gaze and was suddenly blindsided by the view.

There was deep forest on one side and mountain on the other, with bright green hills bobbling between, criss-crossed with rows of vines, slanting and sloping. Pale stone houses punctuated the land-scape, along with a lonely chapel on a hill. A cluster of roofs at the foot of the mountain, with a church spire in the middle, must be the village of Combai.

The late afternoon sun glinted low over the land-scape, turning the vines golden. These were the Colline del Prosecco, the little clay hills that grew the finest glera grapes, to produce the only wines allowed to be designated Prosecco Superiore.

'It's not Tuscany. And it's not champagne,' she finished on a murmur.

'I ran a conference in Tuscany, once.'

'I remember,' Jenn said. 'That was the second time you sent me to stay in Seoul with Halmoni.'

'You're still making me feel guilty about me sending you to your grandmother?'

'I'm just saying! And it's not Tuscany. It's Veneto.'

'Is that where your boss is from? Filippo?'

Jenn groaned inwardly. Her mother couldn't remember where Jenn was, but she did note how much Jenn spoke about her handsome boss. 'No. He's from... further south.' He was from San Vitaliano, near Naples, but her mother didn't need to know that Jenn knew that. 'He's not on this trip, anyway. I have full responsibility.'

'You've worked hard enough for it. It's about time he recognised your abilities. You're ready for *his* job!'

Her highly successful mother meant well, but her comment only poked at all of Jenn's suddenly rampant doubts. If her mother could see inside Jenn's heart she'd be horrified. The things Jenn dreamed about were not fine wines and dollar signs.

'Thanks, Mum. Uh, sorry I missed your calls, but I have to go. I might not be contactable while I'm here. There's a lot to do.'

'I know, Eun-Jin-a. I just need to check you're okay sometimes.'

Jenn swallowed, picturing her mother looking up from a risk calculation and suddenly asking herself if her daughter was still alive. 'Well, have fun driving around in Tuscany. Lovely place, as far as I remember. But drive *safely*.'

'It's *not* Tuscany and—' Jenn cut herself off. 'I will. Love you, Umma.'

'Sa-rang-hae, Eun-Jin-a.'

Jenn smiled faintly as she ended the call. 'Sa-rang-hae' meant 'I love you', but it had always felt like a magic word to Jenn growing up, as it was one of the only things her mother said in Korean. Mary Park had been determined that her daughter's mother tongue would be English and she'd succeeded so well that

Jenn had felt her grandmother's wrath when she'd been sent to Seoul for the summers.

She took a deep breath to pull herself together. Now was not the time to be doubting her career or grumbling about her mother. She and her 'magic nose' had a job to do.

Jenn's keen sense of smell was already operating on overdrive in this unfamiliar environment. She was getting used to the hint of smoke in the air and the constant whiff of manure. The climbing roses were a sweetly fragrant variety. She picked up the tang of tomato stalks, savoury rosemary and the faint bitterness of a distant lavender bush. The cool air settling from the mountain was redolent with pine, zesty and alive.

And she caught a whiff of... was that beer?

The slap of flip-flops on concrete alerted her that someone was coming and then *he* appeared on the terrace below – tractor man. And if that wasn't bad enough, he was wandering around Jenn's farm-stay in his *underwear*. He wore boxers rather than briefs, thank goodness, although the boxers with their *Simpsons* theme and two mugs of Duff beer printed on the cheeks made her cringe.

Tiziano rubbed a hand over his hair and stretched with one arm, while a bottle of beer dangled from the fingers of his other hand. The rest of him was as pale as his face, except for the tracery of a couple of tattoos. He wasn't buff or ripped, but the lines of physical labour marked his arms and chest.

She licked her suddenly dry lips. She'd thought having a crush on her boss was inappropriate, but a farmer? For her? She would have put more effort into her love life in her twenties if she'd known her hormones would get so unpredictable in her thirties. Who was she kidding? Dating had always been a nightmare and it had only got worse as the stakes got higher with each birthday.

Tiziano turned his face up to the sun with a lazy smile and collapsed onto a sun lounger. He took a long slug of beer and burped.

Urgh, you have weird taste, girl, Jenn thought to herself, and looked away.

'Oh, ehilà, principessa!'

Jenn flushed as his nasal accent reached her, but thank God he hadn't caught her staring. She was about to ask him not to call her 'principessa', when he continued.

'You found the place with cellphone rec—'

She glanced down to see why he'd cut himself off and found him blinking and looking everywhere except at her. With a rush of mortification and a desperate – and futile – grab for modesty, she realised she was standing out on her balcony in her bra. She threw herself back inside, slamming the door, as though narrowly escaping a serial killer. Sucking in heaving breaths, she buried her face in her hands and groaned.

She never wanted to see that man again.

3

Jenn's heels clicked on the stone steps as she made her way to the kitchen the following morning. She'd slept late after rolling around on the bouncy mattress, freaked out by the heaviness of the silence. Squawking birds had then woken her at the crack of dawn and she'd forced herself back to sleep by sheer willpower. She'd never again complain about the proximity of her flat to a main road.

Was it too much to hope that Filomena would shuffle off to church and leave her to gulp down a little breakfast alone? The older woman seemed friendly enough, but she left out half of her consonants – in English *and* Italian – so Jenn had little hope of recognising even the few words she understood.

Jenn would put up with a lot for the home-cooked beetroot ravioli she'd eaten the night before, with tender pasta and tangy cheese, but she was worried she'd offended Filomena by repeatedly declining the offer of wine. Surely repeatedly offering was also rude? It had seemed like such a good idea to stay out among the vineyards in a real farmhouse, but she hadn't taken into account this awkward grey area where she felt like a guest, even though she was paying. She'd also assumed she'd have a car to be able to escape when she needed to.

The scent of coffee grew stronger, providing the necessary motivation for the last few steps. She even mustered a smile as she passed under the arched doorway – a smile that promptly died on her lips.

'Hey, bondì, buongiorno principessa.'

Her breath whooshed from her lungs. Had she upset the prosecco gods? Did a driving disqualification bring six weeks of bad luck?

Tiziano wore a threadbare T-shirt today, and another pair of jeans that flapped at the knees but his lack of sartorial elegance wasn't enough to stop her picturing him shirtless, pale skin reflecting the sunlight.

'Good morning,' Jenn croaked, coughing to cover the tightness in her throat. His gaze drifted over her white blouse and black trousers, the outfit finished with a pair of elegant black pumps. A twinkle in his eye suggested he could still picture her in her underwear, too. 'Where's Filomena?' she asked through gritted teeth.

'She gets the eggs.'

'Oh, really? Does she have to go far?' Surely Filomena didn't still drive a car. Jenn imagined the old woman shuffling down to Combai and thought about calling the emergency services again.

Tiziano had the nerve to burst out laughing. 'From the chickens. They're behind the house.'

Jenn's face flamed afresh. 'Of course,' she mumbled.

'Sorry for laughing.' The apology would have gone a long way towards making her feel better, except he kept talking. 'I'm a country boy and... you're a city girl.' And that sounded like a schmaltzy love song. 'You can laugh at me in the city, okay?'

'Okay,' was all she could think of to say in reply. She dreamed of getting up and walking out again. This whole agriturismo experience was her usual social overwhelm multiplied by a thousand.

'Coffee?'

'Yes, *please*.'

His grin was wide and he chuckled again as he

took the moka pot off the stove and poured three shots of espresso.

'Milk?'

'Do you have...?' She cut herself off when she'd finished thinking her sentence through. 'Almond milk' was probably an offensive term in these parts.

'Che cosa? Are you intolerant to lactose?'

'No, it's fine.'

He shrugged. 'The milk here comes from cows, not plants and trees.'

'I gathered that,' she said tightly. 'Thank you.' He poured milk and spoonfuls of foam from a French press into her cup and then he placed a slightly wonky cappuccino in front of her.

The silence stretched, when he sat down, too. Her mind raced, but produced nothing she could say to him. His grin faded and grew awkward, then he took a loud sip of his cappuccino and licked his lips.

A flash of silver caught Jenn's eye and she realised he had a tongue piercing – one of those metal bars straight through his tongue. She only noticed she was staring when he tilted his head and raised his eyebrows. She turned away, her cheeks hot.

Jenn sighed with relief when Filomena returned holding a basket of eggs that made Jenn wonder if there was an army somewhere she had to feed.

Filomena mumbled something and smacked Tiziano on the shoulder.

She turned to Jenn. 'Proper eggs,' she said carefully, with a satisfied smile. 'From proper chickens.'

'Our *own* chickens,' Tiziano explained with a smile. 'And our own eggs. Not proper. But fresher than your supermarket eggs.'

'Right,' Jenn replied.

'Tiziano is lunatic, but he can help you if you don't find me,' Filomena said, giving him another poke. Jenn choked on her milk foam, coughing into the back of her hand.

He cleared his throat loudly, poorly stifling a chuckle. 'She doesn't mean lunatic. She means lunatico – like temperamental, you know? I'm not a lunatic.'

Jenn coughed again. 'Okay,' was all she could think of to say.

'You sleep well?' Filomena asked as she cracked egg after egg into a frying pan. Perhaps Tiziano ate four dozen on a Sunday morning? She hoped he paid more than she did for his board.

'Yes, I slept well, thank you,' Jenn lied earnestly.

Her stomach rumbled at the sudden smell of butter in the pan, accompanied by eggs and salty meat, and Filomena nodded encouragingly.

'Avete fame – good, good. I make more.'

'No!' Jenn insisted in alarm, but Filomena didn't take any notice. Not long after, the table was stacked with plates of bread, cheese and meat and an enormous bowl of scrambled eggs. A crumbly dessert that looked like the lovechild of an apple crumble and a giant Hobnob followed a second later.

'Torta fregolotta,' Filomena said. 'It's fregola, bricioli. What in English, Tiziano?'

'Crumb cake,' he said as he broke it apart with his hands and dumped a piece into her bowl, dolloping mascarpone on top.

'Cake for breakfast?'

'Here in Veneto, you eat like a peasant,' he explained. He seemed to think that was a good thing.

He spread Nutella on his cake and wolfed it down. Piling his plate high with eggs, he grated parmesan on top and gave a satisfied groan when he shovelled in the first few bites as though he hadn't eaten in days.

'Are you a tenant here or something?' she blurted out.

'Or something.' He paused for half a second, before giving her that incorrigible grin. 'She's my grandma,' he admitted. 'I don't exactly pay rent.'

'Oh, I didn't realise. But I'm glad... someone's here to help with the BnB. It seems a bit much.' She added the last part under her breath, with a meaningful glance at Filomena, where she stood at the kitchen sink.

He shrugged as he carried on ploughing through the pile of eggs. 'It's a good deal. I help out when I have time and... I get Nonna's cooking.'

Tiziano and Filomena exchanged a few sentences in combative tones. She pinched him and gestured wildly, but he just laughed. Jenn had no idea how old he was but he looked young when he laughed.

'She's reminding me she doesn't approve of my illegal business out of her barn,' he explained, as though she'd asked.

'What?'

'She's joking.'

'I hope so.'

'She's my biggest customer.'

Jenn plonked her cappuccino down so hard it sloshed over the tablecloth. Filomena exclaimed something and fetched a cloth with surprising speed.

'I'm so sorry,' Jenn murmured, still seeing images of her hostess smoking joints or baking brownies with hash. What was going on in this house? 'Um, I need to... do some work.' She stood suddenly, her chair scraping on the terracotta flagstones.

'On Sunday?'

'Yes, I have an important meeting at a winery this afternoon. If it goes well, I might not have to stay very long...' She coughed to clear her throat. 'Not that—' She cursed under her breath. Why should she even care what this country-bumpkin drug dealer thought of her?

Tiziano stood, too, unfolding himself to his full height. 'Work here at the table,' he said. 'I have to take Nonna to church anyway. Unless you need the internet. Then you have to go on the balcony.'

'Thank you. I— Er...'

'It's grappa,' he blurted out. 'The illegal business,' he explained after she blinked uncomprehendingly at him. 'I was joking. I distil grappa in the barn, just for friends and family.'

'Ohhh, I... That's not what I thought.'

His lips twitched as though he was incapable of fully stifling a smile. 'I could show you my set-up. This place is famous for prosecco, but it's the spiritual home of grappa, too. No Italian meal is complete without it.'

'I'll take your word for it. And... perhaps another time.' Seeing Tiziano's moonshine operation wasn't high on her bucket list.

'Allora, ehm...' He tripped on his chair and gave her another awkward smile as he helped Filomena up. He waved stiffly, his neck flushed. Jenn couldn't think why *he* was embarrassed. 'Se vedemo, as we say. See you later.'

'I might not be here. I have to go to my meeting later.'

He gave her a lazy salute. 'Buona fortuna.' *Good luck.* She was due a bit of that.

* * *

Sitting in the tractor after church, Tiziano couldn't stop brooding about the conversation at breakfast. He gave the clutch a satisfying stamp and shoved at the gear stick until the old tractor lurched into motion, but manhandling the old machine didn't help alleviate the lingering self-consciousness.

'Really suave, old man,' he muttered to himself. Asking a woman if she wanted to see his home distillery was a poor pick-up line, even by his low standards. Not that he was trying to pick her up. She was pretty, but clearly unimpressed with her surroundings – and with him. The idiot in him had asked her anyway.

He swung the tractor around the corner, heading for the main road. He had to help his mate move a wood pile and then take Nonna down the valley for family lunch. But in the afternoon, he'd go fishing.

Did Jenn Park like fish? Imagine if he caught a good trout. She'd... probably look disgusted. Puh, he was supposed to be thinking about something else.

He tipped his head up to the bright blue sky, criss-crossed by wisps of clouds, and chuckled to himself. It was a good day, a good year. The vines were heavy with bunches; the tractor would be busy with the harvest in a month – as would his hands. In the meantime, it was August. The trout might be lazy, but he could be, too.

The engine rattled and coughed as he puttered through the village, nodding and waving as he went. The air was just beginning to swell with heat as the sun beat back the fresh mountain air that descended every evening from Monte Cesen. The forested mountain massif was a familiar presence at his back. He might have grown up on the lower plains, but the mountain had always been there – and his grandparent's farmhouse in the hills had always been his refuge.

Life was good, and he knew how much of a miracle that was.

The old men were still lingering in the churchyard as he turned onto the main road. Hanging from a wrought-iron balcony, the usual pair of faded flags – the red-and-gold lion of Veneto and the blue-and-white of the province of Treviso – rippled in the barely discernible breeze. Everything was in its usual place – except he thought he saw Jenn Park standing at the bus stop.

'Insemenìo,' he said under his breath. But calling himself an idiot didn't help. He wasn't imagining her there. It wasn't a mirage of a pretty, black-haired woman in heels standing in the little bus shelter with a ferocious expression on her face. He heaved the tractor into neutral and studied that impressive expression as he rolled to a stop.

'You,' she said so softly he almost didn't hear.

He'd never thought he was a masochist, but her bluntness made something fizz pleasantly inside him. 'Me,' he said with a grin. 'The bus doesn't go on Sundays.'

Panic flashed across her face. 'I was hoping it was just late.'

'How long have you been standing there?'

'Long enough.'

His grin stretched. It might be his new hobby, pricking her pride. 'Allora, jump in!' he said, holding out his hand. 'I'll take you where you need to go.'

She shook her head fiercely. 'I can't go in *that*. Surely there's a taxi company. I tried one number, but...'

'You expect a God-fearing taxi driver to answer the phone on a Sunday? You need to book in advance. Dai – come on.' He flicked his fingers at her. 'I'm your only choice,' he said, injecting a drop of doom into his tone.

'Where would I even sit?'

He patted the wheel guard beside him. 'I've got space. Come, travel in style – Italian countryside-style! What time is your meeting?'

She checked her smartwatch and then looked as though she wished she hadn't. 'In twenty minutes,' she groaned. 'In Valdo... Valdobbia...'

'Valdobbiadene,' he provided, stifling a smile. 'I'll get you there in nineteen and a half.' He extended his arm again, this time catching her eye. She lifted a hesitant hand and placed it haltingly in his. He closed his fingers around hers and tried not to enjoy it, which didn't work out too well.

He hauled her roughly into the cab and she scrambled to right herself, hands everywhere and her feet flailing for purchase. An elbow caught him in the stomach, making him grunt in pain.

But when he righted her, keeping one arm around her waist until he was certain she stood stable, everything else flew from his mind, except the thought that her face was even prettier up close.

He let her go as though he'd put his fingers in a

fire, popped the tractor back into gear and the vehicle jerked into motion. Jenn plonked onto the wheel guard with a squeak, clutching his shirt for balance, and he had to turn away to hide his grin. *Welcome to the countryside, Miss 'Decent Prosecco'*, he thought to himself, with no small measure of satisfaction.

PROSECCO AND PIAVE

An evening of wine and refreshments from the Conegliano-Valdobbiadene Hills in Veneto, Italy, with notes and a guided tasting from Jenn Park (MW), wine buyer at the Brampton Hotel Group

QUATTRO BREZZE PROSECCO DOCG EXTRA DRY:

With an excellent balance of acidity and sweetness, this confident, cheerful bubbly is the perfect aperitif to drink to celebrate food, family and the great joys in life. Fermented in tanks for forty days, this attractive straw-yellow coloured prosecco has lively perlage and hints of apples and wildflowers on the nose. The first sip is intensely fruity and invites another taste. On the tongue, the wine feels satisfyingly light and velvety and there is a surprising aftertaste of Mediterranean herbs, which also make this wine a good choice to accompany savoury mains with meat or even pizza.

4

Jenn questioned all of her life choices as they bumped and bounced and crawled their way into Valdobbiadene.

She'd been nervous about the meeting even before her latest screw-up, Filippo's years of advice raining down on her thoughts in an unintelligible downpour. Getting this winery to the negotiating table would be a coup that could set her up in her boss's good books for a long time. But she was painfully aware that, the more she wanted this, the more power she gave up from the hotel's negotiating position.

It didn't help that, despite her years of wine training, she couldn't be completely certain that the product was as good as everyone said. Her stupid, prodigious nose let her down when it came to sparkling wine.

Added to the confusion was now the overpowering sensory experience of travelling in this clunking hunk-of-junk on wheels, with a driver who really *wasn't* a hunk of anything, except he kind of was. He must have scrubbed himself clean for church. It should have been a relief, except his aftershave smelled so good, it was distracting – citrus and mountain herbs with subtle woody notes.

There was a faint musty tang in the tractor cab, which only served to remind her that Tiziano was often sweaty with hard work when he sat here. She also picked out a faint hint of cigarette smoke – not enough to suggest he was a regular smoker, but just enough to make her curious – and a little sick.

She couldn't afford to be curious – or distracted – but she was both. When they arrived, her legs were wobbly as she climbed down from the cab and gazed at the elegant winery with its sophisticated touches of contemporary architecture built seamlessly onto a rustic stone building.

The name, 'Elisir di Cartizze', was printed with stylised grape detailing on a subtle sign by the stone steps. The building was set up high, surveying the fluffy hills of vines that stretched in all directions. On one side, the ground dropped away steeply, tumbling into a bright green valley where lush, slightly unkempt vineyards were interspersed with sun-baked clusters of clay-roofed houses and the occasional stone rustico, crumbling in its own idyll.

'You okay?' She jumped at the sound of his voice behind her, and a friendly hand landed on her shoulder.

Her mouth was dry, but she had enough presence of mind to shake off the casual touch that was unexpectedly firm. He handed over her briefcase and she downed half her water in one go. Perhaps dehydration could explain the overload of her senses.

'Shall I wait for you?'

'No!' she quickly insisted. 'I'll be a while.' Hopefully a long while.

'Let me give you my number then. Call me when you're finished and I'll come and get you.'

She thrust her phone into his hands, glancing nervously at the building. She smoothed her clammy palms on her trousers.

'You look... nice,' Tiziano ventured.

She choked on a fatalistic snort of laughter. 'Thanks,' she said drily.

'What?' he said. 'I mean it.'

'No, you don't,' she insisted. 'You mean I look strange – out of place.' He wasn't wrong.

'No...' He seemed to reconsider his words. 'You look like a wine buyer. Good luck,' he said, managing to make 'wine buyer' sound like a bad thing. And why did he think she needed luck?

'You'd better go before they see you,' she urged. She had to find her composure and she certainly couldn't do that with him in the vicinity.

* * *

Jenn was halfway up the stone steps when, without warning, a bouncing ball of orange fluff accosted her. She jumped in alarm, which the little animal obviously interpreted as an invitation to play. It barked and scratched at her legs with blunt nails, leaving marks on her trousers. Jenn snatched up her briefcase, which only encouraged the dog further.

'Down?' she tried, before realising the animal wouldn't understand English. 'Shit,' she muttered, struggling to maintain her balance on the stairs as the dog continued to jump at her and bark in increasing alarm. 'Good dog?' She extended a hesitant hand and patted its head, but that only seemed to startle it.

'Spritz! *Spritz!*' an energetic woman in a simple, but effortlessly elegant linen dress called from the door of the winery. She rushed over. 'I'm so sorry. He's not normally so excited. I think he likes you.'

Jenn glanced down at the velvety snout and big brown eyes and the dog growled, low and full of menace.

'Or... maybe not,' the woman said, taking the dog's collar and extending a hand. 'I'm Valentina Costa. You must be Jenn Park. And this is Spritz.' The dog growled again as Jenn slipped past slowly, careful not to come too close to the bared teeth. 'He'll calm down, I'm sure. Come. I'll show you to the cantina.'

Far from the wheeler-dealing she was used to, Jenn's visit to Elisir di Cartizze was informal – and punctuated by growls and barks from the dog who had decided Jenn didn't belong in his territory. But Valentina, the daughter of the winery's patriarch, was all charm and warmth. She welcomed Jenn like a friend, instead of a buyer, and presented the family's wines with straightforwardness and enthusiasm – and complete honesty.

If one of their wine styles was simple, she described it as simple. One was sweeter and she didn't dress that up as anything except a matter of personal taste. It was nothing like the tastings Jenn had done in other historic wineries, where the winemakers were full of glowing adjectives, superiority and inscrutable smiles.

Valentina might have been open and friendly, but her wines still made Jenn's eyes water as the carbon dioxide bubbles wreaked havoc on her nerve endings. What sparkling wine enthusiasts called 'perlage' Jenn called 'a pain in the nose'. With deep breaths through her mouth, Jenn thought she got through the tastings tolerably well, but Valentina was also honest about the winery's wariness of large contracts, which was a bigger obstacle to Jenn's mission and something she had no idea how to combat. Valentina even suggested Jenn visit other wineries.

'This isn't something we will rush into,' Valentina reiterated as Jenn covered her mouth with her hand and discreetly spat the fifth prosecco into the spittoon. 'We're a small producer and, although you've made your case very well, this would be a big step for us and we have our own business plans.'

Between the paw marks on her trousers, her stinging nose and the unexpected friendliness, Jenn's nerves were wound up so tightly she had no idea what to say. 'I understand,' she managed. Her eyes were watering and she needed to sneeze. 'Ah-ah-I'll come back and see you again when you've had a chance t-to look through our proposal, a-although this is only our first position, o-of course.'

'Of course.' Valentina accompanied her to the door. 'Although with the vendéma, the harvest, approaching, I can't make any promises. Perhaps you could stay through the harvest – see the area at its busiest and really get to know the community, if you're determined to find the *best* prosecco, as you say.'

The dog barked, as though retracting Valentina's gracious invitation, and scratched her leg again.

'I'm sure you'd meet any number of producers willing to work with you.'

Valentina's kind words still stung Jenn with a prick of failure. Filippo would probably have leaned on her harder, talked about all the money to be made, but Valentina didn't seem interested in earning money and the dog clearly wanted her gone. Jenn wasn't brave enough to brush him off, so she simply staggered, holding her briefcase high, as she continued the conversation. 'I-I'm sure you're right.'

Jenn stumbled down the stone steps of the winery to the car park, just as dazed as she'd been when she'd stumbled up them nearly an hour ago. To her horror,

Valentina and Spritz followed her. There were a handful of cars parked so Jenn catalogued them frantically, wondering if she should pretend one of them was hers. She could not imagine explaining that she'd lost her licence and arrived at their lovely winery on a musty tractor. Even the dog wouldn't take her seriously after that.

She raised her chin and was about to offer a confident farewell and pretend she was walking to her car, when a distant rumbling sent unease through her and set the dog off again. As the sound grew louder, Jenn braced herself for more awkward conversation. Valentina strode curiously to the bottom of the driveway and peered down the lane, holding back the barking Spritz.

Jenn's face flamed when the old blue tractor puffed into view, climbing the steep drive with a roar of the engine and rolling to a stop. Tiziano leapt down from the cab with a broad grin, giving Spritz a thorough rub in greeting while the dog preened and whined in ecstasy.

'Bravo cagnolino,' Tiziano crooned, leaning down to offer the dog his cheek for a lick. Jenn's jaw dropped, cutting off her attempt to offer a feeble explanation to Valentina to preserve what professionalism she could.

But before she could say a word, the problem was taken out of her hands.

'Tiziano Lucchetta!' Valentina called out, her tone fond. 'Quanto tempo! You've been avoiding me.' She lifted her arms and he hugged her warmly, pressing kisses to both cheeks.

'Not avoiding you. Just busy.'

'Busy! Lots of appointments with your fishing rod, you mean?'

He opened his hands in a gesture of innocence that looked too well-practised. A lively conversation followed, full of exclamations and affectionate touches and so much history that Jenn wouldn't have known what to say, even if she'd understood all of the Italian. He gestured to Jenn and Valentina turned back to her.

'I didn't know you were staying with Filomena. Is her cooking still as good as it used to be?' The look she gave Tiziano was brimming with suggestion. 'Come in for lunch – both of you. Me pare has been trying to catch you,' she said, poking Tiziano on the shoulder. She turned to Jenn. 'Tiziano is the grape whisperer. Everyone wants him to commit during the harvest. He's very good with his hands,' she said with a chuckle. Dropping her voice, she continued with a conspiratorial smile, 'He has the same reputation with women, if you know what I mean.' Jenn really didn't want to know what she meant.

'Don't listen to Vale,' Tiziano said with an eye roll, but his cheeks were pink. Spritz was still rubbing against his leg as though he were the Messiah.

'Just don't let Tiziano distract you with his grappa. How is the home distillery going?' Valentina asked with a wink at him.

'It hasn't sent anyone to hospital, yet,' he responded drily.

Jenn tried not to overthink the invitation to lunch, but the smudges between business and pleasure made it particularly difficult for her to read the situation, when Valentina bypassed the shop and led them to the rambling stone house behind. The dog continued to nip at her heels, making her trip. He could probably sense her unease.

An older man who Jenn assumed was the founder of the company, Giuseppe, looked less than formal in his socks and Birkenstocks, but he didn't seem to question why Jenn was there for Sunday lunch.

A warm, rich scent hung in the air, but she struggled to identify anything other than garlic. The persistent buzz in her nose made her feel blind, on top of the deep uncertainty about what was expected of her in this social situation. She dabbed at her eyes as

Valentina showed them to a cosy dining room with exposed brick and wood accents.

'Are you okay?' Tiziano asked softly as he took a seat next to her and she nodded fiercely, annoyed that he'd asked *again*. She watched in dismay as Giuseppe popped a cork and poured Prosecco into four white wine glasses. She could only hope they wouldn't notice when she didn't finish hers.

Valentina brought in plates of risotto with a breezy smile and a joke about Tiziano's appetite. 'Never says no to a free meal, does Tiziano,' she said with a chuckle. 'You're lucky I always make too much.'

Jenn reached for the pepper for something to do with her hands, but realised her mistake as the powder swirled. Her beleaguered nose stung. Her vision blurred with tears. Although she turned away from the table, she felt every gaze on her as she gasped and gasped and finally let loose one almighty sneeze after another into her elbow.

A great lunch companion she'd turned out to be.

* * *

'Now promise me,' Valentina said as she kissed Tiziano's cheek, 'you'll drop everything and come to us when the grapes are ready.'

'I always do.'

'I might even buy some of your verdiso next year.'

He grinned. 'You never will.'

A sneeze made them both turn. Valentina stifled a smile. 'She is not what I expected from Filippo Baretti's pupil.'

'Who?'

'Oh, you wouldn't care. A big dog in the wine industry. Works for the Brampton Hotel Group.'

Even he had heard of Jenn's employer. 'Will you supply them?'

Valentina eyed him. 'What do you care? But Filippo Baretti hasn't deigned to visit himself. And did you see she didn't touch her glass at lunch? I don't know what to make of her.'

'She's harmless.'

'She's pretty. Haughty women are your type.'

He laughed her off, but saint heaven, she wasn't wrong. Jenn *was* pretty and very much his type – the type that led to his bomb site of a love life, which Valentina knew too much about for his comfort.

'Thank you for lunch,' Jenn said as she approached, her expression still a little pinched. The dog barked and Jenn jumped.

'Prego,' Valentina replied. 'You'll come and see us again soon? Remember what I said about the harvest.

There's no better way to get to know a terroir and its people than to stand on the hillside together and pick bunches. Giusto, Tiziano?'

'Right.'

'And you'll look over our proposal?' Jenn prompted. Valentina nodded graciously.

Tiziano kissed Valentina's cheek in farewell, roughed up Spritz one more time and gestured Jenn ahead of him in the direction of the tractor, as though it were a horse and carriage and he a footman. Only when they were rumbling back down in the direction of Valdobbiadene, did she let her shoulders droop. Her breath tickled his ear.

'Why didn't you tell me you know Valentina?'

'I didn't know it would make a difference.'

'Of course it makes a difference. You could have warned me that nobody wants to talk to an outsider. And you could have warned me there was a dog. Dogs *hate* me,' she muttered.

'You don't have to be an outsider.' He remembered her untouched wine glass, her clipped conversation. 'And Spritz just needs to get to know you.'

She snorted. 'What, so you're telling me you don't need to go back several generations to belong here? Several generations of my family takes me through four or five different countries – and some of the biggest cities in the world. I've never lived more than a mile from a Starbucks and you think I'm not an outsider here? You have to help me.'

'If you need a wood pile moved or corn or grapes picked – even tying radicchio, I can help. But buying wine is your thing, not mine.'

'You can get me an "in" with Valentina.'

'You have an "in"! She just invited you to come back. She invited you to join the harvest.'

'She was just putting me off. Can you imagine me helping with the harvest?'

Tiziano tried, he really did, but the laugh wouldn't stay down. He howled so loudly that the tractor swerved and she had to clutch his shoulders for balance 'Why is it so important?' he asked when he'd recovered from the mental image of Jenn in dirty old work boots picking grapes. 'There are lots of other producers and some of them sell very good wine at a price even you wouldn't complain about.'

'It's not all about price. It's about—'

'Finding a "decent prosecco" – I remember,' he said with a grin. 'Since cheap obviously means bad.'

She didn't seem to understand his joke. 'Why won't you help me? Is Valentina your ex-girlfriend? You certainly seem to have some kind of history.'

He liked the idea that she was jealous. She couldn't be, since she didn't even like him, but it gave him a little satisfaction to imagine she was. 'Not exactly an ex-girlfriend.'

'Oh,' she said after a moment. 'Well, she was certainly glad to see you. Anyway, the reason it's so important is that Elisir di Cartizze is the only winery I was specifically recommended. Do you know how many producers there are around here? Am I supposed to visit them all to discover the difference between sweet supermarket plonk and fine bubbly?'

'Sweet supermarket plonk?' he repeated slowly with a huff. Pinching his forehead, he asked himself how he could possibly help her when she'd arrived with opinions like these. 'You want me to help you so you don't have to stay very long or get to know anyone.'

'What does this have to do with getting to know anyone? I just want to buy wine!'

'Maybe we want to get to know the person who buys our wine.'

'Why?' she asked, charmingly bewildered.

'Oh, we're just proud, even of our sweet supermarket plonk,' he said with a wink.

Her first response was an inarticulate splutter. 'I apologise. I didn't...' He almost felt sorry for her. 'I realise prosecco is very popular and even the cheapest labels are enjoyable...'

'But not for you,' he finished for her.

'Yes, but it's not what you...' She peered at a sign as he turned off the main road. 'Wait, this isn't the way we came. Where are we going?'

5

'You're breaking up, Jenn! Can't you stand somewhere with phone signal?'

Didn't he think she would if she could? She was halfway up a bloody mountain, standing as far away as she dared from the four men who'd been discussing – or arguing about – how to coax an injured cow into a trailer for the past twenty minutes.

When Tiziano had explained that his friend had called, needing help to move a cow, she'd expected a quick visit to a farm on their way home. Instead, the tiny road they'd followed had climbed, and climbed. The stubborn cow was perched on the side of the mountain above Valdobbiadene, miles from anywhere.

What had he been thinking, that she'd muck in

and help? She could barely stand on the slope in these shoes, let alone tramp up it. Her favourite linen blend trousers had barely survived the dog. After dealing with a cow, they'd have to go straight in the bin.

'Phone signal is an ongoing issue I'm still resolving. But I don't have much to report. You were right. Elisir di Cartizze will need a more personal approach.' An approach that didn't involve using the words 'supermarket plonk' with a local, she thought with a grimace. Tiziano brought out the worst in her. 'I suspect the price isn't a problem, given the relative affordability of even the finest labels.'

Filippo chuckled. 'That's prosecco for you. We'll have to drag these producers into the finest categories ourselves. Take all the time you need. I know you. You'll find a way to reach them, even if it means becoming the godparent of their first child.'

Filippo's warm, deep tone prickled across her skin. *I know you*... Perhaps it wasn't wise to have a crush on her boss, but so few people would say they knew her well and his confidence in her abilities always turned her head.

Jenn's gaze strayed to the group of men who appeared to be hoping the cow would run for mercy to escape their raucous conversation. Tiziano held a bucket of feed in one hand and a can of beer in the other. The man next to him, who was apparently Tiziano's brother Matteo, had a dark moustache and streaks of grey in his brown hair. He had dark circles under his eyes and the air of a prisoner on day release, laughing desperately and sucking on his own beer. The other two men seemed more interested in snacks than moving the cow.

She'd been glad of the excuse of this phone call to cut short the pleasantries, which hadn't been at all pleasant between the language barrier and the nudges and winks in Tiziano's direction. With the ripped jeans, the beer and the goofy grin, he was an unlikely Don Juan, but she had to admit, whatever magnetism he had, she unfortunately felt it, too.

'Hopefully it won't take too much longer,' she murmured.

'You don't like the Italian countryside?' Filippo asked drily. 'Don't worry. I understand. And the closer you get to the Alps, the more miserable the people are.' In that instant, Tiziano roared with laughter and his brother punched him on the arm. 'I'll take you to Naples with me, next time. Show you the real Italy, where the wine is the tears of Christ himself.' She was incapable of replying as her heart stuttered in response. Naples with Filippo was something out of her wildest, most secret dreams, where she also pictured herself surrounded by contented children who played together and were never lonely.

A pair of warm hands closed around her shoulders and she jumped, clutching her chest. 'Tiziano!' she hissed. 'You scared me.' He squeezed her shoulders in apology, his thumbs brushing the back of her neck. She shivered. She must have been more strung out than she thought. She brushed his hands away and turned to him questioningly.

'We're going to have to try a rope. It's not safe to stand here. Do you want to sit in the Lamborghini?'

What Lamborghini?

'Who's *that*?' Filippo's stern voice came over the line.

'Nobody,' she said in a rush. 'I'll call you tomorrow to talk through my strategy.'

Crap, now she needed a strategy by tomorrow and the only idea she'd come up with was taking allergy meds before tasting – which probably wouldn't work because her tingling nose wasn't the only thing making her awkward. Plus, she didn't even know how she was supposed to reach most of her target wineries without investing in a pair of hiking shoes and a time machine.

She ended the call and found Tiziano regarding

her with an exaggerated pout. 'Nobody? After everything we've been through?'

'What we've been through was mostly the near-death experience of travelling in that bucket of bolts!' While squeezed up against his tall frame, trying not to wallow in the scent of him. She'd nearly died several times in his company – of embarrassment.

'That bucket of bolts is Italy's finest Lamborghini.'

Jenn snorted, thinking he was making a joke, until she saw the silver logo on the boxy engine. How fitting that the Lamborghinis around here were tractors.

He dropped his voice. 'There was also that time I saw you—'

'Please,' she stopped him urgently. 'The least you can do is be a gentleman and forget *everything*. I can assure you that I don't usually stand outside in my underwear.'

'I can't promise to forget, but I will sew my lips.' He winked. 'But don't worry. If you go sunbathing by the Piave on a Sunday, you can wear as little as you like.'

Her heart lolloped and her thoughts grew sluggish as she wondered what it would be like to have enough confidence to sunbathe topless, like an Italian woman. She froze when the rational part of her caught wind of what she was thinking.

Jenn lurched into motion, heading for the tractor. She felt the brush of his fingers at her back, but he must have picked up on the way she shrank away because he slowed his steps to create space between them, allowing her to hobble across the grass on her own. Her brain turned over, trying to work out how she'd got into this ludicrous position, navigating a pre-alpine landscape in heels.

She had to admit it was a spectacular landscape. The knobbly hills of vineyards were directly below, tucked between the mountain and a forested ridge. It looked as though the greens had been painted with care by a master artist, in thousands of shades, from the deep green of the pine forests to the bright tint of the summer vineyards. The Piave river curled across the distant plain, sparkling in twisting streams along its bed of white stone. Perhaps there were people down there right now, sunbathing, she thought drily.

The air up here – it was like nothing she'd ever breathed before. There was a healthy whiff of grass-fed cow, but it otherwise smelled of sunshine and crystalline freshness.

The tractor was parked on gravel just off what Tiziano optimistically called the road – a narrow strip of concrete. Jenn clambered into the cab, giving the levers a wide berth as she imagined the Lamborghini careening down the mountain because she'd nudged the brake with her knee. She settled gingerly into the pleather seat.

'Take a selfie,' Tiziano suggested with a grin.

'It's not really my style.'

'You're right. You need a beer.' He retrieved his can from under the dashboard and held it up in salute. He handed her the strong-smelling bag of snacks and a pocket knife before returning to the others.

She stared after him. 'Is it—' She nearly lost her nerve when he turned back in question. 'Is it safe? You won't get hurt, will you?' She pictured the cow's up-turned horns with a shudder.

He pressed a hand to his chest and gave her a grin that was at least three parts mocking. When he spoke, his voice was even rougher than usual. 'I promise, I will come back to you principessa.'

'I'm just worried about having to drive this beast back down!' she called after him.

'Don't worry! I will domesticate that beast when I'm finished with this one.'

She didn't want to watch, but she couldn't look away as Tiziano set the feed bucket in the waiting trailer and coiled a rope around his arm. His compe-tent movements were somehow soothing and she had to admit he'd been kind to her, despite his teasing. Once they roped the cow and tugged in earnest, it didn't take long to coax her into the waiting trailer. Afterwards, they stood around talking again, popping open more beers.

Tiziano gestured to her urgently and it took her too long to realise he wanted her to approach. She climbed out of the tractor with trepidation, confused when he kept waving at her.

'The food!' he shouted. Jenn wasn't sure if she was relieved or disappointed that they hadn't wanted her company, only the bag of cheese and meat. Jenn handed it to him, but he clamped a hand on her forearm before she could escape again.

'Try this.' He fished out something that looked like detritus from the forest floor, but was actually a thick sausage of salami. He flicked open the knife and neatly slit the mouldy casing. Cutting off a hunk in a move she was certain would remove his own skin, but somehow didn't, he held out a piece to her.

She took it gingerly, aware of all the gazes on her. The fragrance was already almost overpowering, but she couldn't stop herself from taking it in, identifying garlic and pepper, cinnamon and thyme over the hearty flavour of the pork. There was a sweet note she hadn't been expecting.

'It won't kill you,' joked one of Tiziano's friends.

'We don't have vegan eggs here, so you will have to get used to our simple tastes.'

'Simple tastes,' snickered the other friend and gave Tiziano a teasing shove.

'I like salami,' she insisted – at least she had on the few occasions she had eaten it. She nibbled curiously, the salt assailing her tongue, along with a savoury flavour that made her think of forests.

'She's having a salami degustazione,' Tiziano said in an amused tone, using the Italian word that was also used for wine tasting, which Jenn had made sure to learn. He cut off a hunk for himself, took a huge bite and chewed with his mouth open. 'This is sopressa, the taste of Veneto. I should have brought a prosecco salami for you to try in this fine outdoor restaurant. We have mucca stars, not Michelin stars,' he said with a snort. But he had to explain that 'mucca' meant cow and by the time she understood the joke, she struggled to muster even a fake laugh.

He passed the salami to his brother and retrieved a hunk of cheese, crumbling off a few pieces and holding them out to her on the flat of his palm. She stared, trying not to think of hygiene or the strange appeal of his capable hands with rough fingertips.

'That cheese could have come from her,' he said,

gesturing to the poor cow in the trailer. 'It's the drunk cheese – seasoned with the waste product from wine.'

'Prosecco salami, drunk cheese – wine really is everywhere around here.'

'Ah, but Tiziano prefers his grappa,' Matteo commented indulgently.

'So do you,' Tiziano shot back.

'Only because I get it for free!'

Tiziano flicked a piece of salami rind at his brother and received a glove in the face in return. 'Since you get it for free, maybe you shouldn't criticise.'

'And maybe you should get off your behind and get a job instead of relying on Nonna to feed you.'

'I have a job!'

'He has about a hundred jobs,' one of the other men pointed out. 'One of which involves making us free grappa.' He winked at Jenn. 'Don't worry, he's a bel toso – a good country boy.'

'Oh, I-I...' *have no idea what's going on or what you want me to say.* 'I haven't ever tasted grappa.'

That was very much the wrong thing to say.

DA LINO PROSECCO TRANQUILLO DOCG:

This fresh, dry white has only the slightest hint of CO_2 and an intense aroma of apples and white flowers. A more vibrant yellow than the more famous varieties, this tranquillo is smoother, but maintains all of the delicate lightness of a prosecco, which makes it an ideal accompaniment for fish. The highlight of this wine is the hint of bitter almond in the aftertaste, rounding out the fruit aromas and satisfying all areas of the palate.

6

'I'm a wine expert. I don't see why you're so outraged that I know nothing about spirits.'

'Wine is the poetry of the land and grappa is water – acquavite, the water of life.'

'I think I'd prefer actual water,' she muttered.

Tiziano ignored her and rummaged in his cupboards, certain he had a pack of dried bigoli back there somewhere. If he'd known he'd be cooking for a woman tonight, he would at least have bought pasta fresh – not that he had any chance of impressing Miss 'I think I'd prefer actual water'. He would cook for her out of stubborn Italian hospitality – and because Nonna was still at his parents' place. Hospitality, that was all, no matter what Matteo and the others had suggested. He didn't invite women here to impress them. Well, he hadn't invited a woman here for any reason in a long time.

It was a good thing he wasn't hoping to impress Jenn, because she was looking around his apartment with her nose turned up in faint disgust. True, it had been a shed for goats in a previous life, but it had everything he needed – *he* had everything he needed.

But he wished he'd had time to tidy up. He banged and crashed the saucepan as he boiled some water trying to keep Jenn's attention on him instead of allowing her gaze to wander to the mess of fishing gear by the TV or the pile of beer cans he'd stacked in a pattern by the sofa over a period of several weeks. Why hadn't he thrown them in the recycling like a normal person?

With the water on to boil, he popped the cork on a bottle of prosecco and poured two glasses.

'One second,' he apologised and legged it to the bathroom, swiping a towel off the floor and closing the door behind him. He grabbed the cleaner and sprayed and wiped with frantic hands. When he returned to the kitchen nook, covering his self-consciousness with a grin and rubbing his hands together, she was looking at him with an amused smile.

'Thank you for cleaning up.'

Heat rose up the back of his neck. 'It was... um...' He gave up.

'But do you mind if we close the bathroom door?'

'Certo, I'll do it.'

'Sorry, I...'

'No need to apologise. I've already made you travel in my bucket of bolts and eat from my hands. And this' – he gestured at the water on the boil – 'isn't the quality you expect.'

'You didn't need to feed me, so thank you,' she said when he returned from closing the bathroom door.

'I can't give you grappa without giving you a meal first. It's a digestivo.'

'Huh,' she said, as though his answer surprised her. 'I'm honestly not sure you should give me grappa at all,' she said with a sigh, her gaze moving everywhere around the room except to his face. She hadn't touched her prosecco. Was she really too proud to eat with him? He knew he wasn't anything special, but he'd suspected there was something else behind her haughtiness than just a sense of superiority. He was probably wrong.

He knew how irrational he could be where a woman he liked was concerned. And, despite that up-turned nose, he liked Jenn. He especially liked her as she was in this moment with her ponytail a mess and her blouse crushed. He grabbed his glass of wine and took a long sip.

'You don't have to stay. You can take the food to your room. Or I can take you back to the village to an osteria if you'd prefer. I'm not trying to force my company on you or sell you my grappa. I'm not allowed to sell it. I'm just... I don't know.' He slugged more wine.

'It's not... I'm not... what you think,' she finally said, her words halting.

His gaze flew to hers. He flicked off the gas burner and plonked himself into the rickety chair opposite her. 'What do you mean?' he asked as gently as he could.

'You think I'm a princess – rude and stuck up.'

'No, I—' All she had to do was raise her eyebrows and he gave up on the platitude he'd been about to give. 'No one's perfect,' he said instead, taking a self-deprecating glance around the shed he called home. 'And I'm only offended because you don't like prosecco,' he joked.

She smiled and he struggled not to stare. 'It's not prosecco that's the problem, it's me. The same goes for your bathroom.'

'What? Prosecco belongs in my bathroom? It's not that bad.' He glanced at the bottle. 'This is made from my friend's best grapes.'

'I'm sure it's exquisite. But I wouldn't know. I can't taste it properly.'

'Can't?' he repeated thoughtfully.

She nodded. 'Can't. I find the bubbles completely overwhelming. It's a hypersensitivity to carbonation, which is all in my head, but knowing that doesn't help me stop feeling it. Did you know that's part of the attraction of carbonated drinks? The fizz stimulates a danger response in the human brain. Drinking prosecco is like watching an action film – and I hate those, too. All the bangs and flashes and the tension.'

'In a glass of prosecco?' he joked to cover the urge to tell her she was gorgeous when she was explaining things, her head tilted just so. 'But it's okay. You don't have to drink it. I'll get you something else.' He was about to jump up and find her a still wine, but there was more uncertainty knit into her expression and so he stayed where he was.

'It's why I'm so stressed about this trip. I feel... blind. Usually, I can pick out every note of the bouquet of every wine I drink, but sparkling wines... one sniff is overload and I... I'm not good with new people. I just wanted you to know it's not... exactly you.'

He sat up straighter in his chair and grabbed his own fist to stop himself from reaching for hers. It was sad, really, that the slightest bit of trust, the most luke-warm praise made his heart pound with possibilities.

'It was the same with your bathroom,' she added. 'I really do appreciate the thought, but the cleaning chemicals...' She covered her mouth and nose with her hand and grimaced. He'd made her gag. It wasn't a promising start.

'Are you serious you can pick out the notes in every wine you drink?'

She gave a casual nod. 'I pursued this career because my sense of smell gives me an advantage. My boss thinks I'm some kind of wonder, but it feels more like cheating, most of the time.'

Tiziano gave in and squeezed her hand, pulling his back when she glanced up in surprise. 'It's not cheating,' he assured her. He stood to turn the gas back on and retrieved a second wine bottle from the fridge.

'Maybe not, but I still can't tell Filippo that the magic doesn't work for sparkling wines. Like I can't tell him I'm taking the bus.' He waggled a finger at her. 'I mean the Lamborghini,' she conceded.

'Why can't you tell him?' he asked as he coaxed out the cork. She pursed her lips and didn't answer. 'What?' The longer he studied her, the pinker her cheeks became. 'Embarrassed? With me? No.' He poured her a glass of the second bottle and set it in front of her.

She peered at the wine. He chopped an onion, trying not to watch her too closely, but he was curious. She certainly looked the part of a fine wine expert, holding the stem of the glass lightly, tipping it, carefully cataloguing the movement of the liquid and then bringing the glass to her nose. She took a small sip, keeping the wine on her tongue for a moment. 'This is prosecco, right? You're tricking me.'

'It is prosecco tranquillo – fewer bubbles, no danger response.'

'Just glera,' she murmured, using the modern name for the grape variety. 'I'm finally tasting everything I read about prosecco. The green apple is very fresh. And it's so light and easy.'

'It wasn't a test,' he commented. 'You can just drink it.'

She blinked at him. 'I never just "drink" wine.'

'Maybe that's part of your problem.'

'I don't have a problem,' she insisted. He turned away from the pan, which was now sizzling with pancetta and cherry tomatoes, and gave her a pointed look. She slumped and reached for the wine. 'You're right, but actually I have several problems,' she mumbled and took a long sip. 'I've also been disqualified from driving and I'm in love with my boss,' she blurted out.

He nearly spilled the cup of grappa he'd been measuring for the sauce. Porca puttana, he should have taken the subtle hints that she wasn't interested in him. He knew he had no right to feel so disappointed about that development. She was only here for a few weeks. Except... He had the sudden urge to search for this Baretti guy on the internet to make sure her boss was a decent sort.

But the expression on her face was miserable and who would he help by growling about whether her boss loved her back? He swallowed the lump in his throat and forced a laugh.

'Let me guess: driving under the influence of alcohol?'

'No! That is one thing I'm very careful of – unlike some people.'

'Beer doesn't count,' he said with a shrug. 'Well then, what was it really? Speeding?' Her silent blush was all the answer he needed. 'Brava! I'm impressed.'

She eyed him. 'I got caught a couple of miles per hour over the limit twice. I wasn't drag racing on the motorway. And the third offence was talking on a mobile phone because my Bluetooth was updating and I had to take a work call. That's all, and now I'm in this stupid situation.' She took another slug of wine. God, he liked her even more as she shed her stiff spine.

'I can drive you, while you're here.' He grinned as she glanced at him in alarm.

'And what will you ask in return? Will I have to wrestle a cow? Or chop wood?'

'How about picking grapes? I need to thin the bunches again up here on our vines. Your little hands would be perfect.' She was looking truly worried, now. 'I'm joking, Jenn. When I'm free, I'm happy to take you wherever you need to go. I'll even promise to do it sober.'

'Are you... is that grappa you're putting in the sauce?'

'Haven't you realised I use grappa for pretty much everything? I wash with it, use it as aftershave. I'm pretty sure I could even put my stuff in the tractor for fuel.'

'You do not wash with it,' she said with a blink that struck him as oddly lazy. 'And you don't use it as aftershave.'

'You're very certain about that.'

She gave a big nod. 'Your aftershave is herbal, not fruity – except for that hint of lime.' She took a deep breath. 'Rosemary, and one of those woody scents.' A little sigh finished her sentence. Tiziano stared at her, his mouth hanging open, feeling hot for all sorts of reasons. *She's in love with someone else*, he reminded himself sternly, but it didn't help much.

'You can't identify the woody scent?' he teased lightly after he'd pulled himself together.

'I haven't trained in perfumes. But wine? Years and years and years of studying and learning and tasting. And I'm still not finished.'

'Being finished learning about wine sounds like being finished with life.'

She squinted at him. 'You don't really think wine is life do you?'

'You don't?' he countered as he tossed the bigoli in the simple sauce.

'Of course not,' she said thoughtfully.

He swung open the window to grab some herbs from the sill. Jenn drifted after him, peering at the plants, her nose forward. He held some leaves out to her. 'Basil.'

She nodded. 'And sage, oregano and... lemon mint?' She brushed her fingertips over the leaves and then held them to her nose. He couldn't tear his gaze away. Sniffing curiously at the basil he'd picked, he wondered what it was like for her to be constantly overpowered by smells.

'What's life for you, then, if not wine?' he

prompted, drawing her back to the table with a light brush of his hand on her back.

'Home, I guess. Family. Work.'

'That, I can agree with – except the "work" part.' He carefully arranged sprigs of basil on the pasta and settled a plate in front of her with a flourish, as though he was serving her at a fine restaurant rather than plonking a plate of pasta onto his scratched wooden table. 'Buon appetito,' he muttered, handing her the pepper grinder, followed by a box of tissues, making her laugh. 'You have a big family?'

'Not at all,' she said glumly. 'I'm an only child. Which is maybe why...' She studied her fork as she wound a few noodles around it.

'Why what?'

'Why... *everything.*' She chewed a mouthful of pasta and he was unreasonably disappointed that she didn't moan in pleasure, as though his grappa was the elixir she'd been looking for her entire life. She washed it down with another sip of wine. 'I can't... I don't admit this very often, but I want... my own family,' she declared with an enormous sigh.

And all the sparks inside him went out.

7

Jenn was dimly aware of what was happening, but the strain of the past few days and the eminently drinkable wine encouraged her to let it happen, like a stone rolling over her life that she was too tired to run from.

Tiziano surely didn't want to know any of this stuff, but that didn't stop her from blurting it all out as the alcohol affected her – strongly, as usual. She kept thinking about his pasty body and those ridiculous boxer shorts, his wicked grin when he noticed her on her balcony less than properly dressed herself – and that comment: 'Embarrassed? With me?'

The food certainly wasn't gourmet, but the hearty flavours of the pancetta and onion, the tang of the tomatoes and the grappa, enveloped her in a warm hug – or perhaps it was just the wine making her thoughts thick and her tongue loose.

'It's not fashionable to want kids more than anything else. And... don't get me wrong, I want a career. I've worked so hard for this and I do... I'm good at it – although it might not look like it to you. But I'm an only child. It was just my mum and me. This family thing that's normal to other people is something I've never had. It scares me that maybe I never will. How old do you think I am?' she asked, just drunk enough not to take it back again.

Tiziano's concerned expression swam in front of her and she struggled to stabilise the image. It was strange. The longer she looked at him, the more attractive his face appeared – his flecked green eyes, cheeks shaded with stubble, his lined forehead that made her question her own assumptions about his age.

'You can't be too young, if you're a wine expert. I know that takes years. So...' He licked his lips, flashing that bar of metal in his tongue and rousing her curiosity. 'Thirty-one?' he guessed.

'Thirty-four,' she declared. 'And how many long-term relationships do you think I've had? None!' she rushed on. Trapped somewhere inside the alcohol haze, her usual self was screaming at her to shut up, but she was so tired and so sick of people judging her

– of judging herself. 'Relationships have always just been... wrong,' she continued glumly. 'And the times I thought it would happen... well, I was way off base. I know that I'm... I can be too direct and I can't always work out what people really mean when they say things, but... isn't there supposed to be someone out there for everyone?'

'There'll be someone out there for you. I wouldn't worry about it.'

'But I want kids – definitely more than one. What if it takes years? You know next year I will already be known as a "geriatric mother"? My mum was thirty-six when she had me and there were so many complications.'

'What if it goes well, happens straight away?' His flat tone rang bells somewhere, but she didn't have the focus to reflect on it. 'I've only had one relationship, and I'm not much younger than you.'

'Yeah, but look at your life. You're happy sowing wild oats and your sperm won't go out of date for years, yet!'

He snorted his wine, which must have hurt, because he was drinking her untouched glass of prosecco spumante and that stuff bubbled. She handed him the tissue box, but he waved her away, coughing and clutching at his chest.

'I'm...' He paused to clear his throat. 'I'm starting to see why you have problems on dates.' Heat rushed to her cheeks, but he was smiling at her in such amusement that she couldn't feel the sting of his words. 'Not that this is a date,' he added.

'Noooo,' she agreed. 'This is an illicit grappa tasting.' The word 'illicit' came out more like 'illllll-thit', even though she'd used all her concentration on the operation of her mouth and tongue.

'Bene,' he said, emptying his glass and slapping the table with his other hand. 'I nearly forgot.' He hauled himself out of his chair and retrieved an array of half-empty bottles from a cupboard. She couldn't help comparing him to Filippo as she watched him. Where her boss was elegant and expressive, Tiziano was careless and emphatic.

Why was she even comparing? And she certainly shouldn't be wondering what would happen at the end of tonight; whether he might try to kiss her and if she would let him.

Instead of the bottom-heavy shot glass she'd expected, he set a delicate, tulip-shaped flute in front of her and tugged off the lid of a suspicious-looking bottle. The scent of alcohol hit her nose and she shrank back. 'Wait,' he said softly, and poured the clear liquid into the glasses with something like reverence.

'You did say that nobody has been sent to hospital because of your grappa, didn't you?'

'Yes. Not yet.'

'What do I—'

'Shh,' he said sharply. 'It's resting.'

She snorted a giggle. 'It's your baby, is it?'

'The only baby for me.'

'You don't want kids?' she asked, squinting at him.

'Can you imagine me as a father? I'll let my sperm go out of date, thank you, and waste my time and passion on distilling the perfect grappa. I'll leave the parenting to you. You'll be an amazing mother one day,' he said with a wink, 'with ten kids, all proud and honest and frank. Ecco qua – you should call your first child Franco!'

Although she suspected he was just trying to make her feel better, it worked. She propped herself up on her elbows, leaning over the table to smile up into his face. He might be mildly infuriating, but he was a good guy. His smile faltered and he snatched up his glass, taking a long sip.

She sniffed hers and almost gagged, but a moment later, a floral bouquet with a hint of honey floated through her sinuses. 'It smells like spring – soaked in alcohol,' she murmured. His grin encouraged her and she took a small sip. The burning sensation in her mouth was intense, but not unpleasant and the second palate was... beautifully complex. She took another sip, bigger this time.

Her thoughts were fuzzy, her senses thankfully dulled and the digestif went down far more smoothly than she expected.

'Wow,' she said, finding her glass empty. The warmth in her chest was exhilarating.

'I'll take that as a compliment.'

She nodded sluggishly. 'Pour another.'

'Are you serious? You don't have to drink it for my pride.'

She gestured to her glass again and he sloshed a little more in. She slugged half of it in one sip. She... glowed. Thank God no one was here to see her except her pasty farmer.

She felt *good*. She sat back in her chair and watched Tiziano fiddle with his glass. He wasn't quite in focus, but she could still appreciate his broad shoulders, hunched as usual. He was nobody's prince charming, but he had... charisma. No, not charisma. He had sex appeal. She didn't understand it, but she was certainly experiencing it.

'There's a... buzz,' she said, swaying lightly from side to side to experiment with the feeling that was something like vertigo.

'Jenn.' His voice reached her as though through a tunnel. 'Are you... drunk?'

'No,' she said firmly. 'I've only had a tiny bit.' At least she thought so.

His fingers brushed her jaw and she wrenched her eyes open to find him peering at her. She secretly liked the goofy smile, but with his brow low and his lips pursed in concern, she was drawn to him, even if the edges of his face wouldn't stay in focus.

'Think you'd better go back to Nonna's?' As he articulated the 'th', his tongue piercing made another flashing appearance. She stared at his mouth, ablaze with curiosity – or perhaps that was the flames of the grappa licking her good sense.

'What does it feel like?' She tilted her head and the fingers on her jaw dropped away. She licked her lips, still staring at his mouth.

'What?' he asked. His Adam's apple bobbed.

'Can you feel the piercing when you kiss? Would I?'

'I f-feel it,' he replied eventually. 'But I don't know...'

'Let's find out,' she whispered.

8

Tiziano hurried into the farmhouse the following morning, wiping the grease off his fingers with an old cloth. Was she awake, yet? Would she be suffering from a hangover? He would have brought a bottle of fernet with him if she'd been one of his mates – the nail to drive out the nail – but Jenn was not one of his mates.

He burst into the kitchen to find her helping Nonna with the dishes. She wore another combination of sleek trousers and low heels and her thick, straight hair had been pulled into a neat ponytail that tickled her shoulder blades. He couldn't decide if he was proud to see she'd recovered well from the mishap last night, or disappointed. He'd liked her with her hair askew and her emotions manifesting in a blast of naivety that was almost painfully sweet.

He was mostly just happy to see her, happy his intuition had been right. She wasn't a wine snob with no respect for the community or the land. She was just shy.

Tiziano let Nonna greet him with kisses on the cheek and a flow of exclamations as though she hadn't seen him for years, but his eyes strayed continually to Jenn. When she mumbled something and turned to go, he rushed after her, catching her at the archway heading out of the kitchen.

But he suddenly had no idea what to say. He stared dumbly at her for several long moments, a smile stretching on his lips. He loved knowing her secrets. He propped an arm on the doorframe and leaned in, trying to gauge how she felt about the *other* part of last night. She was in love with a sophisticated guy and hated everything about his life, but the fireworks last night... He'd be thinking about it – about her – for a long time to come.

She smelled nice, probably her shampoo, and it made him grin all the more, remembering her cataloguing the scents in his aftershave. There wasn't anything serious between them, but he'd forgotten how gripping it was to *be* with someone. He tucked a strand of hair behind her ear but then she bolted, ducking under his arm.

'Did you need something?' she asked.

He opened his mouth, but nothing came out. The cloth in his hand reminded him of what he had to tell her, but his head was swimming, trying to interpret her tone. 'Are you okay this morning?'

'Yes, I'm fine,' she said defensively.

'Bene – good, I...'

'I have a low tolerance for alcohol. At least in a tasting I can spit so it isn't usually a problem.' She touched the backs of her fingers briefly to her cheek. 'I'm sorry I didn't warn you.'

'Not important.'

'No, I... I'm sorry. I think I overshared. Please don't... I must have sounded like an idiot.'

He hesitated, drawing in a measured breath as he carefully screwed up his emotions into a ball and stuffed them away. 'Don't worry,' he assured her, hearing the roughness in his own voice. 'You were cute.'

'Because that's just what every short, Asian woman wants to hear,' she muttered.

'I just meant—' Merda, this conversation had become a minefield. And she was still cute, but it had nothing to do with her stature or her ethnicity. It was actually all to do with that unexpected fierceness, but she didn't want to hear it. 'About the...' He couldn't bring himself to say it aloud and it appeared he didn't need to, because her answer was staring him in the face: she didn't remember. She must have been even more drunk than he'd thought. At least that explained why she'd done it. It certainly wasn't because she liked him.

He blew out a breath, hastily recalculating. He was glad he hadn't said anything and put both of them in a more difficult position. There was no reason to feel put out – except for the suspicion that it couldn't have been as good for her as it had been for him.

'Giorgio! Dato che te si bagnà...' He was glad of the distraction and turned back to see what favour Nonna needed from him.

'Did she just call you Giorgio?' Jenn asked.

'It's my dad's name.'

She stopped him with a hand on his arm. 'Is she... okay?'

'She's eighty-seven. "Okay" was a few years ago. Now... she gets by.'

'You look after her?'

'When she lets me.'

She glanced around the kitchen. 'Your brother doesn't understand how much you do, does he?'

'I don't do much. She's independent, still. And Matteo's right: I let her cook for me as often as I can.'

'Yeah, you *let* her. Like you *let* him think what he wants.'

'Così, I'm your hero now? A superhero who drives a blue tractor?' He flapped his vest top. 'I could rip this off and you could see if my suit is under there.'

'Keep your suit to yourself. I don't need to see it again.'

* * *

Jenn was determined to get herself back on track, after her disastrous first day in the Prosecco Hills. She didn't have time for cows or tractors – or grappa tastings. She didn't want to spend a day longer than necessary sweltering in her not-quite-hotel room, feeling guilty about making an eighty-seven-year-old woman wait on her. She certainly didn't have time for smiling farmers who leaned too close in doorways.

It was impossible to avoid Tiziano completely. He was often in the small vineyard by the farmhouse in the morning, fixing the bird nets, weeding or cutting the grass. In the evening, he was in the courtyard, his hands and shirt smeared with oil, repairing equipment.

But he kept his distance, too, which she was grateful for. Ever since Monday morning, she'd experienced twinges of fear and embarrassment at the thought of talking to him. She hated to think what opinion he had of her now. Perhaps it would have been better to let him think she was a rude snob rather than an eccentric lightweight.

She didn't remember everything that had happened after her two glasses of grappa, but she did know she'd told him how sad and lonely she really was and if that wasn't a turn-off, she couldn't imagine what was. But there had been a moment the next morning when he'd leaned close and a flash of memory at his proximity had made her uneasy. He certainly held different opinions about personal space, so she'd decided she'd read too much into it. She could only conclude that he felt so familiar because of the time she'd spent squashed up against him in the tractor. If something had happened between them, he would have told her, surely.

Who knew why he'd felt the need to look into her eyes with a warm twinkle in his own, or why he rarely wore shoes and belted out rock songs in his raspy voice as he moved among the vines in the morning?

Who knew why she sometimes felt like joining him down there? She suspected it was something

about the way the low rays of dawn sunlight illuminated the leaves, turning the little vineyards golden.
But she'd seen the state of the earth between the rows
of vines. In her shoes, it was a broken ankle waiting to
happen.

She needed to focus on her work, especially after
the rocky start at Elisir di Cartizze. After doing phone-
reception yoga on the tiny balcony, she'd scoured the
internet and the professional database, cross-refer-
encing wineries with bus routes and shorter taxi trips.
She picked ones with a prosecco tranquillo listed,
hoping to ease herself into the tasting, and by timing
her visits well, she could avoid the dreaded Lamborghini – and its owner – and do it all herself.

The trouble was, none of the wineries seemed particularly interested. She was welcomed with open
arms – sometimes literally. The wines were presented
with pride and generosity – and a generous amount of
salami and cheese. She inspected stainless-steel vats
and toured terraced vineyards. But when she presented her proposal, their eyes clouded and answers
became vague.

One winery owner finally mentioned she might
want to visit the consortium of producers for advice
and she could have guessed who the secretary of the
consortium was: Valentina Costa. She spent a few mo-

ments swearing at the website, cursing Tiziano and his strange sex appeal as though it were all his fault.

She'd obviously been blacklisted – yet another failure she could never admit to Filippo. She needed a way to visit a lot of wineries in a short space of time without tipping them off about the Brampton Hotel Group and that was where her new strategy came in.

Getting up early on Saturday morning, she snuck out, leaving a note for the sleeping Filomena, knowing Tiziano would be safely away in the vineyard. She took the first bus to Valdobbiadene. She had time to down a cappuccino and a puff pastry stuffed with vanilla cream, while eying the display of colourful artisan chocolates, before taking the next bus all the way to Treviso.

Although the city was provincial, with narrow, cobbled streets and buildings only a few storeys high, she was comforted by the familiar scent of car exhaust, garlic from a kebab shop mixed with hydrangeas from a nearby florist, and the colourful billboards everywhere.

She was early, and spent half an hour wandering the lanes, snapping photos of the old buildings and charming canals that brought a touch of Venice inland. The warm colours of the stone, the decorative arches, brick crenellations and the pots exploding with flowers were an invitation to explore at a re-laxed pace and she was sorry she didn't have more time.

She followed a group of tourists into a hidden courtyard and stopped up short to see what they'd found. It was a fountain, two streams of water flowing into a marble bowl, but Jenn had never seen a foun-tain where the water flowed out of its nipples before. Not only that, but the empty-eyed figure of the woman was propping her breasts up fiercely.

Jenn studied the sturdy woman, with her unashamed posture, and she had to admit she was kind of impressed. She held up her phone and snapped a surreptitious selfie. Why she wanted to show Tiziano, she wasn't sure. She couldn't, anyway, because then she'd have to admit that she'd come all the way to Treviso to avoid him.

She arrived back at the station to meet her winery tour group with a faint feeling of sheepishness at the lengths she'd gone to for a bit of anonymity and the opportunity to arrive directly at the doors of three wineries in one day. It didn't take long for her to ques-tion the wisdom of coming on the tour. The group was mostly middle-aged couples in hats and bum bags who couldn't pronounce Conegliano any better than she could. And the guide talked to her in slow, clipped

English and declared that she spoke a bit of Japanese, if that would help.

Of course the first question the other tourists had for her was, 'Where are you from?' She reminded herself it was meant harmlessly, especially in this context, but it necessitated a complicated answer that only made her feel like more of an outsider.

'London, mostly,' she said, wondering if they'd let her leave it at that, but they kept looking at her. 'But I was born in South Korea.'

'Ah, Korean! I have a Korean friend back in Kansas. I should have guessed.'

Jenn managed a smile and moved to the back of the bus.

They oohed and aahed as the bus trundled over a long bridge with flapping Italian flags, crossing the sparkling river. A little sign humbly announced the 'Fiume Piave', the Piave river, but the wide expanse of white stone, scrub and alpine blue channels of rushing water looked like its own ecosystem and not just a river. Jenn had caught glimpses of it from many different angles in the week she'd been criss-crossing the area by bus.

In the distance, Jenn caught sight of people picnicking by the water, sitting under umbrellas or lazing in the sunshine. She couldn't help wondering if any of them were sunbathing topless. Tiziano seemed to follow her wherever she went, even when he wasn't really there.

She wondered if she'd have a chance to explore the river while she was here – not to sunbathe, of course, but to admire the view. The water was such a stunning colour and the mountain backdrop was something she'd rarely seen before.

Who was she kidding? Until she had signatures on the dotted line, she wouldn't be stopping for a picnic. If she asked Tiziano to take her there, she'd end up dunked in the water and eating hunks of salami out of his hand, which wasn't her idea of a good time.

The bus continued through the rolling slopes of the gentler landscape to the south. Making a detour to photograph the crumbling mediaeval Castello di San Salvatore with its square stone towers and vineyards in the foreground, they took a narrow road through the hills, that alternated vineyards and woodlands and sweeping views.

The first winery was just outside Pieve di Soligo, with views across the plain towards the distant hills. The cantina, the tasting room, would have been modern fifteen years ago, with its minimalist counter of wood in a metal frame and deep burgundy paint that reminded her more of red wine.

The tanks had pride of place, sealed with their stainless-steel doors, like spaceships for wine. A few nostalgic touches – a wooden winepress with rusty brackets, a scratched mask with an enormous nose for Carnevale, lacy doilies and checked cloth – completed the rather hectic interior décor. It was nothing like the elegant châteaux wineries she'd visited in France, or the almost invisible contemporary glass of the best wineries in Australia.

The owner of the operation, a man called Stefano, who was in his fifties and the son of the founder, greeted them himself. He had a handlebar moustache and he shook hands with each of them for what Jenn felt was far too long. The pride in his voice was evident as he explained the history of the vineyard and winery, pointing out the oldest vines and the newest fermentation tanks.

Jenn pricked up her ears as he explained the organic certification of the vineyard and how the resulting tough-skinned grapes produced a more complex wine. She wished she could confirm it with her own nose.

When it came to the tasting, the group was full of both enthusiasm and ignorance, with one couple even asking how to hold the glass correctly. The good-natured Stefano poured generously and Jenn blinked in surprise to see the tourists slurping their first tasting glass of the dry prosecco spumante. No one spat.

One American managed to describe her first sip as, 'Frothy and floral,' but the others only managed, 'Delicious,' or, 'Ooh, that's lovely,' from the jolly pensioner from the north of England.

Jenn turned her glass slowly by the foot. The colour was an elegant middle ground between straw and pale and the froth looked satisfyingly creamy. Before she could complete her assessment, Stefano approached with a coaxing smile. In a moment of panic, she lifted the glass to her lips and slugged it like the others.

She had a fleeting taste of honey and sour apple as it went down, but mostly she felt a little like the cork must have felt when Stefano had popped it with a whoop – tingly and electric.

'Delicious,' she said emphatically.

Stefano smiled warmly and gestured to the plate of cheese and cured meats. 'Our wine is an artisan product, but we are simple farmers at heart and caring for the land is our most important job. This is drunken cheese from local cows – a natural pairing with prosecco. It has very few carbon miles as I collect this from the dairy on my bicycle myself.'

Jenn smiled, reminded again of Tiziano. 'I love the

sound of drunk cheese.' She selected a piece, taking in a long breath before popping it into her mouth. 'On the nose, it's tangy and spicy, but the sugars from the grapes kick in on the tongue.'

'You are an intenditrice – una esperta – about cheese!'

At least he hadn't suspected her of being an expert about wine. 'Does the dairy take milk from the cows up on the mountain pastures?'

'Sai, I'm not sure. I'll have to ask Egidio next time I collect the cheese.'

Jenn gulped the next glass, too, the extra dry. The difference in sweetness was minor – at least according to her irreverent tasting method – and she was almost enjoying herself. The brut, the driest prosecco, went up her nose a little, but she managed to recover with Stefano thumping her on the back and recommending that she taste the wine a little slower.

'I'll know for next time,' she croaked and he poured her another – a little bigger this time. With his bushy moustache and kind smile, there was no way she could say no, so she braced herself and took a sip, willing her eyes not to water. All she noticed was the creamy texture of the froth.

Her cheeks were hot and she was a little wobbly as the tour group boarded the minibus in the direction of

Pieve for lunch, but she downed most of her bottle of water and suspected she'd be okay if she didn't have any wine at lunch.

Hopping off the bus near the osteria selected by the tour operator, she was feeling quite proud of herself. A bustling weekly market filled the piazza, with giant tubs of plump tomatoes separated according to quality, peaches and red currants, fresh beetroot and little packs of zucchini flowers tied up with string. A trailer with a chilled counter offered fresh meat, from sausages to skinned rabbit.

The chaos of voices and smells was disorienting and she marched through, keeping her eyes on the tour guide and mostly ignoring the vendors and their colourful wares – until she heard a voice behind her.

'Jenn? Jenn! What are you doing here? Introduce me to your friends!'

QUATTRO BREZZE PROSECCO ROSÉ MILLESIMATO DOCG:

A blend of 90% glera and 10% pinot noir, this prosecco rosé has all the joy and immediacy of a fruity prosecco, with the blush-pink colour of a summer sunrise and a hint of raspberry from the pinot noir. The perlage of this vintage is particularly creamy and the experience brings to mind Italian gelato and hot sun.

9

It took her so long to locate him that she started to question whether she'd imagined his voice.

'Eccomi! Smell the cheese!'

But she knew she wasn't imagining him when she saw him standing in the cheese trailer wearing a white hat and a toothy grin. 'You're a cheesemonger today?'

'Who are you calling a monkey?'

'A laòro, Tonno!' called a woman in a matching hat who was serving a customer further along the counter.

'Now she's calling me a tuna,' Tiziano said, ignoring the woman. 'I'll be a zoo by the end of the day if enough women walk past.'

'I didn't say monkey, I said cheesemonger –

someone who sells cheese. Why is she calling you a tuna?'

'It's an old joke from when I learned English in school with her and her husband. It came from my family name. Lucchetta became lucky, which went back to fortuna, to tuna and then tonno in Italian. We were bored in school,' he said with a shrug.

Jenn gave a wide-eyed nod, just about following.

'But I'm just helping today. I'm not a cheesemonkey, as Laura reminds me.' He jerked his head in the direction of the fierce-looking woman. 'She is my friend's wife, but he has a rugby game today, so she is angry with us both. But why are you at the market? I could have brought you. You could be a cheesemonkey too, for a day! Here, try some.'

Jenn tried to refuse, but after he'd thrust it in her face, she didn't feel she could. She took it with an apologetic smile for Laura. 'Thank you. I'm... I have a wine tasting, of course.' She took a surreptitious glance at the tour group, wondering if Tiziano might not notice them, but they were standing in a clump in the middle of the thoroughfare, watching her curiously in their hats and bum bags and they couldn't have looked more out of place if they'd been draped in the flags of their respective countries.

Tiziano waved them over and presented the different types of cheese with too much flair. 'Here you have real mountain cheese, the aged montasio. This is the old man cheese, chewy and spicy, if you like that sort of thing. Personally, I like the soft, younger man cheese.' He winked at Jenn and she stifled a groan. 'This is caciotta, made with prosecco wine.'

The tourists lapped him up and even Laura couldn't complain after most of them bought something. When the tour guide moved them on towards the osteria, Jenn began to hope that he'd forgotten to ask about her 'friends' in the tour group. But his raised eyebrows as he waved goodbye suggested she hadn't quite got away with it.

The worry about being caught out intensified in the afternoon as the bus pulled out of the second winery and made its way to higher altitudes for the third, motoring through stone villages with rustic rooftiles, surrounded by the lush green of vines and forest, with spots of pink from the roses planted at the edges of the vineyards. The hills became more familiar and, as they turned off the main road to reach the last winery, a blue tractor puttered past. Anywhere else, she would have assumed it was a different blue tractor, but Tiziano was omnipresent this close to Combai.

They took a tour of the vineyard before the tasting, walking among the rows of fluffy vines, and who else should have been there but Tiziano himself, waving emphatically from the driver's seat of a ride-on lawn-mower, his cap low over his eyes.

He came into the cantina when they were halfway through the tasting, smelling less than fresh and tracking in grass clippings. His boots clomped on the floor, but at least he was wearing shoes. He ignored Jenn completely, leaving her to indignantly watch as he conversed with the owner of the vineyard in bois-terous tones and shared a – very large – glass of some kind of cloudy drink out of a wine bottle.

He leaned his elbows on the bar and turned to the tour group, who were watching him as though he re-ally was an animal in a zoo. 'E quindi? You like the wine, English tourists?'

'We're actually American, but yes, it's perfect for summer,' one of the men replied.

'And the hills? They are beautiful, no?'

'Just fabulous. I never imagined the landscape would be so mountainous!' the American wife gushed. 'It's such a shame we have to go back to our hotel in Venice tonight.'

'Ah, Venessia is the queen of cities. We poor farmers are here because of her power.'

'Are you a farmer, then?' asked the middle-aged woman from the north of England, whose name was

Carmen or Carmel, but Jenn hadn't quite caught it. 'I thought we saw you selling cheese.'

The owner of the vineyard, a balding man called Lorenzo who smelled vaguely of tobacco, cackled and clapped him on the shoulder. 'Ah, Tiziano is a tutto-fare! He does everything – and sometimes nothing. In fact, he says for days he will come to cut my grass and he appears without warning today! I thought he would be fishing. Ecco qui, if you are interested,' Lorenzo be-gan, dropping his voice. He opened a cabinet behind the counter with a key and took out an unlabelled bot-tle, setting it on the counter with a flourish. 'La grappa. You want to taste? This is Tiziano's very own creation.'

He tugged off the lid and, even though Jenn was six feet away, the smell gave her goosebumps. Her gaze snapped to Tiziano. She remembered his face close to hers – so close she'd caught the scent of the grappa on his lips. Staring at his lips triggered another ripple of memory she couldn't quite grasp.

She shook herself. There was no way anything could have happened. He teased her and thought she was wrong about wine – and about life. Plus, he wouldn't have kissed her after she'd embarrassingly admitted her feelings for Filippo.

The men enthusiastically accepted glasses of

grappa, as did Carmen (or Carmel) and the pair of Polish pensioners.

'Grappa always made me think of the mafia,' the chatty American said as he sniffed his glass. 'That was until the Big V, of course.'

'The Big V? Were you a virgin?' Carmen joked.

'It's the brand name,' the American continued. 'Hasn't it arrived in England, yet? It's all the rage in the hipster bars in New York these days. VG and T they call it: Big V Grappa and tonic. It really puts hair on your chest.'

Jenn couldn't help thinking that hadn't worked for Tiziano, but she couldn't say it out loud and she didn't dare catch his eye in case he read her mind.

'Isn't the Big V from here? I thought the V stood for Venice,' the tourist asked Lorenzo.

'Forget this Big V. I don't know where it's distilled. It uses the V for Veneto, the birthplace of grappa, to sound authentic, but we don't know it here. La grappa needs history – preferably generations. Tiziano – his Nonno distilled grappa. It's *tradition*.'

'I'm sure there was a Big V prosecco grappa released this year,' the American continued thoughtfully. 'It would have to be from here, right?'

'To use the name, the grapes must be grown within the Prosecco DOC area, which is this part of Veneto and some of the neighbouring region of Friuli-Venezia Giulia,' Jenn said. The tour group turned to her in surprise.

'Aha, a wine expert in our midst!' Tiziano said with a grin.

After tasting the range of wines, including a sparkling rosé Jenn suspected hotel guests would lap up at the bar, the decidedly relaxed tour group gathered in front of the old stone building, gasping afresh at the view of the terraced hills and the mountain massif. The minibus crunched its way up on the gravel to collect them.

Jenn sensed rather than saw Tiziano drift closer to her. Was he finally going to acknowledge her? Did she want him to? She took a step in the direction of the others, torn.

'Are you really going to get on that bus?' he asked in a low voice. 'You'll go back to Treviso? Or did you depart from Venice? Please don't tell me you went all the way to Venice just to avoid me.'

'Treviso,' she said defensively.

'I see you don't disagree with the part about avoiding me. Are you sure you're not embarrassed about... Sunday night?'

Her gaze swerved to his. 'No... Why would I be?'

'No reason,' he reassured her, but his reassurance

had the opposite effect. 'You just... told me a lot of things. Not that I judged!'

'Are you sure that's all?'

A flicker of dismay crossed his features. 'What else do you think would have happened?'

The confusing mix of signals she got from him made her head ache and she had the urge to punch him on the arm. If he was disappointed that nothing had happened, that meant he liked her, but then she didn't understand why he seemed to enjoy riling her up.

'Allora? Are you coming home with me? If you don't, I'll *know* you're avoiding me.'

'I have to go back, now, or they'll ask why I took the tour!' she hissed.

'What were you going to do if you wanted to buy Lorenzo's wine?'

She froze, giving herself an inward kick. 'You're infuriating when you're right.'

'All included in my services. Here, I'll explain to him.'

'No—' He was gone before she could manage anything further, ambling over to Lorenzo. He crossed his arms and started up a conversation in that low brogue, which Jenn had realised was the local dialect, punctuated by exclamations that were full of testosterone. He

waved her over and she scowled in return. His behaviour was presumptuous and patronising and...
whatever he'd said seemed to work, damn it.

Lorenzo held out a hand to shake hers. 'Come back
another time, Miss Park, and we can talk about what
you need.'

'Thank you – and for the tasting. I'm sorry—'

'Psht,' Lorenzo said, cutting her off. 'Tiziano explained everything.'

'He... did?' She didn't have a chance to ask anything more, as Tiziano said goodbye to Lorenzo and
motioned for her to follow him.

Her annoyance with him only grew and she
wished she had left with the bus when Tiziano led her
through the vines to where he'd parked.

'Where's the Lamborghini?'

'You expect me to put the grass cutter in a trailer
just to drive it two kilometres away? It uses less fuel
than the tractor anyway.'

'You mean we're riding the lawn mower home?'

'What? The motor is as powerful as a Vespa.'

'It's *not* a Vespa, Tiziano.'

'A little imagination and you'll be in the middle of
your own Italian cliché.' He hopped up onto the seat –
the only seat – leaving her to squeeze on behind him.

If she'd thought the Lamborghini was an uncomfortable ride, the lawn mower was a death trap – or at least a grazed-knee-trap. It doodled along the side of the road at granny-in-a-Fiat miles an hour, giving her cramps in her fingers from clinging to the seat. Tiziano whistled and turned his face up to the sun as though he hadn't a care in the world.

'Doesn't this thing go any faster?' she asked over the puttering motor.

'Not everyone is a speed fanatic like you!' he called back.

'I thought you said you wouldn't judge me.'

'Speeding I'll judge, and taking an anonymous wine tour when you have the world of prosecco at your feet, but not the geriatric mother stuff.'

She vaguely remembered talking about those secret fears, but the stark evidence that she'd definitely overshared made her blanch. Swallowing her embarrassment, she said through gritted teeth, 'I'm doing what I can under my own steam. You can't judge me for taking the tour!'

'I said I can drive you. I have some time to help.'

'When you're not sunbathing or fishing,' she muttered.

'Exactly!'

'Is that why you turned up today? Don't think I

didn't notice Lorenzo saying he hadn't expected you. Did you come just to embarrass me?'

He stopped the motor suddenly and turned, a heated expression on his face. 'I know you think I'm a vulgar farm boy, but I'm not trying to drive you away!'

'Stop with the farm boy stuff! Firstly, you're a grown man, even if you live with your grandmother and work part-time jobs. Secondly, I know we've argued about wine and pride and different tastes, but I never belittled you for being from the countryside.'

'Maybe not, but you also haven't hidden how much you dislike it here.'

'That's my problem, not yours! All of this is my problem. And I'm solving it my way.'

'And I'm trying to help – in my way.'

'But you haven't helped. Your ex-lover has black-listed me and I have nothing to show for a week spent visiting vineyards and hours wasted at bus stops!' She was satisfied to see her point land.

'You think Valentina's angry because I broke her heart and she's taking it out on you?'

'If you hadn't shown up when you did, things might have gone differently.'

'Allora, Valentina is not jealous or secretly pining for me. It was only two or three times and only be-cause... I don't know. She felt sorry for me or something. If she's being prudent, it's because you came in not understanding how things work. Prosecco is more than a product to stock the shelves here. Do you know how little money some of these vineyards make? The demand for prosecco exploded, but no one wants to pay. On the plains, they can increase yields, change crops, but here? The hills limit the scale of the vineyards and the ground limits the yields. They have to choose quality over quantity and you're asking for a lot of trust with your big contracts.'

Trust was a commodity Jenn wasn't used to trading. Her stomach twisted as she realised just how poorly she'd handled her assignment so far. Her hand fisted in Tiziano's flannel shirt as her mind raced. 'I don't know,' she began haltingly, 'how to build trust.'

'Definitely *not* by joining a tourist group,' he muttered, tightening the knot in her stomach.

'I didn't mean to insult you – or anyone else.'

'You just don't like us,' he said, softening his words with a pout, but Jenn still felt the sting.

'I don't understand you,' she muttered.

'I've been trying to show you. We're simple people,' he said with a dismissive shrug that annoyed her, because he wasn't simple at all to her.

'We're a farming community. The grapes and the ground are our treasure. We have a word in Veneto that means money – schei. But it's a pride thing. We don't want too much schei. That's greedy; that's not what we live our lives for here. You come in talking about deals and we think of winners and losers, of business types who just want the schei, talking about markets and price pressures. In Valdobbiadene, in Veneto – in Italy – the product comes first, not the market.'

'I... I like your attitude. I admire your farming community – I honestly do.'

'Then why did you take a tour? Why do you keep us at a distance? That's not the way to get people on your side. We rely on each other here.'

'You mean you stick together to make things difficult for the outsider. Even that dog hated me.'

'You're the one making yourself an outsider.'

'That's charming, Tiziano, but I was born an outsider. I'm half-Korean – I don't fit in there and I don't quite fit in in London. I grew up all over the world. My family, such as it is, lives on three continents. You were born in these hills.'

He studied her, brow furrowed and lopsided. 'Is that really how you feel?'

The question landed uncomfortably between her ribs. 'It's not a feeling. It's a state.'

'Bene, we'll have to change your state, then.' His

smile returned, wide and slow. 'You'll be like a butter-fly, finding your colours and flying off.'

'I'm not a butterfly,' she said drily. 'And if I were, I'd only have two weeks to find the perfect prosecco be-fore I *die*.'

He choked on a cough. 'Okay, not a butterfly.'

10

The conversation on the mower stayed with Tiziano in the days that followed, lending him an unexpected feeling of protectiveness towards their guest. She certainly didn't understand the lifestyle in this region and he wasn't convinced she wanted to, but the way she'd quietly admitted she didn't know how to build trust had touched him.

Every morning, she stumbled out of her stifling hot room onto the balcony, to stretch and yawn in her pyjamas. He made sure he looked busy among the vines, but bleary-eyed, clumsy Jenn made him smile. By the time she came down for breakfast, she was decked out in a fresh outfit and heels, an elegant tortoise-shell clip in her hair and pearl earrings in her lobes. She was always deferential to Nonna, polite and helpful and she even dipping her head to show respect on occasion, which he guessed she didn't realise she was doing.

I was born an outsider. He thought more about her statement than the throwaway comment warranted. There was nothing he could do about it. The people from his world would show her generous hospitality and fair cooperation, but she didn't belong here, either.

That didn't stop him deciding to adopt her for the little time she was here. After doing his own chores early in the morning, he waited until she was ready and then dropped her where she needed to go. If he had time, he picked her up again afterwards, but he didn't always manage it and she clearly didn't want to rely on him too much.

It was petty, but he decided to show her the full range of transport available in the countryside. He took her, gasping and yelping, through the forest on his friend's all-terrain vehicle on Monday. Tuesday was a rickety tandem bike that wobbled as it careened down the winding road to Valdobbiadene, the soles of her shoes slipping as she tried to pedal. Wednesday was comparative luxury when he wheeled out his Piaggio Ape, the tiny, three-wheeled truck that was a symbol of rural Italy.

'It has the motor of a Vespa – literally this time,' he explained with a wink as he popped the door open. 'But vespa means wasp, whereas ape means bee,' he explained.

'Ah-peh.' She repeated the Italian pronunciation doubtfully. 'Is there a reason for the stinging insects?'

'Maybe the buzzing engine,' he joked, swinging himself into the seat. 'But it has the heart of a lion.' He shoved up his sleeve to show her the tattoo of the winged lion on the inside of his forearm.

'That's... loyal,' she said tactfully, but he hoped she found it kind of hot, too. 'Where do I sit? On the floor?' He shuffled over a fraction and she perched on the edge of the seat, banging her knees when she pulled the door shut.

She used the opportunity of relative safety to call her boss on the drive, which hadn't been part of his plan.

'I'll talk to this consortium next week, but at the moment, I'm still gathering information. I'd like to briefly discuss with you what our guests will want in a prosecco.'

She paused to listen. 'I'm thinking about the tasting notes rather than my... experience – what will sound good on the wine list.' Another pause. 'Of course, I'm not being swayed by a good pitch. Yes, the consortium seems powerful, but I think we need to work with them and not against them.'

He glanced at her when she hung up. Was it wrong to be a little bit proud of how she'd pushed back about the consortium? But, of course, he couldn't let her suspect that was how he felt, or she might have to admit she'd been wrong. 'No, "Bye honey, I'll be home soon?"' he teased.

'Shut up,' she muttered. 'You took advantage of my vulnerability while I was drunk to get my darkest secrets.'

'I would never!' He gave her a pointed glance. Would she ask him straight up what happened that night? 'I only hope he's worth it. I'm not that impressed so far.'

'Luckily you're not the one who's interested in him.'

'I'm sure if he was that great a guy I could be convinced. What would happen if you got together? Would you quit?'

'No,' she insisted.

'You would,' he said casually. 'You'd think about how you want to have kids and it would make sense for you to be the one to stop working and he still gets a better deal.'

'Now you're the one talking about deals. Loving someone isn't a deal.'

'No, but there's power involved, especially if we're talking about you and "Big Piece" Baretti.'

'Big piece of what?'

'You know. A big guy.'

'You think I don't have a chance, is that it? That it's a juvenile crush?'

'I'm the last person to accuse someone else of being juvenile. If he knows what's right for him, he'll fall for you too.'

'Oh, I... Thanks,' she mumbled. It was almost too easy, getting a reaction from her. 'And he's not as heartless as you think he is.'

'I'm not judging, Jenn. It was a stupid idea to have an opinion. Don't listen to me.'

He waited for her to quip that she was used to ignoring the junk he said, but instead she studied him. 'What about you? Your ex-girlfriend? What was she like?'

'Which one? I told you Valentina wasn't really a

girlfriend. I took Laura the cheesemonkey out for a few months in liceo – in school. Dated her before her husband, too, but she got smart after a month and kicked me on my butt.'

To his surprise, she smiled smugly at him and goosebumps sneaked up his arm. 'I do remember some things from Sunday night. You said you'd had one relationship. A big-R *Relationship*. So tell me.'

The flash of goosebumps became a sting as memories surfaced against his will. He wished he could bury it all in the past, but several unopened letters in a drawer in his nightstand proved it wasn't over, yet. Just the Milan postmark was enough to make his stomach clench.

She drew back suddenly. 'You don't have to... Sorry, Tiziano.' She pressed her lips together. 'I should have guessed you wouldn't want to talk about it.'

'No, it's fine,' he lied. Lying to her, ignoring the letter – he couldn't seem to do anything else about this shit. 'Just imagine me trying to be in a serious relationship. That's more or less what happened. It was a long time ago.'

'You're a free spirit,' she said with an apologetic smile that he didn't deserve.

'Free as a butterfly,' he joked. 'Speaking of butterflies, how is the tasting going? Getting any more flavour? Or just sneezes?'

'At the risk of admitting you were right, tasting the tranquillo helped. They think I'm crazy for not sticking my nose in before sipping, but I'm getting more on my tongue.'

'I'm happy your tongue is busy,' he said, trying his hardest to keep a straight face while he fiddled with his piercing, enjoying her suspicious look. Did she remember *anything* from Sunday night after the grappa? 'Spèta, wait, I know what you need!'

'I'm terrified to hear.'

'Prosecco in context. You shouldn't be standing in a cantina feeling shy when you drink prosecco. You should be together with friends and family, laughing and talking.'

'Friends and family are somewhat lacking if you hadn't noticed.'

He gave her a disapproving pout. 'No friends? We must discuss that. But if you don't have your family here to drink prosecco with you, easy – you borrow mine. You are coming with us to Montebelluna on Sunday. We have a family baptism.'

'Oh, I... I'm not family. And I won't understand the ceremony.'

'Psht, the ceremony is not important. Just don't

snore. It's the lunch you should experience. Maybe you can even hold the baby.'

For someone who had admitted that she wanted children more than anything else, she looked very startled at the idea of holding one in real life.

'Will they let me?'

He chuckled. 'You'd be better off asking, "Will I be able to avoid it?" Poor baby Alessandro is always tossed around the family like a rugby ball. He had the bad luck of being born second and his big sister is... a force of nature. You'll have a great time.'

* * *

'You have a car?' Jenn cried on Sunday morning. She should have expected it.

'No, this is Nonna's car.' *That* didn't surprise her. The boxy red Fiat looked as though it had survived the fighting along the Piave in the First World War.

'Does it actually work?'

'For now,' he said with a shrug. 'But we can't turn up to church in the Lamborghini.'

'*Now* you see that's a problem?'

The other surprise was Tiziano in a suit. It was an ill-fitting number – he had such long arms that no off-the-rack suit would work – with a rockstar tie and an odd yellowish sheen to the black, as though it hadn't been stored properly, but it made him look almost... normal. His hair was swept off his forehead with gel. He cut a completely different figure from Filippo in his tailored Armani, but he looked good.

Tiziano helped Filomena into the passenger seat. His nonna wore a loose summer frock with a busy pattern, her short hair combed back to reveal the grey roots. Jenn felt the now-familiar urge to help her, this time to colour her hair and maybe put on some prettier shoes. But that would surely be overstepping, as Filomena was not her halmoni, her fiery Korean grandmother, who had taught her the meaning of family, respecting her elders and tough love.

The Fiat made it down from the hills, albeit with coughs and splutters that made Jenn picture them stranded on a lonely road in the middle of fields of corn. But they safely crossed the Piave and arrived at the brick church in Montebelluna with its neogothic tracery and gold icon of Mary above the portal.

The congregation was just as well turned out as the elaborate church interior. Among the women milling around before the service, she catalogued all manner of dresses, most above the knee (some *far* above the knee), from floral print to wraparound to little black numbers with transparent shawls draped over bare shoulders in a nod to modesty in church, all paired with chic heels. Jenn suspected the mobile hair-dressers in the area had been busy this morning.

Jenn felt a moment of fear that she was under-dressed – after two weeks of feeling like a sore thumb among the rural population of Valdobbiadene. She should have worn her patent heels with the buckle, and maybe a skirt.

'You look fine,' Tiziano assured her, tugging on his collar. A bead of sweat had already popped out on his forehead.

'I suppose I should have expected it to be a semi-formal event if you put on a suit.'

'Do I look good? Is it a story of Cenerentola? Or I mean Cenerentolo. What is it in English again?'

'Cinderella?' Jenn guessed. 'Your fairy godmother has her work cut out for her. But... you look fine, too.'

'It's not a fairy godmother. It's my grandfather's Armani.'

'That would explain the smell, although you doused it well with aftershave.'

He blinked at her. 'I keep forgetting I can't get away with anything because of your nose. But you like my aftershave.'

'It's okay,' she said, failing to stifle a smile. 'Which reminds me, do you smoke?'

His expression was a study in innocence. 'No,' he said slowly. 'Why? Would that be a reason for breaking up a relationship?'

She crossed her arms. 'We're not in a relationship, so it doesn't matter.'

'Ah, but if we were...'

She refused to react to that, although it was difficult to ignore the uptick of her heartbeat. 'You'd quit smoking?' she prompted.

A ripple of emotion crossed his features, but he banished it in a moment, fiddling with his earring and giving her a lopsided smile. 'I don't smoke much. Sometimes with my guys while we're fishing. But I quit years ago. Shouldn't have started. It was a teenage thing. When I got my first tattoo, I stopped smoking.'

'Huh, I suppose that's an improvement.'

It wasn't long before the hordes descended on them. Everyone wanted to kiss Tiziano – and a few cuffed him lightly, too. Jenn hung back with Filomena where she didn't have to answer too many questions. Tiziano's brother Matteo, rocking a mewling baby in a long, white dress, greeted her with a harried smile, pointing out his wife, who appeared to be wrestling a small crocodile with ponytails.

'That's my wife Maryam and our daughter Dinah,' Matteo said. As they watched, Dinah shouted something Jenn couldn't understand and promptly burst into tears. Matteo gave Jenn an apologetic smile and headed into the fray.

To Jenn's surprise, Tiziano beat him to it and hefted the little screaming person out of his sister-in-law's arms. Propping the girl up on one arm, he caught Dinah's eye and gave her an exaggerated pout. He spoke to her in an animated tone, while smoothing his hand down her back.

'Ah, Tiziano has the... attitude with children,' Filomena said softly. Jenn had to agree that he had a whole lot of attitude in general and she was inclined to think it was a good thing. 'But so discomfort and disgrace, il povero.' Her voice trailed off. Jenn contemplated her words for a moment, but couldn't make anything of them. '*Il povero*' might have been 'poor thing', but 'discomfort and disgrace' sounded like bad things so why would Filomena in the same breath express pity towards her smiling, irreverent grandson?

She watched Tiziano with his niece, taking in every nuance of his smile. He hunched himself over her, bringing his face to Dinah's and ignoring everyone else.

Jenn's breath caught, and she felt a thousand things at once. Was there more to Tiziano than she'd thought? The possibility stung her conscience because she would admit she'd underestimated him. But, more confronting than that, was the way the simple image of an uncle comforting his niece made her think of everything in life she wanted and couldn't have.

Was that what love looked like?

DA LINO PROSECCO CONEGLIANO-VALDOBBIADENE DOCG BRUT:

This zesty, 100% glera prosecco has green-gold colour highlights and leads with a fresh note of sour apple and hints of wisteria. The bubbles are brilliant and persistent and the texture is silky and round. A balanced finish with more floral notes and hints of chalk make this a prosecco for all tastes and occasions – a prosecco to drink while you're making memories.

11

Jenn pulled herself together enough to sit demurely in the pew with Filomena as the service started. The priest intoned in Italian and she zoned out, her gaze wandering. She took in the vivid colours of the stained-glass windows and the detail of the vegetation sculpted where the columns grew into the vaults.

Tiziano explained that there were six baptisms taking place, so the church was packed. The children fidgeted and babies interrupted the proceedings with sudden wailing. Professional photographers captured the solemn ceremonies from all angles as the robed priest poured water onto little heads with a shiny, golden shell, making echoing pronouncements.

When it was Alessandro's turn, it looked as though

the whole congregation decamped to the altar. A middle-aged woman helped Filomena climb the steps and Tiziano took his place behind Matteo and Maryam, but he soon came forward to take Dinah, whispering in her ear and making her laugh as the priest took the wriggling baby, holding him as though he were a sack of potatoes.

Dousing complete, the family took their places in the pews with a collective sigh of relief. When the mass had concluded, the festive ambience ramped up. In the past, families might have celebrated that the child had been placed into the hands of God in case anything happened to them, but that day it seemed as if everyone was now thinking about lunch and perhaps ditching their shawls when they exited the church.

They piled back into the car. From the way Tiziano spoke about the restaurant, Jenn was looking forward to a refined venue with elegant glassware and crisp, white table linen. She had her first suspicions that her assumptions were wrong when they headed out into the wheat fields rather than staying in the cobbled centre of Montebelluna. Climbing through a pine forest, they came to a stop outside a rambling white building with clay rooftiles and wooden shutters that looked more like a farmhouse than a fine restaurant.

The terrace was shaded by a lush vine and set for an event, with checked tablecloths and glassware and decorated with strips of white material, but the effect was rustic and welcoming, rather than chic. Then Jenn noticed the view.

She looked out over a vast valley, with the mountains in the background. Jenn recognised the Monte Cesen massif and the Prosecco Hills nestled in front. If she hopped up on her tiptoes, she could catch glimpses of the winding Piave below.

'We can almost see your house from here,' she commented to Tiziano with a smile.

'How are you doing, your Shyness?' he asked in reply. 'Too much company already?'

'I haven't had to talk to anyone, so I'm okay.'

'If you get stressed, just give me a secret signal and I'll make up an excuse for you.'

'What kind of secret signal?'

'I don't know, rub your nose?'

'That won't work. I'll be summoning you like a genie every time I take a sip of prosecco.'

'Speaking of which, I have a plan.' He took her elbow and dragged her to a table where bottles of prosecco and white wine sat in ice-buckets alongside rows of red wine bottles. 'Soave or pinot grigio? Or this Conegliano red?'

'I thought I was supposed to drink prosecco in context.'

'Oh, that's coming,' he said with mock foreboding, making her roll her eyes.

She accepted a glass of soave, picking up the melony tang in the scent even as the server poured. But before she could take a sniff, Tiziano snatched the glass out of her hand and downed half of it.

'Lout!' she blustered.

His smile was deliberately provoking. 'I'm saving you from your wine. Now take tiny sips. No one will realise you're not drinking.'

'Because that would offend the hosts?'

'L'acqua marsise i pài, as we say. Water just rots the pilings, but wine is for drinking. If you prefer, I could let you get drunk and tell them all about your love life. Why don't we just be honest and tell them you get drunk on one glass?' he suggested with a chuckle. 'I'm assuming your boss doesn't know.'

'Of course not!'

'I can't imagine what kind of marriage you guys are going to have then,' he mumbled, then sidled away before she could respond – or give in to the urge to whack him.

'What do you know about marriage?' she said to

his retreating back, receiving only a careless wave in reply.

He clearly knew more about family than she did. Tiziano spoke to everyone, kissing cheeks, clapping shoulders and then bumping fists with the younger guests. Jenn picked a corner and stayed there, nursing her half-glass of wine.

The only blessing was that there was very little expectation that Jenn would say anything. Everyone was merry and high-spirited except her, but how could she be when she understood nothing and no one understood her? Although, she thought morosely, it wasn't that different from any other party she'd ever attended.

For the meal, she found herself between Zia Monica, who may or may not have been Tiziano's real aunt, and a man called Mauro whose relation to the family wasn't clear at all. Monica spoke excellent English because it sounded to Jenn as if she spent most of her life on cruises.

The tables were spread with bites of bread and polenta, soft and hard cheese, salami and a variety of white pickles. Busy waiters rushed to fill every glass with prosecco. One of the men who'd helped with the cow stood and gave a toast, which Zia Monica translated with questionable accuracy, especially because she kept calling the man the 'priest', when the real priest was cosseted in a corner with the old men, pouring glasses of some kind of wine out of a one-litre bottle with a swing cap instead of a cork.

When the company raised their glasses, Jenn did the same, her heart pounding with trepidation. She braced herself and took a big sip. For a moment, she thought she'd managed to drink with only a stifled grimace and no other consequences, but a moment later, before any of the conversations had resumed, a violent sneeze ripped through her.

She pressed the backs of her fingers to her mouth and nose, feeling every eye on her and, not for the first time in her life, wished she was invisible.

Then she heard Tiziano's voice from two tables away. 'Salùte!' he called merrily. 'Bless you!'

'Bessoo,' Dinah parroted from where she was wriggling on his lap, making Tiziano and his family roar with laughter.

Jenn was soon forgotten when lunch was served: a primo piatto of rustic gnocchi in sweet tomato sugo and a secondi of pork with polenta. Jenn's trusty glass of straw-yellow soave remained by her plate with just enough wine left in it to discourage the attentive waiters.

She couldn't discourage the attentive Monica as

easily, though, and she felt as if she'd explained the geography of South Korea several times before lunch was finished, as well as the fact that she was *half*-Korean and she didn't know her father. Monica seemed to think that was some kind of tragedy, which only made Jenn's cheeks pinker.

On the few occasions that Monica paused to muster her next story, Mauro would begin an emphatic pronouncement that Jenn didn't understand and proceed to mumble the rest after shovelling another piece of polenta into his mouth.

'I putèi!' he repeated many times for emphasis. In the ensuing silence, Jenn felt pressured to ask Monica what he'd said.

'Verissimo, Mauro,' Monica agreed with an indulgent smile. 'He's talking about the children. Here in Veneto, the children are the greatest richness, the most precious thing we have. Without the children, we have nothing.' Jenn attempted a wobbly smile at Monica's bitter-sweet words. Shedding a tear would make her look like even more of a weirdo.

As soon as the first guests rose to mingle and converse, Jenn escaped inside for a breather. The interior of the restaurant was even more naff than the outside, with walls painted terracotta and an enormous stone fireplace with knick-knacks on the mantelpiece. She assumed they got away with it because the gnocchi was to die for.

But who was she to judge the décor of a place where so many happy people were celebrating? She wanted to kick herself for her mood. Was there such a thing as 'Freudenschade', where other people's happiness made you sad? The Lucchetta family were so *at home*, here. They all spoke the same brogue, knew the same people, and the extent of their experience of far-off places was from behind a tour guide. What could she possibly have to bond with them over?

As she was giving herself a stern pep talk, Maryam came rushing in, holding baby Alessandro like a hot potato. She rushed past Jenn and banged the door of the toilets.

'O fioeo mio!' came her voice a moment later in an exasperated tone. It sounded like the standard Italian phrase 'figlio mio', which Jenn thought meant 'my son'.

Before Jenn could decide whether to say anything or to rush away so Maryam didn't feel embarrassed, Tiziano's sister-in-law emerged from the bathroom, juggling a changing bag. She gave Jenn a harried smile and took a seat next to where Jenn was standing. She reached inside the straps of her dress and tugged one side all the way down. Jenn turned away in a hurry.

'Don't worry. So many people have seen these now, that— Casso! What now?' The shrill cry currently paralysing the terrace was piercing even through the panes of glass. From Maryam's reaction, it had to be Dinah. 'Jenn, is it? Please! Just take him!'

Panic shot through Jenn as the wobbly bundle in white cotton and lace was thrust into her suddenly clumsy arms and then Maryam disappeared back outside. Jenn clutched at the baby and he gave a pitiful little whimper that broke her heart. Still no parental instincts kicked in.

Worried about his head, she tucked him into the crook of one arm. He was not impressed. His tiny mouth opened wide and he grizzled for his mother, not exactly screaming, but certainly sounding as though Jenn were poking him with a stick instead of trying to hold him safely and securely. He nuzzled her blouse, turning away to make another pitiful cry, then returning to root around her chest in earnest.

'Oh, crap,' she muttered when she realised what the baby was doing. She yanked him away from her breasts and he yelped in earnest.

'Need some help?' came an amused voice from the doors to the terrace.

'He's looking for milk!'

'That's basically all he does. He's like me as a teenager – always searching for tits.'

Jenn was too flustered even to tell him off. Alessandro unexpectedly kicked out his legs and Jenn felt certain an armful of playful kittens would be easier to keep in hand. 'What do I do? He's hungry, but Maryam didn't have time to feed him. He's going to scream any second – or I'm going to drop him!'

'Psht, you're not going to drop him. Here.'

Jenn could only stare as Tiziano's callused fingers lifted the baby calmly from her arms. He pressed his warm little nephew against his chest, holding him in place with one big hand that spanned the tiny back. Baby Alessandro clucked in contentment and brought a fist to his mouth. Tiziano turned his head, brushed a kiss on the baby's downy forehead, and rested his cheek there. He crooned something in a low, rough voice and brought his other hand up to stroke the baby's hair.

The tender image and the softness of Tiziano's body language made Jenn feel wobbly in her shoes. This was a man who insisted he would never have his own children?

12

Tease her and make a joke – presto!

Jenn was staring at the baby with such a heart-breaking mix of longing and wariness that he regretted taking Alessandro from her – or regretted bringing her to the baptism entirely. He should have realised he'd be twisting the knife in. Well-meaning but naïve questions from Zia Monica wouldn't make her feel welcome and a party was the worst possible place to introduce Jenn to the realities of a large family. Although perhaps this could serve as a cautionary tale to help her realise that the things she longed for, the things she'd never had, were not all they were cracked up to be.

He blinked back the sting of emotion at that thought. He was a product of all of the worst things that could happen. If he told her everything... No, that wouldn't be fair. She wouldn't have to go through what he had – at least he hoped, with everything inside him, that she wouldn't have to.

'For someone who wants children, you don't seem to like babies,' he blurted out to break the charged silence.

That made her snap out of it. Good. 'I can't help it if I've never held a baby before. For someone who insists he *won't* have children, you seem awfully good with them!'

'It's like that thing with cats,' he deflected carefully. 'They always like the people who are allergic to them. But are you serious? You've never held a baby before?'

She shook her head. 'Aren't you worried about his head?'

'He's got a hard head like his father.'

'I mean his neck. Aren't babies' necks fragile?'

'He's three months old. He's fine. Besides, Maryam and Matteo's kids could both hold their heads up the day they were born.'

She took a step closer and he turned so she could see the little face currently nudging his collarbone and dribbling on his shirt. 'Tough, country kids?' she asked with a hint of a smile.

'You're getting the idea. Ecco, do you want to hold him again?' She opened her mouth to say something, but he wouldn't let her refuse, so he barrelled on. 'Sandrino likes to be upright or face down, like a rugby ball.' Jenn's eyes went round as he slung the baby over his arm, supporting his little chest with his hand.

'That looks like advanced baby whispering. I just need Baby 101 – how to not injure him.'

'Forza, Jenn! Stop thinking like that. Look, he's cute. He's got these tiny little hands. Take him!' She accepted him gingerly, holding him as though he were a priceless vase she didn't want to get her fingerprints on. 'You know the thing babies want most of all?'

'Milk?'

'Okay, second of all. They want to be cuddled. Stroke his back. He can't see very well and you smell strange, so make sure he knows you're there for him.'

'I smell strange?'

'I don't think Maryam has much time to shower these days, so you're too clean. And move a little, side to side, whatever feels natural.'

'I thought all of this was supposed to feel natural.'

'Nothing feels natural the first time. You're fine,' he said emphatically. *You're fine*, he repeated for himself.

The memories that came rolling back would retreat again, like the waves at Jesolo beach. This was Sandrino, who luckily had Matteo's genes instead of Tiziano's.

Jenn dipped her head and breathed in through her nose, a faint smile on her lips. 'It's true. There is a particular baby smell.' Alessandro fussed, grumbling at the amateur hold she had on him, but she rocked him and patted his back, beaming at Tiziano when the baby stopped grouching. Tiziano's throat grew tight. Why was he still surprised when he caught glimpses of the woman beneath the haughty veneer?

He turned his attention to the baby instead, clearing his throat. 'Drino, she's not Mama, but you know what? Jenn uses her nose to learn about the world, just like you. You find your milk and she finds the nectar of the grape.'

'That's a weird mental image.'

He glanced up from the precious little face of his nephew to find her watching him with a smile that gave him a touch of vertigo. Her dimples made him think of pressing kisses to her cheeks – a strangely mundane fantasy, but he realised he hadn't kissed her cheeks, yet.

'You've called him Alessandro, Sandrino and Drino. Which one will stick?'

'All of them, and we all get called Lucky at some point too.'

'An auspicious name,' she said, that soft smile still on her lips.

'What about Jenn? Is that short for something Korean?'

She shook her head and the furrow on her brow had him wondering what her childhood had been like, between two cultures. 'I have two names,' she admitted quietly.

'You have to tell me now.'

'Jenn is my English name – just Jenn, not Jennifer or even Jenny. I don't think my mother realised how much that would confuse people. And my Korean name is Park Eun-Jin.'

'Do you speak Korean? Your accent changed when you said your name.'

'I speak it badly, but I can pronounce my own name. Embarrassingly, when I write the characters for my name, my calligraphy is terrible. They are the only three characters I know and I still struggle to get them right. I can write standard Korean, but for auspicious things we use Chinese characters. I think my mother sees it as a personal failing that she worked instead of making me practise calligraphy.'

It all sounded unbearably lonely. Tiziano licked

his lips and watched her closely. 'I think you... turned out well, Park Eun-Jin.'

Just then the doors banged open and he jerked back. 'There you are!' his mother said with a sigh. She paused for a second when she took in the scene, Jenn rocking the baby and Tiziano hovering close, but it didn't stop her for long. 'Come, we need to take the family photo.' She approached with a quick smile for Jenn and switched to English. 'Hello, I'm sorry we didn't meet, yet. I'm Elena. I hope you enjoyed lunch.'

Jenn mumbled something in reply. Tiziano could only assume she'd picked up on the frosty undertone of his mother's greeting. The aloofness of both women annoyed him.

His mother lifted Alessandro out of Jenn's arms and turned to go, beckoning Tiziano to follow her. He hesitated for a moment, glancing between Jenn and his mother. Jenn flicked her fingers at him and mouthed, 'Go.'

'Are you... okay?' He rubbed his nose pointedly at her.

'Of course,' she insisted too quickly.

'Don't stay in here by yourself for too long. Zia Monica has many more stories to tell.'

At the last minute, he couldn't resist. He leaned down and pressed his lips lightly to her cheek and she sucked in a startled breath, her eyes wide. He escaped before he was tempted to do anything else, catching his mother's narrowed gaze as they headed back to the terrace.

Elena's enormous sigh gave away exactly what she was going to say – that, and the fact that they'd had this conversation every time his mother had caught wind of one of his relationships.

'Really,' she grumbled. 'A guest at Nonna's agriturismo? That's a poor choice, even for you.'

'At least she'll leave a nice review,' he muttered, looking out over the river and the mountains instead of at his mother's pinched expression.

'Tiziano, I'm not suggesting it hasn't been hard for you. I'm your mother and I was with you every step of the way. But it's been eight years. We've all given you the space you needed, but at some point you need to accept that the past is gone. These casual relationships won't help you. Don't deny it. I know you choose these women because there is no chance it will grow into anything more, but none of them treat you well.'

He counted down silently, waiting for his mother to say the word he knew was coming and bracing himself for it. 'All these women are just like Marzia!'

He stifled a grimace. It still hurt. 'I don't "choose" women! I just... let it happen.'

'Exactly! No goal or purpose. It will only make you more depressed.'

He wanted to bite out that letting things happen was the only way he could find to go forward, but his mother had no idea. She thought the past was gone.

'I'm not sleeping with Jenn. She's just... it's not what you think. If you could be nice to her, I'd appreciate it.'

'Why? I won't see her again, will I?' Elena asked.

Tiziano couldn't bring himself to answer. Why did he feel the urge to sabotage Jenn's work and make her stay longer? She'd hate him for it, but she didn't like him anyway so that didn't matter. It was just a shame he liked her so much – disdainful attitude and all. Or was his mother right and he only liked her because he knew she would leave again? It wasn't because she reminded him of Marzi. She didn't – it was just a coincidence that she was ambitious and clever like his ex.

He didn't want to think about Marzi. He still had those unopened letters taunting him and he was trying his best to ignore it all.

He stood at the back of the family photo, slinging his arms over two of his cousins and smiling his signature toothy grin. But his gaze kept returning to where Jenn stood, off to one side, her arms tucked around herself. When he stood with his beaming family, celebrating marriages and births, anniversaries and successes, he felt like an outsider too.

* * *

Jenn suspected it was a pointless exercise, but she couldn't stop trying to puzzle Tiziano out. His mood had swung decidedly downwards after the weird moment with the baby and his mother. Perhaps he *couldn't* have children. That would explain a lot. But how would he know that? Unless that one relationship he hadn't wanted to talk about had blown up because they couldn't have children. That didn't seem fair. They could have adopted. It was obvious that Tiziano liked children.

Urgh, none of it made any sense and it wasn't her business anyway, although it would have been nice to know something about him, given everything she'd blabbed about herself.

The car made it safely back to Combai by some miracle, gurgling and grinding up the driveway and giving out with a cough once there. Tiziano cursed it with phrases that Jenn didn't understand, but which sounded flagrantly colourful. He helped Filomena inside and disappeared again. Whatever had piqued him at the party obviously hadn't cleared, yet.

She went up to her room and peeled off her blouse and tailored trousers in favour of a T-shirt with Mickey Mouse on it and light cotton capris. She ducked out onto the balcony to read her emails. A few always dropped in on a Sunday, but luckily she hadn't missed anything from Filippo.

She could have replied to one or two, but instead, she flicked through her photos, pausing on the best ones with a smile. There was Stefano with his bushy moustache, holding his organic prosecco, his eyes twinkling with pride. There was a great shot of a bunch of plump grapes, brownish-yellow, now they'd passed the ripening stage of veraison. She'd captured the looming mountain in the background, as well as the fluffy, horizontal rows of vines, out of focus. But the ones she kept returning to were the faces of the growers.

Her photos from the baptism were of the church and the view from the restaurant. As uncomfortable as she'd been, at times, the family had been kind to her and Tiziano had been right to say she needed to appreciate the wine in context. She chided herself for wishing she had a picture of him to puzzle over. Sometimes, tight lines at the corners of his mouth seemed to be whispering his secrets.

A rustling among the vines made her look up and

she saw him there, his head bobbing above the leaves. She'd never explored the little vineyard attached to Filomena's farmhouse, or found out what it meant to Tiziano. Maybe he'd be more likely to open up to her among the bunches of golden grapes.

13

The vineyard was a scorching sun trap. The soil was crumbly and radiated heat. Jenn had thought her little balcony was hot, but it was a breezy haven in comparison to the stifling microclimate of the hillside. She wasn't clueless enough to wear heels, but her strappy sandals were the only other option she had and they soon slipped and filled up with dirt, and the incline was so steep that she had to grab for the metal posts at the ends of the rows.

The vines emerged from the soil as fat, twisted trunks, clinging to the hillside with their spindly, leafy arms. The slope was cut into low-set terraces, which was the only way Jenn could imagine anyone being able to prune and harvest in such steep conditions.

The earthy, sulphury smell of lime tickled her nostrils, but it wasn't unpleasant, especially because it suggested a soil that could produce grapes full of complex mineral flavours.

Tiziano was right at the top and he smiled when he saw her – well, he laughed at her. Clods of dirt crunched under his boots as he made his way to her, reaching out to haul her into the row with him.

'I see time with your grapes has restored your mood – either that, or laughing at me,' she said. His smile faded. 'Sorry, you're allowed to be grumpy,' she insisted, looking out over the dazzling green hills. 'I didn't come out here to upset you.'

'Why did you come out here?'

'Is this Filomena's vineyard, then?' she asked, brushing off his question.

He nodded. 'Her father bought the land between the two wars. It's not much – not enough to be worth learning winemaking for, but the grapes are... something special.'

'Has it been a good year?'

'Magari,' he replied immediately, a thoughtful smile on his face. 'You don't have that word in English. It's like hope and fear and lots of... maybe.' He glanced at her and something in that look made her think about kisses and whispered secrets. Magari... She took a deep breath to clear her thoughts.

'Have any of the vines survived since your great-grandfather's time?'

'A few.' But Jenn could tell he was being modest. At the top of the vineyard was a gnarled row of ancient vines, interspersed with younger plants filling the gaps where the old ones had died. The oldest bore only a handful of bunches, but they were pungent and golden.

'This is your real job, then,' she said with a reproachful smile.

He shook his head. 'It's too small to make any money and I'm not trained. My parents wanted to sell the land when Nonna couldn't look after it any more. I just take care of it so they don't have an excuse.'

'I thought you said that money wasn't important to the community around here.'

'I said it wasn't the *most* important thing. My parents should sell it, from a business point of view. The top wineries would pay an eye for this land, but they rarely buy the grapes. Plus, these vecchie viti, old vines, here are verdiso, not glera. A small amount is allowed in prosecco, but the trend is for 100% glera. My grandfather had no way of anticipating that. When he was working this land, prosecco wasn't much known outside of Veneto, and I think Nonno kept the vines working mainly so he could get back the grapes after pressing to make grappa. That was his true passion.' He grinned at her suddenly. 'We're peasants, not a noble family.'

She returned the smile. 'And you think *I* have too much pride.'

He watched her intently for long enough that she busied herself inspecting the grapes. 'I'm sorry about today,' he said softly.

'What? Why?'

'You hated it.' He sighed. 'That wasn't my intention.'

'Just because I find something difficult doesn't mean I hate it. Everyone was friendly – except maybe your mother.'

'Yeah, she thinks we're sleeping together,' he said casually, plucking off a leaf as though he hadn't said something outrageous.

'Why on earth does she think that?' Jenn choked out.

'It's my fault. I brought you. I'm sure it wasn't because she picked up on the sexual tension,' he said with a wink. 'And I couldn't tell her you're actually in love with your boss so she doesn't need to worry about me.'

'Worry about you? As if *I* would be the one...' There was a concerning twinkle in his eye. He grinned, catching his tongue between his teeth, and Jenn was struck again by niggling, vague memories. Had they kissed? The more she thought about it, the more she could imagine the feel of his mouth on hers – in a lot of detail. 'Are you... sure nothing happened that night?' she asked before she thought better of it.

'Why? Do you remember something?'

'No,' she insisted.

'Are *you* sure?' When she looked up, he was suddenly closer, his tall frame hunched over her with one hand on the wire that supported the row of vines. That woody scent, heat and sunshine did bring back memories – taste memories. She froze and stared. She *had* kissed him.

'You told me nothing happened!' she cried.

'You obviously wanted to think that. I only obliged.'

'Nothing... else happened, did it?'

'I would feel even more annoyed – and very guilty – if you didn't remember sleeping with me. No, nothing else happened. I wouldn't even have kissed you if I'd realised how strongly alcohol affects you.'

'You kissed me then,' she muttered, releasing a relieved breath.

He opened his mouth, but hesitated, and her worries rushed back. He swallowed and the prickle of memory over Jenn's nerve endings grew stronger. He didn't have to say anything, she could almost see it now. She'd smooshed her lips against his and challenged him to game of tonsil hockey. But why? She was supposed to be in love with Filippo. She was even more baffled by relationships than she'd thought.

'It's okay, Jenn.' Tiziano's voice crooning in her ear reminded her of how he'd been with Alessandro – strong and capable and infinitely gentle. 'It was a drunk kiss and you didn't betray anyone.'

'Only myself,' she muttered.

He laughed darkly. 'A guy like me... a woman like you – I know it doesn't make sense, but... it wasn't that bad, even if you don't remember it.'

'I didn't mean to hurt your feelings—'

'You can't hurt my feelings – or my pride. They're not as fragile as yours.'

'I'm not—' She cut herself off when she realised he was teasing her again. 'I don't believe you,' she blurted out. 'I apologise for accosting you while drunk and then forgetting all about it, and I apologise for suggesting that kissing you was beneath me or that I didn't mean to do it. It's *not* that.'

'You mean you *did* want to kiss me?'

That was the question of the hour.

Her cheeks heated, but she decided to blame the sunlight that was also scorching her hair. His eyes twinkled and that blasted smile, all teeth and cheekiness, distracted her.

'It's not really fair that you don't remember,' he said, his voice so quiet it rasped.

Remind me...

Holy crap, that was a bad idea. Besides, she remembered more and more the longer she stared at his mouth. She'd wondered what it would feel like to kiss him with that piercing and... boy, she'd found out. They'd gone from zero to making out in about two seconds. She was hot inside *and* out, now. He licked his lips and she wondered where she'd left her breath.

She was about to panic and either kiss him again or step away and go tumbling down the hill, when she was saved by the trill of her phone ringing. She took a hasty step back as she fumbled in her pocket. Her foot landed awkwardly on the churned earth and she stumbled, teetering. Her phone went flying and she lunged after it, registering in the same frenzied moment that she was heading straight for the wires and that Filippo was calling.

Her progress down the hill halted suddenly and

she caught her phone with a relieved gasp. As she connected the call, her, 'Hello?' was breathless.

There was a pause on the line. 'Everything okay, Jenn?'

'Yes!' she insisted. 'I was just... walking.' That was when she noticed a tattooed arm wrapped around her waist and felt a gust of Tiziano's breath in her hair.

'Walking? Did something happen to the hire car?'

She opened her mouth, but the vibrations at her back from Tiziano's laughter stopped her from weaving the lies more tightly. She planted her feet and peeled his arm off her.

'I'm in a vineyard,' she explained instead. 'What's up? Can I help with something?'

'Yes, you can. I've decided to attend the Vin Excellence conference in Milan after all and I need you with me.'

'Need me...' Had Filippo always spoken about her in such strong terms? She was so mixed up. It must have been the relentless humidity. 'Sure. I can take a few days out from my work here. Things are coming along. I'm getting to know the... producers.' The tips of her ears were hot.

'Good, I knew you'd be a prosecco expert in no time. Bookings are strong for your tasting event already and I'm looking forward to it myself. You'll drive and bring the hire car to Milan?'

She gulped. 'I could take the train. I don't know how far it is.'

'No, no, from where you are? The trains probably only run once a day and go at the speed of a snail. You can pick me up from the airport. I'm taking my friend's Lamborghini to Rome after the conference so it doesn't make sense to get my own car in the city.'

Jenn blinked, picturing Filippo driving Tiziano's clunking tractor all the way to Rome until she realised he meant another kind of Lamborghini. 'Sure,' she said, her voice wavering. 'I'll pick you up at the airport.' Tiziano gave her a nudge and she eyed him.

'Perfetto,' Filippo said, falling back into his usual Italian tic that Jenn found irresistible, except when she was panicking about all the lies she was spinning. 'I'll send you the details of the hotel booking and see you in a few days. My contacts in Milan are keen to meet you. They'll be interested to hear all about your prosecco adventures.'

'They... great,' she said weakly. 'I'll... see you then.'

'Why did you say that?' Tiziano asked as soon as she disconnected the call. He threw up his arms. 'How are you going to pick him up from the airport? On a bicycle?'

Jenn's mind raced, but she already knew what she had to do, what she'd known she would do ever since she'd panicked and agreed with Filippo's suggestion. 'Would you...' She choked on the request. 'Help me?' she mumbled.

His brow shot up. Then his mouth twitched with a smile. He hunched over. 'What was that? Can you say it again, loudly?'

She crossed her arms. 'Can you help me? Can you drive me to Milan and pick Filippo up from the airport?'

He matched her stance. 'You should tell him the truth.'

'He's just starting to trust me with more responsibility. His opinion of me will completely change, when I've been working so hard for this. Me losing my licence has nothing to do with how good I am at my job. It was one mistake.'

'If he thinks you don't make mistakes, he doesn't know you very well.'

She forced herself to ignore the jibe. 'Please, Tiziano. It's important.'

'I can see that his opinion is very important to you. If he's the type to drive a fucking Lamborghini to Rome, he can overlook your little mistake.'

She raised an agitated hand to her hair. 'Are you saying you won't help me?'

'Why should I?'

His tone made her stomach drop. 'No reason, I suppose,' she mumbled, turning to pick her way back down to the farmhouse. She'd find another way to work this out, but she was oddly disappointed.

'Jenn.' Tiziano's voice came behind her, his tone flat. 'Because we're friends, giusto? That's why I should help you. That's what you meant to say, right?' When she turned to him, his smile was gone, replaced by a surprisingly vulnerable frown slanting his brow.

'Of course we're friends.'

'You're just saying that because you want my help.'

'No, I just didn't realise friendship was a good enough reason.'

He slapped a hand to his chest. 'Do you not know me?'

She couldn't help but smile. 'I'm starting to,' she said softly.

'But remember I'm doing it for you, not your boss. And *I* like you better when you make mistakes.'

14

Patetico sfigato…

It wasn't news to him that he was a pathetic loser, but begging for friendship had been a new low. Although he couldn't regret that undignified moment because she'd smiled at him and because she now sat in the passenger seat of Nonna's Fiat for the four-hour drive to Milan. Helping her was the perfect distraction from the pile of letters he'd stuffed into his bag and the Milan address he needed to visit, if he could gather the courage.

'Why did we have to leave so early?' she asked with a yawn. She wasn't wearing any make-up and her hair was tied back in a messy ponytail.

'This isn't early.'

'Okay, why did we have to leave at farm o'clock? Filippo's flight doesn't land until this evening.'

Tiziano's smile vanished at the mention of Filippo. He hated the guy already. 'We have to stop at least twice. The car overheats on the autostrada. Hopefully we'll get all the way to the McDonald's in Peschiera del Garda before we have to stop.'

'McDonald's?' she asked, her nose wrinkling.

'Would you rather the autogrill? What's that in English again? A truck stop? In Italy they have those toilets in the floor.' He'd expected her to shudder in distaste, but she glanced at him with a smile.

'I can do squat toilets. I spent time with my grandmother in Korea. It's actually quite ergonomic.'

'You continue to surprise me.'

She gave him a smug look that only amused him. 'Where did you learn English? I'd usually say motorway services rather than truck stop.'

'In school, we learned British English, but not that stuff. I was terrible at English until I went to the States a few years ago.'

'You went to the US? For how long? What did you do?' she asked with far more interest than he'd expected.

'A year and mainly I outstayed my visa. How much time have you spent in Korea?'

'I spent summers there when I was a kid.' Her voice was flat. Her memories of Korea were obviously as problematic as his year in the US.

'Not idyllic summers with your family in the countryside, then?'

'Not at all. My grandmother lived in an apartment on the twenty-eighth floor – in Seoul.'

'Lived? I'm sorry.'

She nodded, a deep crease between her brows. 'At least I got to know her well...' Her voice trailed off. 'My grandmother wasn't like Filomena, though – I mean, except the feeding. Halmoni loved to prepare food for me and it was amazing. Have you eaten Korean food?'

He shook his head. 'Maybe I'll find a restaurant in Milan while you schmooze. I don't think we have any Korean in Treviso – Venezia probably. But why wasn't she like Nonna?'

'My family in general is nothing like yours. I told you, didn't I, that I don't know my father? Well, my grandmother freaked out and disowned my mother after she got pregnant and wouldn't say who the father was. I think he was probably married.'

'What?'

Jenn shrugged. 'It was the eighties. Even today,

single parents are rare in Korea. But my mum was smart and moved somewhere she could make it on her own. We spent a few years in Hong Kong, where she could afford a nanny and then we were in New York until I was eight, then London. It was only when Mum's career really took off that she struggled with the amount of childcare she needed so she went back to my grandmother, begging her to take me one summer when she had a string of high-profile deals.'

'Seoul, Hong Kong, New York, London – your life is like a band's stadium tour.' He had to force the smile to match the joke. He was trying to lighten the mood instead of drawing attention to how brittle her voice sounded. Her mother had to beg her family for help? Talk about a tangled mess of pride and grief. 'Did you grow close to your grandmother?' he asked warily.

'Yeah,' she said after a long hesitation. 'As close as she could manage. My whole existence was a bit shock to her pride and it took a lot for her to get over it. Mum's success in her career helped Halmoni to soften her stance. Mum's a genius with numbers. She's high up at a private bank these days.'

'You're making me feel bad for resenting my mother's interference in my life.'

'I didn't mean to. What does she interfere with?

Does she think you should get a job? Do they know you work like four jobs?'

He gripped the wheel and looked straight ahead as they cruised along the autostrada, disproportionately pleased by her defence of him. She was only being fair.

'Or is it the pressure to get married and have babies like your brother? I find that so insensitive. You never know why someone doesn't have kids and, even though I want my own, I don't like people always asking when I'll finally "decide" to settle down and have them, as though it's within my power and I'm just being stubborn.'

He gave a huff, hoping she didn't notice the bleakness of his laughter. 'You're right, of course.'

'You're a fantastic uncle, though.'

He choked, clearing his throat before he managed to respond with mumbled thanks. 'Allora,' he began, shoving away the gloom of the past to change the subject, 'when signor Baretti finally realises what he's been missing and begs for a chance with you, how many little Korean-Napoletani will you have?'

Only after several moments of silence did Tiziano suspect he'd said the wrong thing.

'You're a real nutcase sometimes, you know,' she

said. 'I assume you're not trying to piss me off on purpose, but then you say something like that...'

'I am a nutcase, but I didn't mean to piss you off. What did I say?'

'It wasn't what you said, it was the way you said it. He's not going to beg for a chance with me and you make it sound like wanting kids is a grand joke! I should never have told you!'

Tiziano took a deep breath and eyeballed the bridge ahead, pricked by guilt. She didn't realise how close she'd come to poking his wounds. 'I'm sorry, Jenn,' he said through gritted teeth. 'I didn't mean to criticise you. It's my problem, my attitude to parenthood, and no reflection on you. But I do think Baretti should beg to deserve you.'

He glanced at her in time to see her throat ripple as she swallowed. Merda, he'd turned it on too strong again. 'Th-thanks,' she stammered, staring at her hands, 'for the vote of confidence, at least.'

'What's the plan, then? Do you need me to strand you two somewhere so you have to talk? Getting stuck in an elevator could work, except it's not well ventilated and that's no good for your nose.'

She relaxed in her seat and he was glad to take a breath after the emotion strung tight between them. 'I don't think getting stuck in an elevator is a good idea.

Filippo is more likely to combust with frustration than with sudden lust for me.'

'I'm sure he feels the lust part already. I thought you were aiming for true love.'

She eyed him and he realised he'd sounded cynical again. 'He's my boss.'

'He's still a man.'

'Not every man is as undiscerning as you,' she said, giving him a withering look. 'No, I don't want to lose my job over a crush. I should probably give up on it.'

How strange, that he felt sympathy and glee at the same time. 'Give up without trying? I'm not saying you should do anything differently, but a weekend like this is a great opportunity to work out how he feels about you. Maybe we can give him a nudge. I might make him jealous,' he added with a grin. 'Shall we do that? I could pretend to be interested in you, and he might get jealous or defend you.'

'And what am *I* supposed to do? If I encourage you, he'll get the wrong idea, but if I fight you off... No, Tiziano. It's a terrible idea. I just have to look for an opportunity to be honest.'

'You'll tell him how you feel?'

'Of course not!'

'Oh, it was only me who thought that's what being honest meant.'

'Very funny. I mean, letting things happen naturally, if they're going to.'

'Does that usually work for you?'

She blushed fiercely. 'No,' she admitted, her voice tight. 'Fine, since you've had all this experience, how do you get girls to sleep with you, then?'

He said her name, his voice gentle. 'Jenn, you're right. You have a much better attitude to relationships than I ever had – much more honest. But you're not being honest with him.' He patted her shoulder, keeping his eyes on the road. 'Has he ever seen you without make-up? Have you let him see that glint in your eye when you argue? Or that Mickey Mouse shirt? That one's cute.'

'I'm not cute. I'm *successful*, for God's sake!' she muttered.

'You can be sweet *and* successful.'

'Yeah, whatever,' she muttered. 'I look successful when I'm wearing make-up and a suit, not a stupid Mickey Mouse shirt!'

He sat back in his seat, releasing a deep breath. What did he know, anyway? He'd loved someone and it had been a disaster. Perhaps he should be putting her off the idea entirely.

'Well... you're hot in make-up and a suit, too, so... daghe! Go for it. If I can help you, I will.'

'Thank you,' she said, but her voice lacked conviction.

'What about the car? Have you worked out a story? I don't want to say the wrong thing.'

'We'll keep it simple. And if this car is so temperamental, that's a good excuse for you having to drive it. You don't have to hang around. I think the wine show is walking distance from the hotel so you can just drop us off.'

'How do you manage these events without getting drunk?'

'That's easy. I spit. It's not that strange that someone who can't tolerate alcohol is a wine expert.'

Her defensive tone spoke for itself. 'Good point. It's not something you have to hide, then.'

'I'm not hiding it. I just don't want to advertise the fact. It's hard enough being taken seriously as an Asian woman in this industry. Filippo is introducing me to a few of his contacts. Do you think I want them making their first impressions based on that?'

He wished he could tell her to let it all go, to screw the people who didn't believe in her. But if he'd grown up under the pressure she had, he would have crumbled a long time ago. His family wasn't perfect, but at least they'd held him together when he'd needed it.

'I can't have him thinking I'm a weak link, especially if… if I'm trying to see if he has feelings for me. Urgh, I sound like such a loser. Maybe I should just go on Tinder like a normal person – but I hate dating and I like Filippo.'

'Yeah, dating sounds like the seventh level of the inferno, which is why I've never tried it. So, what's it going to be, then, for Filippo? New dress? Low neckline?'

'*That's* your suggestion? After the summers I spent with my grandma where those kinds of clothes would have got me grounded, I can't pull that sort of thing off.'

He grinned at her. 'He might be signor sofisticato, but if you want to see if he's attracted to you…'

'First you suggest sunbathing by the Piave and now you think I should wear a low-cut dress. I don't think you know me very well, Tiziano,' she muttered.

He didn't know her well, he had to remind himself. It only felt that way, sometimes. 'Aren't you a bit curious about what it would be like, the sunshine on your… skin?' She choked and spluttered and he kept teasing because it was easier than having a serious conversation. 'What did you think I was going to say? Sunshine on your nipples? It's a good feeling, unless the piercing gets hot and then it's—'

'I don't want to know about your—' She cut herself

off with a harrumph. 'You're teasing me. You don't have a nipple piercing,' she accused in a peeved tone.

'Would you like to find out?'

'No!' The alarm in her expression was funny, even though it pricked his stupid pride. 'You're unbelievable,' she muttered.

15

Jenn hated that she was nervous. Her knee-jerk reaction was to blame Tiziano and the conversation they'd had in the car, but that wasn't fair. He'd only made her see how naïve she'd been to indulge her crush on Filippo.

She'd never even allowed herself to imagine getting somewhere with him – because it was hopeless. Or was she just nervous that Tiziano would let slip that she'd lost her licence? God, she owed him for this, and she hated having to rely on other people.

No matter her tangled motives, it was the most awkward meeting she could have imagined when Filippo stepped through the sliding doors into the Arrivals lounge. Jenn stretched onto her toes without thinking, and Filippo leaned down with the same instinct before they both froze and their gazes flew to each other.

Jenn drew back and coughed. 'I've obviously been in Italy too long,' she mumbled.

Filippo laughed – his low, rich chuckle – and Jenn waited for the little thrill of attraction she always felt at that sound.

He looked just the same: wavy black hair with hints of grey at the temples, thick lashes, stern mouth and dark eyes with the firepower of Mount Vesuvius. But he might have been a stranger, Jenn felt so different. What was wrong with her, aside from the usual inability to understand the emotions of others? Did it apply to her *own* emotions, now, too?

'I hope the car isn't far. It's suffocating outside. I had to walk across the tarmac,' he said with a dashing frown creasing his forehead. 'I know I'm Italian, but the London air has tamed me, it seems.'

'Um... about the car.' She caught sight of Tiziano, hanging back by the doors, clutching his hands in front of him, and ignored his grin at her discomfort. 'It broke down.'

'What? Do we have a shitty Renault instead? Or did they upgrade you to a convertible?'

'No, they...' She resisted the urge to cross her fingers behind her back like a naughty kid. 'There was a problem at their main site and they had no cars left at all.'

'At all? What kind of idiots run the company? We won't use them again. But you found something better?'

'Not... better, exactly. It all happened at the last minute – this morning.' She was a terrible liar. Surely Filippo would notice.

'Spit it out, Jenn,' he said tolerantly – and a little patronisingly, if she was honest. 'I won't fire you for a screw-up at the hire car company. You're my best nose.'

'Actually, the host from the agriturismo offered to help, so the car is...'

'The little nonna lent you her car? Of course she did.' He clapped her on the shoulder. 'But it's probably an ancient Fiat with merda di mucca on the seats. Don't worry. A bit of cow shit won't kill me.' He headed for the doors and Tiziano waved his arms urgently at her. She grimaced in return, giving a shrug.

'Filippo,' she said as firmly as she could. 'It is a little Fiat, and there's no cow shit, but there's a little more to it. It's... temperamental – the car. The hosts at the agriturismo are actually an older woman and her grandson, so her grandson offered to drive us so I didn't have to... deal with the old car.' Filippo didn't appear to have anything to say, so Jenn flapped her arms in Tiziano's direction. 'This is Tiziano, from the agriturismo.'

Tiziano stepped forward with a grin, hand outstretched. Filippo blinked at him for a moment, before slowly shaking his hand, his mouth hanging open. 'Ciao, Filippo, don't worry. I won't get in the way. I'll take you to the hotel and then you'll have Jenn all to yourself.'

Jenn groaned inwardly. He may as well have winked at Filippo, he'd been so obvious. Her boss looked him up and down with thinly veiled distaste, pausing on the studs in both ears, the unbuttoned flannel shirt and the gaping holes in the knees of his jeans. It made Jenn's head hurt. She was annoyed with Tiziano for being too familiar with her boss, but she was also annoyed with Filippo for judging on first impressions – especially when she knew Tiziano played up that first impression for his own curious reasons.

It struck her that, although she felt she knew Tiziano surprisingly well, there was still so much she didn't know.

Filippo and Tiziano chatted stiltedly in a mix of English and Italian as the Fiat puttered noisily through the streets of Milan to their hotel. When Tiziano began talking about tractors, Jenn decided to intervene before Filippo's mystified silence in response became more oppressive.

'You remember I mentioned I'd found someone to make introductions for me, to make connections with this consortium? That was Tiziano. He knows everyone in the hills and runs a small vineyard himself.'

Filippo was thankfully satisfied, although Tiziano's dubious look made her scrunch her nose at him when Filippo wasn't looking.

Arriving at the hotel, Tiziano gave them a lazy salute and gargled a farewell in what Jenn suspected was dialect, if Filippo's sneer was anything to go by. Tiziano pecked Jenn's cheek and whispered, 'Daghe, principessa!' When he'd loped away through the re-volving doors, Jenn felt strangely naked. *Must be the nerves...*

'What a strange man,' Filippo muttered as they ap-proached the reception desk. 'They're all farm people in Veneto – even the prosecco producers. It's all about the land and not about the wine. But you get on with him?'

What did he mean by that? Was he suggesting there was something... amorous going on between them? Why would he think that? 'Uh, he's been helpful.'

'If *you* approve, then he must be a good contact.'

'What do you mean?' Filippo's smile slipped at her blunt question, but she had to know.

'Well, you... you have a reputation – in the company and increasingly in the market.'

'What kind of reputation?'

'Calm down. It's a good thing, Jenn. Everyone knows you're selective and... demanding, and you say what you think. It's something I would be proud of, if I were you.'

She nodded dumbly. Did her colleagues really think she was demanding? And could that be a good thing, as Filippo obviously thought it was? She wasn't sure she wanted to be perceived that way, even if Filippo seemed to like it.

'It's why I wanted you here, Jenn,' Filippo said, squeezing her arm. 'You're my secret weapon and I want to know what my contacts make of you at dinner tomorrow night.'

'Oh... we'll see... shall we?' What dinner? Had she missed a memo?

'Do you think we should invite your country bumpkin?' Filippo asked suddenly. 'If he thinks he knows wine it might be... entertaining.'

Heat flooded Jenn's cheeks, as though she'd just taken a shot of Tiziano's grappa. She didn't want

Tiziano hanging around to spill her secrets, but she especially didn't want to expose him to Filippo's disdain. It pricked her to think she'd treated him with the same disdain only three weeks ago. Just because he chose the life of a farmer didn't mean he couldn't understand the intricacies of the wine world. 'I'm sure there's no need to do that. He's just a... a guide. He's not in the wine industry.'

'Perhaps he'd like a glimpse into the real business of wine, instead of his rural idyll. I have not heard dialect as strong as his in years. It would be quite amusing to introduce him to our Italian colleagues.' His chuckle was rich and deep, but Jenn only felt cold inside hearing it.

She stifled a groan, wishing Filippo didn't feel the need to pick on the farm boy. She wanted to stand up for Tiziano, explain what she'd learned about fine wine from the people of the Prosecco Hills, but it was clear Filippo didn't want to hear it.

Safely in her room after they'd checked in, she snatched up her phone and dialled Tiziano's number.

'I expected you to miss me, but not this much.'

'Shut up. This is important. Filippo might invite you to join us at the networking dinner tomorrow night, but you need to tell him no.'

'A networking dinner? You didn't tell me about that. Do I need to drive you to the restaurant?'

'Shit, I don't know. Wait, no, you can't. You need to have some other plans or Filippo might insist you join us. We can get a taxi if it's far.'

'Won't you be expected to drink at a networking dinner?'

A fresh trickle of anxiety dripped down her throat. 'I'll manage. I always do.' Except she hadn't attended a networking dinner like this before, in Italy, with Filippo's contacts who drove sports cars and conducted business over dessert. She couldn't even use the excuse that she was driving.

'I'll be on my best behaviour. I promise I won't embarrass you,' Tiziano continued.

'It's not that. I'm worried Filippo is inviting you to make some kind of point.'

'He is jealous after all.'

'No! Not like that. He has his opinions of prosecco and seems to think that everyone from Veneto is unsophisticated. That's why he sent me instead of coming himself. I think he wants to laugh at you with his cronies.'

He hesitated for a long moment. 'Okay, I see why you don't want to be honest about your intolerance for alcohol in this company.'

'And why you should stay away.'

'Don't worry about me. Now I want to come and see this for myself.'

She groaned. 'Maybe he won't invite you after all.'

'Then I'd miss out on all the free alcohol and nice food. It doesn't bother me if they want to make fun of this campagnolo – your country boy. I will even speak dialect for their amusement. Then I can drive you.'

She was tempted to protest that she could look after herself, but she didn't want to offend him any further. And part of her was unexpectedly glad to know he might be there.

* * *

The following night, it was obvious that Filippo's outfit was the result of several hours with a tailor and Tiziano's was not. She didn't want to know how much Filippo had paid for his sharp dinner jacket, but the effect was striking. He cut a dashing form, all crisp lines and edges, with just enough salt-and-pepper stubble to make women imagine waking up next to him in the morning.

Tiziano loped into the lobby, in a stiff cotton shirt that still showed the lines where it had been folded in the packet and a thin black tie that made him look like a sallow rockstar who never saw the sun.

Jenn hoped she looked vaguely appropriate for the event. She'd bought a black silk dress with flounces at the shoulders from a boutique around the corner. Filippo had given her outfit a once-over and a warm nod when she'd emerged from the lift into the hotel lobby, but she couldn't tell whether he was approving the impression she would make on his colleagues or enjoying her appearance himself.

Tiziano and Filippo greeted each other with a firm handshake that was approaching an arm wrestle and Filippo headed for the doors, his fine leather shoes clicking subtly on the marble. Tiziano turned back and gave her a wink and two thumbs up.

He kissed her cheek and whispered, 'Nice plan. If he doesn't notice you in that dress, he's not the man he thinks he is.'

'Uh, thanks – I think,' she replied with a wry smile and heat in her cheeks.

Filippo insisted on taking a taxi, claiming he wanted to share a drink with Tiziano, as though they were old friends. It was Filippo's specialty, turning on the charm like that, but Jenn had never seen so starkly how well he could fake it.

'Even you aren't allowed to spit tonight, Jenn,' he

said with a broad smile that did nothing to counteract the chill racing down her spine at his pronouncement. 'Let your hair down.' Her hand flew to her ponytail Did he mean that seriously? She was even more adrift than usual and the night hadn't even begun.

The restaurant was a fine affair with a requirement for jackets that they reluctantly waived for Tiziano, at Filippo's insistence. When they were led to the private dining room in the back, dimly lit, with reflective surfaces everywhere, Jenn's unease grew.

Half of the party was already seated, sipping fragrant aperitivi with wedges of lime or sprigs of mint. Her nose was bombarded with sweet elderflower, burnt orange and herbal notes from all of the drinks at once. Filippo greeted them all boisterously, clapping the men on the shoulder and giving the only other woman a kiss on the cheek.

He introduced Jenn warmly as his 'secret weapon', mentioning her 'extraordinary nose'. She began to think it would start growing, like Pinocchio's, if she spent too long in this company – which was probably only right, given all the lies she'd told lately.

The worst part was, rather than making her proud of her ability, she felt like Filippo's performing monkey, the freak she secretly feared she was. She struggled to ignore the different notes of cologne and perfume and tried to focus on finding the right words so she didn't embarrass herself.

When all the diners had arrived, there were twelve men and only two other women, both taller and more confident than Jenn was and effortlessly... Italian.

Everyone took their seats, Tiziano plonking himself next to her as Filippo sat opposite. They would be served a four-course menu with wine pairings. Four glasses of wine. She'd be singing karaoke after two and snoring on the table after the third.

Someone ordered the restaurant's finest prosecco for everyone, to start the meal, nodding at Tiziano, and Jenn couldn't help feeling that, one way or another, this dinner would end in disaster.

LEOA'I L MACE

16

Jenn was so nervous, she somehow got her glass mixed up with Tiziano's. He patted her hand under the table when she murmured an apology, and proceeded to mix their glasses up on purpose, drinking most of both glasses himself. If they'd been alone, she would have laughed and given him a shove, but she felt as though all eyes were on her.

She soon discovered Filippo's monkey was required to perform before every course. She was handed the wine blind and expected to identify what it was and adlib her tasting notes. Although it made her feel like a burlesque performer with an unusual skill, it wasn't as bad as the dread she felt at having to drink the glass afterward.

She didn't have much experience with soave, but her suspicion that an Italian wine would come first and the distinct bitter almond note at the back of her mouth helped her to guess correctly and she could rattle the tasting notes off in her sleep. Her audience was impressed and Filippo gave her an approving smile.

That smile was usually enough for her to work through the weekend, but that night it wasn't even enough to stifle her annoyance.

The next time Tiziano surreptitiously swapped her full glass for his half-empty one, she nearly told him off for going too hard on the free booze but he winked at her and she froze, realising he was doing it on purpose – doing it for *her*.

Relief sweeping through her, she finally tasted the food – which was fortunate, because she adored carpaccio and this one melted in her mouth. She relaxed enough to enjoy the primo piatto of gnocchi with shrimps and follow the conversations about terroir and marketing, about educating the customer's palate or adapting traditional winemaking.

Only the occasional barbed question was thrown in Tiziano's direction, but if he realised they were treating him disdainfully, then he ignored it and went on talking about the province, his Nonna's cooking or fishing for trout in the Piave, as though he wanted to confirm all of their prejudices.

By the time the secondo piatto, the main course of veal with artichoke and tempura zucchini flowers, arrived, Tiziano was slouching suspiciously low in his chair and he was adding s's onto the beginning of everything he said. The poor man had drunk six glasses of wine, although the two of prosecco had been small.

She caught him heaving an enormous sigh when he grasped the glass of moscato that accompanied the apricot sorbet with rosemary mousse for dessert. He downed half of it in one swallow.

'You're enjoying your meal, Tiziano,' Filippo commented.

'S'delicious. Thank you.'

Worried about him, Jenn reached for the glass to finish the rest before he could, but his hand landed on top of hers. She stared in alarm at their intertwined hands, in full view on the table. His thumb brushed her skin.

She tugged her hand away and Tiziano cleared his throat and beckoned to the waiter, ordering coffee in his raspy voice.

'Why not coffee for everyone?' Filippo said, repeating himself in Italian.

'Even better, caffè corretto!' declared an older man.

'What's caffè corretto?' she asked warily after Tiziano stifled a groan.

'Coffee with grappa,' he muttered.

'And grappa per tutti!' Filippo declared, a little rough around the edges himself, although he'd only consumed half of the amount Tiziano had. Jenn had her answer to what that meant a moment later, when little tulip glasses of clear, brownish liquid were placed in front of each of them, as well as an espresso.

Tiziano held his glass up to the light, as though appreciating the colour of the finest wine. 'It's aged. The colour comes from oak barrels.' He sniffed the liquid and Jenn did the same out of curiosity, but she gagged and sneezed when the alcohol fumes drifted up her nose. 'Four years?' Tiziano muttered, ignoring her. She took a sip and it burned down her throat. The burst of flavour was unexpected, filling her mouth and her sinuses with a fruity, oak-scented smoothness that lingered.

Filippo roared with laughter. 'You are a grappa connoisseur, a prodigy in grappa, like Jenn is with wine? I'm surprised your nose can pick up any kind of bouquet when grappa is designed to knock out your taste buds, not stimulate them.'

Tiziano chuckled in return. 'Don't take away the

few pleasures of the peasants,' he said in a low, amused tone, and sipped his grappa. 'But I don't pretend to be a prodigy like Jenn. What brand is this? What grape?' Filippo beckoned to the waiter with impatient fingers and held a short discussion in Italian. Tiziano burst out laughing before anyone could translate it for Jenn.

'What?' she asked, but he kept laughing, rubbing a hand over his face, his shoulders shaking.

'It's,' he eventually began, before pausing to laugh again.

'It's the Big V?' Jenn guessed.

'You've heard of it?' Filippo asked. 'I was shocked it's become so popular – grappa, of all things, in trending cocktails in America.'

'It's from Veneto,' Jenn explained. 'They have a prosecco grappa, apparently.'

Tiziano was still chuckling, only quieting when she shot him a sharp look. He downed his glass in one go and then, with no concern for his audience, snatched hers and downed that, too.

He glanced around the silent table with a shrug. 'When it's free,' he mumbled, but he didn't seem capable of finishing the sentence.

'Perhaps Tiziano would like to leave,' Filippo suggested in amusement, 'before someone has to mop him up off the floor tomorrow morning?'

Jenn shot to her feet. 'I'll... I should...' She couldn't explain what she owed him. 'I'll call him a taxi,' was all she managed, but she knew she wouldn't be coming back. She'd needed to make a good impression, but she owed Tiziano more.

In the taxi, he groaned and slumped against the window. The taxi driver talked at her in Italian, growing louder when it became apparent that she didn't understand. She shook Tiziano guiltily. 'Where are you staying?' She hoped it was with a friend who could look after him.

'Just go back to the hotel. I'll be fine from there,' he slurred.

'No, you won't! There is no way I'm going to let you drive like this. God, I'm so sorry.'

He squeezed her hand, but it seemed to take all of his strength. 'Don't worry. I've been drunk before.'

'That doesn't mean I would ever forgive myself if you lost your licence for drunk driving or had an accident or... choked on your own vomit!'

'I'm not going to vomit.'

The driver called something over his shoulder in relief that suggested his English was better than he'd led Jenn to believe.

'S'go back to the hotel.' Tiziano gave the name of the hotel to the driver, who pulled away from the kerb with a shake of his head and an eloquent hand gesture.

Jenn tried one more time. 'Where are you staying? Where did you sleep last night?'

His eyes didn't open as he murmured, 'In the car.'

'What? Why didn't you tell me you were broke?'

His hand groped for her head and he smoothed her hair jerkily. 'Calma. It's a long story. I have money.'

'But you can't sleep in the car when it's parked at the hotel!' That finally made him pause.

'It's a hotel. I'll sleep there.'

She offered to pay for a room for him, but of course he refused.

The taxi pulled up at the hotel and she dashed around the car to open his door. She had to catch him when he spilled out onto the kerb. He leaned his head on her shoulder and groaned. The scent of his hair gel reached her nose.

She was usually unsettled by the scents of other people in her personal space, but the pleasantly clean smell only reminded her of everything he'd done for her that evening – everything he'd done for her over the past few weeks.

'Come on, you,' she said softly, patting his cheek.

'I don't like Filippo,' he mumbled, shifting his head on her shoulder. At that moment, Jenn wasn't so fond of her boss either, but it was a problem that would have to wait until tomorrow. 'But I like you,' he continued softly. A smile touched her lips. Only Tiziano could still like her after everything she'd put him through. Then his lips feathered over her neck and she froze.

'Tiziano,' she warned, her breath short. 'Time to get out of the taxi and sleep this off.' He plopped one leg out and sighed. She helped him haul himself up and dragged him into the foyer with some difficulty, his long arm slung over her shoulder. She gritted her teeth and tottered towards the reception desk, trying to think ahead and not wonder what he'd meant by his mumbled confession that he liked her.

'Good evening, Miss Park,' said the receptionist, who obviously hadn't got the memo that chirpiness wasn't called for at this time of night especially when the guest was dragging in a drunk man.

'Could I book another room for my... friend?'

Given the way the evening had played out, she should have expected the receptionist's earnest apology. 'I'm so sorry, Miss Park, but we're fully booked tonight.'

'Car,' Tiziano said, his breath tickling her ear.

Jenn shifted him to save her smarting shoulder. 'Oh, okay. No problem,' she said tightly to the receptionist, and turned for the doors. After a few steps she stopped and sighed. There was only one solution. They staggered to the lifts and up to Jenn's floor, tumbling into the room after she unlocked it. He blinked wildly when she turned the lights on, his pallor grey and his eyes dull.

'You might feel better after a shower. Will you be okay?'

He fumbled for the wall and nodded. Whether he'd forgotten she was there or simply forgotten social niceties, she didn't know, but he tugged off his tie and unbuttoned the shirt where he stood, pulling it off over his shoulders.

Jenn suspected she shouldn't, but she couldn't help herself. She looked down at his chest. There, winking in the light, was a little barbell through his left nipple. She grimaced.

'It hurt a lot less than a tattoo,' he mumbled, tweaking the barbell and making Jenn gasp. He chuckled and lifted an arm to rub the back of his head, revealing the dark tattoo on the inside of his arm. She picked out a pair of wings, a few skulls and stylised lions, all woven together with swirling patterns. She could imagine that would have hurt. 'Hai finito? Uh, you finished looking?'

She managed some kind of choked response and ushered him into the bathroom, gulping in an enormous breath when he was safely behind the door.

But her uncertainty wound up again when she emerged from her own shower half an hour later. He was sprawled on the bed – her bed – his hair a tangled mess. He appeared to have kicked off the covers already. Jenn stared, no idea how to make the situation bearable and not at all sure what she wanted.

She pulled back the sheet and slipped into bed, trying not to disturb him. She wished she couldn't smell him so intensely, but not because he smelled unpleasant. He smelled like the opposite of loneliness, whatever that was.

She turned off the light and curled up next to him, not quite touching. He turned his head towards her and she stared, her eyes slowly adjusting until she could make out the line of his jaw, his full lips – not smiling, for once.

He murmured something unintelligible and the persistent hint of alcohol on his breath pricked her afresh with guilt.

'Shhh,' she said softly, brushing her fingertips over his cheek.

'Marzi...' he said on a sigh. 'Te vojo ben. Tutto va bene.'

Jenn froze, drawing her hand back slowly so he didn't wake up. Had he just confused her with someone else, someone called Marzi?

17

The sunlight was disorienting when Tiziano woke up. It was approaching the vendèma, harvest time – September was ticking along. He should have been up before dawn, checking the grapes for botrytis and getting on top of equipment repairs before the requests for help with the harvest flooded in.

He started to rise, but the pounding in his head stopped him a few inches off the pillow. Unfamiliar light slanting through the blinds tipped him off that he wasn't at home, in his dim converted shed, in his own stinking company.

He froze. He didn't dare look to his left, but he knew, anyway, that he wasn't alone. A flash of concern about boundaries and drunk sex lit up in his brain, but he shook his head to clear it. He remembered most of the night before, although it grew hazy at the end. Had he really tweaked his nipple at her? He hoped not.

He grimaced and squeezed his throbbing head with one hand. Forcing himself upright with a stifled groan, he slipped out of the bed before he was tempted to stare at her across the pillow. He escaped into the bathroom to see if there was anything he could do to make it less terrible that she'd had to share a bed with him.

The packaged hotel-brand toothbrush he'd found in the cabinet last night was a godsend and he swallowed his guilt and rummaged in her toiletry bag for toothpaste. It was worth it when he also came away with paracetamol. Leaning on the sink, he stared at his reflection, at the lines of age that felt overdue on his face, after everything he'd lived. He was only thirty, but he felt seventy, and not only because of the alcohol. Two nights in the city were enough. At least Jenn had saved him from a second night in the car in front of *that* apartment building, too cowardly to ring the doorbell.

A smile ghosted his lips as he thought about Jenn. She was something special. So lost, so worried, and yet, she was so much stronger than he was.

He slipped out of the bathroom and accidentally

caught sight of her, curled up peacefully in a pair of tiny shorts and a strappy pyjama top, her hair brushing her cheek. Yep, gorgeous. He hoped that turd Filippo never got to see her like this, or, if he did, that he was humbled by how lucky he was.

Tiziano knew he should go before Jenn woke up, but his self-discipline wasn't great at the best of times, so he snatched up her room key on his way out. Ten minutes later, he was back with coffee in a takeaway cup for Jenn. His own double espresso, knocked back at the bar, had gone a long way to clearing his head.

She was still asleep. It was a Sunday morning, so he understood if she wanted to sleep late, but he'd worked in agriculture for so many years that he'd forgotten people did that. Plus, this was some kind of working weekend for her and he wasn't sure what her turd boss wanted from her. Tiziano hesitated for a long moment, coffee cup in hand, wondering if he should wake her. It seemed cruel, but cold coffee was also a travesty.

He set the coffee down on the night table and she rolled over, as though drawn to the earthy, rich smell of the coffee. Trust Jenn to wake up for a smell. She blinked lazily and stretched and if Tiziano's smile grew much wider, it would hurt.

'Buongiorno, splendore,' he said with a soft

chuckle, glad she wouldn't understand the endearment that had slipped out too easily.

She slowly opened her eyes and met his gaze. He swallowed, wondering what her reaction would be to the memories of last night. Then she smiled, warm and a little bit amused and he gulped for a different reason.

'How are you feeling?' she asked. 'Do you remember what happened?'

He perched on the edge of the bed, careful not to touch her legs. 'I wasn't that drunk. I unfortunately remember everything.'

'You *unfortunately* remember admitting you like me and kissing my neck?'

He straightened so suddenly that he bounced on the bed. He *hadn't* remembered that, although he did, now, vividly.

She laughed wryly. 'I don't know what happens to us when we're drunk, but at least it affected you, too.'

'Sorry, I—'

She shushed him with her fingers against his lips and he felt an idiot for enjoying the touch. 'Don't worry, Tiziano. I know you didn't mean anything and I owe you. I really owe you for your help last night.' She dropped her hand and he went after it before he could stop himself, gripping it between both of his.

'You don't owe me. I'm not sure I made anything better for you. And saying I liked you wasn't a part of the night I regret.'

She sat up slowly, rubbing her upper arm. Legs crossed, perched in front of him, she was suddenly very close. His fingers itched to brush her hair back over her shoulder. She peered at him from beneath a furrowed brow and bit her lip.

Oh, crap. His mind raced. Surely she wasn't inviting a kiss. Didn't she realise what would happen? With every second that he hesitated, she swayed closer.

'Jenn?' he asked, his voice breathy.

'Mmm?'

'You're not... still drunk are you?'

Finally, some reason intruded. 'I didn't drink much last night. What are you talking about?'

'I just... It seemed like you wanted me to kiss you, but if you're not drunk, why would you...'

She drew back – thank God. 'If you don't want to kiss me, you can just walk away. You don't need to spell it out for me.' She pulled her knees up and moved to get off the bed, her face turned away.

'You still don't remember? The night with the grappa?'

She flashed him a frown. 'You told me we kissed

and nothing else happened. I even said I wasn't sure I could believe you,' she groaned.

'Technically, we didn't go further than a kiss, but...'

'Technically?' She stared at him, wary, but curious and he bit his tongue to stop himself from blurting out how much he wanted to kiss her again. 'Did we touch?'

Heat swept up the back of his neck. 'A bit,' he admitted.

'Where?'

Her blunt question made him smile, but he was also panting like a poor greyhound. 'Ehm, I don't know how to describe it.'

Her back straight, she eyeballed him and asked, 'Was it... was it like this?' She lifted a hand to his face, her fingertips drifting into his hair.

He cleared his throat. 'Not exactly.'

'This?' She tucked her legs under her and came closer, lifting her other hand to frame his face. Sparks crackled across his skin. This touch wasn't drunken fumbling, it was sober tenderness and he wasn't sure he could take it.

'Jenn,' he mumbled in warning.

'Did we... remove clothes?'

He shook his head vehemently. 'You were drunk.'

'I can't help thinking that it's a shame I can't re-member properly.'

He whipped his gaze to hers, finding her expression so soft he was done for. 'I thought that,' he admitted, trailing his fingers from her shoulder to her waist.

She watched the progress of his hand. 'Did we touch like that?' He shook his head and settled his forehead against hers. 'But it was good, whatever we did?'

'Too good,' he said with a dry laugh. 'I'm worried it'll happen again.'

'That's one solution.'

His breath had taken a vacation without him and his brain was fog. Did she really want it to be out in the open how much they were attracted to each other? It was a bit late to be worried about that, when her fingers tangled in his hair and she brought her face close. His eyes squeezed shut.

'Is this your way of thanking me for last night? Because you really don't have to.'

Her lips skittered across his jaw to his ear and he thought he would burst. 'That would be a bad reason to kiss someone.'

A smile touched his lips. 'I've kissed people for worse reasons.'

'But I haven't,' she whispered in his ear. And that was the problem. He could afford to mess around, have a good time without thinking about the future, but Jenn? Her lips feathered across his cheek and that was all it took for him to toss his reservations aside. If she regretted this later, then that was fair. At least they could have a good time, now.

He tugged her into his lap, one arm tightening around her waist and the other in her hair. 'It was more like this, that night,' he muttered, the recklessness rising in him again. He tilted his head and let it happen.

* * *

Whatever pride Jenn had sacrificed to start this was more than replenished as Tiziano clung to her like a drowning man, breathing her in with open-mouthed kisses that made her wonder if the aircon in the room had broken in the night. She felt his piercing, smooth against her tongue, bringing back flashes from that Sunday night.

How could she have forgotten the feeling of his erratic breath gusting her skin? She hadn't – not entirely. He felt familiar. The *wanting* felt familiar. She could barely think. She *had* to think. She had to work out what was going on and why his mouth felt so good on her neck, but... *God*, his mouth felt good on her neck.

She mumbled something, but she forgot what she

wanted to say as soon as she started the sentence and she didn't seem capable of language right now, anyway. Tiziano didn't have that problem. Everywhere he touched, he also admired with rasping praise, switching between English and Italian.

'Bellissima,' he murmured, swallowing the l's as he usually did in his rural dialect. 'You're so beautiful. God, even your hands are beautiful.' Tingles ran up her arm as he kissed her hand and the inside of her wrist, where her pulse was pounding. She didn't think of contradicting him, even as his fingers drifted under her shirt.

She slipped off her own top, feeling hot and tight, and started on his buttons with hands that didn't seem to work properly. She breathed him in, with a strong premonition that the scent of them together would be a powerful memory.

He stilled her all of a sudden with one hand on her thigh and tucked her hair behind her ear. 'Are you on contraception?' he panted, his expression unexpectedly pinched. 'I always use condoms as well, but... are you?'

Jenn froze, her doubts rushing back with force. This was Tiziano, who flirted with all of Veneto and didn't want kids. Sex would complicate everything and mean nothing.

He rubbed a hand over his face, giving her a smile that didn't reach his eyes. He had the nerve to still look cute, his hair a mess and a tired kind of honesty in his green eyes. She should get off him and try to work out what happened next, now the unpremeditated sex seemed to have stalled.

'I didn't mean to spoil the mood. It was a miracle that we got this far.' His smile was wry, but she glimpsed the hurt underneath. It was difficult to hide your feelings from the person sitting almost naked in your lap. She understood he didn't want kids, but there'd been something in his voice when he'd asked about contraception that made her wonder if there wasn't more to it than he let on.

And who was Marzi? She thought he'd murmured in his sleep that he loved her.

He shifted and she wondered if he was trying to dislodge her. The heat of a blush began on her chest, but she was more confused than embarrassed – it was just Tiziano after all.

'I take contraception,' she blurted out. 'It's a responsible question. It's okay to ask.'

His mouth opened, but he didn't say anything at first. It was on the tip of her tongue to ask him what had happened to make him so careful, what heartbreak he'd suffered. It wasn't any of her business, but that wasn't what stopped her. If she asked him now, he'd be out the door so fast he'd probably give the hotel guests an eyeful of his tattoos and she hadn't finished admiring them herself.

She wanted to clock out of life with Tiziano for a little while. She grabbed the open sides of his shirt in two fists and looked him in the eye. 'I want this. Stop wallowing in your inferiority complex and believe me.'

His mouth turned up on one side in a bewildered smile. She loved the way he gazed at her, as though everything she did was right. 'I really, *really* like you, Park Eun-Jin,' he murmured. He dislodged her fingers from his shirt and stripped it off. Dumping her off his lap, her propped himself up with hands on either side of her and leaned close until she tumbled back onto the bed.

After that, there was no more hesitation. Tiziano was all eagerness and fervour – and rough hands and heavy touches. He pushed the rest of the world away with kisses that felt like deep, cleansing breaths; occasional giddy smiles and murmured, urgent words. She didn't feel uncertain or vulnerable, as she'd feared. She felt... enough. Her touches were enough to make Tiziano lose his words and squeeze his eyes shut as he moved with her. Her body was enough to draw out a fierceness in him that made him nip her shoulder and clutch her tightly.

She felt safe enough to loosen her own bonds of pride and feel everything that washed over her, even when his avid touches caught her by surprise. And, after the intensity of the final moments had rolled through her, leaving her gasping and digging her fingernails into his skin, she felt content.

18

He'd never seen anyone sleep so soundly. He'd been smugly satisfied when she'd conked out a few minutes after sex, although it also worried him that she'd wake up with very different feelings about him than when she'd fallen asleep with her head on his chest.

'Principessa?' he said softly. 'Rosaspina?' He chuckled at his own joke, calling her Briar Rose – Sleeping Beauty from the Brothers Grimm. 'I ordered breakfast from room service and I have to get back to check on Nonna.' When her only response was a snort and a sigh, he gave her shoulder a shake. 'Principessa?'

'Don't call me princess,' she groaned.

'Good, you're awake – and yourself again. I got a bit worried you liked me.'

She lifted a wobbly hand to slap him on the arm. 'The number of times I thought about doing that,' she mumbled. He leaned down, offering her his arm again, flexing his biceps. She giggled, clapping a hand over her mouth to stifle it. 'Put some clothes on. You're making me laugh.'

'That's not the reaction I was looking for.'

She sat up, pulling the sheet with her in an absurd, but sweet, attempt at modesty. 'I'm sorry, Tiziano,' she said with an indulgent smile. 'But your muscles aren't your best feature.'

'Psht, they're very impressive and they don't even come from the gym!'

'I didn't say I didn't like them,' she said, her eyelids drooping as her gaze skimmed his bare chest. 'But did you say something about breakfast?'

He grinned. 'Room service will be here soon. Maybe you should...' He gestured vaguely at her body.

'Right.' She glanced at her discarded pyjamas, lying suggestively on the floor, then back at him, biting her lip. 'Is it silly to ask you to turn around?'

'No,' he said firmly.

'You think it is a little bit.'

He gave in to the temptation to kiss her, trying and failing to keep it short and sweet. 'Don't start caring about what I think just because we had sex. If you don't want to walk around naked, then don't. I can get you a robe, or – even better.' He scooped his own shirt off the floor and shook it in front of her.

Giving him an amused smile, she turned and shrugged into his shirt. When she turned around, clutching the sides together, his mouth was as dry as the Piave in a summer drought.

She disappeared into the bathroom, putting him out of his misery, but into the new misery of restlessness. They should talk. He was enough of a coward that he'd kept at bay all of the reasons sleeping with her had been a bad idea, but they crept in on him when she wasn't there.

A knock at the door startled him, but he leapt for it, glad of the distraction of room service from his concerns. He pulled the door wide – and froze. Curses of an increasingly foul nature scrolled behind his eyes and his brain refused to kick into gear.

He nearly panicked and shut the door in Filippo's scowling face.

'Ahi, buongiorno Filippo,' Tiziano said, moving awkwardly from foot to foot. He raised a hand to smooth his hair self-consciously, but dropped it in a hurry when he realised he was flashing his armpit at the man. 'Vuoi venire dentro?' He gestured wildly at the room as he invited Filippo in, stopping abruptly when he caught sight of the mess of covers on the bed. *Fuck.*

'No, no,' Jenn's boss said in his infuriatingly rich, deep voice. It was Sunday morning and the man looked as though he'd just stepped off the cover of a magazine. Whereas Tiziano was standing in front of him in only a pair of rumpled trousers – *casso*, a pair of *unbuttoned* trousers.

The bathroom door opened and Tiziano turned and ran. He skidded to a stop just as she was stepping over the threshold into the room. Gripping the door with one hand and propping his other one against the wall, he blocked her path – and blocked her from view.

'Is that room service? What's going on?' He opened his mouth to explain the disaster unfolding behind him, but his throat clogged and he had no idea how he was supposed to make this okay again. 'Tiziano? What's going on? If you want to show me your muscles again, then you can wait until after I've had some breakfast.'

He coughed, his stomach twisting in anticipation of the way her expression would crumple when she discovered who had heard that statement. *Stop being a dick and tell her*, he instructed himself forcefully. 'Filippo's here,' he ground out. 'I'm sorry.'

Her eyes went round and she gaped, fumbling for the doorknob as she swayed in shock. 'Filippo?' she mouthed.

He nodded. 'I know. Fuck. Get dressed,' he mouthed back, gesturing to her – his – shirt. He ushered her back into the bathroom, giving Filippo a tight smile as he leaned back against the closed door. Catching sight of her little suitcase in the corner, he realised another problem and stifled a groan.

'Aspetto fuori,' Filippo said drily, frowning when Tiziano met his gaze. All Tiziano could do was nod in agreement at Filippo's suggestion that he wait outside, but, when the door was closed, the situation felt even more hopeless. He propped his hands on his hips and grimaced.

Remembering Jenn in the bathroom, he raced back to the door and called out, 'Sorry. He's outside. Quick, get dressed!'

She tore open the door and bolted to the other side of the room to rummage in her suitcase. Now apparently not caring if he saw, she stripped off his shirt and manoeuvred into a bra, quite a pretty one in grey with little—

He turned abruptly away. He swiped his shirt up

from where she'd left it on the bed and shrugged into it. He didn't have a fancy sense of smell, but even he could tell his shirt smelled like her soap. By the time he'd tucked the crumpled shirt into his trousers, closed the button this time and located his belt, Jenn walked into his line of vision, dressed in one of her usual combinations of tailored trousers and a flowing blouse and drawing a brush through her hair.

'Maybe he won't think—' He couldn't even finish his own sentence.

'What else is there *to* think?' She buried her face in her hands. 'I'm going to lose my job,' she moaned. It probably wasn't very big of him, but he was glad she was upset about her job and not the man.

'What have you done wrong?'

'This is a work trip!'

'It's a Sunday! He's the one who wants too much of you. Does he know how many hours you've worked this month?'

'You think I've done so much overtime that I earned a bit of casual sex?' He knew she was being sarcastic, but it still stung. He'd forgotten that he was a bad luck charm for relationships and he was only supposed to sleep with people he didn't care about.

'Scolta, you can scream at me later all you want,

but don't let him make you feel bad. Everyone has a private life.'

'Not me, usually,' she muttered.

'Maybe he needs to learn that you do.'

'Why? It's not like this is ever going to happen again.'

He turned away before she saw him flinch. Of course it wasn't going to happen again. It was clear to him, too, that they shouldn't have slept together, so why did it still hurt? He stared at the blinds as though he could escape through the window and undo all of the damage he'd done.

There was another knock at the door, followed by the muffled call of, 'Room service.'

'Go and meet him in the bar,' Tiziano suggested.

'And let you eat all the room service?' His gaze swerved back to hers. There was a little smile on her lips. 'I'll meet him at the bar and come back. Save me some food,' she said, patting his arm. 'I might need something if I get fired.'

He was a little dizzy trying to gauge her emotions. 'You won't get fired.'

'I've never done anything like this before. Did he look really angry?'

He was stupidly flattered. 'Angry with me? Yes, but maybe he was just jealous.'

'He was not jealous,' she groaned.

'If you can't believe he could have feelings for you, how is anything ever going to happen between you two?' He kept his tone jokey, but of course she didn't laugh. She looked stunned.

'There's not much chance of that, now, is there?' she said with a sigh that got him in the ribs. 'I should go.'

'Wait,' he called after her before she reached the door. He wanted to kiss her, do something to reassure her but all he could do was fix the little tangle of hair at her ear. 'Tutto a posto,' he murmured. 'All ready. Okay?'

'Okay,' she repeated with a grimace.

* * *

When Jenn found Filippo out in the corridor, he was smiling, putting her entirely off-balance. Was he looking forward to firing her? Or did that smile mean her job was safe?

'Coffee at the bar, hmm?'

She nodded mutely and followed him down the hall. She couldn't help thinking of Tiziano's suggestion that they get stuck in a lift together as they descended to the lobby. If the lift stopped right now, she would be crawling up the walls to get away.

What did that say about her supposed feelings for her boss? She suspected she'd been a fool.

'I'm off to Rome this morning,' he commented. What kind of opening was that? Would he say she didn't even need to come back to the office?

He didn't continue and she wondered if he was expecting her to say something. 'Right. In your friend's Lamborghini.'

Filippo's lips twitched in another smile. 'You remembered. I'm leaving soon, but I thought we should quickly discuss next steps.'

Next steps like Jenn's resignation? 'Sure,' she muttered. Sitting up at the bar with a cappuccino in front of her five minutes later, she was just as lost as she'd been when she'd left Tiziano behind in her room.

'How much longer do you think you'll need to get a few wineries to the negotiating table?'

'If you need me to get it sorted quickly, I can—'

'No, no. Perhaps I should have warned you that these relationships with producers can be difficult to build. From what you've told me, you're making good progress. You want them to trust you, but have a healthy respect for you when it comes to negotiations. It doesn't pay to get too... friendly.'

Jenn stared at him, but she couldn't tell if he was making a reference to Tiziano or not. 'I would guess another two to three weeks. The cheaper price brackets are closer.'

'Good. I might join you myself when our lawyers come, so keep me informed, of course.'

'Of course.'

'And I have another task for you while you're there, since you appear to be getting to know... the area... rather intimately.' Heat rose in her cheeks and she realised with a start that she wasn't wearing any make-up. She felt naked without it. 'We need to stock this Big V grappa. I'm hearing about it everywhere. I think of grappa as the group of men gathering after dinner with cigars, but this one seems to be making the crossover into aperitivi and cocktails. I also hear that the caffè corretto will be popular this winter.'

'I-I don't know anything about spirits,' she stammered, still confused about what was going on and trying not to think of Tiziano and his home distillery – or the night she'd sampled his wares.

'Don't worry. You don't need to taste it. I will email you the two varieties I want to order. They're closed to new contracts at the moment, so you'll need to do some convincing.'

She swallowed. 'Convincing... isn't really in my skill set.'

He smiled again and if it weren't for this absurd situation where he'd almost discovered her naked with Tiziano, she might have thought there was some fondness in his eyes. 'You'll do fine,' he said smoothly. 'Remember the next step in your career. I understand it's not easy and the things that make you an exceptional wine expert are not the things that make someone good at doing deals. But you did okay last night. And you will learn, especially when you can learn from me.'

Given his superior tone, she implied that he meant she could learn from 'the best'. 'All right,' she muttered. 'I'll chase up this Big V distillery as well.' She only hoped it was on a bus route.

'Excellent. I should go and you should...' He appeared to be struggling not to smile. 'You should enjoy... Milan before you go back to the countryside. Or are you getting used to rural living?'

'I wouldn't say I've got used to it but I have developed an appreciation for the area. It is very beautiful.'

He lost his battle with the smile and flashed his perfect teeth at her. 'I'm glad you're taking the time to thoroughly appreciate what the countryside has to offer.'

'Are you talking about Tiziano?' She clapped a hand over her mouth, wishing that question away again as soon as it came out of her mouth. But she couldn't bear the confusion. She wanted to keep her job, but it would be better to know straight up what the consequences of that morning would be.

'Yes,' he confirmed with a chuckle. Jenn clutched her hand into a fist, waiting to see what he would say. 'There's no explaining taste, I suppose, if that's what you like.'

'I'm so sorry, it... Nothing happened on company time. I would never... And there's no conflict of interest.'

'Calm down, Jenn. It's fine.'

She blinked, so surprised by his words that she didn't understand them for a few moments.

'You're not the first person to mix a little pleasure with business,' he said with a wink. She sucked in a startled breath. Filippo had never *winked* at her before. Tiziano, sure, but his were cheeky and endearing. Filippo's made her feel uncomfortable. 'I'll be honest, Jenn, it's a relief. You're a genius and an asset to the company, but sometimes I suspected there were electrical circuits under your skin. It's good to see you're hot-blooded like the rest of us.'

'Of course, I'm...' She sighed. 'We all make mistakes, don't we?'

'Davvero. Just don't feel too guilty when you break his heart.'

'Oh, I... It's not a heart thing.'

Filippo laughed and slapped the bar. 'Good to hear it, Jenn. Good to hear it.'

19

When she got back to the room, Tiziano was in a foul mood. He barely gave her time to inhale a croissant and a piece of toast before he herded her out the door and into the Fiat. No matter how many times she tried to tell him everything was okay and it seemed she hadn't lost her job, his mood didn't budge.

'I've never seen you so grumpy,' she muttered as they waited at the fifth set of traffic lights they'd encountered on their way out of Milan.

'There's too much traffic. I *hate* the city,' he muttered, fiddling with the dial until the radio spluttered to life with a crooning ballad. Tiziano grimaced and punched at the buttons until it changed to static and then eventually found another station that was blaring punk rock. He grunted in approval and turned up the volume.

The sun beat down on the little Fiat relentlessly and Jenn's hair was stuck to her forehead and the back of her neck before they'd made it out of Milan. When they reached the highway, she was even less comfortable with the wind flubbing through the windows loudly, whipping her hair and clothes, but Tiziano breathed a sigh of relief.

'You're looking forward to getting home,' she said loudly, over the music and the throb of the wind. His only response was a wordless nod. 'I thought you were Mr Happy-Go-Lucky.'

'There's always more to people than what you see,' he snapped.

She eyed him warily. There was more to people than what they *let you* see. After mistaking him for someone who preferred a simple life, she was starting to suspect that he was one of the most complex people she'd ever met. But if he didn't want to talk, she couldn't make him and the journey progressed in silence until she eventually fell asleep.

For the second time that day, he woke her, but this time he was much less gentle. His fingers bit into her shoulders as he shook her. Her protest died on her lips when she noticed the strong, sweet smell in the car and the feeling of being a chicken in the oven, it was so hot.

'You'd better get out,' he said. 'The engine's over-heated. I had the heat on to try and get the temperature down, but it didn't work.'

'You... what?' He grasped her hands and hauled her out of the car, where she finally breathed again. Outside, on a sweltering hard shoulder, it was still about a million degrees, but at least she wasn't grilling any more. 'Oh, God,' she groaned.

'I'm sorry,' Tiziano mumbled. Holding her chin steady, he swiped her sticky hair off her forehead and neck. His expression was still pinched, but the simple action made Jenn wonder if they would soon be okay again. She was unexpectedly relieved at the prospect.

'What do we do now?' she asked, following him to the boot – if you could call the boxy little compartment a boot.

He popped it open with some difficulty and handed her a bottle of water, which she snatched from him greedily, but her first sip was almost as hot as a nice cup of tea and she choked and spluttered, spilling some over her hand.

'Casso, I'm sorry. How many fucking times have I said that today?'

'It's not your fault,' she said, squeezing his arm.

Since when had she been so touchy-feely? 'Stop blaming yourself.'

'I can't blame you, though. You're the one who doesn't like making mistakes.'

She drew back, studying him. 'Are you upset that we slept together?'

He looked up from where he'd been rummaging in the boot. 'I'm not upset!' he insisted vehemently. 'I'm Mr Happy-Go-Lucky! Even though that sounds like a name for my—'

'Tiziano!' she choked out, cutting him off before he could finish the crass joke.

He grabbed a threadbare towel and a bottle of liquid from the boot, closing it again. 'It's clear you don't want to do it again and that's fine,' he called over his shoulder.

'What?'

He hesitated by the driver-side door and she suspected his pink skin was not only because of the heat. She was rather gratified to see him looking uncomfortable. 'You said... Do I have to explain?'

'I have no idea what you're talking about.'

With a cough, he continued, 'You said you wouldn't sleep with me again. That's not a... problem. I'm not complaining. It's not that I expected...'

'Is that why you're grumpy?'

'No!' he insisted. 'Not exactly,' he qualified himself. 'It probably shouldn't have happened anyway, right?'

She frowned at him and came closer. 'Is that what you think, or is it what you think I think?'

'Eh?'

'Do you want to sleep with me again?' she asked, slowly and clearly.

He licked his lips. 'You still have to ask? But I'm a guy, not a pazzo. If you don't want to, then fine.'

'I never said I wouldn't sleep with you again.'

'Yes, you did. You freaked out when you realised Filippo had found out. Then we were talking about him learning that you have a life and you said it wouldn't happen again.' He flung the door open and leaned in, fiddling with something before slamming it shut again. He stalked around to the bonnet and opened it with some difficulty, then he buried his head in the engine.

Jenn hesitated, trying not to notice that he looked kind of hot, leaning over the engine like that, and wondering how to respond.

'I didn't mean that I wouldn't sleep with you again.'

He straightened so fast his head clipped the bonnet and it came crashing down on top of him. She rushed to help as he spat curses and cried out in pain.

Lifting the bonnet, she slipped the prop back into place and helped him up.

'Today is not our day,' she commented.

'It started well,' he said, his voice low. His smile was dangerous – all light and disarming. 'Allora, what *did* you mean?'

'Well, this is the first time I've ever slept with someone in a hotel at a work event and... I imagine it will be the last.' Surely he wouldn't read anything into that. Maybe they'd end up in bed together again. If she was honest, she hoped Nonna was at least a little deaf and they would spend the night together at the agriturismo. For that to happen though, she needed him to sprinkle his magic dust and keep it all light and fun. But he didn't get the memo.

'What about Filippo?'

She stifled a groan. 'I panicked this morning and probably overreacted.'

'That's not what I mean. Wouldn't you be hoping one day for something to happen with Filippo on a trip? One time when I'm not there to screw with your priorities.'

'You can't think... I've been a bit of an idiot where Filippo is concerned. I see that now. You saw it.'

'I didn't. I saw that you believed you weren't good enough for him, which is bullshit.'

'I was never going to jeopardise my job for him. What does that say about my so-called feelings? I'm pretty sure you saw that.'

'You work hard. Why should you have to risk that?'

'Do you *want* me to be in love with him?' She had the sudden thought that he might, that he had only got involved with her because she was unavailable.

'Of course I don't,' he muttered, but she wasn't sure if she could believe him. 'I think he's a stronzo di prima classe – a... first-class turd. But if you like him...'

Now was not the time to laugh at the way he carefully enunciated 'first-class turd', but she was tempted. 'He said something similar about you this morning – not the turd part!' she hurried to correct herself when he hooted with laughter. 'He said something about my strange taste.'

He cocked his head and gave an exaggerated frown. 'Maybe there is something off about your taste.'

'Maybe there is,' she muttered, gritting her teeth. 'The point is, I'm less certain about Filippo than I was last week. He was weird this morning, like he suddenly respected me more because of what happened.'

'That's a good thing, right?'

'No! If he respected me more because he caught *you* in my bedroom half-naked, then what does that say about him? I had him built up as someone I could spend my life with. Don't try to tell me you didn't think that was at least naïve, if not stupid.'

'What I think doesn't matter.'

'I still want you to understand. I... my outlook has changed over the past twenty-four hours. I don't know what to think any more.'

He looked up at the sky and sighed. 'It's not because of me, is it? I never wanted to change your outlook.'

Sometimes Tiziano made zero sense to her. 'I wouldn't say it's entirely because of you, but if I was truly in love with Filippo, why would I have wanted to sleep with you?'

He shook his head with sudden vehemence. 'It's not so simple. People aren't black and white like that – *love* isn't black and white.'

'It's not?' she asked stupidly.

'No, it's not,' he repeated.

'Are you talking about—'

'Jenn, don't provoke me right now. Do you know how hard it is to keep being Mr Happy-Go-Lucky sometimes?' he asked, leaning heavily on the front of the car. His brow was knit tight over pained eyes. His lips were thin and tense. She didn't know what to say and it was wretched.

He reached for the old towel and she eagerly

handed it to him. He eyed her, but turned his attention back to the engine.

'Stand back,' he warned her, before opening a cap that hissed angrily. He poured some of the liquid inside and screwed it shut again with the towel. He fiddled with a few more bolts and hoses and eventually straightened, wiping his hands on the towel. 'That might get us to the next service station,' he said grimly.

'You... don't think we'll get back?'

'There's a leak. No chance of driving all the way back.'

'Shit,' she muttered, feeling terrible for dragging him into this, when he had his grandmother, his grapes and numerous other responsibilities waiting for him. She felt extra guilty because she was secretly happy with the idea of having him to herself for a bit longer, argument or no.

'If you're against the idea of another night with Mr Happy-Go-Lucky, then we can probably get the train to Montebelluna and Matteo will drive us home.' He slammed the bonnet, tossed the towel and the bottle into the boot and opened the driver door. 'Let's see if this works.'

20

Damn it, the engine started. To make matters worse, the rest of the afternoon passed so smoothly he barely recognised his life. The car made it all the way to Verona before Jenn couldn't handle the suspense of waiting for the car to conk out. Teasing her about not being able to take risks and secretly hoping they'd still be stranded somewhere overnight, Tiziano put her out of her misery and agreed to find a garage.

But not before taking a detour around Verona to see Jenn's face light up as she took in the warm colours of the rendered buildings along the river, the crenellated castle and the many arched bridges.

He was stupidly gratified when she exclaimed, 'The river looks a bit like the Piave.'

He insisted on stopping for lunch at a little osteria on a narrow back street, exploding with flowers and ivy. For the first time in what felt like years, he wished he didn't have to rush home.

Jenn had some kind of app that told her the best public transport options and, after dropping off the car at a mechanic's garage, it took surprisingly little time to reach Montebelluna. That unfortunately meant one thing: they couldn't escape dinner with his brother.

He was on edge already. He wasn't proud of his recent decisions. The letters he hadn't dealt with in Milan still hung over him and he didn't know when that would come back to bite him. He'd confused Jenn about her entire future, when he should have known better than to get involved. Now he had to step up and help her get the producers she wanted on side quickly, so she didn't waste any more time on him.

Maryam and Matteo lived in a two-storey stone house with red shutters, climbing red roses and plastic children's play equipment littering the big yard. Jenn's eyes lit up when she saw it. God, he hoped she found what she was looking for one day.

Maryam came to the door with Alessandro on her arm and greeted them with her usual warmth, kissing both of Tiziano's cheeks and clutching him to her with one arm. He appreciated the hug that day, and pulled her and Sandro close for a moment longer.

'Jenn!' she cried, repeating the kisses and hug. Jenn looked flustered, probably remembering the awkward baptism.

'I'm sorry to arrive at such short notice. I know you have so much to do...'

'Ma no! If you bring Tiziano, you can come any time! Dinah asks for him at least once a week – if not once a day.'

'I always tell you I can babysit,' he said defensively.

Maryam patted him on the arm. 'As soon as this one's not breast-feeding any more – I'm drinking. And then you'll have so much babysitting you'll regret offering.'

He grinned. 'Or we go drinking together, like we did in school. Matteo can babysit, since he gets drunk on three shots these days anyway.'

'Te sento, Tiziano!' Matteo called from inside the house. Of course Matteo could hear him. That was the intention. His older brother appeared and pulled him in for a hug, clapping him on the back. 'Stop joking about getting my wife drunk.'

He was about to snap a defensive reply, when Maryam rolled her eyes and then handed Matteo the baby. 'Òhi, he knows how I wish I could go out and drink right now,' she joked, switching to English with a glance at Jenn.

In no mood to tolerate his brother, Tiziano played a magnetic fishing game with Dinah at the kitchen table, leaving Jenn to fend for herself. She offered to help Maryam, but Matteo sat her down and asked if she'd prefer red or white wine.

'Actually,' Tiziano said without looking up from his efforts to snag an octopus, 'Jenn is intolerant to alcohol.'

'What?' Matteo asked.

Jenn blushed, and opened her mouth to say something, but Tiziano didn't let her. 'She doesn't react well to alcohol. She gets drunk quickly and goes all sweaty and red.' He gestured to his face for emphasis. He caught Jenn's furious expression and threw his hands up. 'Fine! Accept the wine. At least it's easier for me to carry you to bed drunk than it was for you to get me to the hotel last night.'

'You were drunk? I thought you helped Jenn with a meeting at a nice restaurant, but you inbronbà la buelo? You... you... wet your stomach?'

'I think the correct expression in English is, "got trashed". Right, Jenn?'

'You didn't—'

'What was it in the end? Seven, eight glasses of

wine and some grappa? Big V grappa, too.' That still made him chuckle.

'I thought you don't drink like that any more,' Matteo said frustratingly gently. Did his brother think he was going to lose it in front of Dinah? In front of *Jenn?* 'And why don't you let her decide if she wants wine or not,' Matteo continued.

'I know. I can't do anything fucking right,' Tiziano said, turning away again. The kitchen fell silent and he felt everyone's eyes on him, especially Jenn's.

'Fucking ra,' Dinah repeated enthusiastically and Maryam snorted with laughter from her position at the kitchen bench.

'I will have to explain, if she says that in front of the nursery teachers,' she said. 'But they probably expect it.'

'Sorry for adding English swear words to her vocabulary on my account,' Jenn said.

'This is one time I can legitimately take the blame myself and not you,' Tiziano muttered.

'What's that?' Matteo interrupted. He glanced between them suspiciously.

'*Niente,*' he mumbled. He didn't need to hear again that he shouldn't be sleeping with guests, especially when he wasn't sure if it would happen again.

'If you are sensitive to bad language, never go

fishing with Tiziano,' Maryam said, her hands busy pulling apart a fresh lettuce.

'I won't,' Jenn said with a laugh and he couldn't help pouting at her.

'You really don't want wine?' Matteo asked, stealing her attention.

'Actually, no,' she said. 'Thank you, but... Tiziano's right. I'm sensitive to alcohol.'

'There!' Tiziano said, waving his hand at her. 'That wasn't too hard, was it?'

She lifted her chin and it took all his effort not to smile.

'Now, if you're just going to sit there, you could join the game.' He gestured to the shiny octopus he was trying to snag with his magnetic fishing rod.

She hesitated, glancing warily at Dinah, but then took the seat next to Tiziano's niece and accepted the rod he handed her.

'Varda,' he said, leaning down to catch Dinah's attention. 'Daghe, venseremo!' He lifted his fist.

'Daghe!' Dinah repeated with her own little hand clenched into a fist, giggling at his expression. He glanced up to find Jenn watching him doubtfully.

'Are you two ganging up on me? Daghe means "come on", doesn't it? I've heard you say it a lot.'

'Some friendly competition, that's all,' he insisted.

'Right.'

He tried to hold his tongue, but he should have known he had no chance. 'I knew you secretly wanted to come fishing with me.'

* * *

By the time they finished dinner, it was past nine o'clock, but the house wasn't exactly quiet. Matteo had been gone for half an hour, trying to get Dinah to be quiet and go to sleep – a nightly struggle, Jenn understood. Occasional shrieking and stomping could still be heard from upstairs.

Tiziano paced the other end of the kitchen, swinging a grumbling Alessandro to and fro and crooning strange songs in his rasping brogue.

Jenn took the plate Maryam handed her and dried it vigorously. Anything to keep her mind off the picture Tiziano made holding a baby – a slightly ridiculous picture, because of all the funny faces he pulled, as though his cheeks were made of rubber.

Jenn turned her attention firmly back to Maryam. 'Thanks so much for dinner.'

Maryam nudged her with her elbow. 'No, don't thank me. It's good to have people at the table and time to get to know you properly.' She washed and rinsed furiously and Jenn took the time to hide the heat in her face. Why would Maryam want to get to know her?

'Did you really go to school with Tiziano?' Jenn asked, changing the subject.

Maryam smiled instantly. 'Yes, we are the same age. Bene, I turned thirty a few months before he did. One of my earliest memories of arriving in Italy from Morocco was this boy with the white face pulling my hair. But he played with me and we became friends. I met Matteo because of him and now we've been together for thirteen years.'

'Wow,' she said. Maryam was only thirty and had a husband and two kids. And *Tiziano* was only thirty. It wasn't a big age gap, but she felt it – perhaps because he didn't always act his age.

'Dimmelo, Jenn – tell me,' Maryam began conspiratorially, dropping her voice low. '*Please* tell me you had some fun with Tiziano in the hotel.'

Jenn spluttered a denial that came out completely unintelligible. 'Why would you want me to tell you that?' she managed after she'd coughed away most of her embarrassment.

Maryam shrugged theatrically, the plate in her hand dripping everywhere. 'I don't want to change anything, but... I was too young when I found Matteo and I didn't get time for all that young and wild stuff.'

'I'm sorry, but I'm not that young any more and I was never wild,' Jenn admitted flatly. But she had had fun with Tiziano in the hotel room. She bit her lip to keep quiet. 'I'm thirty-four,' she volunteered to distract Maryam.

'Oh, but you look so young! And I look so old! That is what kids do to you.'

'To be honest, I'd prefer the kids and some grey hair,' Jenn said lightly.

'Ohhhh, there's still so much time and you're so beautiful you can pick the right husband.'

'Psht, Maryam,' came Tiziano's voice. 'She'll think you regret having kids. And so will this little guy.' He gestured with the baby, who was sucking heartily on his finger. 'How can he do anything bad to you. Varda – look.' He lifted the baby to his eye level and gave him an exaggerated wink. Alessandro gurgled and cooed. 'He makes you smile. That's what babies do to you.'

'Ha!' Maryam said, her hand on her hip. 'That's what they do to men. Do you have any idea what that progenie del diavolo did to me before he was born? And on the day he was born? And every night since?'

'Are you calling Matteo the devil?'

Maryam threw up her arms. 'I did in the hospital!'

Jenn couldn't help grinning. She stared at Maryam, with her wild hair and her vigorous energy and wished they could be friends. It wasn't the kind of wish she'd ever expressed before, even to herself. But Maryam was so passionate and straightforward, so warm and generous with her honesty and Jenn indulged herself for a moment, imagining long afternoons with food and wine, enjoying a lush, green garden, bright with magnolias and fragrant with jasmine, watching the children play and not thinking about everything she had to achieve the following week.

It didn't sound like Jenn Park at all. It sounded like her grandmother's definition of laziness and her mother's worst nightmare and *they* were the family Jenn had, not Tiziano's larger-than-life relatives. And what did Tiziano want, if not this life his brother had, with love and conviviality, food and *family*? Why did he live in his garage up in the hills looking after his grandmother and working for everyone but himself?

Maryam continued, 'I will complain if I want to and everyone knows it doesn't mean I regret a thing. I have two kids hanging off me *all day* and—' She cut herself off. When Jenn glanced at her in surprise, her expression was full of dismay. 'Me spiase, Tiziano.' It sounded enough like 'mi dispiace' in standard Italian that Jenn guessed she was apologising. She continued in a rush of Italian. Her tone was beseeching and Jenn was intolerably curious.

Maryam and Tiziano talked over each other for a few minutes, arms flying, until Matteo's voice drifted down the stairs, his tone sharp, and they fell silent abruptly. Tiziano stalked out. His exit would have been more dramatic, except that he had to shuffle Alessandro up his shoulder and the baby had the audacity to coo sweetly, even as he was carted out of the room.

Maryam took a deep breath, hands on her hips. She whipped up the tea towel and set to the dishes again with fury, muttering to herself. Perhaps this family thing wasn't as idyllic as Jenn had pictured.

'Is… everything okay?'

'Yes don't worry.' Maryam leaned heavily on the sink and turned fiercely to Jenn. 'Are you sure… nothing will happen between you two?' She was staring at Jenn with big eyes. 'Only, it looks to me that he likes you and after everything he's been through—' She snapped her mouth shut. Jenn's expression must have given her away.

'Everything he's been through?' Jenn asked warily.

'Ops,' Maryam groaned. 'Everyone here saw it happen and what it did to him, but I didn't think…'

'What? What happened?'

'Casso,' Maryam muttered, turning back to the sink. 'Forget I said anything – *please*. It was stupid to think he would... again... even for someone he liked.' She sighed deeply, studying the ceiling. 'It would take a miracle and I think he's given up on those.'

21

Jenn was jolted awake the following morning by a tap on the door of the balcony. She'd slept like the dead and even now she was wondering if she could afford to roll over and get another hour. Even when she worked late, she wasn't usually so sluggish in the morning.

Another tap sounded on the door and she blinked in confusion. Dragging herself out of bed with a groan, she pulled on the door until streams of bright sunlight attacked her eyes.

'Bondì, dormigliona!' she heard from below. She stumbled out onto the balcony to see Tiziano standing on the terrace, a grin on his face. He was back in his usual ripped jeans and a band T-shirt, without the plaid, so she suspected he wasn't off somewhere to work. If she had to guess, he'd recently showered. His hair was neat and he looked fresh. She thought she could smell the familiar fragrance of his aftershave, even at this distance. 'I missed you this morning.'

'What?' Her thoughts flew back to the night before, when Maryam had dropped them back. Matteo had fallen asleep next to Dinah, so Maryam had packed Alessandro into his baby seat and driven them herself. By the end of the half-hour drive, the baby had been grizzling fiercely, so she'd stopped to feed him one more time, waving through the windscreen as she nursed him.

'I missed you when I checked the vines,' he explained. 'Usually I see you drinking your tea on the balcony, but not this morning.'

He looked out for her? If he'd admitted that a week ago, she would have stopped sitting out on the balcony. But just then, she felt pleasantly fluttery thinking about him glancing up at her as he did his work. She leaned her elbows on the railing. 'I must have slept in.'

'Nice for some of us.' He crossed his arms, drawing her eyes to the tattoos on his forearms. His earrings winked in the sunshine. 'I have to get the car. The garage said they will finish it by the time I arrive on the train. You'll be okay on the bus today?'

'Sure.' She nodded. 'I need to do some research

first. Filippo wants me to get this Big V grappa place to the negotiating table,' she said, rolling her eyes. 'Everything I know about grappa is what you taught me.'

He snorted a laugh. 'I can give you a tour of my grandfather's distilling equipment in the barn if that'll help.'

'Do *you* want to supply Brampton with grappa?' she asked with a smile. 'About ten thousand bottles, I think.'

'Not if you offered me the world,' he said emphatically, which was all Jenn needed to know about his attitude to her job. But that wasn't anything new. She'd managed to forget for a few days how different they were. 'I need to go... catch a bus,' he said musingly. 'I never thought I'd say that, but you've taught me some things, too.'

'Have you downloaded the app?' she called as he turned to go.

'I'm not taking it that far.' He flicked his hand behind him in some kind of wave and rubbed the back of his head, making his hair stand up. He had his usual spring in his step. It was a relief to see him back to normal.

'Tiziano!' she called out before she lost her nerve. He turned back, shielding his eyes from the sun. 'I...'

Her courage faltered. 'I wanted to go home with you last night, but... in front of Maryam, I wasn't sure...'

His grin was instantaneous and bright. He stepped back onto the terrace, craning his neck to look up at her. It was a moment that fizzed with possibilities – the landscape opening out in front of her, the morning sunshine slanting over the vineyards and Tiziano staring as though he'd happily miss his bus in order to keep smiling up at her.

'There's always tonight,' he said, his voice deep.

She nodded, tempted to grin right back. 'I wasn't sure if we... what we...'

'It doesn't matter,' he said with a little shake of his head. 'If you want to come, come. You can doubt yourself, but don't doubt me.'

His simple invitation robbed her of any reply she might have produced. She didn't know what their relationship meant, or how long it would last, but he'd invited her to trust him and she couldn't bring herself to refuse, when his smile was so wide and his words so touching.

'Se vedemo, Juliet,' he said with a wink and a kiss to his fingertips.

'So long, Romeo,' she called after him drily. 'Have a good trip to fair Verona!'

* * *

Tiziano whistled and sang along with the radio, beating the old pleather steering wheel in time to the music, as he cruised home from Verona. He was pleased Jenn wanted to keep this... thing with him going a little longer. Even seeing the letter still crumpled and stained in the boot, only caused a momentary twinge of guilt He would deal with that after Jenn left. For now, he had at least a week and the perfect idea for how to help her.

The grappa issue was a problem, though, and he was having trouble deciding what to do. He'd nearly choked when she'd told him about the new addition to her assignment that morning, although she hadn't seemed to notice. He'd think about it later. For now, he wanted to think about how she'd looked, leaning on the railing and grinning down at him, her hair mussed and her pyjamas so short. He even liked the hint of diffidence in her smile, now he understood it wasn't arrogant pride, as he'd first thought.

Dinner last night had been unexpectedly pleasant in a lot of ways. Jenn had seemed surprisingly comfortable and although he'd been worried that Maryam would say something, it was clear she hadn't. Jenn wouldn't have flirted with him and teased him and grinned shyly down at him if she'd known. He shuddered to think how her attitude would change if she found out everything he'd been through. She'd be like all the others back then, when it had happened – all soft, pained words and concerned looks reminding him that he was falling apart.

He didn't want that from Jenn. He wanted her to think he was a carefree country boy who avoided responsibility. He didn't want her to know why he couldn't think about the future.

He could have a vacation from his real life with her, someone who didn't know his history, and she could have a vacation with him and then decide afterwards, with a clear head, what she wanted to do about Filippo. Niente danno, niente affanno – no harm, no worries.

The car rattled across the Ponte di Vidor, the expanse of the Piave river bed on both sides, and he gave a sigh to be home. The white stones and criss-crossing streams of blue-green looked inviting and he imagined bringing Jenn here to swim.

He enjoyed wondering what she was doing as he passed through Valdobbiadene and headed into the hills. The sun was baking and it had been weeks since they'd had any decent rain. His fingers itched as though they could sense the impending harvest.

Feeling like an eager puppy, he coaxed the groaning little Fiat up the drive and turned into the courtyard to park while he opened the garage. But he stamped on the brakes when he found another car already there.

It was a silver BMW that he didn't recognise. The first shiver of misgiving prickled on his skin when he noticed the provincial code on the licence plate: MI for Milan.

Yanking on the handbrake, he threw open the door of the Fiat and hoped he was wrong – or at least that he wasn't too late to avert disaster. Casso. Was she already inside? He clutched his hands over his mouth and took a few deep breaths. *Fuck*. He was such an idiot. If he'd been a grown up and rung her doorbell in Milan, he wouldn't be dealing with this, now. If he didn't reach her first, she might upset Nonna.

The door of the BMW opened – slowly, as though releasing the poisonous gases of his memories. He forgot to be relieved that Nonna hadn't seen her, yet. He had to look at her, now, and after eight years, he still wasn't ready.

22

Jenn vaguely registered the sound of a car driving up, but it didn't sound like the Fiat, so she dismissed it and focussed on the report she'd finally managed to download onto her computer. A moment later, the familiar putter of the Fiat followed and her concentration was shot. She closed her computer, vowing to come back to it as soon as she'd said hello.

But before she could even set her things down, the sound of voices drifted through the balcony door. She heard Tiziano's mumble, but his blank tone filled her with alarm. She rushed down the stairs, through the kitchen and out into the courtyard, but she stopped short when she saw another woman.

She was dressed immaculately in summer-weight

linen that hung perfectly on her frame. Her features were sharp and attractive, her make-up subtle, but perfectly applied. Her expression was grim with exasperation.

'Marzi?' Jenn blurted out, surprising herself. Both gazes snapped to her, but now wasn't the time to explain that Tiziano had murmured her name in his sleep.

'Go back inside,' Tiziano bit out, stalking over and ushering her back to the door of the farmhouse when she didn't immediately go. 'You don't need to see this.'

'But what—?' His deep sigh cut off anything else she might have said. He turned away, leaving Jenn frustrated and clearly unwanted. Glancing inside, she saw Filomena watching from the kitchen window and rushed to join her.

At first, the couple outside exchanged only clipped sentences, standing too far away from each other for a proper conversation. It seemed very sudden when Marzi threw up her hands and shouted. Less than a minute later, things escalated and Jenn watched on in horror. Even Filomena stood stock still, her mouth hanging open, as they yelled at each other, voices wavering and breaking.

The woman said something slowly, her voice

breaking, and even Jenn understood the last word she spat with great emphasis: 'Divorzio.'

'They're married?' Jenn blurted out. She felt ill thinking about it. They were obviously separated, but she didn't feel much better for pointing that out to herself.

When Filomena nodded, a cold feeling spread through her. It wasn't guilt, although she fervently wished she hadn't let things go so far between them, now she understood the complexity of his life. It was the feeling of being wrong about him. She'd thought he'd mumbled in his sleep that he loved Marzi. What did that mean about this marriage?

He wasn't who she'd thought he was and that hurt more than she wanted to admit.

Filomena continued to mutter exclamations and then she beckoned for Jenn to follow her into the lounge. She searched among the clutter of photo frames, her frown deepening. Jenn saw a few familiar faces: Matteo and Maryam on their wedding day and again with a baby in a long, white dress, which she guessed was Dinah; Tiziano's parents on holiday somewhere with islands and turquoise water; a pile of Zia Monica on the decks of cruise ships.

'Ahi!' Filomena exclaimed, gesturing in frustration. Jenn could guess why she couldn't find Tiziano's wedding photo. The old woman opened a few drawers and then she found it. By then, Jenn wasn't sure if she should even look. Tiziano obviously didn't want the photo on display. He hadn't wanted her to know anything about Marzi.

But when Jenn caught sight of the photo, she couldn't look away. The air rushed from her lungs and tears came to her eyes. Her feelings churned afresh. What had Maryam said? *Everything he's been through...* Looking at the photo, Jenn almost didn't want to know.

There stood Tiziano, with his familiar grin, earrings winking. His hair was neatly slicked back and he had his arm around the woman Jenn now recognised, although her hair was longer in the photo and coiffed at the front. She wore a white dress with a pretty square neckline and clutched a bouquet of pastel roses as she leaned into him. It was a lovely photo.

But Tiziano's face was narrower and, although Jenn suspected he wore the same suit he'd worn to the baptism, it wasn't as faded and there was more room in the shoulders. Marzi's hair wasn't the pale blonde she now dyed it and she had braces. They looked like a pair of A-Level students going to prom, except Marzi's dress was obviously a wedding dress.

And she was clearly pregnant.

Jenn hated to think of the possibilities, but she

couldn't stop. Did the child live with Marzi? Jenn couldn't imagine Tiziano separated from his child, despite the carefree image he liked to project. Had they disputed custody? But they weren't even officially divorced. No... Jenn suspected something much worse had happened, something that would make Tiziano refuse to even consider having children in the future.

The sound of raised voices drew them back into the kitchen before Jenn could decide whether to ask Filomena about the baby, even though it was clearly none of her business. Tiziano's grandmother eavesdropped shamelessly. Jenn was desperate to understand, even though it was probably for the best that she didn't.

Marzi hauled out a bunch of papers and slapped them onto the hood of her BMW, shaking a hand at Tiziano as she did so. He shrugged and took the papers with a comment that sounded barbed. The courtyard fell silent, but it was more like the pause between lightning and thunder than the sun coming out again.

Then Marzi burst into tears. Tiziano approached her warily, his hands up to touch her shoulders, but she warned him off with sharp words and he pulled back. She turned to the car, shouting between sobs and throwing up her arms. She slammed the door behind her and the car revved to life. With one last cry at

Tiziano through the open window, she set the car into reverse and stomped on the accelerator.

The BMW didn't get far. With a crash, it shuddered to a halt. The red Fiat on the driveway jumped with the force of the impact and skidded a few feet. Undeterred, Marzi drove the car forward and turned the wheel before reversing up the grassy bank next to the driveway to avoid the Fiat. Swiping her fingertips under her chin at him, she backed up nearly to the vines, turned the car and bumped down to the road on the grass.

Tiziano stood utterly still as the sound of the engine receded. His gaze was on the grey flagstones, but Jenn doubted he saw anything. The sheaf of papers in his hand flapped in the breeze.

'Oh, sò stùfo!' Jenn heard from behind her and turned in alarm to see Filomena groping for the back of a chair.

'Halmoni!' she said, rushing to take Filomena's arm and help her to the sofa in the lounge. She blinked when she realised what she'd said. Perhaps she'd heard Tiziano call her 'Nonna' so often that the concept had stuck. 'Rest,' she said gently, helping the old woman to prop her legs up on the sofa. 'It's all right.'

'Tizi... ano,' she said faintly.

'I'll talk to him,' Jenn said soothingly. She paused,

again realising that she'd spoken without thought. Would he want to be alone? And what about her own feelings?

As she pulled the crocheted blanket over Filomena's waist, Jenn felt surprisingly little doubt. She couldn't leave Tiziano on his own. She'd only found out a portion of what had happened and it was enough to make her worry about him.

Mr Happy-Go-Lucky indeed. How badly she'd misjudged him.

* * *

The courtyard was empty by the time she'd tidied the kitchen and checked on Filomena. Thinking of her conversation with Tiziano from her balcony early that morning with unexpected sadness, she made her way out with some trepidation. The heat of the afternoon still hung in the air, heavy and scented with jasmine. The mountain cast its creeping shadow and the rest of the hills were bathed in slanted, golden sunlight, showing off the pale greens of the vines, the bright red of the roses and the weathered clay roofs. The church bell rang, a jaunty peal followed by five gongs. It was distant enough not to disturb but close enough to have become a familiar sound – the slow, comforting passage of time, continuity and agelessness, rather than the haggard rush of traffic she was used to.

She found Tiziano's dark converted shed empty, with only the lingering scent of his aftershave and the herbs on the windowsill. The next place to look would be the vineyard. Her hands felt empty as she contemplated the conversation she would have with him, so she rummaged in his fridge, which held only a single wedge of cheese, and his cupboard, which was better stocked – with alcohol and salami, at least. A bottle of grappa in the corner bore the label 'Big V', printed to look hand-written, but clearly mass-produced. She chose another bottle instead, and made her way across the porch and over to the vineyard.

It was still hot, but not scorching. The bunches hung heavily among the leaves, yellow-green and plump and lightly spotted. She hadn't asked him where these grapes would end up this year. She hoped he had a winery lined up. She wanted to buy the wine next year after the fermentations were complete. It was a surprisingly inviting fantasy: popping the bottle and forcing it down, getting drunk and sneezing and thinking about these hills – and these people – months after she'd left.

She reached the bench at the top of the hill and still hadn't found him. What now? The bottle of grappa hung limp and heavy in her hand. And then it gave her an idea.

She slipped and slid back down, hurrying back to the courtyard, where she stopped and studied each of the old farm buildings in turn. In which one would she find Tiziano's famous home distillery? Poking her head in one rotten wooden doorway, she found a musty old barn full of farm equipment. The next one was stacked with crates of wine. But as she reached the third door, the faint sour smell told her this was the one. She opened it gingerly and peered into the dim space, lit only by two dirty windows.

He was at the back of the barn, puffing on a cigarette in the gloom. She followed the smell of smoke and the little glow of the cigarette end. He might have been watching her, but he said nothing, taking another drag, blowing out smoke. Even that wasn't enough to make her turn back, although the smell rankled.

Bracing herself, she plonked down next to him. He watched her as she set the salami and cheese between them, as well as the bottle of grappa and two glasses. The cigarette dangled in his fingers. She gritted her teeth against a sneeze. If he kept smoking, she wasn't sure she could stay. The wary look in his eyes suggested he knew it, too.

With a little cough, she opened the cheese and cut off a few hunks with the sturdy bone-handled knife she'd found in his drawer. Peeling the salami with some difficulty, she managed to cut off a hunk, although she had the white mould from the rind all over her fingertips. And still, Tiziano just watched her.

She hesitated with the salami in her hand. If she offered it to him and he didn't take it, she'd have to accept that he didn't want her there. She didn't know what to say – she never did – but that didn't worry her so much just then. She only knew she wanted to sit in this shed with him until he was ready to come out.

So, she shoved the piece of salami in her own mouth, trying to ignore the smell of cigarette smoke and focus on the taste of the cured meat. The hearty, savoury flavour was pure comfort food, designed to be eaten in thick, salty slices.

Tiziano huffed and she turned to him warily. 'Are you going to share?'

'Maybe,' she said. She kept her gaze on his, lifting her chin. She wouldn't go without a fight – or at least without him realising that he was choosing to wallow alone. He regarded her right back, his eyes shining in the dimness. Her heart rate stuttered. Why did she feel as if she knew his face so well?

He turned away first, with a sigh. He lifted the cigarette to his lips and Jenn braced herself. But instead of sending her away, he leaned over to the open window to blow out the smoke, wafting it away from her with his other hand. And then he stubbed the cigarette out, half-smoked.

'Sorry. Seeing her made me want to kill my lungs a little bit.'

Jenn hoped she wasn't going to cry.

23

'Why are you here?' he asked.

She cut another slice of salami, thoughts flitting across her face as she considered her answer. He couldn't help comparing the woman sitting next to him now, her body language still and patient, to the straight-backed powerhouse who'd arrived three weeks ago. She almost looked at home.

'I didn't want you to be alone,' was all she said. She handed him a slice of salami and reached for the bottle of grappa. He watched curiously out of the corner of his eye as she sloshed a little liquid into each glass. She'd brought solid shot glasses instead of the little tulip glasses. She nudged one glass in his direction and picked up her own. She took a sip, scrunching her eyes shut and shuddering as the liquid seared down her throat.

He lifted his own glass and saluted her before downing the whole lot. In summer, the punchy warmth of the alcohol was strangely cooling, even as it burned through his chest. 'This one was aged in those barrels right there,' he murmured, pointing to the far corner. 'Slovenian oak, used to age Conegliano rosso before Nonno bought them.'

He poured himself another shot and nursed it, warming the liquid with his hands to release the aromas. He took a deep sniff and sighed. 'I always feel like I'm drinking this grappa with him, with Nonno,' he muttered. 'He used to make this type from merlot pomace from his best friend's vineyard near San Pietro di Feletto.'

She sniffed it. 'Yes, I'm getting a plum note, now you mention merlot.'

'The famous nose needed a tip?'

She eyed him. 'Grappa knocks me out a bit – figuratively.'

'Literally, too, if you drink all of that.'

She took another small sip. 'Gosh, it's different from drinking wine. It's like I'm used to a pleasant ride on a gondola in Venice and you've put me on a roller-coaster.' She took another sniff and coughed as the fumes shot up her nose. 'I don't need to drink it. Just smelling it is an extreme sport.' He laughed at her, taking another sip with an appreciative sigh. 'You used to drink with your grandfather? Please tell me you were over the legal drinking age.'

'Yes, don't worry. Even we weren't tough enough to drink grappa from the bottle at teenage parties. I had my Coke and Malibu years like everyone else. I used to sit with him in the courtyard like an old man – you know the way.' He spread his legs and sprawled, hand resting near his crotch. He looked up at the beams in the ceiling, but, in his mind, he was watching the stars pop out as Nonno muttered something and he listened with only half an ear.

Jenn chuckled. 'I do recognise that pose.'

'No one could sit and do nothing like Nonno. It was an art. You wouldn't be able to do it,' he said, flashing her a smile.

'You're probably right.'

'You want to see the still?' he asked. She met his gaze, as though she was also thinking of that first morning when he'd offered.

'Show me,' she said.

He tugged the canvas cover off the gleaming copper equipment with a flourish and tapped the bulbous pot with his knuckles, making it clang. 'I don't know what this stuff is called in English. We put the grape pomace in here, after fermenting it in a tank for a couple of days. Nonno used gas, but I use electricity, now – put solar panels on the roof – to heat it.'

'When you heat it, the alcohol becomes fumes and... condenses here?' She brushed her fingers over the copper pipe.

'This is where I find the heart of the grappa. The first part is not good and the last part also, but the middle part is where the aromas are, and the pure alcohol to bind them.'

'How do you know when you've found the heart?'

'The way Nonno taught me – by feeling. And also checking the temperature and alcohol level.'

'Is it a science or an art?' she asked. He grinned at her and she came closer. This dark room held so many good memories, but he'd never been so aware of making a new one. He knew she had to leave, soon, but she was here, now. He could picture her face in an old photo.

He slipped his hands around her waist and tugged her close. 'It's a craft,' he answered her question. 'And a tradition – something that lives on after us.' *Sometimes that's all we have*. 'Nonna doesn't come here often,' he surprised himself by saying. 'Too much of him is here. But I still need him sometimes.'

As she studied him, her eyes huge in the dimness, he nearly told her everything. He almost *wanted* to. But then she'd know he was always bluffing.

'Tiziano,' she said softly, her voice strained.

'Did you mean it when you said you wouldn't leave me alone right now?' he asked, cutting her off. She nodded, but he suspected she knew he was avoiding her unasked question. He'd just thought of a better way to keep avoiding it. 'Then let's go fishing!'

'Fishing?' she repeated doubtfully. 'Are you sure that's the best—?'

'Fishing solves everything. And you promised you'd come with me one time.'

'I'm not sure I—'

He hurried back to the bench, shoving a few hunks of cheese into his mouth and downing the rest of his grappa. 'Come on!' He stood, gathering the food and handing her the bottle. 'You can take your top off in the sun by the river!'

Her only response was an inarticulate splutter.

* * *

He regretted the cigarette more than usual half an hour later when Jenn was squashed up against him in the cab of the Piaggio Ape, his little three-wheeled truck. She could obviously still smell it and he much preferred her reaction to his usual scent, rather than the scrunch of her nose whenever she got a whiff of him.

He stopped at his nearest fishing spot, just outside the protected section of the Piave, with a small grassy bank, a stony beach and a fast-flowing stretch of water that was full of trout. Carrying the equipment to the beach, he set out a blanket and a low camping chair. He settled into the chair, fetched a can of beer from the cold bag and reached for his rod with a sigh of contentment.

'Ow,' Jenn complained as she sat on the blanket. She rubbed at her bottom and tried to settle more comfortably on the stones. It was passive-aggressive and he kind of liked that she had that fault, too.

'Don't worry,' he said happily, 'you can have the chair in a minute.'

'Where will you sit?'

'I'll be standing – in the river. You didn't think I'd just set the rod in a holder and drink beer all evening?'

'No, I... actually, yes. That's what I thought fishing was.'

He winked at her. 'Then you've got a lot to learn. I'll show you how to cast later. I even know the right words. I did a lot of fishing in the States.'

'Men are the same the world over, are they?'

'Noooo,' he said with a snort. 'There's nothing like me fioi – my boys from Veneto.'

'I'm starting to believe you,' she said with a chuckle.

A few minutes later, he'd strung a fly and was heading for the river in his rubber boots. Pretending to ignore Jenn, he waded into the water and tried out a few casts. The shady spots were cool in the evening air and the water crisp and fresh, but the sun still shone harshly, turning the river a golden green. The white stones were warm and smooth, loose from centuries of river flow. In the distance, low cliffs rose on one side, where the river had cut away at the rock too long ago for anyone to remember, even the Venetian historians of old. As usual, the river was wild – and welcoming – as it twisted its way to the Adriatic.

'I'm not looking,' he called over his shoulder.

'What?'

He gestured encouragingly. 'Take your shirt off! When are you going to get a better chance? I know you're wondering what it would be like.'

'What if someone comes?'

'Would you rather head straight for the Lido di Venezia and fling off your bikini for the movie stars?'

'Are you teasing me? Do you think I won't do it?'

He very carefully peeled all traces of a smile off his face before he turned to her. 'I'm not provoking you. If you want to do it, prego. If you don't want me to look, I won't. If you *do* want me to look... then whistle.'

'I'm *not* going to whistle.'

'Spetta a ti,' he said, cocking his head and turning back to the river. 'You decide. I'm going to fish.' He cast for emphasis, but the line got caught in some low-hanging branches and he swore. Wading across the gentle rapids that soaked his shorts, he propped the rod under his arm and untangled the line. 'Still not looking,' he called over his shoulder as he kept his eyes on his fingers.

'Don't turn around,' she called out.

'I won't,' he promised, swallowing the lump in his throat.

'But Tiziano,' she began, her tone surprisingly matter-of-fact for a woman who might have been topless in the evening sun, 'are you really okay?'

He turned towards her instinctively, caught sight of her bare foot and whirled again before he broke his promise. He sighed and lifted his gaze to the twist of the river and further, to the shadow of the mountains in the distance. He was okay – as anyone ever was. He could set her mind at rest.

'How much did you understand?' he asked conversationally, managing another wobbly cast.

'Not a lot, but probably more than you wanted me to.'

'Tell me,' he instructed gently.

'Er... I gather that she's your... ex-wife and maybe you're still married?'

'All correct,' he said flatly. 'Her name is Marzia. And she's engaged to someone else. My agreement to appear at the town hall for a divorce meeting is the only thing standing between her and a happy life. Did that surprise you? To hear that I'm married?'

'You know it did.'

'Which is why I don't know why you're still being nice to me. I hid it from you. I didn't tell you on purpose.'

'But not because you were trying to deceive me,' she said softly.

His head swivelled again, but he managed to stop when she was only a smudge in his peripheral vision. 'Are you defending me?'

'Someone has to,' she mumbled. For a moment,

the only sounds to be heard in the bend in the river were the splash of the rapids and the chirp of insects. He still didn't understand. She sighed deeply. 'Nonna showed me your wedding photo,' she said quietly.

He froze, fishing rod halfway through a cast. An understanding of just how much she knew washed over him. It was more than he'd imagined, but nowhere near the full story. Measuring his breaths, he reeled in his fishing line and cast again.

'You don't need to tell me anything,' she continued quietly. 'But I also don't want to create misunderstandings.'

He knew what she was asking, but he couldn't bring himself to tell her that part, even the bare minimum.

'Tiziano,' she said, her voice shaking. 'The baby...'

He shook his head vehemently. 'I don't have a kid,' he mumbled.

'I... that's what I thought. I didn't imagine you'd—'

'Please don't imagine,' he muttered. 'I don't want you to even imagine.'

'I'll try not to. But I'm... sorry, for whatever happened.'

'Trust me when I say that pity does fuck all.'

'I believe you,' she said after a pause. 'Maybe I

shouldn't have brought it up. I'm sorry for disturbing your fishing spot.'

He blinked, remembering his rod all of a sudden and reeling in again, slowly. When he drew in another breath, he felt lighter, as though the rays of evening sunshine could pass through him. He inhaled again, deep and loose, river air entering his lungs to attack every molecule of smoke he'd stupidly allowed to accumulate there. It was done for today. He turned his face up to the sun. It was done.

He was glad Jenn had brought it up. He wasn't ready to go into the details, not tonight, but he was glad she knew. Strange as the feeling seemed, he was proud of her for bringing it up, for having the courage to reset whatever this was between them, so it was right again.

He cast, but it was half-hearted. Nothing was biting today. His head wasn't as blessedly empty as it usually was when he fished, but he didn't mind. Knowing she was behind him – potentially topless, he suddenly remembered – more than made up for the disappointing catch.

Birdsong reached his ears and made him want to turn, but he forced his eyes along the river. The chirping sounded again, giving the amusing impression that the bird was trying to get his attention. It was an unusual sound for a bird to make, almost like—

He froze. A whistle. It sounded like a whistle. His mouth dropped open. She didn't...

The whistling sounded again, this time in a droll, impatient singsong, and his grin stretched off his face. Reeling in and tossing the rod onto the bank, he turned eagerly.

24

Tiziano paused when he saw her. She was sitting forward in the folding chair, clasping her hands in uncertainty. A few buttons of her blouse were undone, but she was still fully clothed.

'Are you disappointed?' she asked, squinting in the sun.

'Of c—' He cut himself off. 'Strangely, no. Not that I don't like your...' Her eyes narrowed and he cleared his throat. 'And I do think you should try it, since I know you're curious. But I don't want you to feel nervous.'

'I wasn't nervous, exactly.'

'Yes, you were – you are,' he said with a smile. 'But that's okay.'

'Fine, I'm nervous. But what I meant was, we

needed to have that conversation and it would have been weird to talk while I was topless, so... I hope you don't mind – the conversation, not the toplessness.'

'Davvero, I don't mind, Jenn.'

'I suppose I feel guilty for judging you.'

He sighed and tramped over the stones to reach the blanket. He lowered himself onto it, sprawling his legs in front, and took a sip of beer. 'Don't worry. I still like you,' he said, shooting her a smile.

'Oh, I... good.'

He peered at her out of the corner of his eye as she gazed at the treeline of the bank opposite. She still clasped her hands between her knees in uncertainty. 'It might help you to just do it,' he said with a chuckle. 'Sometimes thinking about doing something is worse than actually doing it.' If only he'd taken his own damn advice in Milan, today would never have happened.

But, with a cold beer in his hand, the sun shining on his favourite riverbend, and Jenn next to him thinking about taking her top off, he had to admit he was glad today had happened, despite the mess with Marzi.

'Really? I should just do what I'm thinking about?'

He lifted his eyebrows. 'Definitely.' Her expression was hesitant but light-hearted. It made him smile. Her hands rose to the top button of her blouse and his gaze fixed there.

She leaned closer and his gaze snapped up to hers. She feathered her fingers along the side of his face and his throat clammed up. 'This is what I was thinking about,' she said softly and a moment later, she kissed him.

He clamped a hand around the back of her neck to hold her where she was, but she showed no signs of wanting to draw away. It was a slow, languid kiss. He adored letting her lead, listening for her hitched breaths and waiting until she came closer.

She kissed him deeply, and he kissed her back, as the sun hung suspended in the sky, casting its timeless rays on one of the last days of summer. The riverbend was silent, except for the burble of the water and the occasional call of a starling. He could almost hear her pulse, where it pounded under his thumb.

He was overwhelmed for a moment at so much contentment. With anyone else, he might have been asking himself if he had a condom in his fishing gear and having a go at her buttons himself. But he didn't want anything more than that moment, moving his fingertips over her skin, sharing kisses as hot and lazy as the evening. He never wanted the day to end – he never wanted the minute to end.

* * *

Jenn wasn't sure exactly what happened in that moment, but she was too dazed to question it. She felt as though time existed differently on that riverbank – no past, no future, just the present. Never before had she realised how appealing that prospect could be.

Her life had always been lived for the future: a good education for a good job, to be someone and be worth something. But the future had no place in that present, where her hands slowly explored the furrows of his face; his jaw, which now bore two days' growth of bristles; and the short, cropped sides of his hair. And she kissed him.

Perhaps she shouldn't have done it. He'd had a draining afternoon. He was technically still married. He didn't have a job, or a house, or a proper car and he didn't want any of those things. But the kiss was perfect.

The only smells that reached her were the fresh greenness of the river and Tiziano's familiar scent, tinged with beer. Nothing concerned her. She'd even forgotten why she was here, in this strange part of the world where the earth was richly fertile, producing fine food and wine and people who understood how to appreciate it.

A great bird flew overhead, its call piercing the idyll. The sound didn't startle Jenn, not when she felt part of the landscape of this great river, but it returned her to awareness and she broke the kiss gently, pressing another and then another to his mouth as a promise or an apology – she wasn't sure which.

When he grinned at her, his eyes crinkling and his mouth kicked up on one side, she drew back enough to look at him properly. His smile was astonishing. She liked his face. She liked *him*.

'I like this river,' she murmured.

'Él bèl Piave,' he said softly. 'It's a bit wild and that's the way we like it.'

Jenn leaned her head on his shoulder and gazed up at the bird that was still circling. It had wide, straight wings and swooped elegantly in the air currents. The first hints of the cool of evening were creeping down from the mountain, while the pebbles by the river still baked.

'The stones are so white and the water is so turquoise, I could almost imagine I'm in the Maldives.'

Tiziano snorted. 'The Piave is not the Maldives. Have you been there?'

'No,' she said with a laugh. He tugged her off the chair and onto the blanket, ignoring her outraged grumble of, 'Hey!' She wasn't as outraged as she wanted him to think, and she might have been quite happy to snuggle closer to him anyway. But then he took the chair for himself and her outrage grew more real.

'Shhh,' he soothed, which only prompted more indignance, until his hands landed on her shoulders. He increased the pressure until he was massaging gently, his thumbs unravelling the knots in her muscles. It was heavenly. Her head lolled forward. The sound of the lapping water stilled her and his glorious hands softened her.

When she felt certain she was now made of marshmallows and she was struggling to stay upright, he rose and helped her back into the reclining chair, his cheeky grin back in place.

'What mdid you do to mmme?' she mumbled, leaning back in the chair with a sigh.

He pressed a kiss to her hair and tiptoed away. 'I'm going to do a few more casts and then I'll take you home. If you're asleep, I'll tuck you into the tray on the back,' he joked.

She wasn't sleepy, exactly but she did like the idea of him taking her home. Perhaps the day would end the way she'd pictured that morning, despite the wrong-turn it had taken after lunch. She peered lazily at the birds circling in the sky, the wide river and the dense greenery on both banks. They were completely alone and she was deeply comfortable.

There would never be a better time.

It started as a small, unthreatening idea that made Jenn smile. All of Tiziano's advice came back to her at once and she knew one thing was true: sometimes thinking about something was a bigger deal than actually doing it. So, while he untangled his line and made a wobbly cast, whistling absently, she undid her buttons and whipped off her blouse as quickly as she could. Her bra followed a moment later and she sat back in the chair, squeezing her eyes shut and focusing on the sensation of the breeze on her skin.

Biting her lip against the weird thrill, she reclined decadently and she couldn't quite smother a snort of laughter. She laughed again when Tiziano did a double take, his mouth agape, but he wrenched his gaze back to his rod. God, if her mother could see her now...

'How does it feel?' he asked.

'Good,' she responded tentatively. 'Not very "me",' she admitted a few moments later. 'But I'm glad I tried it once.' That feeling of being enough stole over her, again.

He glanced back with a smile and even managed to

keep his eyes up, which she found oddly disappoint-ing. 'Want to burn your bra?'

'Nope. It's my prettiest one.'

His smile stretched. 'I'll study it in detail later.' She found herself grinning back.

'You're not great at fishing, it seems,' she said, not even sure if she was hinting that she wanted to go back. Part of her wanted to stay here all night, with time stopped, even if it meant they didn't make it into bed.

'I'm distracted,' he said in mock defensiveness.

'Don't blame me!'

'If you want trout for dinner, you might have to put your pretty bra back on. And to tell the truth, even that might not work.'

She smiled and scooted down in the chair, stretching her arms and legs. It probably didn't look dignified or attractive, but only Tiziano would see her. She hadn't even been this relaxed on holiday in Hawaii last year.

She was so tranquil and Tiziano was so deter-mined to pay attention to his fishing, at least for a few casts, that at first, they entirely missed the distant rustling noises. By the time they heard voices it was too late.

Jenn threw her arms around her chest in panic as

first one man, then another, appeared through the bamboo by the river bank.

'Tiziano!' she hissed and he turned so fast he slipped, scrabbling on the stones to reach her. He dived in front of her, chest heaving, and drew himself up to block her from view. She clutched his arm and peered over his shoulder, vainly hoping they'd just leave again before they even realised she was topless. She groped for her bra with her other hand, but she couldn't quite reach it without coming out from her hiding place.

'Ciao, Tiziano! Ehi! Bona sera, fradel!' the first man called out, raising a hand in greeting and heading their way. Jenn's stomach plummeted. She cursed Tiziano for knowing everyone in this bloody country – and for assuring her that no one would come.

'What do I do, now?' she whispered urgently.

He reached behind and tugged her flush against his back, so his body completely hid her from view as he mumbled some kind of greeting to the man in return. She tucked her head between his shoulder blades, as one of his long arms swiped up her bra.

And that was the moment the newcomers realised Tiziano had company.

25

Jenn squeezed her eyes shut and clutched her fists in Tiziano's T-shirt. The fervent wish that she could disappear among the stones was futile, but she certainly hoped she'd never, ever have to see these two guys again in her life.

After a moment's pause, laughter started up and one of them wolf whistled. Jenn couldn't understand the words, but the suggestive, teasing tone was obvious. Surely, if they thought she and Tiziano had been... amorous out here, they should leave them alone, but they appeared to have no intention of doing so. Tiziano mumbled something in reply and shoved her bra at her, fetching her blouse a moment later.

Swallowing a mortified groan, she slipped into her bra, fumbling with the clasp.

'Antonia? Silvia?'

'Giovanna, no?'

Oh, God, they were trying to guess who she was. Had Tiziano really brought so many different women here?

She shimmied into her blouse and started frantically on the buttons as Tiziano mumbled something in their defence – rather feebly, she thought. Last button done up, she took a few deep breaths and stumbled out from behind him, clutching her hands together nervously. The sooner the horrible moment was over and they could go, the better. For the first time, she was looking forward to seeing the Ape, that bee vehicle again.

She stared at the smooth stones instead of meeting the men's gazes as they looked between her and Tiziano. 'I didn't know you like fishing? Jenn, isn't it?' Her gaze snapped up and she recognised one of the men from the cow incident.

'Yes, h-hi,' she managed. 'Tiziano was fishing. I don't know how to fish.'

The man rubbed his hands together and gave her a wink. 'Looks like he was very busy... fishing. You can take a break and share our pizza.' The other man protested loudly at that idea and Tiziano laughed.

'I can get more pizza. Jenn, do you remember Carlo? And Luca?' She nodded, even though she hadn't remembered their names. She was distracted by Tiziano's offer to get more pizza.

Another two men crashed out of the undergrowth and greeted Tiziano with back-slapping and exclamations, and they were followed by three women in tiny shorts, the strings of their bikinis tickling the backs of their necks.

One of them, Jenn noted in alarm, was Valentina Costa – and, at her heels, was a familiar flame-coloured dog. The woman from Elisir di Cartizze lifted her brow when she saw Jenn and glanced curiously at Tiziano.

Spritz was less circumspect, making a beeline for Jenn, tail up, with the fur on his back quivering in discontent. He gave a bark and Jenn sighed. She should just go. Even the dog understood she had made a fool of herself in front of people she didn't know.

'Miss Park, what are you doing here?' Valentina asked, soothing the dog with a stroke down his back.

'I, uh, wanted to see the Piave and Tiziano wanted to go fishing, so... we came here.'

'How is your work going? Have you found what you need, now?'

'Valentina!' Tiziano approached and kissed her cheek while Spritz jumped in joy and licked his hand, thankfully distracting him from Jenn. 'Not the place for work, *giusto*? Jenn works all the time. It's a miracle I got her here.'

'I didn't know you could perform miracles, Tiziano,' Valentina joked.

Jenn watched the exchange closely, her head spinning slightly from all the subtext. Was Valentina jealous? Or teasing? Or just patronising Tiziano, the way everyone did.

The quiet riverbank transformed rather quickly into a party. Someone made a firepit in the stones and the group formed a ring around it with folding chairs and picnic blankets, punctuated with cool boxes full of beer. Tiziano fended off the numerous offers of beer for Jenn and, although she couldn't understand what he said, she suspected he wasn't blabbing her secret this time.

'Do you want to go?' Tiziano asked her, quietly enough that none of the others would hear. 'I really didn't expect them all to be here on a Monday night.'

The scent of the pizza reached her as someone

opened a box and her stomach responded with a gnawing rumble. The familiar flavours of the tomatoes and oregano were combined with the hearty, mountain aroma of the local salami and her mouth watered.

'Stay for pizza?' Tiziano asked with a grin.

She chuckled, experiencing the unexpected urge to hold his hand. 'Mmm,' she said with a nod.

Tiziano lowered himself to a picnic blanket and accepted another beer, but Jenn hesitated a moment. Where was her place in this circle? Although Valentina and Carlo had spoken to her in English, the conversation slipped back into Italian as soon as she wasn't part of it.

'Jenn!' The other man, Luca, beckoned to her, patting the reclining chair. 'Dai, sit down.' She gave a nod that she was sure must look as shy as she felt and picked her way over the stones to take her place. Settling in the chair, she smiled uncertainly at Luca. She felt Tiziano's gaze on her, across the circle, and glanced up. Lifting his beer in salute, he grinned at her and she found herself grinning back.

'No beer? Davvero?'

'Vero,' she assured him.

'She's driving me home later,' Tiziano said with a wink.

Luca handed her an enormous slice of droopy pizza, the base thin, with the perfect hint of stretch. She stifled a moan even before she bit into it; the flavours were so rich in her nose.

'Pizza con sopressa e chiodini,' Luca explained. 'Sopressa is our salami. The chiodini are these.' He pointed to the tiny mushrooms that were such a stereotypical shape they could have had fairies living under them.

The circle went quiet, watching Jenn take her first bite. With a nervous laugh, she tucked in, nodding and making the expected appreciative noises. And when they weren't watching any more, she analysed the flavours for herself. Nothing was subtle. The mushrooms were meaty and the salami had a hearty savouriness that made her think of full tummies after a day of hard work.

The pizza disappeared quickly, but not as quickly as the time. Jenn missed much of the conversation, but there were obviously a lot of jokes, which one of them would try to explain to her. As far as she could tell, they were either rude or mocking, but always completely irreverent. She got the impression Filippo wouldn't have appreciated half of them.

With the last glow of sunlight fading behind the

mountain, Valentina drew an unlabelled bottle from a cool box, along with a stack of plastic cups. Jenn peered at it curiously. Was that a beer bottle cap on the top?

Valentina caught her eye and laughed, turning the bottle upside down for a moment. 'The finest from Elisir di Cartizze, Miss Park,' she called out. 'But this is not a tasting. You drink it or you leave it.'

'Of... of course.' Jenn was far too curious to leave it.

Valentina held the bottle carefully away from her as she popped the cap. With a loud hiss, a burst of froth exploded from the top. The rest of the party cheered and Valentina sloshed the liquid generously into the plastic cups. She had to open a second bottle before everyone had a cup in their hand.

Jenn sniffed hers warily. Anything that exploded from its bottle was not going to be fun for her nose, but she was keen to taste it. She picked up the aroma of flowers and perhaps lemon. It definitely had the fruit-forward freshness of prosecco, but the bubbles calmed right down before she even sipped.

'Cheers!' Valentina muttered and knocked back a generous gulp. Everyone else did the same, so Jenn braced herself and took a slug. She coughed as the remaining fizz bounced around her sinuses. Valentina laughed at her. 'Not even our traditional col fondo is to your liking?'

Jenn didn't reply for a moment. She was struck by the flavours developing on her tongue. The wine was dry – very dry – but so vivaciously fruity that she almost forgot about the bubbles. She hadn't detected pear in the aroma at all, but on her tongue, it was obvious. And the texture was smooth and creamy.

She peered at the liquid but she couldn't see well in a plastic cup, in the gathering darkness. 'The texture is... unexpected.'

Valentina gestured with her cup. 'Not a tasting!' she insisted again.

Jenn nodded and took another sip, spluttering a little, but the bubbles had dissipated enough that it didn't burn as much as she'd come to expect. 'It's just the bubbles that bother me,' she said, clearing her throat. 'The wine is... delicious.' She took another big gulp to make her point. It was fresh and enjoyable, complex enough to be an experience on her tongue, but not enough to detract from the simple pleasure of drinking it. 'What did you call it? Col fondo? What does that mean?'

'Americans will like it,' Tiziano commented. 'They call it "Farmer's Fizz". Maybe not your taste.' He flashed her a smile.

'Looked like farmers were her taste when we arrived!' Carlo quipped, giving Tiziano a shove.

'It's a pét-nat?' she asked, ignoring the teasing. 'Traditional fermentation?' She didn't know a lot about the pétillant-naturel style of sparkling wine, but Tiziano was right that it was a growing trend in the US. The in-bottle, slightly unpredictable fermentation would explain the pyrotechnics when Valentina opened it. The wine would be a hard sell to Filippo – if Valentina even produced this at commercial quality – but it was a joy to drink.

'Yes, this is bottle fermented our traditional way,' Valentina explained. 'I mixed the yeasts, but you can leave the sediment settled at the bottom of the bottle and it is more like your expected prosecco, just a little wilder.'

'Like the Veneto country boys,' Jenn said with a smile and was rewarded with raucous cheers from Luca, Carlo and the others.

Valentina caught Jenn's eye and they shared a laugh. Jenn's head began to swim, but it was a pleasant, cosy fog. She hoped Tiziano hadn't been serious about her driving them home. Not only would it have been completely illegal – not that Tiziano seemed to care – but on one glass she was already too tipsy to trust herself. If Tiziano got drunk, perhaps they'd have to camp out here by the fire and curl up together when it got cold.

What had happened to her, that she wasn't horrified by that prospect? She usually needed walls and a floor – preferably several storeys up. But, here she was, pleasantly tipsy by the dying fire, contemplating stretching out and sleeping under the stars.

It was because she wasn't alone...

She hoped she'd forget that thought when she woke up tomorrow morning. It was only an *illusion* of togetherness. These were not her friends and Tiziano was not her... anything. But it was a nice illusion.

Carlo retrieved a guitar and played absently, others joining in, or talking in increasingly hushed tones. Tiziano himself was a very nice illusion, the flickering firelight on his face and his arms propped on his knees, singing a line or two along with Carlo, Spritz asleep at his side. Jenn should have felt sad that she didn't know the songs or share the nostalgia, but it didn't matter so much.

For once, her heart was full.

Not stopping to question herself, she rose and tramped around to where Tiziano was sitting. She sank down next to him and scooted up until her shoulder was pressed against his, hugging her knees.

He watched her curiously until she settled beside

him, but didn't ask any questions. He just nudged her softly with his elbow. She felt the flickered gazes of the others, but Tiziano didn't seem to mind and the attention didn't last long.

A few minutes after the conversation resumed, he took a deep breath and stretched his arm around her, drawing her close against him. Jenn knew she had a goofy smile on her face, but she didn't care.

The flickered gazes became furtive smiles. The lazy evening became a cool, dark night and the mellow party wound down with contented lethargy. Jenn didn't want to move, but the decision was made for her when the others made mumbled comments about something that sounded like 'lavoro', which she knew meant work.

She leaned her head on Tiziano's shoulder for a moment, and felt him press a kiss to her hair.

'Stay there,' he murmured and rose to pack up his fishing rod, but Spritz startled awake and she stumbled to her feet before he could express his displeasure. She was sure the dog would be jealous if he realised she'd been snuggling into Tiziano, too.

Luca and Carlo switched on the torch function on their phones in preparation for the tramp back through the undergrowth. Jenn drifted back to

Tiziano's side and he took her hand, entwining his fingers through hers a moment later.

Valentina approached, her thoughtful expression illuminated by the light of the half-moon. 'You will call me again after the harvest, no?' was all she said to Jenn.

Tiziano tugged on Jenn's hand until she stumbled against him. 'I said no work tonight.'

A puzzled smile touched Valentina's lips as she turned her thoughtful gaze on Tiziano. 'Bene, bene,' she said, holding up an arm in surrender. With one last quizzical smile, she followed the others into the bamboo at the riverbank.

Jenn hung back with Tiziano, walking slowly in the moonlight, growing accustomed to the feel of his hand curled around hers. He didn't let go until after they'd said goodbye to the others and he had to pack the gear into the Ape.

Instead of feeling squashed and uncomfortable on the bumpy road in the funny little vehicle, she spent the trip back leaning her head on Tiziano's arm while she stared up at the luminous moon.

The peaceful little parallel world came back to the farmhouse with them, to Jenn's delight. Tiziano kissed her even before she'd unfolded herself from the seat.

Unlike the kisses at the river, this one was eager and impatient and she knew exactly where it was going.

But when she was stretched out on his bed, trying not to cry out as his mouth and his hands and his body brought all her emotions to a peak, her future didn't seem so clear any more.

ELISIR DI CARTIZZE PROSECCO VALDOBBIADENE SUPERIORE DOCG SUI LIEVITI BRUT NATURE:

As the name suggests, this is a complex, unique wine, bottle fermented with limited production. Golden and lightly cloudy, the bubbles in this 'col fondo'-style naturally fermented wine are less aggressive than traditional prosecco and it boasts a starker minerality. With zero residual sugar, this wine is as dry as it comes, but the intense fruitiness of the glera grapes, as well as the notes of melon and citrus, make this wine an easy pleasure to drink. On the tongue, the pear aroma dominates, balanced with limestone chalkiness. Each bottle is unique, like a moment in time.

26

Tiziano managed to plait her hair before she woke up. It wasn't neat; he didn't have a hairbrush. He'd expected her to wake up before he was done and ask why the heck he was plaiting her hair. But she slept on, occasionally stirring and shifting, as he studied the bones in her shoulders, the imperfections on her skin that she would probably hide if she were awake.

Even after everything that had happened earlier in the day, he'd been happy yesterday evening. The thought didn't pain him as much as it should have. All the years he'd had to work so hard for a scrap of happiness, and now he couldn't seem to stop it. What was wrong with him?

He tied the end of Jenn's short plait with the wire

from a pair of old earbuds he found in the night table. He brushed a finger over her jaw and she stirred again. She probably had work to do, so he told himself he could wake her gently. He pressed the tip of his thumb to her bottom lip. So beautiful...

Her phone on the other night table lit up all of a sudden, buzzing and trilling with a loud ringtone. Her eyes finally snapped open, looking glazed and wild, and she sprang up with a shudder, groping for the phone.

'Hello?' she rasped, clearing her throat. One hand rose to her hair and she patted it in absent confusion. 'Filippo! Um, yes. Good morning. No, no – no problem.' Tiziano froze. So much for keeping her happy and relaxed like last night. He should believe her when she said she preferred to be working. 'Of course, you didn't wake me,' she continued, making him stifle a chuckle. Her pride had also awoken from its slumber.

He couldn't resist, he pinched her waist lightly, making her squeal. She glared at him, but he grinned back. She must have had no idea how ridiculous she looked, naked and completely dishevelled. Her straight back and cool expression were right out of a boardroom somewhere.

'Nothing, I'm just... sometimes I have to do yoga

for phone signal out here,' she lied. Tiziano sighed and gave up.

He swiped a fresh pair of boxers and headed for the bathroom, dunking his whole head under the tap in a futile attempt to wake up from this dream where everything Jenn did turned him on and made him feel good. He reached for his toothbrush and grimaced at himself in the mirror as she continued to talk. He tried not to actively listen, but it was difficult not to. And then she said something that made him freeze mid-brush.

'Yes, I've made contact with the Big V. They gave me an outright "no", of course, but I'm going to go out there myself and try to speak to someone. Maybe I'll find a contact. I'm working on it, anyway. Surely they have plans to expand production, especially since everyone around here tells me the Big V is only about making a buck. I thought I might actually find someone sensible to talk to after all the wineries that are too proud to admit they need to earn money.'

The prick of guilt was deeper this time. He should tell her before she found out herself. But it turned out some of his own pride had survived the past ten years and her comments about making a buck and being sensible ticked him off. She still thought her deals were more important than these people – *his* people.

'Oh, I do have a bit of a lead, which I think will be quite promising for our US hotels. What do you think of a prosecco pét-nat? I know I'll have to find one we can rely on, but don't you think it would be great to have a natural wine on the list? I tried one last night and, although it's distinctly a prosecco, it's very complex.'

Tiziano stared again at his own reflection in the mirror, toothbrush hanging out of his mouth, as he listened to Jenn transform back into the wine snob he'd first met. He wasn't being fair, but the disappointment sluiced him like water from the tap. He was the idiot trying to find meaning in their time together. She was only here to do business.

The wrinkles at the corners of his eyes seemed suddenly pronounced. It shouldn't have been news to him that happiness was fleeting and had to be enjoyed in the moment.

He stalked out of the bathroom to find some clean clothes, refusing to be gratified when her words faltered at the distraction of his almost naked body. He shoved his arms through the sleeves of a fresh flannel shirt and tried desperately to clear his head.

His own phone rang and he snatched it up in relief, greeting Lorenzo with enthusiasm. His friend had good news for him. He exchanged a few cheerful words over the phone and assured Lorenzo that he'd be there shortly, before hanging up. He should have dragged himself out of bed earlier.

'Are you... okay?' came Jenn's voice, her call now over.

'Già, certamente. I'm always fine.'

'Tiziano,' she began.

'How are *you*?'

'Fine,' she said hesitantly. 'Are you going to see Marzi today?'

'Can't,' he said, tugging on the laces of his work boots. 'Work to do.'

'Are you... but you will, won't you?'

He clomped over to where she still sat clutching his sheet to her chest, her haphazard plait sticking out to one side. He'd intended to give her a quick kiss and leave her to her work and her assumptions, but seeing the obvious concern in her expression stilled him. 'Thank you... for yesterday,' he managed haltingly. 'And I'm sorry for the drama. I'm dealing with it,' he lied spectacularly. He suspected she knew it. 'Good luck with the Big V,' he said with a twitch of a smile.

'Thanks,' she said in confusion at the sudden change in topic.

He leaned over to give her the quick kiss he'd hoped would smooth over the goodbye that didn't feel right, but the way she sighed with relief and lifted her face to his picked at the stitches of emotion he'd hastily applied over his heart that morning. He slid his hand around the back of her head to prolong the kiss but it couldn't last forever – nothing did.

With one more gentle brush of his mouth over hers, he pulled away and hurried for the door, giving her a breezy salute to cover his roiling emotions. 'Gotta go. It's time for the vendéma – the harvest begins!'

* * *

Jenn stared after him for a long moment, hearing the Lamborghini sputter to life and wondering what had just happened. She'd thought for a moment that Tiziano was going to pretend their conversation at the river yesterday meant nothing. She told herself it was his right not to share his life story, but the moment when he'd allowed some dark emotion to creep into his voice and been honest with her had felt like something real.

But now he'd withdrawn this morning and she couldn't help thinking he was keeping things superficial between them on purpose. She should welcome it. What could their relationship be except superficial?

Did she really want to know what had happened to him after that wedding photo was taken?

She noticed the time with mild horror. Thank God she hadn't admitted to Filippo that he'd woken her.

She dressed quickly, feeling something tapping her back repeatedly, although when she turned to find out what it was, there was nothing there. When she caught sight of herself in the mirror after going to the toilet, her jaw dropped. Her hair was not only a knotty mess, it had been carelessly plaited into a fat braid that gave her big hair on top. When she reached for the end of the braid, she found a pair of earphones holding her hair in place.

Tiziano... Would he ever stop surprising her?

After hastily tugging out the braid and smoothing her hair as best she could, she tiptoed back to the farmhouse, a blush already beginning on her chest. She'd made it through the kitchen and was heading for the stairs, when the voice she'd been dreading sounded behind her.

'Buongiorno, bea! Fai colazione, ecco qua. Siediti.'

She had no desire to explain that she'd actually been creeping upstairs and not coming down to breakfast, so she sat obediently at the table and ate, hoping Nonna wouldn't notice her messy hair and yesterday's clothes.

'Tiziano no breakfast?' Nonna asked.

Jenn shook her head. 'He said the harvest is here.'

'Ah!' Nonna's smile was bright. At first Jenn thought Nonna was excited about the harvest, but then she realised what she'd given away with her thoughtless words. She kept her eyes down and shovelled some of Nonna's proper eggs into her mouth to shut herself up until the embarrassment passed. 'The vendéma. He will not be disposable so much.' Jenn blinked. Disposable? She assumed Nonna meant he wouldn't be available and she'd simply chosen the wrong word again. 'Very busy in the harvest. Tiziano is good with grapes.'

Yes, and women, as Jenn had now been told many times.

'Vendemmia in Italiano. My hands, they have the work of many vendemmie – and my heart.' She smiled and the sudden resemblance to Tiziano stole Jenn's breath. She felt a prickle of anticipation. The most important time of year in the winemaking calendar had arrived in Veneto. A measure of frustration accompanied that realisation, as the busy vineyard owners would have even less interest in meeting her, but it was the birth of a new vintage, the few days or weeks that would determine the next year for Prosecco DOCG.

What was harvest time like in this unique pocket

of Italy? She wished Tiziano hadn't left, so she could ask him all of her questions.

Her questions would have to wait, though, because she had work to do – after a shower. She phoned Lorenzo first, as his rosé was at the top of her list at the lower price point, but the call rang out and, when someone finally answered half an hour later, she received only the terse answer that the winery was closed for the harvest. She received the same response when she called a nearby vineyard.

Feeling discouraged, she decided it would be better to head out to the Big V, as she could at least be certain that they weren't busy with the harvest. Walking down the steep road into Combai, she was surprised to see the shops closed already. Even the hairdresser had the blinds down. She found the reason on the one shop that had bothered to explain: the macelleria had taped a scrap of paper on the window in front of the giant sausages of salami that said, 'Chiuso per vendéma.'

Jenn hadn't seen anyone at work on the leafy hillsides as she'd walked into town. Where was this harvest?

She waited fifteen minutes for the bus to Pieve di Soligo and then half an hour for her connection. Standing in the insufficient shade of a spindly tree in a dusty square was a new level of uselessness. Perhaps she should have told Filippo about her licence and if he'd decided not to send her, she could at least have accepted it with grace and been respected for her honesty.

She could almost imagine her mother's reaction to that idea. *Honesty is well and good, but people need to respect your competence.* Competence was another resource Jenn seemed to be running low on right now. She'd been here three and a half weeks and she hadn't made any firm recommendations and now she was wasting her time on some grappa distillery that didn't want their business either. At this rate, the tasting evening in October would be sparse indeed.

If she'd known this was where she'd be in the middle of September, her August self would have had a pre-emptive meltdown, so why wasn't she panicking, now? She was frustrated, certainly, but she wasn't finished – with prosecco, with these baking clay-roofed towns and lime green, terraced hills. How odd that she was no longer even thinking about missing the salad bowl takeaway on the corner of her street or the anonymous bustle of central London.

Although the buses could come a bit more often.

When her connecting bus finally turned up, she showed her QR code and sat behind the driver. She wanted to be sure she got off at the nearest stop. Since she was currently the only passenger on the bus, she hoped the driver wouldn't mind her questions.

'Erm, scusa, parli inglese?'

'No,' he said casually, not taking his eyes from the road.

'Ah,' she muttered, sitting back in her seat. No English. She pulled out her phone. Google was preferable to an actual human anyway. She followed their progress on the map, with a pin dropped on the distillery. When the bus took an unexpected turn, she gritted her teeth and asked, 'Big V grappa distilleria?'

The driver turned and blinked at her for long enough for her to get nervous about his driving. 'Bassano del Grappa,' he said, thankfully paying attention again. 'Poli, Nardini.' He gestured back the way they'd come. 'Big V grappa fa male!'

She thought that meant it was bad, but it was downright odd that these proud country people refused to get behind a local brand just because it didn't have generations of history. 'Big V per favore,' she managed to say.

Ten minutes later, he pulled into a bus stop with a sigh she thought was a little overdone. He hopped down the steps of the bus after her. He held his arm straight. 'Trecento metri, poi gira a sinistra, poi a destra e poi di nuovo a destra. Su via Borniola, sempre dritto, dritto, dritto, okay?'

Jenn swallowed and nodded. 'Okay.' There was always Google. But, when she opened the app, the distillery appeared to be over three miles away.

Jenn looked frightful by the time she trudged along the gravel path at the Big V: sweaty and dishevelled and an embarrassment to the Brampton Hotel Group. It was past lunchtime and she was starving. This was the worst business meeting of her life and it hadn't even happened, yet. Perhaps now was the time to panic.

27

Two hours later, Jenn discovered that sacrificing her pride was a valid business strategy in this part of the world. Her stomach was full and she had a warm grappa buzz in her throat and her chest. A friendly marketing executive called Antonia had not only taken her out to lunch and given her a tasting, she'd also been apologetic about the difficulties ordering and had even promised to speak to the CEO.

And now Jenn was sitting in the passenger seat of Antonia's car on her way back to Combai. Tiziano would find it all hilarious. Thinking of him out picking grapes somewhere brought her thoughts back to Lorenzo's winery and that rosé. She might be able to get some photos of the harvest for the tasting night.

'Actually, Antonia,' she said on impulse, 'perhaps you could drop me off at the Quattro Brezze winery in Premaor?'

'Certo, no problem. You are helping with the harvest?'

Jenn chuckled until she realised Antonia wasn't joking. 'Uh, not in these shoes.'

When they pulled into the driveway at the winery, Jenn caught her first glimpses of the harvest. A tractor with an empty trailer was pulling out of the shed and another one puttered in after it, full of yellow-green bunches that shuddered gently as the tractor rumbled by. Among the vineyards on even ground behind the winery, a red grape harvester was at work, rolling slowly along one of the many rows.

Jenn stepped out of the car, wondering if she should just get Antonia to drop her back to the agriturismo instead. She would surely be in the way, here. She didn't even know why she was so curious. She didn't expect they'd stomp on the grapes with their feet like the Portuguese vineyard she'd visited last year, although it was something she could imagine Tiziano doing for fun.

Before she'd decided what to do, a familiar, mud-splattered blue Lamborghini juddered into the drive with a laden trailer. Had she secretly hoped this would happen? No comment.

When the tractor pulled to a stop in front of the shed, she rushed over, shading her eyes from the sun as she looked up into the cab to see... a complete stranger. She suspected her face fell because the weathered man with the bushy moustache frowned pointedly at her.

'Dov'è Tiziano?' she blurted out.

The man gargled something and gestured behind him. 'Nella vigna!' he said at the end.

'You know Tiziano?'

Jenn turned back to find Antonia regarding her curiously. Oh dear, she had no excuse for the sudden jab of jealousy. 'Doesn't everyone know Tiziano? I'm staying at his Nonna's agriturismo,' she explained, which seemed to surprise Antonia.

'There they are – up there.' Jenn's gaze followed where Antonia was pointing. The sloping vineyard was teeming with people among the rows of terraced vines. 'Come on!'

The hillside that looked idyllic from across the road was intimidating from below. Jenn tramped after Antonia, wishing she was wearing at least a pair of sneakers, if not hiking boots, instead of her court shoes. She had to stop for a breather halfway up the steep path, propping herself up on her knees. Laughter and voices echoed among the vines, along with the snip-snip of secateurs.

The drop down to the road was dizzying. Jenn could imagine herself falling on her backside and tumbling all the way down, taking out a few of the fine old vines as she went. Up ahead, a man emerged from the foliage, hauling two heavy buckets up the almost vertical slope as though they weighed nothing. He tipped them into the tray of another little farm vehicle and she snapped a few photos of the heap of plump grapes, wobbling like jelly.

She heard Tiziano before she saw him, recognising his teasing tone. The rasp in his voice was more pronounced, as though he'd been shouting along the rows all day. Antonia said something from up ahead and the message was passed down. As Jenn approached, he was making his way laboriously up the hill, his feet slipping on the dry earth. His cheeks were pink, his cap was soaked with sweat and his arms were tight with strain as he lugged two heavy buckets up with him.

Scrambling to the top, he ducked under a wire and said something to Antonia, a broad smile on his face. He kissed her cheeks in greeting and Jenn tried to reason with herself. If there had been anything between them, it was in the past. She would not feel jealous.

Except she did feel it. She stamped her foot, trying to clear her head. Perhaps she shouldn't have come. Would he think she'd come looking for him? Would he worry she was turning this thing between them into something serious?

'Jenn!' he called out and it was too late to do anything but smile awkwardly. He set his buckets down and approached. Tugging off his gloves, he leaned down to her, causing a definite flutter where she was trying to keep hold of herself.

At the last minute, he sent a furtive glance behind him and then kissed her – not on the cheek, straight on the mouth.

She stumbled in surprise and he grasped her waist, holding her still until he was ready to end the kiss. The embarrassed and confused part of her wished he would, but she still grasped a fistful of his shirt to hold him where he was.

He eventually pulled away with another covert glance at the rest of the workers. No one appeared to have seen – except probably Antonia, who approached with a puzzled expression. She obviously wasn't jealous, the lucky thing.

'You've come to help with the harvest!' he said with a grin.

'Oh, I... No. I can't. I don't know... what I'm doing.'

'You don't need training to cut grapes. Everyone gives a hand – or two.' He grasped both of hers and tugged her into the vines.

28

Tiziano knew he should leave her alone. She pulled against his grip and it was obvious she didn't want to be here. She had fancy qualifications in wine, not his agriculture certifications. She'd lived in London and New York and Hong Kong and thought eggs only came from shops.

She slipped and gave a panicked whimper as gravity got its claws into her. He caught her heavily, his hand landing on her backside. Cheers and wolf whistles surrounded them as he embraced her among the vines, feeling guilty, but also very, very happy to have her in his arms. She peered at him from where she was clutching his shoulder, her expression deeply uncertain.

'Okay?' he asked.

'Not really,' she muttered. 'Look, it's... really not my thing. I-I have done a day of harvesting before and I really don't want to—'

'Ecco qua,' interrupted one of the other pickers, shaking gloves and a pair of secateurs in front of him and Jenn. 'Torna al lavoro, bòcia! Anche le tose!' There was a glint in the old man's eye as he mock-scolded Tiziano for shirking off work, but Jenn obviously didn't pick up on it. As Tiziano held onto her for a moment longer – to make sure she was stable on her feet, of course – Jenn accepted the gloves and secateurs with one of her unconscious nods that was almost a bow.

'I'll take care of you,' he whispered in her ear, but the look she gave him suggested that promise didn't put her mind at rest. To her credit, she squared her shoulders and slipped the gloves on, even as she scowled at the vines.

Antonia accepted a pair of gloves herself with a wry smile. She was obviously dying to ask him what was going on, but he couldn't explain it in front of Jenn. 'I'll tell you later,' he murmured to her in Italian as she breezed past.

She gave an amused chuckle. 'She's nice – too nice for you.'

'Lo so bene, Tonia,' he said with a shake of his head: *I know that.*

He grabbed a few buckets and led them halfway down the hill to a new row. Antonia mucked in immediately, but Jenn stared at the vine in front of her with the same trepidation on her face as she'd shown the cow weeks ago.

'Just hold the bunch and cut.'

'What if I squeeze it?'

'It's fine, Jenn.'

'But what if the berry breaks and the juice comes out?'

Was she serious? 'You're not going to accidentally make wine. Just cut and put the bunch in the bucket. It's already better than mechanised picking, even if you burst a couple, and they'll sort them at the winery, so if you include a few bad bunches, it's not a problem.'

Taking a deep breath, she grasped the nearest bunch as though it were a newborn baby – and he knew too well how inept she was at holding babies. Raising her secateurs haltingly to the stem, she carefully aligned the blade and snipped, but she accidentally slipped the safety clasp back on and the secateurs wouldn't open again. She shook them and the whole vine moved, right down to the roots that disappeared into the dusty earth.

'Shit!' She pulled her hands back. 'I'm going to break it!'

'You're not going to break anything,' he said smoothly, eyeing her suspiciously. 'I thought you said you'd done this before?'

'Technically I have, but I was so... inefficient in the vineyard that I ended up working with the press instead.'

'Don't worry about efficiency here. We have strength of numbers. The grapes will get picked today, and we're doing it together – that's what matters.'

Her gaze flew to his. 'We, you mean everyone – all these people?' Actually, he'd meant him and Jenn, but if she preferred to think that way, he'd let her. 'I'm all thumbs with this stuff,' she admitted.

'That wasn't so hard to admit, was it?' he teased. He detached the secateurs and handed them back to her.

She tried again and although she managed to slice through the stem this time, she fumbled and both the grapes and the secateurs slipped from her hands. She muttered a filthier swear word and he had to stifle a laugh.

She tried to pick up the grapes, but she struggled

to grip the generous bunch and ended up scraping it out of the dust with both hands, gritting her teeth. 'I told you,' she muttered as she dumped the first bunch into the bucket.

'Maybe the gloves are too big,' he suggested, tugging them off. 'Look at those little hands.'

'They're not little. It's yours that are big. Now leave me alone to embarrass myself in peace.'

He watched her for a long moment as she went for the next stem, snapping it so unexpectedly quickly that she dropped the bunch again. Was she truly so worried about making a mistake? Or was it being part of the group that troubled her? He suspected she had hang-ups about both.

He approached her slowly, as though she were one of the skittish hares that ranged over the vineyards early in the morning. He reached around her to grasp the hand holding the secateurs. 'Ecco, like this.'

He brought her left hand up to hold the bunch. Then he brought her other hand up and squeezed, snipping the stem. Then they both fumbled with the grapes. A moment later, the secateurs had tumbled to the ground again and the grapes were squashed between his hand and her chest. She looked down, stunned.

He cleared his throat, bringing his other hand up to support what was left of the bunch that was now dripping sticky juice down her silk blouse. 'Sorry.'

To his surprise, she snorted and her shoulders shook against his chest. 'Can we save this bunch?'

He settled his chin on her shoulder and gave her a squeeze before extricating himself with one final kiss to the side of her neck that made her shiver. 'I was distracted,' he murmured into her ear before he drew away to pick off the crushed berries.

'I never guessed I had to squeeze the handles of the secateurs like that,' she said drily. 'It's so damn complicated I'm glad you were here to show me.'

'I'm glad you're here, punto. It doesn't matter how quickly or how well you do it. Just join in,' he continued, hoping she'd let his confession slide. 'I guarantee, it will get you on Lorenzo's good list. That's what you want, right?'

'Of course,' she said. She tugged her damp blouse off her skin with a grimace. 'I just didn't think Lorenzo would appreciate us making wine on my boobs.'

He burst out laughing. 'You're giving me ideas! But why are you so worried? You can't be good at everything.' He tugged his own secateurs out of his pocket and began casually snipping bunches from the vine, the movement habitual. He caught two or three bunches in one hand before he dropped them into the bucket and her eyes widened watching him.

She stared at the vine before her and grasped the bunch, snipping it and dropping it into the bucket with a sigh of relief. 'You're right we can't be good at everything. So, shouldn't we stick with the things we're good at?'

'There are a lot of things I shouldn't be doing, then,' he joked. Her brow furrowed, as though she disagreed. 'Sometimes we have to do things we're not good at.'

'Ha. I'm well aware of that, but that doesn't mean we shouldn't play to our strengths.'

She sounded so convincing, he almost forgot his suspicion that the reason she made herself an outsider wasn't out of pride, but fears of inadequacy. 'Is that why you're a wine expert? Because of that magic nose?'

She nodded. 'Except...' She paused to study another bunch. 'The more senior I get, the more the skillset changes and what if I'm not good at it any more?'

What should he say? Not a joke. *Definitely don't joke.* 'You're not going to turn into Filippo, and wear tailored Italian suits and drive a Ferrari. Is that what you're worried about? You'll have to get your licence back, first.'

'Since you never push yourself to do well at anything difficult, I assume you wouldn't understand,' she said breezily.

He reached over and snipped the bunch she was inspecting and it fell to the ground in front of her. 'Since you try so hard at everything you do, big and small, I don't think you have anything to worry about. You'll find your own way to do things without the tailored suit.'

'You have a lot of faith in me,' she muttered, 'considering I've been here nearly four weeks with nothing to show for it.'

'Nothing? How many of these people do you know, now? *One* of them, extremely well. Isn't that part of your job, to get to know the terroir? The terroir means the people, the traditions. Look.' He gestured behind them at the view. 'These vineyards have been here for hundreds of years, since before anyone kept records. And this year, you are part of the tradition. Surely you understand by now that we are farmers. To an Italian, growing wine is just as important as growing food!'

She gazed at the view, her fingers moving absently over an unfolding red rose growing beneath the vine. Her cheeks and nose were pink and her hair was a mess and she was so beautiful, with her thoughts and fears all over her face. 'You're right. I've learned a lot. And you're right about the people. I'm not good with people, but maybe it's something I can learn – and not the way Filippo wants to teach me.'

'I've heard you say you're not good with people before, but I don't think it's true.'

'You're just blind and deaf! I never say the right thing. It used to drive my grandmother crazy, how I either kept having weird conversations with her acquaintances or I wouldn't say anything at all. She'd blame my mother. That's why my mum always had something to prove, why she always told me I needed a niche, where I could stand out for success. So, I'm the family wine expert with the sensitive nose.'

'You stand out in any field,' he mumbled. At least at this moment, when she felt so uncertain, she wouldn't question exactly how much he meant that.

'But not necessarily for success,' she said with a humourless laugh. 'And if I don't succeed, then Halmoni was right and Mum made the biggest mistake of her life keeping both me and her career.'

Tiziano's throat clogged up. 'That's a lot to put on you.'

'It is what it is. I don't blame my mum for pushing me to succeed – or for prioritising her career so she could provide for me. All the other options were more terrible.'

'Yeah, I know,' he said before he could stop it. She glanced at him, picking up on his tone, but he wasn't about to explain that Marzi had given up her study when she was pregnant. Then he'd have to tell her everything that happened after and he wasn't ready for Jenn to know how not okay he really was.

'You know from your own experience?' Jenn asked gently – warily.

'No pity, remember,' he joked with a warning glance. 'And also, we were talking about you. Weren't you still a child when you stayed with your grand-mother? When I was a kid, I spoke to dirt more than I spoke to adults. She shouldn't have been so hard on you.'

Jenn snorted a laugh. 'I can only imagine what Halmoni would have said if I'd spoken to dirt. She was always so worried I was weird.'

'You are weird. That's why you fit in so well, here!'

'I am not and I do not.' She snipped a bunch – rather expertly now – and dropped it into the bucket.

'Did you see that? You're learning. You can have honorary citizenship of Valdobbiadene.'

She smiled and he cocked his head to watch her. 'I

kept getting cramps the time I did this in France. Why do you think my hands are okay this time?'

He leaned over to whisper in her ear, 'Because you're doing it slowly – and my company is relaxing.'

'Your company *is* relaxing – when I'm not fighting the urge to give you a shove.' She hesitated for a moment, then nudged him playfully with her shoulder. He struggled to tone down his grin. 'Do you plait all the girls' hair, then?' she asked with studied casualness. 'The headphones were a nice touch.'

'I was trying to wake you up, but you slept like a stone.'

'Fine, don't answer,' she murmured flatly. 'I probably don't want to know the answer anyway, and it's none of my business.'

He adored the tinge of jealousy in her words. 'I think it was the first time I've done the hair of a woman in bed,' he admitted thoughtfully. When she flushed with a small smile she was trying to curb, he grinned at her. 'Usually, I'm too busy with other things in bed.'

'Did I mention I regularly experience the urge to give you a shove?'

'I have that effect on all the girls.' She scowled at him and even that was gorgeous. God, she unravelled something inside him and he couldn't get enough. It was unexpected and he wasn't sure if he should run the other way or beg her to stay. 'But be careful on the hill. Lorenzo likes me a lot. If I land with a splat at the bottom of his vineyard, you'll never get your contract.'

'You seem to have an outsize influence on my efforts to secure contracts.' She had no idea how true that was, but he wasn't about to admit that, now. 'Even Antonia. Why didn't you tell me you knew someone who works at the Big V?'

'I didn't think you wanted to use my contacts.'

'Maybe I've resigned myself to getting to know all your ex-girlfriends for my work.' She was refusing to look at him and her tone was much more obvious than she probably thought. He wanted to kiss her again.

'Is that what's bothering you?'

'What? Nothing's bothering me – except the heat. My hands are sweating and I can't hold these scissors properly.' She rubbed at her forehead with the back of her hand, leaving a smear of dirt. He took the secateurs from her and popped them in his pocket. Then he wiped her hands on his T-shirt, pressing her palms to his chest.

He ducked his head to catch her eye and grinned. 'Jealousy suits you, but you have nothing to worry about. Antonia's not an ex of any sort. I haven't slept with *everyone*.'

'Sorry, I—' she began.

'Just *most* people,' he continued with a grin, poking her in the waist until she squealed. Then he held his arms wide in surrender. 'Daghe, I'm waiting for the push down the hill. Give me your best.'

29

By Saturday evening, Jenn was more exhausted than she'd ever been in her life. The back of her neck was peeling from sunburn. Her hands were blistered and dry and, when she closed her eyes, she saw bunches of grapes swinging behind her eyelids.

But it wasn't such a bad view. Those grapes in her mind's eye were hanging from beautiful old vines on steep hillsides, with fragrant roses below, giving up their scent in the beating sunshine. She couldn't quite believe she'd been up there, moving slowly along the leafy rows high above the road, among the little hills dotted with old stone buildings.

After finishing the harvest for Lorenzo, she'd

tagged along with Tiziano as the workers continued to another vineyard near the hamlet of Colbertaldo. She'd spent the days up on the ridges, pausing for breaks in an old stone rustico with no glass in the windows and a hole in the terracotta roof. She suspected no salami would ever taste better than the sopressa that was handed around in the shade, along with hunks of bread. She'd wolfed it down, needing the calories and the salt.

At lunchtime, they would all head down the hill to an osteria with simple décor, but the most beautiful terrace, verdant with grape vines and wisteria that made her wonder what the region looked like in spring.

And in the evenings, she would try not to fall asleep at the table while eating the salad and pasta that Nonna fed her. After a shower, she'd used her last drips of energy every day to sneak back down the stairs to Tiziano's shed, where she put up with his teasing because he also gave her poor shoulders a massage.

She'd asked herself once if he might want a night to himself, but she was conscious of her time in his idyllic little world winding down. Besides, it was only Tiziano. He'd tell her if he didn't want her there.

Sometimes Tiziano dropped her off for dinner

with Nonna and headed back out to do a few final jobs with the Lamborghini, coming back with his hair slicked with sweat and the sticky-sweet smell of juice on his hands. He worked corporate London hours during the harvest and she was glad he'd been so free with his time in August in preparation.

After the grape harvest, he would head down to the plains for the corn harvest and then radicchio, until he got a break again at Christmas. She'd made a joke about everyone wanting his hands and his tractor and he'd quipped that he was extra busy with his hands since she'd arrived.

Lorenzo had proved eager to discuss contracts and Jenn had been showered with whole cases of prosecco and not just tastings, after helping with the harvest. She'd bugged Antonia until she'd promised to set up a meeting with the CEO of the Big V and that had been pencilled in for Wednesday the following week, depending on the prosecco harvest, for some reason.

As though joining the harvest was a key in a lock, the other two wineries she'd asked for a formal meeting also finally agreed and Jenn was busy contacting the legal department in the evenings to draw up draft contracts, and planning for the arrival of a company lawyer to attend the meetings.

But her sudden progress wasn't as satisfying as

she'd expected. Completing her work meant leaving and that thought always left her cold, despite the warm September weather. If Valentina agreed to a meeting, Jenn could finish within a week. She wasn't ready. She wasn't even ready to think about it.

She'd loved watching proud Lorenzo's face when she'd complimented his rosé, but she found herself hoping Filippo and the lawyers wouldn't drive too hard a bargain when they agreed terms. The lawyers didn't understand the community, the pride in the land and the way they worked it.

The most important thing for Jenn was seeing this place thrive. Filippo would tell her they could thrive by selling thousands of bottles to the Brampton Hotel Group at a reasonable price. Now that Jenn had picked the grapes with her own sweaty hands, in a landscape of rich contours and unique views, she'd lost all perspective on what would be a reasonable price.

She'd lost perspective on a lot of things. The countryside was supposed to be a harsh and foreign place to her. Before, she'd craved the convenience and anonymity of city life, to say nothing of the reliable public transport. The city didn't care if she was only half-anything, with a background everywhere and nowhere.

Now, she'd grown entirely too comfortable in the country and it tempted her to ask a range of difficult questions about why she'd chosen the wine buying career path to begin with. She tried not to think too much about that, as it only led to Jenn hearing her mother's voice crying in alarm about years of her career wasted. But Jenn was more worried about the years of her life wasted.

Like the years she'd wasted obsessing over Filippo. She needed some serious self-reflection on that point, but not now, not when she could curl up with Tiziano, pushing the world away and never worrying what he thought of her or whether he felt as happy with her as she did with him. She had no doubt he did. He made it very clear every time he touched her. And if their time together could be coming to an end in as little as a week... she couldn't bear to think about it.

That Saturday night had the slightest bite in the air that slipped in through the open window, and a late summer heaviness that felt like imminent change. Tiziano would be out in the morning, finally meeting Marzi. Some kind of change would come into his life and Jenn hoped it would be positive. She was glad of the warmth of his body against her back as she drifted to sleep.

But she didn't sleep so deeply that she missed the knock on the door several hours later. Coming awake slowly in confusion, she felt Tiziano rising. She propped herself up sluggishly on one elbow as he flung open the door.

Matteo stood on the doorstep and burst into rapid Italian before Tiziano could even greet him. He was juggling a restless Dinah on his hip and the agitation in his voice was obvious. Jenn blinked at the little clock radio on the kitchen bench: 2.23 a.m. What was wrong? She came to the door to see if she could help. 'Tiziano? Devi aiutarmi. Portala, te prego!'

Jenn only understood the word 'help' and the urgency in Matteo's tone. Peering past Matteo, she saw Maryam in the car, sitting in the back with one hand protectively over the baby seat. But Tiziano seemed to have frozen and said nothing.

'What's happened? Can I help?' she blurted out.

Matteo blinked, as though noticing her presence for the first time. He shifted the wriggling Dinah. 'We have to take Alessandro to the hospital. His fever is high and he has had an... attack. I'm worried.'

'Oh, no,' Jenn whispered. She turned expectantly to Tiziano, wondering why he hadn't taken Dinah, yet. He was staring at the little girl as though she pained him. 'Tiziano,' she prompted him. 'What's the matter?'

Matteo sighed deeply. 'Not now, fradel. I need your help. Maybe it's nothing and Alessandro will be okay. Do I have to wake Nonna so she can take Dinah? We already took the risk of coming here instead of waking a neighbour.' He said something sharply in Italian, his tone high with worry, but even that wasn't enough to snap Tiziano out of it. He just stared, his face contorted.

Jenn blew one long breath out through her nose. 'Here,' she said to Matteo. She lifted her hands for Dinah. 'Give her to me.'

Raising his eyebrows, as though he'd only just worked out why Jenn was at Tiziano's in the middle of the night, in her pyjamas, Matteo scowled at his brother and then nodded, crooning something softly into his daughter's ear. He tried to hand the toddler over, but she clung to her father, as though her hands and feet were fitted with talons.

Jenn took a hesitant step forward. 'Hi Dinah,' she said softly. 'Come to Zia Jenn. Zia will look after you.' She knew the frightened little girl couldn't understand anything except the word 'zia' for auntie, but the words kept flowing. 'Look, here's Zio Tiziano. Come in with me. We'll give him a cuddle and it'll be okay.' She brushed a hand over Dinah's tangled black curls. 'Don't worry We'll be okay. Come to Zia. Shhhh.'

Dinah shrieked when Jenn hefted her out of Matteo's arms and for a panicked moment, Jenn was worried about dropping the little girl, but she hurried inside, waving Matteo off. Tiziano at least had the presence of mind to shut the door and then Jenn set the restless toddler down with an enormous sigh. Dinah raced for the door and threw herself at it, screaming for her father.

The car started up outside and Jenn's heart broke for all of them. The feeling of helplessness was horrendous. She followed Dinah to the door and dropped to her knees, speaking to her again, but the crying only got worse. 'He'll come back. He's not gone. He'll be back,' she repeated, having no idea what else to do.

Her ears were ringing by the time Dinah's cries settled to whimpers. Dinah looked exhausted, but that was another problem that felt too big for Jenn to solve. She suspected picking the girl up and carrying her to bed would be entirely counterproductive. Out of her depth, she did the only thing she could think of: she lay down on the floor herself.

A few long moments later, a little finger poked her in the nose. That was followed by sticky hands in her hair. Jenn kept her eyes shut, relieved she'd at least distracted the girl. 'Ow!' The tug on her hair was harder than she'd expected. Dinah giggled and Jenn's smarting scalp didn't seem like a high price to pay.

'Dai, tósata.' She heard Tiziano's voice as his footsteps approached. Dinah held up her hands and he snatched her up off the floor. She threw her arms around his neck and he tucked her tight against his chest. His expression was still alarmingly blank, but a flash of something painful crossed his features as he pressed her close.

I don't have a kid... Jenn had tried to leave her curiosity at the door out of respect, but she couldn't ignore it, when the truth was stark on his features. He rocked Dinah gently, smoothing her hair and pressing a kiss to her forehead. He carried her into the kitchen and rummaged in the cupboard, one-handed, until he found a bread stick. She munched it immediately, resting her head on his shoulder.

Next, he filled a glass and held it to her lips, tipping it for her so she could drink. She slurped down the water and went back to eating. Between the chewing and the sipping and the rocking, she calmed down and her eyelids drooped.

He beckoned for Jenn and she rushed to turn back the covers for him. Dinah didn't immediately let him put her down. She clung to his neck, shaking her head.

But after ten minutes of rocking and sips of water, she resigned herself to sleep and settled on the pillow.

Jenn pulled up the blanket, tucking it securely around Dinah's little body. She felt Tiziano's eyes on her and was relieved to see a hint of his smile returning. 'She'll only kick it off in five minutes.'

'Then maybe it's for me, not her,' she said with a faint smile. Tiziano was the only person she knew who could tell her she was wrong without making her feel inadequate.

His smile grew warm, but with a thoughtful wariness that made her breath catch. 'You were amazing just then,' he murmured.

She looked down at her bare feet. 'I don't know if I did the right thing.' She felt his fingertips on her cheek, brushing her hair back from her face.

'You did more than the right thing. You *cared*. She understood that.' He smoothed Dinah's hair, making Jenn lift her hands in alarm. Would she wake up? She didn't think she could go through all that again. But Tiziano didn't look concerned. He took Jenn's hands, threading his fingers through hers. 'Shh, don't worry. She won't wake up, now.'

'Are you sure?'

He tugged her close. When she relaxed into his arms, she sensed the ache of sadness in him. Why hadn't she recognised it before? He settled his cheek on the top of her head and Jenn was suddenly fighting tears.

'You weren't exactly right,' he murmured.

'Hmm?' was all she could manage in reply.

'I did need a cuddle, but it doesn't make anything okay.'

30

Jenn wouldn't let him go, even after he kissed the top of her head and gave her a little squeeze to signal that she could pull away if she wanted to. Her wiry arms were still locked around his body. He was thinking about turning off the light and switching on a lamp instead. Maybe he'd grab a beer from the fridge for what would be a long night of waiting to hear from Matteo. But Jenn still had him in a squeeze.

'I need to sit down, principessa,' he whispered. Her arms sprang open as though she hadn't realised what she'd been doing and she swiped at her eyes with the backs of her fingers. 'Jenn,' he groaned. 'Are you crying? Because of me?'

'Yes, because of you,' she said with a scowl. 'Because I tried not to imagine anything, like you told me, but I keep... imagining. I know you don't want kids and that's fair, but I keep thinking about you as a father and it makes me cry. I'm sorry.'

He sighed, her words confirming his suspicion that he would need to tell her and burst this little bubble of happiness, let her see who he really was. It was going to burst anyway and she obviously wanted to know.

He stalked to the fridge and grabbed a beer, popping it open as he walked to the ancient chenille sofa, collapsing onto it with a sigh. Taking a long glug, he wondered where he should start. Jenn perched next to him, completely still, as though afraid of scaring him off. Smart woman.

'Marzia was at university,' he mumbled. 'We'd been together since liceo, since school, and doing the long-distance thing for a year, with her at university and me doing an agriculture certificate at technical college – you see I have a thing for women who are out of my league.'

'Skip the self-deprecating commentary and tell me what happened.'

Yeah, strong, intelligent women were definitely his weakness. 'What do you think happened? We screwed up one time – a couple of times, to be honest – while she was back in the summer. She returned to Milan and got a shock a few weeks later. We had... the discussions you can imagine. I was young. I didn't understand what she would go through. Maybe I was too strong with her, insisting I wanted to keep the baby, get married, save up for a house and all that stuff. She went along with it all – she didn't disagree, anyway. Not openly. She quit her course and moved home and bought a wedding dress. But I should probably have guessed that it wasn't what she truly wanted.' He took another sip of beer. 'And then he was born and everything changed.'

The memories flooded him – not specifics, nothing that he remembered seeing or hearing or even smelling, but the freight train of emotions that had flattened him in those weeks after he'd first held his son. He was trying to tell the story coherently, but his thoughts shot off in all directions.

'It's difficult to explain.' He risked a glance at her. She was hugging her knees to her chest and watching him with wide, troubled eyes. 'Marzi got depressed, really badly. Some of it was post-partum, but she was depressed even before she gave birth. Her whole life changed and she felt like it wasn't her choice. She went from having a world of possibility to... just me and Veneto. I was off work a lot. Marzi needed someone to look after her and Rico as well – that was his name. Enrico. It feels so strange to say his name out loud. Why should it be strange to say my son's name?'

He cleared his throat, catching himself before his thoughts spiralled. He didn't realise she'd taken his hand until she squeezed it reflexively. He didn't squeeze back. He was holding himself together by a thread.

'I don't even remember that time very well. It was chaos and we had no money. I was a twenty-year-old farm worker on flexible contracts. We were borrowing money from everyone and she'd never had a great re-lationship with her parents. I understand why she hated her life. I was... Rico was the best thing that had ever happened to me and I was still stressed, so, yes, I understood why she was depressed. Jenn, I'm not even at the bad part,' he warned when a tear dropped onto the back of her hand.

'Keep going,' she said with a sniff. 'I'm crying so you don't have to.' Her grip on his hand tightened. It was a lovely idea, but he wasn't sure it would work.

He cleared his throat. 'We got through it somehow and, for a while, I thought maybe things would be okay. I tried to convince her to go back and study at the University of Padua, but I knew it wasn't that easy. We argued about a little sister or brother for Rico and I definitely shouldn't have pushed her. It was easier for me. I had a cute kid who was a year old. And then one night... I didn't any more.'

He tore his hand from hers. This part was not allowed to be okay. Calmly explaining how his son had died could never show enough respect for the little life that everyone else had forgotten. He needed to hurt.

'He got sick? A fever?' she guessed, her voice shaking.

He nodded. 'We waited too long to take him to the hospital. Kids get sick all the time, right? But it wasn't a virus. It was meningitis.' He slid off the sofa and onto the floor, leaning his head on the cushion and staring at the ceiling. He could seep into the earth, now.

Jenn was silent and still and a glance confirmed she had tears rolling down her cheeks. Then she asked a question he never would have expected. 'Can I see a photo of Rico?'

'What? Why?'

'I'm sorry if it hurts too much. You don't have to.'

He hauled himself up and strode to the bedside table. Pulling the photo from the top drawer, he felt guilty to realise how creased and covered in fingerprints it was. He thrust it at Jenn and went to the wardrobe, pulling out the shoebox of other prints. 'I don't know why my family thinks this should all have gone away by now. He's my *son*. I don't *want* to forget, even for a minute, even if it means every minute I have to remember he's gone. I don't want another child and I don't want another wife, because Marzi is his mother!' He caught himself before he went any further. The anger was one thing he'd learned didn't help.

Jenn still didn't say anything. She was probably planning her escape route.

'I know everyone deals with loss differently. I have to let Marzi go and she didn't deserve some of the things I said to her on Monday, but if I can't say them to her, who can I be honest with?'

Jenn glanced up from the photo she'd been studying. 'Aside from me, you mean?'

He stared at her, his breath short again. 'Aside from you,' he repeated on a whisper. 'For now,' he added with a grimace. He tugged her to her feet and pulled her against him, wrapping his arms tightly around her. 'At least I've learned my lesson. I've gotta let you go.'

* * *

Jenn squeezed her eyes shut. She was processing fiercely. Pressing her face into his T-shirt, she breathed in. He smelled the same – like lazy summer days and the wild river. His hold on her was tight, in contrast to that sentence he'd uttered that had mixed everything up inside her.

I've gotta let you go.

She still clutched a photo of his son. It should have surprised her that Tiziano was a man who loved deeply and irrevocably, but it hadn't. A part of her, deep inside, had recognised that already – she *knew* him, even though she hadn't known exactly what he'd gone through.

Her heart was breaking in several places and he'd said he had to let her go. Her place was in the city, in another country, hopefully one day with her own family, and he would never ask her to stay, as he'd asked Marzi. He would let her go before she became another person in his life who hurt him, because he was tender and loyal and passionate.

'Not yet,' she muttered, unable to stop herself. 'Don't let me go, yet.'

He chuckled. It was such a *Tiziano* thing to do that her eyes pricked with fresh tears. His arms tightened even further. 'I won't,' he promised softly.

'I'm sorry it hurts, and I wish I could make everything better with a cuddle, but I...' *love you for remembering.* 'It's admirable how you honour his memory.'

'Admirable?' he repeated with a huff, as though he suspected that formal word had been her second choice. But there was no way he would suspect the L-word had almost slipped out of her mouth. 'You might not think so if you'd seen what I did to myself in the years after he died. It took me too long to work out the difference between honouring his memory and regretting my existence.'

'*Tiziano,*' she choked. The tremor in his voice revealed more than he'd probably intended. She suspected 'regretting his existence' was an understatement. 'That's something I don't want to imagine.'

'What? Me spending the day drunk while working with heavy equipment? That happened. Or how I wandered around America with nothing except my clothes, spending all my cash in hand on bourbon and waiting for someone to arrest me and send me back to Veneto?'

She shook her head, pressing her cheek to his chest. 'I meant imagining you didn't exist.'

He opened his mouth, but nothing came out. 'Unless we become pen friends, I'm not going to exist to you in a little while anyway.'

'You'll always exist to me,' she admitted, surprising herself with her honesty. 'I don't know if, after this, we can just be friends. But I won't ever forget.'

He smoothed her hair back from her face, making her wonder how *she'd* ever existed without these affectionate touches. 'I'd come and visit you, but you might have married your soul mate and be expecting your fourth child by the time I actually get on a plane. I don't think I'll like your husband.'

He was joking, but it hurt so much it caught Jenn by surprise. She didn't much like this hypothetical husband, either. She could only imagine he would be a poor substitute for this... whatever she felt in Tiziano's arms right now. And her own children? Instead of the idyllic family she'd always pictured, when she thought of her future, she suddenly imagined herself at a small child's bedside, clutching him helplessly as he slipped away, taking her whole reason for living with him. How would she be able to open herself up to that kind of hurt when she could barely open herself up to well-meaning friends? What would it be like raising a child – loving a child?

She'd been so naïve. She'd dreamed of having her own family, of truly belonging somewhere, but children weren't a solution to a problem. They were people and she wasn't good with people. She suddenly realised she'd spent her life longing for connection, while simultaneously keeping everyone at arm's length, afraid of being judged.

Until now. Tiziano had judged her, teased her, found her lacking, and yet, he took her in his arms and touched her as though he never wanted her to change. What was she supposed to do with all these feelings?

'Shit, I'm sorry, Jenn. I was trying to make you laugh, not... that.'

'Just, no husband jokes. Not when the way I feel about you is so confusing.' She pressed her lips shut and closed her eyes, not sure if she should have said that. 'And don't *ever* regret your existence. If I hadn't met you... Well, I'm glad I did, no matter what. Don't doubt that.' She couldn't doubt herself any more, either. *I love you.* She would tell him before she left and hope that he could at least feed his ego with it for years after she was gone.

'I would never doubt you,' he murmured against her hair. 'You're too strong for doubt.'

'You are the strong one, Tiziano – much stronger than you think. Everyone relies on you and you're always there for them.' She glanced at the sleeping form of little Dinah, remembering the way he'd held his niece with the confidence of practice and a vast dose of love. 'And you're always there for Rico, in your heart. That takes enormous strength.'

'I wasn't there for him when it counted.'

'Yes, you were. You were handed the most difficult thing a parent can ever experience. It wasn't fair and it wasn't right. But you're trying, and that's brave.'

When she glanced up, his eyes were glistening and there was a tremor in his jaw. She loved his cheerful and cheeky smiles, his expressive face, but that look lodged inside her where understanding was instinctual, not rational.

She raised the photo still clutched in her hand. The little blond boy was adorable, with his father's bright smile and his hair so long she could have plaited it neatly like her mother had always done with hers. He was up in his father's arms and Tiziano, his face leaner with youth, was leaning against an old tractor. The sweet photo showed starkly everything he'd lost.

'Two babies,' he muttered, taking the photo and studying it, a faint smile on his lips.

'You were really young, to deal with all of this,' she said softly. 'When I was twenty, I was discovering how incompetent I was for the first time, terrified I'd made a mistake by choosing to study oenology.'

'Nothing's changed, then?' She poked him in the

chest, which would have had more impact if she'd been willing to move out of his arms to do so. He gathered her close again. 'You're not incompetent. You're a person – a beautiful, powerful, thinking and feeling person.'

'Feeling' was right. *Had* nothing changed since she was twenty? Was she still floundering through life with only the appearance of success and none of the satisfaction?

'He's just beautiful, Tiziano,' she said, brushing a fingertip over the image of the little boy. She wanted to cry again, but not just for Rico or his father this time. Her mother had taught her to go after what she wanted at all costs, but had she ever truly understood what she wanted?

She stretched up to give Tiziano a halting kiss on the cheek. He turned his head and brushed a kiss over her mouth. When she responded in kind, it started a different kind of kiss, slow and wary. When she drew away for breath and a futile grasp for clear-headedness, she could so easily have uttered the three words. She'd never imagined it would feel like this.

Tiziano tugged her back to the sofa, where he stretched out, tucking her against him. He picked up one photo after another, occasionally telling her the background of the shot, or some small event that had happened – more often than not a minor accident that had left Rico bruised or bleeding from his own recklessness.

He painted a picture of a family full of flaws: Marzi often emotionally absent, Tiziano learning about parenting by doing and not always doing it right, and poor Rico. But they'd been a family. Jenn found herself wondering what Marzi thought about that.

When Tiziano's phone rang, Jenn opened her eyes, startled to discover she'd fallen asleep and her head now rested on a pillow, not Tiziano's chest. He paced the polished concrete floor, his phone to his ear.

He released an enormous sigh and muttered something and Jenn realised it must be good news, as she thought he'd said, 'Grasie al casso,' which she was pretty sure was a ruder, dialect version of, 'Thank God.'

She dragged herself upright when he hung up. 'Alessandro?'

He grinned at her; Mr Happy-Go-Lucky was back, but with a rawness that made her want him even more. 'He's okay. He has a chest infection, but he's already responding to antibiotics and they've got the fever down.'

She held out her arms. 'Come here.' He approached with charming eagerness and lay down next to her on the sofa. She looped her arms around his shoulders and tugged him against her. He turned his head into her chest with a smile and she grinned and ran her fingers through his hair. There was no one quite like her big-hearted country boy.

31

The house hadn't changed a bit in the years since Tiziano had last been there. He steered the Fiat up onto the grassy shoulder and parked, peering at the single-storey brick construction with the giant magnolia in the front garden. It still bore one or two flowers in honour of late summer – as big as dinner plates with tough, white petals.

He'd been in and out of this house for years as a teenager, sometimes sneaking around and other times on his best behaviour to face Marzi's concerned parents – concerned their daughter had hooked up with the wrong kind of guy. Then there was that one time they'd had to tell them she was pregnant and Marzi's mother had lost it.

He felt unexpectedly detached that morning; eight years felt like a long time, all of a sudden.

He was early. It had been a busy morning already, since the moment Dinah had woken up with the first glow of light on the horizon. He'd tried to keep her quiet with snacks while Jenn grabbed a bit more sleep, but it hadn't worked for long.

He wondered what they were doing, now. Matteo and Maryam were still at the hospital with Alessandro. He'd offered to bring Dinah with him to see Marzi, but Jenn had insisted he should go alone. Tiziano only hoped Dinah hadn't destroyed too much of Nonna's crockery and Jenn's sanity.

He needed to sort everything out and head back. 'Sort everything out' was probably optimistic, but he could hand over the documents she needed to file with the court and get back to the harvest.

The vineyards began at the end of the street – a flat, sunny field of parallel vines. A grape harvester was already at work, making a rumble that was only tolerated on Sundays during the harvest. The house was on the outskirts of Conegliano, where he and Marzi had gone to school.

With no hesitation, he banged the car door shut behind him and jogged through the rose-covered arch and up the front steps. Marzi's mother opened the door, now going grey, but just as disapproving as ever.

Marzi appeared mercifully quickly and led him to the terrace at the side of the house, offering refreshment half-heartedly, which he refused before she'd even finished talking. She sat slowly, as though she was worried about upsetting a wild animal.

'I'm sorry,' he went in with. 'I shouldn't have got angry on Monday.'

'I do understand why you were angry, you know,' she said, her shoulders stiff. 'You think I've forgotten him.'

Tiziano stilled, letting the words have their intended shock factor. If he hadn't talked about this just last night, he'd be terrified of breaking down in front of Marzi. He nodded slowly. 'I don't "think" you've forgotten him. I'm *afraid* you've forgotten him. Deep down, I know you never can. You're just looking for a way ahead – like me.'

Her hand covered his and it felt strange – *he* felt strange, because he knew the feel of Marzi's hand well. 'It's okay that you were angry. Tiziano,' she began. The sound of his name in her voice also felt like a kind of benediction, a goodbye. After all this time... 'The reason I was upset was that you're right. I left that time behind. It was easier that way. I could just go back to my life before.'

'I can't imagine life was the same,' he said, shaking his head. How had they gone from shouting at each other to defending each other?

'I managed, just about. And do you know why I could do that without hating myself every minute?'

'Marzi...'

'Because of you,' she explained. 'I need to acknowledge this. I could leave him in peace because I knew you would be there to keep his memory. You paid the price and I rebuilt my life. You always made up for my mistakes.'

'They weren't mistakes—'

'My inadequacies – whatever you want to call them.'

'You were young.'

'So were you!' She sighed. 'And if I was upset with you on Monday, it was just because I'm old enough now to worry that I took advantage of you.'

'You didn't.'

She eyed him doubtfully, as though she was angry with him for *not* being angry this morning. 'There is something else I have to tell you.'

'I know you're engaged to Paolo. News still travels, even when you've been gone as long as you have. You can file the deeds with the court. I'm not going to stop you just because part of me is still desperate for him to be alive. But... part of me has to keep loving you, Marzi. Over time, that part gets further and further away and sometimes I can ignore it, ignore the way it pulls me in two. But it has to stay there. Just... don't be angry with me for it, and don't feel guilty.'

'Do you think I don't understand that feeling?'

'But you love Paolo?'

'Yes!' she said helplessly. 'I know you find it hard to believe, but I loved you with everything I had. That part is still in me, too. But things heal over and change.' Her hand tightened on his. 'That's why I have to tell you... I'm pregnant.'

His gaze snapped to hers. It took a moment for the world to stop spinning. Another baby? How could there be another baby? It didn't matter that it wasn't his. He couldn't understand how she'd been able to make that decision. His eyes stung and he turned his hand over to hold hers in return.

'I don't want to upset you again. I know you must think I'm replacing him. *I'm* worried I'm replacing him. I couldn't justify the decision to have another baby in any way, so I just did it, I stopped taking contraception and let it happen.'

His emotions swam in all directions.

'If it makes you feel any better, I'm terrified. Now it's real, I'm not sure I can do this. I should have thought it through, but it happened so quickly and I'm so worried, I'm struggling to think about the baby.'

He clasped his other hand over hers. Her confession didn't make him feel better, but it clarified what he was feeling. 'You can do it,' he murmured. 'I'm happy for you.' He meant it, although he could barely believe that. 'The baby's Rico's brother or sister, you know.' He blinked back tears.

Marzi's gasp suggested she'd never thought of her pregnancy that way. Then she broke down in tears, pulling her hand from his and burying her face in her palms. 'You're right,' she mumbled. 'And that's wonderful and so terribly sad at the same time and I spent so long avoiding all of this.'

'I think now is a better time to address it than after the baby's born.'

She peered at him, her blue eyes so familiar. 'I'm also worried about... Paolo doesn't know anything about kids and he works such long hours. The first feeling I had when I found out I was pregnant, was panic that I had to do it without *you*.'

He squeezed her shoulder. 'As soon as he's weaned, I'll be your babysitter. I've grown up enough to look after other people's children these days.'

She studied him with a narrowed gaze. 'What's happened, Tiziano? You're so calm. What's changed?'

I fell in love with someone else, too. The answer presented itself without an invitation. But he said, 'Maybe things do heal over and change, even if we don't want them to.'

'Is there... no one for you, yet?'

'Too busy,' he said with a shrug.

'Too busy helping everyone else and neglecting yourself. Some things don't change.'

He shook his head with a dry smile. 'I don't neglect myself.'

'Mmm, I hear rumours, too. But that's not what I mean. You're the type to settle down.' *And have a family...* No, he wasn't that type any more.

The thought pricked him with guilt. Jenn wanted kids. Maybe he loved her, but he couldn't promise her that. Either he'd follow her to London and be a constant thorn in her side or she'd have to risk her entire happiness and come here. He didn't want that responsibility. And besides, Jenn was soft-hearted, not reckless. He might be staring the L-word in the face, but she must have protected herself better.

'I'm okay, Marzi,' he assured her. 'And that's enough of a miracle for me.'

* * *

The scent of garlic and pancetta greeted him as he pushed open the door of the farmhouse. He couldn't hear a sound. He frowned and slipped quietly inside. The kitchen was in chaos, with pea pods exploding from the compost caddy and the remains of a pasta lunch still on the table.

Finding nobody, he continued down the hall to the lounge, wondering why the curtains were drawn. He saw Nonna first, stretched out on the sofa, snoring lightly. It was a little early for her to be napping, but he imagined she was exhausted from her morning with Dinah.

He squinted around the room, his gaze finally settling on Jenn, a silhouette on the other side of the room. She was moving strangely and she had earbuds in. When she turned, he saw Dinah in her arms, hanging limp, her pacifier in her mouth.

Mamma mia, he loved her, all right.

Taking a few breaths to calm himself down, he strode over to her with a casual smile. She didn't see him until he was right next to her and she jumped, then gasped, staring at Dinah in panic. 'Shh,' he said, pulling one of her earbuds out. 'She's fast asleep. You can put her down, now.'

Her eyes wide, she shook her head fiercely. 'You have no idea how long it took me to achieve this.'

'I do and I am amazed.' He pressed a kiss to her lips over the top of his niece's sleeping body. The intimacy of the moment wrapped around him. Had agreeing to a divorce unlocked this dangerous prickle of hope?

He blinked it back. He'd spent too long working out how to exist without hope to have it creep up on him again, now.

'Aren't your arms hurting?' She sighed and gave a reluctant nod. 'Dammela. Give her to me.' He grasped Dinah under the arms and lifted her against him. She stirred, but the moment of vigorous sucking on her pacifier boded well. Leaning right over, he transferred her gently onto the other sofa, where she immediately curled up.

When it was clear she'd settled back into a deep sleep, Jenn sighed and dropped her forehead to his arm. 'You look ready to join her,' he commented.

'How did it go?' she asked, tucking herself closer.

He stared at the strip of sunlight peeking in between the curtains as his arm crept around her. 'Okay,' he murmured.

'Just okay?'

'She's pregnant,' he blurted out.

Jenn stilled. 'That must have been difficult to hear.' He nodded silently, unable to say anything else. He thought about trying to explain to her that his reaction to the news hadn't been the panic and grief he'd expected, but what would it change? He was still mixed up in the past and he'd only ruin Jenn's future.

He didn't want to ruin the present.

ELISIR DI CARTIZZE VALDOBBIADENE SUPERIORE DI CARTIZZE DOCG BRUT:

The tender, creamy bubbles and the combination of tropical fruit notes and chalk make this a memorable and exciting prosecco. Only the finest hand-picked grapes from the small, steep Cartizze growing zone are used to produce this rich, rounded prosecco. The hint of hazelnut and almond in the finish make the Superiore di Cartizze a truly complex drinking experience, with all the character of the land and its people.

32

An alarm was raised across the region on Sunday night. There was a forecast of heavy rain for Wednesday. At dawn on Monday morning, all hands congregated in the Cartizze to harvest in the cool morning conditions. As Jenn balanced on the hillside, filling her bucket one snip at a time, the slanted rays of sun on her back, there was no hint of rain in the air. But there was one thing she needed to understand about the weather in this corner of Veneto, the pickers assured her: storms blew in suddenly.

The year had been hot and dry, with so little rain that some of the vines hadn't made it. The heat boded well for the yield and the flavour of the wine, but rain now would endanger an otherwise promising vintage, especially in the Cartizze, the little hexagon of steep, contoured hills with ancient vines and mineral-rich soil.

Tiziano was busy rigging up a pulley system for the buckets, to save many trips up and down the almost vertical sections. Jenn was glad of a pair of boots borrowed from Valentina.

That afternoon, Filippo called unexpectedly. She missed his first two calls, she was so engrossed in her work, and the irritation in his voice when she finally answered pricked her with guilt. Her mind raced with ways to explain that she'd spent the last week helping with the harvest instead of planning or developing her notes – or catching up on the rest of her work that hadn't simply gone away, just because she was in the land of prosecco.

But she didn't need to explain anything, because Filippo did all the talking, announcing his own arrival the following evening with the lawyer, for the meetings she'd scheduled that week, including with the Big V on Wednesday.

It took a minute or two for Jenn to process her disappointment at the news. Filippo was an intruder on the life she'd been rather naïvely living in the countryside with no thought to the future. She couldn't help wishing he'd wait a bit longer.

To make matters worse, he wanted to stay at Nonna's agriturismo and wouldn't be dissuaded. Then he ended the call with, 'Why don't you book onto the same flight home on Saturday? I'm sure you'll get Elisir di Cartizze on board, if you're up in the vineyards today. You've done a great job and your draft tasting notes are wonderful.'

The unexpected praise would usually have given her satisfaction, but instead dread settled in her stomach. She was supposed to book a flight – a flight that would take her away from here. And her last days would be spoiled by Filippo's presence and the necessity of sneaking around to be with Tiziano.

Tiziano tried to tell her it would be fine, he could make up another room and Nonna would manage, but Jenn felt terrible landing Filippo on them.

She couldn't help thinking that that night would be their last, although the thought wasn't rational, or at all like her. 'I'll sneak down when Filippo's gone to his room,' she murmured as she kissed along his jaw, making him smile. His only response was to touch her more ardently, which brought back her worry that tonight could be their last.

On the Tuesday morning of Filippo's arrival, Tiziano was moody. She would have teasingly called him 'lunatico', if she weren't so on edge herself. She stopped him before he jumped down from the Lamborghini when they arrived at the top of the hill in Valentina's vineyard, determined to clear the air. But he insisted everything was fine and proceeded to kiss her as though he needed oxygen from her mouth. The sidelong looks she noticed as they joined the rest of the team suggested there had been a few witnesses in addition to the old Lamborghini she was starting to think of with a great deal of fondness.

Tiziano and his skilled hands were much in demand and Jenn was disappointed she couldn't spend the morning quietly with him, talking about nothing, or about the most important things, while they kept busy picking the grapes. But she'd got to know a few of the other pickers who were willing to try out their English and, after lunch, Valentina herself took up a position next to her.

'How is the pressing going?' Jenn asked, glad of the opportunity to satisfy her curiosity.

'The volume of free-run juice is a little less than last year so far, but the balance of acidity is good. Today we focus on the grapes. Usually we only pick morning and evening, because those times are the best, but today we work all day. The rain will come this evening,' she said with certainty.

Jenn glanced up at the wide blue sky with scepticism. 'I thought the forecast was for rain tomorrow.'

Valentina smiled. 'It will come from behind the mountain. The wind comes from the sea and the rain from the mountains; that's what makes our weather so variable. We don't trust the forecast.'

With a nod, Jenn set to work again with new fervour. They picked companionably, falling silent for long periods of concentrated labour, then chatting about London or Rome, or the wine industry.

In the afternoon, Valentina tapped her on the shoulder and gestured to the top of the hill, where a bench was placed in front of a wooden cross, with roses blooming at either side. 'Let's take a break.'

Jenn followed, accepting Valentina's hand when she skidded on the dry dirt of the hill. At the top, they both paused to catch their breath, gazing out over the countless little hills and hamlets. 'I never grow tired of this view,' Valentina said with a smile. 'I adore Rome and I love Verona, but I couldn't do without these hills.' She trudged to the bench and sat down heavily.

Jenn took a seat next to her, the exhaustion creeping into her consciousness the moment she sat down. 'It is a unique place.'

'And we are unique people,' Valentina said with a grin.

As if on cue, Tiziano waved from a few rows down. 'Enjoy your rest while we work!'

Valentina flicked her fingers under her chin. 'Have you forgotten who's paying you?'

'You're paying me? It's such a tiny amount, I'd forgotten.'

'Sometimes I want to shove him down the hill,' Jenn muttered.

Valentina burst out laughing. 'Everyone knows that feeling!'

'It's nice to know you're talking about me up there. Don't forget to mention how good I am in bed!'

Jenn was glad her face was already red with exertion and no one would notice her fierce blush. But it was clear the whole region knew they were sleeping together and it didn't seem to matter to anyone.

'And no talking business!' he called out before turning back to his work. 'There's time for that later.'

Valentina whistled for Spritz, who'd been trotting worshipfully by Tiziano's side and only reluctantly left his hero in favour of his mistress. Valentina handed Jenn a dog treat and Jenn froze. 'Go on. I think he'll take it from you now, and then he'll be your best friend – if you want him to be.'

Jenn took the treat and gazed warily at the happy little dog, expecting him to start growling at any moment. Perhaps it was because she was wearing his mistress's shoes but, instead of growling, he dropped low to the ground and approached her uncertainly. 'That's a feeling I know,' she murmured with a smile. 'Here, Spritz. Good boy.' He darted up to take the treat and then dropped back again, not yet comfortable with her, but it was progress. She rubbed his head, adding some firmness since he seemed to like Tiziano roughing him up.

Valentina turned to her with a smile. 'See? He just needed time. And I don't mind talking business, but Tiziano's right. We need to talk properly later. I'm sure we can reach some kind of arrangement and I hope you don't mind that I was circumspect. This land, this wine... for us, it's a way of life, but outside the region, it's a trend, a fad – a market.'

'I understand,' Jenn assured her. 'I certainly didn't appreciate the terroir before. To be honest, I'm glad you pushed me to get to know the region, first. It was important for me to spend the time here. I would never have joined in the harvest, even two weeks ago!'

'Tiziano has that effect on people.'

'He's the heart of this place, isn't he? You all are.'

A tractor puttered laboriously up the hill and came to a stop at the top, its trailer empty. Valentina greeted the driver as he emerged and they exchanged a few words. The man handed her a bag and she returned to the bench with a grin.

'Sostentamento!' she explained, pulling out a fat stick of salami and a knife. She peeled it expertly and cut a piece for Jenn. 'Sustenance? Is that right?'

Jenn nodded. 'You certainly eat well during the harvest.'

'Food is important all year round – and this!' She lifted a bottle out of the bag. The clear liquid inside definitely wasn't wine and Jenn wasn't sure if she was relieved or not.

'Grappa?' she asked.

Valentina nodded. 'Made from our own *vinaccia*, the pomace. There's nothing like clearing your chest after hard work. Here.' She produced a little glass and pulled out the stopper with a pop.

'Um,' Jenn began, fighting the urge to save her pride, 'just a small one, please. I'm... alcohol affects me very strongly and I don't want to end up entertaining all the pickers with my bad karaoke.' She snapped her mouth closed. Valentina just looked at her for a long moment and Jenn waited for the questions she couldn't answer: *If you can't handle alcohol, why are you a wine expert? Why didn't you say something earlier? Why are you even here if you can't drink with us?*

But all she said was, 'Bad karaoke? I'd like to see

that.' She poured a splash of grappa into the glass and handed it to her. 'Just enough to get the burn in your throat. This was how we kept warm in winter before gas heating.'

Jenn took the glass and waited for Valentina to pour her own. She rubbed her fingers over the glass absently, remembering Tiziano doing the same, and sniffed the warmed liquid curiously. She recognised the bite of a young grappa, but she also detected a pleasant floral note.

Valentina sloshed some into her own glass and raised it to Jenn's with a grin, before knocking half of it back in one gulp. Jenn sipped at hers cautiously. It had a cleaner taste than she'd expected, less full.

'That's... different.'

'Different how?'

'Oh, I don't know my way around grappa at all. I just noticed it's different from Tiziano's.'

'Yes, well Tiziano is rather an artist when it comes to grappa.'

'Tell me,' she began, 'why does everyone hate the Big V? My boss wants a supply contract with them, even though they seem to sell more than they can make. It tastes similar to Tiziano's, which everyone loves. And it's local, even if doesn't have the long history of the other brands. I don't get it.'

To Jenn's shock, Valentina burst out laughing, clutching her stomach. 'Are you serious?'

'What?' she asked, her uncertainty creeping back. Why was Valentina laughing at her? She'd thought they'd been getting on well. People were so difficult sometimes.

Valentina stopped laughing, studying Jenn. 'I thought you would know.'

'Know what?'

Valentina tensed and glanced out over the vines. 'It's a poorly-kept secret. The Big V *is* Tiziano's grappa.'

Jenn blinked, even more confused than she'd been before. 'He sold them a recipe?'

'No, he founded the distillery. He came back from America with financing, a whole lot of contacts and some Californian oak barrels and it took off.'

Jenn's stomach flipped and tumbled to her toes. It took her a long moment to process what she'd heard. Tiziano was supposed to be a penniless farm labourer who didn't believe in money. At least that's what she'd judged him to be when they'd first met. That's what he'd *claimed* to be, while scolding her for focusing on business.

She wouldn't have been able to get a word out in reply, even if she'd known what to say. He'd lied to her. He'd known she was under pressure to get the Big V to the negotiating table and he'd let her make a fool of herself anyway. He'd had ample opportunities to come clean. Was he punishing her for judging him? Was he laughing at her?

Her pride cracked and slipped, but it wasn't the worst thing she felt. Disappointment coiled around her throat. If he wasn't the man she'd thought he was... then the man she'd fallen in love with didn't exist.

She'd been so stupid making their relationship into something deeper. He'd never suggested she meant more to him than any of the other women who'd slept with him out of pity, or for fun, or any of his other reasons for keeping people at arm's length.

He'd been forced to tell her about Marzi and Rico – it hadn't meant as much to him as it had to her. The first time she'd felt safe enough to allow someone close, and it had turned out her poor instincts for people had let her down again.

Her phone rang and she brushed her hand on her shorts before fetching it out of her zipped pocket. When Filippo's name flashed up, a new shot of panic struck. Filippo was here to meet with the CEO of the Big V. But the owner was Tiziano himself. Jenn had screwed up again. She connected the call with trep- idation.

'Jenn, hi. I need you to pick us up from the airport in two hours,' Filippo said without preamble.

Oh, shit. In the shambles of her most recent screw-up, she'd forgotten her earlier blunder. 'Um, that might be a problem,' she said, rubbing her eyes.

'Whatever appointment you have, cancel it. I didn't realise Grevener doesn't drive,' he explained, referring to the lawyer who was travelling with him. 'Bad timing, but I had to hand in my licence yesterday. One speeding ticket too many, apparently,' he said with an audible shrug. 'I assume your hire car has been repaired.'

It felt as though steam was puffing out of her ears, although it could have been the heat. 'To be perfectly honest, Filippo,' she said with a sigh, 'I lost my licence, too. I'm sorry I didn't tell you. I...' She fell silent, waiting for the consequences of her mistakes, her lies, to crash over her.

But Filippo burst out laughing. 'We're two of a kind, Jenn! Fine, then get that country bumpkin you found to drive to the airport to collect us.'

She gritted her teeth. 'All right, Filippo. I'll ask him.'

'Jenn, we have to get on our flight now. Meet us at the airport no matter what. I'm sure you'll find a way to make it worth his while,' he said with a dark chuckle. 'I'll see you in a couple of hours.'

She took her phone from her ear with the strangest feeling of coldness inside, while the sunshine beat down on the outside. If only she'd kept her eye on the ball. She wasn't in Italy on holiday, to go fishing or to have a damn summer fling. She was here to work, to prove herself to her boss on her first buying trip. What could she do to avert disaster?

33

Tiziano dragged himself up the hill, swiping his hair off his forehead with a dirty hand. He should leave Jenn and Valentina together to talk. Jenn had more than proved herself and he suspected Valentina was ready to consider a contract with Brampton. Jenn could go home successful and Filippo should give her a fucking bonus.

He stuffed down the irrational jealousy that had got hold of him yesterday when the news of Filippo's imminent arrival had landed with a splat. He was behaving like a child, but it matched the helplessness that was plaguing him at the thought of her leaving. She had to go. He had nothing that would make her stay – and a shock for her tomorrow when she walked into her meeting at the Big V. But it didn't stop him railing against what had to happen.

He'd keep his raging jealousy to himself as best he could. He'd caught the hint of embarrassment in her tone when she'd talked about Filippo staying in Nonna's old farmhouse with the green 1970s tiles and the cracks and the fuse box that tripped in a stiff breeze.

She was right, the agriturismo needed work – work he'd intended to do for the past couple of years, but he'd been strangely reluctant to change the place that had been his haven in many difficult times. It pricked his pride that she was ashamed of the place – of *him*, he thought in his more petulant moments.

He shouldn't be so annoyed. He'd gone into this relationship – this *casual* relationship – knowing he wasn't even remotely her type. It wasn't her fault that he couldn't keep a hold of his own feelings.

He saw her chatting with Valentina and experienced the first tingles of alarm when he noticed her expression: tight and full of dismay. He hurried forward, stupidly ready to run to her defence but her phone rang and she stepped away to take the call.

After listening to someone on the other end of the line, she lifted a hand to her forehead, raking it over her face in distress. The agitation was clear in her voice, even though he was too far away to make out any words. He approached in a hurry, although his footsteps slowed when he heard her say, 'All right, Filippo. I'll ask him.'

'What's up?' he blurted out as soon as he reached where she was standing at the top of the hill. She stilled and turned slowly to face him. When her gaze met his, he experienced the distinct sensation of something valuable being snatched from his fingers. It was over already. He'd lost her. He didn't know what had happened, but this was it. When she spoke, they weren't the words he'd expected, but her wooden tone was somehow worse. 'I need you to drive me to Venice.'

'To get Filippo?' He invented several colourful nicknames for Filippo in his head.

'I'm sorry about the harvest, but... in the circumstances, I think you can make the time to help me.'

'Why can't he hire a car?'

The pink in her cheeks was usually something he admired, but he was too uneasy. 'He got a driving ban and the lawyer doesn't drive, either. If I had another option, I'd take it.'

'A driving ban? Why does that sound familiar?'

'You'd better take her,' Valentina murmured in Italian. 'I didn't realise you hadn't told her about the Big V.'

A flush swept up his throat. Merda. 'I'll go and get the Fiat,' he mumbled, rubbing the back of his neck.

'Get someone to drive you both back to Combai,' Valentina suggested. 'We could still use the tractor.'

'Certo,' he said, kissing Valentina's cheek in an absent farewell.

Jenn was alarmingly silent. In ten minutes, they were back at the farmhouse and she ducked inside to change before they set off. He should probably do the same, but he'd decided it would be his passive-aggressive reaction to her distancing herself that she'd have to spend the trip smelling his sweat.

When she returned in one of her usual blouses and the court shoes that were a little worse for wear after a few trips into the hills, he had the car waiting and had lowered himself into the driver's seat with a huff. She came around to her side, got in and slammed the door.

As soon as he'd turned out of the driveway, she let loose and it was almost a relief. 'What do *you* possibly have to be annoyed about?'

Adrenaline flooded him to hear the emotion in her voice. 'You have no idea why I'm annoyed? You didn't think *I* might have a drop of pride myself?'

'What are you talking about?'

Could he admit he was angry she was drawing

away from him the instant Filippo was in the country? 'Even now, I'm your last choice. If you had another option, you'd take it,' he said, paraphrasing her words from earlier.

'That wasn't what I meant!'

He knew she'd meant she didn't want to inconvenience him, but it was also true that she would never have been interested in him, if they'd met in London. She'd never give up her life to take a chance on him and he didn't want her to, but that didn't mean it didn't hurt.

'Don't talk to me about pride,' she continued. 'You know how hard I worked for the meeting at the Big V tomorrow and you were planning to ruin it!'

'I wasn't!' he denied vehemently. 'I was planning to sign a fucking contract that I can't really afford – for you!'

'Oh, that's so touching, Tiziano, after you lied to me and forced me to make a fool of myself in front of my boss!'

'When did I do that?'

'Do you think Filippo will be happy to discover you're the owner? After the way he treated you in Milan? And it's all my fault!'

'It's *not* your fault. If it weren't for you, Filippo wouldn't have a chance in hell of a contract.'

'You've been pulling strings behind the scenes this whole time. Did it amuse you to see me doing all the wrong things? I was trying! You can't blame me for not knowing how things work around here when no one cut me any slack!'

He fell silent. She'd misunderstood him entirely, but that was nothing compared to the hurt that bloomed in him that she'd think him capable of that.

'Ever since I got to know you, I've only helped you,' he insisted. 'If I let you make a few mistakes at first, it was because I didn't think they were a big deal.'

'*This* is a big deal! I've not only humiliated myself, I'm going to humiliate my *boss*! You *know* how important this trip is to me!'

'Yeah,' he said with a huff. 'I know. I know how important your *boss* is to you.' He could see in her face that he'd struck a blow, but the regret wasn't enough to stop him. 'A bit awkward that the guy you've been sleeping with has to come with you to collect the man you really want.'

* * *

Just great. Jenn was enough of a mess and now Tiziano wanted to have this conversation, too. She was nervous about seeing Filippo, now her stupid former crush on him was a source of embarrassment. She was scared of failing in her job and equally wary of success. She didn't know what she wanted any more, but the freedom she'd found to explore life was also crumbling with every word out of Tiziano's mouth. She'd been *wrong*, about so many things. She'd never been so wrong in her life, even though it had all felt right.

'That hurts, Tiziano,' she managed to say, her voice choked.

'Life hurts,' he scoffed.

'Don't use that excuse. For someone who doesn't like pity from others, you have a remarkable amount for yourself!' She almost wished she could swallow the words, but these feelings of disappointment and hurt were all that were left of a relationship that had meant too much to her and she wanted to wallow in them for a bit longer. 'How dare you even *think* I could still want Filippo after everything that you and I—'

'I'm not blaming you! I know what this was, between us.' The 'was' hurt. 'We were always honest with each other. Why shouldn't you have some fun before that idiot sees what's right in front of him?'

'I can't believe this! It wasn't *fun*. You don't know me very well if you think I could be with you the way we were while still having feelings for Filippo. I felt something for him, but I realised in Milan it wasn't what I thought and I know now...' *I know now what it's like to love someone.*

'Jenn,' he said, his voice rough, 'don't try to tell me you ever thought our relationship was serious. You know I'm a lazy ass who lives in a shed and works casual jobs. This thing with the Big V doesn't change that you don't like who I really am.'

She wanted to shout that he was wrong, make him pull over and shake him and then kiss him and then climb in his lap. He wasn't lazy, he was committed to enjoying life after surviving a period of depression. She *loved* who he really was.

But he certainly didn't seem to think they'd been serious, and he'd lied to her for weeks. She was a fish out of water in the country and he hated the city.

'It's okay,' he continued. 'We both know this "us" was a temporary thing. Sure, it sucks that Filippo's coming to the agriturismo to steal our last couple of nights, but it was coming anyway, right? I'm sorry about the Big V. I didn't want you to know because I'm not some fucking CEO, even though that's what Antonia calls me. I started the business and some contacts in America made the marketing easy, but it's not my life. I didn't want you to get the wrong idea, or for anything between us to change. I'll fix it. Filippo would be an even bigger idiot than I already think he is, if he makes you pay for my shit.'

'You pretended you had no money and no job security and – nothing! How is that not giving me the wrong idea?'

'Would you have taken me more seriously if you'd known I have a bank account with some savings from the little I take from the Big V? Trust me, it's still nothing compared to Prince Filippo's "assets" I'm sure. Yeah, I could afford a car and maybe a few other things, but I'm not swimming in cash and thank you so much for making me admit that the stupid business I started when I didn't even really want to be alive became such a success it embarrasses me!'

Jenn fell silent. His hands clenched on the steering wheel. She hated this feeling of being ripped in two directions. 'I understand,' she murmured. And she did. She even understood why he went around the countryside rubbishing his own business. It was just like him to do something ridiculous like that. It was part of the reason she loved him so much.

'You don't understand,' he insisted. 'I lied about the Big V, but it's always been the truth that I can't give you what you want in life.'

Her skin prickled at his veiled reference to her desire for a family. He didn't know the doubts that had been plaguing her. 'You can't always control these things. Some people can't have kids, but they don't let that stop them finding a partner.'

He glanced at her in alarm. 'You're not thinking straight, Jenn. You'll be the world's most amazing mother and to give that up... is just wrong.'

To give up on you is wrong...

'I'm not giving up,' she muttered, not sure if she meant her dreams of having kids or her attachment to him. 'Not entirely. I'm just saying it's an excuse. I understand what happened with Marzia hurt you, but it's not reason enough to believe that no one will ever love you again.' She bit her lip, wondering if those words had been wise. She should be steering clear of the L-word.

'Why not?' he scoffed. 'Because *you* love me?'

34

Jenn's heartbeat echoed in her ears. His words were full of vulnerability, but uttered in such a mocking tone that any hope she might have foolishly entertained withered immediately. He wouldn't accept her feelings.

'What if I said I did love you?' she asked, hoping the bitterness in her tone would disguise the disappointment. 'You don't even *like* me. You think my priorities are screwed up and I do business the wrong way.'

'You'd certainly be wrong if you thought you loved me,' he said through clenched teeth, looking away. 'I shouldn't have got upset. Maybe not Filippo, but go find a nice guy and make all your dreams come true, Jenn.'

It was Jenn's turn to avert her gaze. She stared firmly out of the passenger window as tears gathered. They were really ending this... whatever it had been. The future yawned before her, suddenly empty. She had three awkward days of meetings, with Filippo barging into this little community that had begun to feel like hers, ruining the comfort she'd found at the old farmhouse. And after that... back to normal, which wouldn't feel normal at all. Tiziano had barged into her life and she didn't know what to do without him any more.

She didn't know what to do about a lot of things. She couldn't drift through life the way he did and he couldn't allow her to rely on him for anything more than a lift to the airport. It was a silent trip to the airport, after they'd exchanged so many words that had got them nowhere.

Jenn hated how Tiziano acted towards Filippo, when they arrived: polite and full of deference. She might have tolerated it if he'd winked at her or shared the joke, but he was playing straight and that wasn't like him.

When they pulled into the agriturismo, he apologised over and over for the state of the rooms and it still didn't stop Filippo making a snide comment to

Alex Grevener, the lawyer, after Tiziano had left. He commented to Jenn with faux concern, wondering how she'd managed so many weeks in the place, and she brushed him off with as few words as possible.

She thought she detected a patronising undertone when he spoke to her and she wondered if it had always been there. He didn't talk to Alex that way. Had Jenn been too eager to please? It was counter-intuitive, but she was worried that Filippo respected her less because she'd been so available. She couldn't win, and Filippo probably didn't even realise it.

The larger question was: how could she go back to her normal life when she'd lost so much respect for him? She didn't *want* Filippo's job in the future. Playing the game, doing deals and keeping her cards close were what she found most difficult – and least satisfying.

The night was unseasonably warm and muggy for the middle of September, but she kept her ceiling fan off, knowing that Filippo would have his on and she didn't want to trip a fuse. She would have slept terribly anyway.

At about eleven, the first rumbles of thunder echoed over the hills and, with a crack of lightning, the deluge began. Jenn hopped out of bed and threw open the balcony door to watch, breathing in the fresh scent of earth and rain after the sweltering humidity.

The storm was spectacular, illuminating the dim hills with blinding flashes, the heavy drops of rain battering the roof and slowly filling the valley with mist. Valentina had been right. Jenn hoped they'd finished the harvest in time.

She huddled by the door to the balcony, learning with dismay that wonderful memories could haunt her just as much as the difficult ones. She didn't want to lose everything she'd discovered in prosecco country.

She craned her neck to see the terrace near Tiziano's poky little shed. A window shutter flapped and made her wonder if he was there below, staring out, as she was. On a whim, she stepped onto the balcony and leaned over the railing, letting the rain splash her shoulders and soak her vest top.

She'd felt something in this place. It hadn't all been good or easy, but it had been genuine – she had been genuine. She had to take that with her back to London, even though it might make her reassess everything she'd thought was important. Success and failure looked different to different people.

And love had nothing to do with either.

A light flashed on in Tiziano's shed, sending a

beam over the fluttering vines. She leaned further out, her hair plastered to her face by the driving rain, but she couldn't see inside. She wanted to talk to him so badly. She was still angry – no, disappointed – that he'd kept the secret, but she understood why he'd done it and she wanted to push past it.

But there was no pushing past the problems that had always existed between them. Even without the professional and geographical challenges, she'd always be waiting for him to realise he was punishing himself for losing Rico and Marzi, and what if he never did?

* * *

When Wednesday morning arrived, it was still raining and Jenn was bone-weary. After so many weeks away, her blouses were all crushed and she felt overdressed in her heels. Filippo eyed her when she came down to breakfast, but she ignored him.

She didn't know how they were getting to the Big V this morning. She didn't want to take Filippo on the bus, but neither could she ask Tiziano. He didn't show up for breakfast, which was probably for the best. She was surreptitiously checking the bus times again, when she received a text message. After translating the

Italian, she was still confused. It appeared to have come from a taxi driver who thought she'd booked a taxi for that morning. Then she realised Tiziano had booked it for her. The driver was probably a friend of his. Tiziano had told her he'd fix things, after all – in that impassive voice that had made her feel helpless and disappointed.

When they arrived at the distillery ten minutes before their appointment, Jenn felt strangely calm. Things couldn't get any worse than they already were. Filippo would take credit for this contract, if it happened, and she didn't even care, because she would rather be on the riverbank of the Piave.

But when the CEO appeared for their meeting, Jenn got a shock. It was an older man she'd never met. Although gruff, he was polite to Filippo, but he looked uncomfortable in the ill-fitting collared shirt and trousers.

Tiziano...

'Uh, I'm just going to make a phone call,' she said, ignoring Filippo's astonished look. 'Don't wait for me.' As soon as Tiziano picked up, she hissed, 'What are you doing? You can't just pretend someone else is the CEO.'

'Why not? I thought you'd approve of this solution.'

'But if he signs something, it won't be valid.'

'There won't be any signing today. They'll just agree terms. I prepared Adriano and it will all be confirmed in writing afterward. Did you want me to suddenly appear and embarrass you? This way, he'll never find out.'

'I can understand why you thought I'd approve of this solution, but I'm tired of pretending.'

'Jenn, you've said yourself many times, your job is important to you. In a couple of days, you'll leave, and you'll remember everything you love about London.'

Since when was he the sensible one? But his words cut through her confusion with a dose of panic. If he was wrong, as she wanted to insist, then what awaited her when she got home?

On Thursday and Friday, Jenn, Filippo and Alex visited the four wineries she'd selected. She and Filippo fell into a good-cop, bad-cop routine that seemed to startle him at first, but he eventually commented on how well it worked. Jenn was careful not to say that she wasn't just playing the good cop, she genuinely cared about these wineries and their people and the traditions of their products, rather than driving a good deal for the hotel group.

When they made their way out of the tasting room at Elisir di Cartizze on Friday, the rain now cleared and the sun trying to turn the leaves yellow for autumn, Valentina pulled Jenn aside as Filippo and Alex headed for the taxi.

'Filippo is... proud, isn't he?' She wrinkled her nose, making Jenn wonder if her first choice of words had been something stronger. 'I thought you were the same, when we met.'

'I'm not like Filippo,' Jenn commented softly.

'No,' Valentina agreed, squeezing her arm. 'You're one of us.'

Jenn smiled, even though the words brought as much hurt as satisfaction. 'Next year when the time is right, call me and I'll jump on a plane with my bucket.'

'You want a bucket as a souvenir?'

'Thanks, but I've got a stick of salami as a souvenir.'

'It's a shame you're going, just as we got used to you. You must come back – to visit, not for the harvest. You're not very good, anyway, and we can't talk freely if we're working.'

Jenn didn't disagree, even though she'd discovered that harvesting grapes together was the best way to get to know someone. She hugged Valentina, amazed that she'd wanted to demonstrate her feelings so openly and get close enough to smell Valentina's subtle perfume. With a quick kiss to each other's cheeks, Jenn turned to go before she made an even greater fool of herself by crying.

'Come back to visit!' Valentina called again as Jenn hurried down the steps. 'We'll all work on him!' But Jenn knew she couldn't come back – not for a long time, no matter how much she wanted to see Nonna and Valentina, Maryam and Dinah and little Alessandro.

In the taxi on the way back to the farmhouse, Filippo and the lawyer chatted about the tasting night planned for three weeks' time. Jenn usually enjoyed those events. She found it less stressful to present wines in front of a large group than to converse with someone one on one. But she didn't want to even think about London, yet, and sat silently in the passenger seat, her gaze glued to the familiar landscape of the little stone villages in the shadow of the mountain.

'I'm not going out tonight,' she said absently over her shoulder, without looking at Filippo.

'Spending your last night with farmer boy?' Filippo asked. 'I thought you'd got rid of him rather efficiently.'

'I'm going to eat with Filomena. She's been kind to me.'

'Suit yourself.'

But when the taxi pulled into the courtyard, the slanting rays of the sun illuminated a very different scene to what she'd expected.

35

'Jenn! Jenn!'

Jenn stepped out of the car with a hint of lightness she hadn't hoped to feel again. Maryam waved frenetically from the other side of the farmhouse, at the foot of the vineyard. Her car was parked at the bottom of the hill, along with an assortment of odd vehicles. Not only were the Lamborghini *and* the Piaggio Ape lined up, there was also another tractor, a car with a trailer and a little farm vehicle with a tub on the back. The vineyard was teeming with people.

Jenn rushed to Maryam and threw her arms around her, earning a delighted smile. 'How are you? And Alessandro?'

'Okay, now. These kids! I'm going to have a heart attack one day.'

'You're helping with the harvest?'

'Just Nonna's. It's tradition. She tasted a grape at lunchtime and declared the harvest!'

Jenn couldn't believe she'd nearly missed it. 'What about the kids? Do you need me to watch them?' she surprised herself by offering.

Maryam shook her head. 'You have to help pick the grapes. Look.' She pointed to where Dinah was sitting at Nonna's feet, playing with the leaves as the older woman wielded her secateurs on the lowest vines. 'Alessandro comes with me too. Watch!' She winked, reminding Jenn painfully of her brother-in-law.

Maryam retrieved a long, light cloth and wound it around her waist in practised moves that looked complicated to Jenn. She lifted the baby out of his car seat and onto her hip, tugging the cloth up his back and tightening it. Then she hauled Alessandro around onto her back and tied off, crossing the fabric around herself until the baby was secure. The whole process had only taken a minute or two and Jenn stared in awe.

'Ta-da!' Maryam said, lifting her arms and turning in a circle so Jenn could admire her handiwork. 'Time to get started! You will want to take your shoes off.'

Jenn grinned, gazing up the steep hill and spying Tiziano halfway up, hauling buckets. Matteo was there, too, as well as their parents, Carlo and Luca, Adriano and Antonia from the Big V and Jenn even spied Mauro and Zia Monica from the baptism.

Tiziano did an amusing double take when he saw her, which she wasn't sure if he'd intended to be funny. He gazed at her uncertainly.

'Jenn?' she heard Filippo calling from behind her. 'Looks like they're busy. The taxi is coming back for us at seven-thirty for dinner.'

'Go without me!' she called back. 'I've got work to do!'

'Work?'

'Yes, work!' she said with a laugh, meeting Tiziano's eyes and watching the tentative smile grow on his lips. Then she kicked off her heels and headed barefoot up the side, after Maryam.

'Harvesting barefoot! That's a great idea!' Carlo called in greeting, handing her a pair of secateurs before producing a spare pair for himself. 'How about you take your shirt off, too!'

'How about we all just harvest naked?' she quipped, refusing to blush. '*That* would be a good marketing ploy: "Naked Vines Italian Verdiso, picked by hand, in the nude". Do you think Tiziano could sell that in America?' She shot him a meaningful look as Luca and Carlo hooted with laughter.

'Naked Grappa sounds good, too. Want us all to pose for the label?' Luca joked.

'I thought you wanted to actually sell the product,' Jenn deadpanned, moving to cut her first bunch from the vine.

Carlo looped his arm around Jenn's neck and hooted with laughter. 'You're okay.'

Jenn's grin stalled when she caught sight of the flash of emotion on Tiziano's face, his brow low as he eyed Carlo. 'Back to work, fioi,' Jenn said, putting Tiziano out of his misery and causing another bout of laughter as she referred to the 'boys' in the local dialect.

Maryam joined her and they made their way through the vines together. Jenn chatted companionably with her, marvelling at the twisted grandfather vines, but her gaze strayed up the hill to where Tiziano directed the pickers and filled his own bucket. She found him looking at her enough times to know he was similarly distracted.

After about an hour of picking, he appeared at her side so suddenly that she jumped and stubbed her toe on a rock. 'Ow!' His hand landed on her shoulder and she leaned into him instinctively. God, perhaps it was for the best that she was leaving, if she was going to react like this to the simplest of touches.

'You could have hurt your feet already. Here.' He dropped to his haunches and snagged her ankle. He brushed off her foot and slipped a sock on, fitting a musty running shoe over the top, then he repeated the action with her other foot. The trainers felt like clown shoes on her small feet. She must look terrible, sweaty and dusty, with her blouse and trousers crushed and dirty, and the old trainers that definitely had a particular stench. But she didn't care.

When he stood, he regarded her grimly. 'You can't harvest barefoot.'

'Thank you, Health and Safety officer,' she said with a mock salute that made his frown deeper. Then he was gone again.

The evening felt like one last chance – for what, she wasn't sure, but she was determined to embrace it. She tramped down to Nonna, pointing out the shoes with a smile, and watched her wrinkled hands deftly snipping the bunches from the vines.

'You are familiar, now,' Nonna said with a smile.

'I hope so.'

'Family, Nonna!' called Maryam from further up the hill. 'Familiare means family, not familiar!'

'I still kind of hope so,' Jenn murmured to herself.

Nonna smiled and patted her cheek. 'Che bella ragazza. You not rest here? Not rest with Tiziano? Tiziano mio, bravo ragazzo, e molto bello, no?' she asked, gesturing to her face. Jenn struggled to keep a straight face, torn between laughing and crying.

'*Molto bello*,' she agreed. Tiziano was very beautiful, and a *bravo ragazzo*, too – a good boy.

'Siete una bellissima coppia!' Nonna said, patting her arm and then taking her hand. 'Good husband! Beautiful children.'

Jenn's throat thickened and she squeezed Nonna's hand. 'Magari, Nonna,' she said softly. 'Magari.' That word had a world of meaning to her, now: a wish that things were different, a wish that this didn't have to be the end and, perhaps, if she was honest with herself, a grain of hope that they could still work things out.

She looked up to find him watching her again. 'Is she trying to arrange our marriage?' he called out jokingly.

'Yes!' she shouted back.

His eyes popped and she gave a helpless smile. Something had come over her since she hadn't had Tiziano to balance her out. 'Tell her not to pick a date during the harvest,' he called back when he'd recovered.

'Okay!' she said cheerfully and he eyed her again.

It was a perfect evening to end her five weeks in the Colline del Prosecco. An autumn freshness crept down the mountain with the sunset, damp and rich with the promise of things to come. Jenn was enveloped by the gentle breeze in the leaves, jolly laughter, friendship and... family. The only problem was the 'end' part.

With the departure of the sun over the mountain, the merry harvest party began to wind down. Nonna went inside to cook and prepare refreshments, then Matteo and Maryam collected Dinah and headed for their car. Jenn skidded down the hill to throw her arms around Maryam.

'You really leave tomorrow morning?' Maryam asked. Jenn nodded, not trusting herself to speak. 'Che insemenìo, Tiziano,' she continued. Grasping Jenn's hands, Maryam gave a sigh. 'I had hoped...' She seemed to reconsider what she'd been about to say and Jenn feared it was for the best.

'Perhaps, so had I,' she murmured. 'Thank you. For being a friend to me.'

'Of course! Come and see me. Or I come and see you! We can have a girls' night in London. I like that idea.'

'Maryam will keep you out all night.' Tiziano appeared behind her. He kissed his sister-in-law on the cheek and clapped his brother's shoulder. Not long after that, they left and Jenn began to realise just how much goodbyes could sting. And she hadn't even got to the most difficult one, yet.

* * *

Shortly after sunset, moisture hung in the air and the landscape was dim and quiet. Only a gibbous moon sent a glow over the vines. The lamp on the wall of the farmhouse gave off some feeble light, but the deep blues and greens of the vineyard at night bled together, making it increasingly difficult to see the stalks to cut them.

Tiziano fetched his headlamp out of his pocket, but he didn't put it on. Instead he climbed slowly down to Jenn. She was squatting to cut some low-hanging grapes, her face tilted up. He paused to take her in, this woman who felt she didn't belong anywhere, but who would leave a gap inside him when she left. Her eyes were wide and dark in the moonlight, and she had a smudge on her cheek. Her hair clung to her forehead with sweat and stuck out around her head.

He'd thought she was fascinating the first time he saw her, but now, she was stunning.

She glanced up and saw him and he hated the wariness that crept into her gaze when he approached. He lifted the headlamp and stretched the elastic around her head, giving in to the temptation to brush her cheek with his thumb, even though it left a fresh smudge. Then he switched on the lamp and he couldn't see her face properly any more. It was probably for the best. He had work to do.

'Don't cut your fingers in the dark.'

'Okay,' she replied softly. He hesitated for another moment, before he forced himself to get back to work. They were racing against the thickening dew.

As the time wore on, he expected Jenn to disappear back inside, but it became clear she was determined to stay to the bitter end. He tried not to read too much into that. It didn't mean she'd stay here – with him. When they finally waved off the last trailer of grapes, headed for a winery on the other side of Vittorio Veneto, a decided chill had descended from Monte Cesen and it was past nine o'clock. Tiziano said goodbye to his parents and Luca and Carlo, but he hesitated halfway down the hill, watching Jenn out of the corner of his eye.

She tramped up and stood beside him with a sigh. 'Happy with the harvest?'

He nodded. Retrieving a bunch from the couple

left in his bucket, he plucked one grape and held it up. She watched him in surprise as he popped it unceremoniously into her mouth. 'Can you understand the wine?'

'A little. It's acidic – sour. But it's bright and fruity. Like its grower?' she said with a smile, spitting out the seeds.

He eyed her, but 'bright and fruity' probably described him well. And he certainly felt the bitter aftertaste, knowing she was leaving tomorrow. 'You can't taste this one until at least two years' time. It's going to the cooperative to make passito wine this year. Not prosecco, so you won't want to buy it.'

'Shh,' she said softly and reached into his bucket. Pulling out a grape, she pressed it into his mouth. He held her gaze as the sour berry burst on his tongue. 'I don't want to talk about buying wine.'

'What do you want to—' She cut him off with another grape through his lips and he chewed slowly. 'Jenn, what are we—' He was ready that time, and swiped his lips across her fingers as she popped the grape inside. Her breath hitched.

Maybe they were supposed to be angry with each other but he missed her. He would miss her more when she left. He wanted this last night.

'Tiziano—' He was ready with a grape and she

chuckled as she chewed. 'Another,' she murmured, lifting her face. He took his time slipping the grape between her lips.

'You're leaving—' She quickly shoved a grape in his mouth to cut off that particular sentence.

She leaned on his crossed arms and lifted her face. 'Can't we just forget, for tonight?'

His mouth was a breath from hers even before she finished speaking. Dropping the bucket and lifting his hands to her face, he kissed her, deep and slow. The way she clutched at him, opening her mouth and pressing close, gasping for quick breaths between drawn-out kisses, reminded him of the first time they'd kissed – except tonight she was sober and she knew exactly what she was doing.

He pulled her hard against him, the fingers of one hand sinking into her hair. All the heated words they'd exchanged, their differences, all the competing goals, didn't matter. All that mattered was being together tonight.

Safe on the moonlit hillside, they stood for a long time, his hands roving under her shirt and his lips over her neck. 'Come with me,' he finally whispered, hauling her into his arms when she stumbled on the uneven ground in the dark.

He sensed something shifting inside him as he carried her, laughing, into his dingy converted shed and straight to the little bathroom to shower. He didn't want to understand what these feelings meant, so he unloaded it all onto her, making her feel every inch of her skin under the spray and, afterwards, every pulse point as he pushed her higher.

She stayed with him through the onslaught of emotion and he was gratified by her cry as he bit her shoulder and pressed her heavily into the bed. He couldn't hold back and, as he followed her over the edge and collapsed next to her, heaving for breath, he knew he would suffer for letting her mean so much to him.

36

Jenn had expected it, but she was still disappointed when the sound of the Lamborghini woke her early the following morning. He was gone. That was it. They wouldn't have gained anything from a messy goodbye, anyway. She'd been clinging to the hope that Tiziano would give her one last lift. But she understood that a goodbye would be too difficult – especially after last night.

She rose and opened the curtains, but it was barely daylight outside. A delicate mist hung between the vines, the yellow tinge to the leaves growing more distinct with each dawn. Time moved on, even when she didn't want it to.

Perhaps she shouldn't have pushed for one last

night, but she didn't regret it. She'd never made love with someone like that: no inhibitions or apologies. Instead of being awkward it had been... beautiful.

Now, she might never see him again. She flopped back onto the bed, breathing deeply. What would she give to be able to stay here? She was certain of one thing: she was tired of hiding, of fearing failure and the disapproval of others. Her definition of success had shifted and she wanted more out of life than constant striving.

Unable to face her dirty blouse from the day before, she opened Tiziano's cupboard to steal a T-shirt. Her gaze caught on the shoebox she knew was full of photos of his precious little boy. Her feelings catching her by surprise, she couldn't stop herself from opening the lid and looking through a few. Fresh tears pricked her eyes, even as she tried to be stoic and accept how hopelessly she loved Tiziano – the reliable friend, the joker, the farm boy, the father.

She closed the box again and pulled herself together with a few deep breaths. She wasn't part of his family, no matter how badly she wanted to be.

She slipped back to the house to shower and of course Filippo caught her in the hallway. 'Buongiorno,' he said with a curious glint in his eye.

'Good morning,' she replied with a tired smile. Let him think what he wanted.

She slipped the shirt back on for breakfast, enjoying the glint in Nonna's eye. The heavy old table was overflowing that morning, making Jenn feel keenly the love of an Italian grandmother.

'You were brave last night, tesoro,' Nonna said, patting her hand. For a moment, Jenn thought she meant she'd been brave to approach Tiziano and let that spark take over one more time. But she was probably talking about the vendéma, the heroic harvest. 'It is delusion, no? Leaving us?'

Jenn blinked. If only it *was* just in her imagination that she was leaving, but unfortunately it seemed to be more of Nonna's confused English. 'A big delusion,' she agreed anyway.

'You have a marvellous estate with us. Your work, you realised?'

Jenn smiled, glad she'd learned that 'estate' meant summer in Italian and she understood at least that much, now. She wasn't quite sure what Nonna meant by 'realised', but it struck her that she *had* realised a lot of things about her work. 'Work is only part of what I realised,' she murmured.

Nonna took her hand again. 'I miss me, bea tósa.'

'You, too, Nonna,' she said with a chuckle. 'I will miss you.'

'Before you miss, you *eat*,' Nonna declared and spooned a dollop of mascarpone onto her fregolotta chunks. A moment later, toast with pancetta and three different cheeses appeared on one side and a fried egg with thick slices of fresh tomato on the other.

'Proper eggs,' Jenn said earnestly.

'Always proper eggs! And proper pomodori.'

Jenn thought with chagrin that she would never find proper eggs in London. Proper eggs needed to be prepared with proper love.

* * *

Tiziano was supposed to be thirty kilometres away helping a friend prepare for the Biancoperla corn harvest, but instead, he switched off the motor of the Lamborghini outside a familiar set of stone gates and gave an enormous sigh. He should have expected he'd end up here, today.

What *was* surprising, was the sense of disappointment in himself. Usually, when he came here, it was for clarity, to make sense of his life as it was, now. But he was here and still confused. He wrenched open the door of the tractor and leapt down.

When he got to the little plot, he only felt worse. Propped against the monument, was a bunch of wildflowers in blue, yellow and white, tied with ribbon.

A pained smile touched his lips as he thought of Marzi leaving the little bouquet there with her regrets, thinking about all the flowers Rico never got to pick. He waited for the anger, the helplessness, and when it didn't come immediately, he felt guilty for grasping for it. Rico's memory didn't deserve that desperation. That was Tiziano's problem and he wished he'd found a way to leave it outside the cemetery years ago.

The little bouquet of hand-picked flowers honoured the memory of their son so much better than Tiziano's frustration. Glancing at his watch, he headed for the gate again, sitting on the wall to eat the bread and cheese he'd brought with him. It had taken him over an hour to putter down to Montebelluna in the tractor. He could have been sitting in the kitchen eating with Nonna but he hadn't been able to face that.

He couldn't do goodbyes.

Feeling restless and useless, he hopped back up into the cab of the tractor and slumped down in the seat. Glancing at his watch again, he closed his eyes and tried to doze. She'd be in the taxi by now. He just needed to stay here until she left. Then he might feel normal again, and not tempted to tear up his life.

Casso, what was he doing? He started up the tractor and took off, cursing himself for chewing through petrol. He cursed himself even more vehemently when he arrived at his next destination. Was it really necessary to punish himself like this, just because he'd been a little bit happy with a woman? It was enough punishment that she was leaving.

Unfortunately, his brother appeared before he could noisily back the tractor out of the driveway again. Stupid vehicle.

Matteo was wiping his hands on a tea towel. 'Turn that thing off before Alessandro starts wailing again!' Tiziano cut the motor with a grimace and climbed down. 'Maryam said you'd be here, today. 'Ndemo, let's sit out the back.' Tiziano trailed him through the house, which was strewn with toddler toys and washing. A shriek sounded upstairs. Matteo paused in the kitchen to pull two bottles of beer from the fridge.

'I thought you weren't one for morning beers these days,' Tiziano commented warily.

His brother opened one bottle on the other and took a swig as he shuffled out onto the terrace like an old man. 'Dinah woke up every two hours last night and I was sleeping in her room because a baby has taken my wife's affections. If I'm going to deal with you, as well, I need a beer.'

'I admit I enjoy being the difficult one,' Tiziano said with a smile. They collapsed into the plastic chairs and gazed out at the yard full of toys and half-finished projects.

Maryam appeared, her hair wild and the look in her eyes even wilder. 'If you're going to sit down and relax, take her!' she hissed and shepherded their daughter onto the terrace. 'Why won't that boy sleep?'

'Speaking of the difficult one,' Tiziano said with a grin and beckoned for Dinah to come to him. He settled his niece on his lap, wrapping his arms around her. The thought struck him that she was already bigger than Rico. He expected to feel sad about that, to wrestle with the relentless passage of time that swept Rico further and further away, but watching Dinah grow was some kind of miracle and he valued that too.

'Good, you're making yourself useful,' Matteo said, leaning his head on the back of the chair. 'So,' he continued, eyeing Tiziano, 'what time's the flight?'

'Eleven-thirty,' he answered immediately, glancing up at the sky with a frown. 'Don't worry, I'm not going to pretend I'm here for something else. I just need to stay here until she's gone.'

'Why? You don't want to cry on your own?'

It was Tiziano's turn to scowl, but Dinah poked his cheeks, so he contorted his face into a sillier expression, making her laugh. 'Maybe it's to stop me doing something stupid.'

Matteo sat up in alarm. 'Something stupid?'

'Calmati, fradel!' Tiziano said with his hand in the air. 'Something stupid like going after her! Madre de Dio, what did you think I meant?'

Matteo punched him on the shoulder. 'You know what I thought.'

'Shit, how bad was I... back then?'

The grim look in his brother's eyes sobered him. 'Pretty bad.'

Tiziano rubbed a hand over his eyes and tucked Dinah's little curly head under his chin. 'Even so, I never... okay, maybe once, but not seriously... not for long, anyway. You know I'd never do that to you.'

'That doesn't fill me with confidence,' Matteo muttered. 'Why do you think going after her is a stupid thing to do?'

'Pffft,' was the first answer that reached his lips. 'I have some pride.'

'What does that mean, Tiziano? You think she'll laugh at you for telling her you have feelings for her?'

'What good are *feelings*? We had a good time together, but you can't imagine I can make her happy in the real world – in her real world. Or do you think they need farmhands in London?'

'Make something of the distillery, start taking it seriously.'

'You think if I put on a suit and play the boss, she'll want me? You didn't see how annoyed she was when she found out I own it. That's not the way to impress her.'

'That means she likes you for *you*, not for your job or what you have to offer. Perhaps she's crazier than I thought.'

Memories of last night flashed through him with a squeeze of his chest. She was crazier than *she* thought. It was gorgeous. 'But the distillery is here. I can't make her come here for me. You know I can't.'

'Judging by the couple of times I've met Jenn, I don't think you can *make* her do anything. But you can ask.'

'Wow, grasie fradel. What a great idea. "Allora, Jenn, would you think about quitting a job you work hard at to move here to the countryside which you hate, so we could have a bit more hot sex?" Is that what you pictured?'

'*Don't* even *mention* hot sex right now,' Matteo growled. 'You idiot.'

'This is the advice I came here for,' Tiziano said with a nod. 'Davvero, what did you think I'd say? "Marry me?"' As the words tumbled from his mouth, he felt the strangest conviction that he might have accidentally said those words if he hadn't taken off this morning. Talk about doing something stupid. 'I'm not fucking divorced, yet!'

'Va bene!' Matteo said with a dismissive wave of his hand. 'You've made your point. But...' His brother had an unexpectedly pained expression on his face. 'Don't close the door. London's not that far. You could visit. Give her some time – give *you* some time.'

I don't need time... '*You* liked her, did you?' was what he said instead of admitting his true thoughts. 'Might not be a point in her favour.'

'Not as much as *you* like *my* wife,' Matteo replied with a scowl.

'You know how much I love Maryam,' Tiziano said with a wink. It was far too easy to rile up his brother. 'Does it worry you?'

'It's worried me a lot less the past few weeks,' Matteo shot back, 'since you've finally been fantasising about someone else.'

'What do you mean "finally"? I've fantasised about a lot of people over the years.'

Matteo snorted and took another sip of beer. 'You only ever looked at other women to make yourself feel bad about Marzi. Don't try to tell me this is the same. For one thing, you've spent years doing absolutely fuck all and now you're worried you'll do something to make yourself happy. People change, Tiziano. *Jenn* changed, didn't she, in the weeks she was here? Maybe there aren't as many obstacles as you think.'

The back of Tiziano's neck prickled as he allowed himself to wonder if his brother was right. But Matteo didn't understand just how many of Jenn's dreams she'd have to give up for him.

Maryam poked her head around the back door. She grinned at Tiziano and kissed his cheeks. 'Hi, pasticcino.' Matteo grumbled something inarticulate at his wife's use of the endearment, but she ignored him and stole his beer.

'Mamma!' Dinah called. Maryam rolled her eyes, but beckoned for her daughter to come and settled Dinah in her lap, stroking her hair.

'Tell me the plan,' she demanded.

'He has no plan,' Matteo said, 'only problems.'

A high-pitched wail sounded from one of the open windows upstairs and Maryam groaned. 'That fucking kid. It's too early for teeth, but he bites like the devil and still doesn't settle down.'

Tiziano stood. 'I'll go. You guys can argue about the plan. Matteo has already called me an idiot and given me bad advice. Maybe Sandro is the distraction I needed after all.'

He was glad to escape, but when he hauled Alessandro out of the cot, he sensed he wouldn't find the answers he wanted, here. He might only find answers he *didn't* want.

'Don't need to sleep, eh?' he crooned to the baby. Opening the shutters to let the light in, he sat in Maryam's armchair and held Alessandro at his eye level. The baby blinked and gurgled and gave him a gummy smile, shoving a tiny fist into his mouth. Tiziano pressed a kiss to his little bald head and breathed in, remembering Jenn holding him and commenting on the baby smell. God, how had someone so intelligent and perceptive tolerated him for so long?

Tiziano slumped in the chair with Sandro tucked into his arm. He managed to slip the dummy into the baby's mouth at an opportune moment and Sandro stilled, eyes heavy. 'Need to sleep after all, hmm?' Tiziano murmured, leaning his head back.

He'd held Sandro often since the day he was born, but each time he felt he learned a lesson about trust and love. *Love...* His feelings truly were a mess.

It turned out that he had no distractions at all when a plane cut across the sky a few minutes later. He didn't need to look at the time to know it was her flight. He clutched his warm little nephew as he watched the jet slowly draw its line and he accepted the fact that he *wanted* to move forward, to think about the future.

'Are you wondering what it would feel like if he was yours?' came Maryam's voice.

Tiziano opened his mouth to deny it, but he couldn't. 'Maybe,' he murmured.

'And? How is it? Because you can have him if you want. He can chew on *your* nipples – unless you still have that piercing. That would be a choking hazard.' She grinned at him, but her eyes were soft. She knew the jokes made his feelings bearable. 'Did you talk through everything already with Matteo?'

He nodded. 'Keep the door open, people change, London isn't very far away, I'm an idiot – it was something like that.'

'Argh,' Maryam groaned. 'That man is hopeless, sometimes! Listen to me: I've already decided Jenn is my sister-in-law. Dinah needs a cousin quickly before the age gap is too great, but a cousin in London is no use to her. The solution? Get your backside on a plane and *bring her back*!'

Like a game of Tetris set on fast, all the blocks fell into place in Tiziano's mind. Jenn wanted family, a place to belong? She already had that here, if he could make her believe it. Her job was a complication, but Matteo was right that she wasn't the same buttoned-up wine snob that she'd been when she arrived and Tiziano had enough connections to find some kind of solution.

And kids? Goosebumps crept up his arms as he imagined the journey with Jenn, not only the worries, the exhaustion and the fear, but the joy and wonder, the promise of the future.

He wanted that future.

'I like your thinking, sorellona.' He made to get up, full of sudden enthusiasm, but Maryam was there in a flash, waving a finger.

'Don't you dare move! Get on a plane and bring her back *after* Sandro's nap,' she hissed.

37

Jenn collapsed onto the sofa in her own living room and waited for the familiar sweep of relief at being back in her own space. She had the internet on tap in every square inch of her apartment. She could shower three times a day and even walk around naked – not that she'd ever done that before.

Her neighbours didn't know or care what she did. They were going about their own business, too. She rose and closed the gauze curtains over the bay window. She was going to cry and she didn't want the neighbours to see *that*.

Casso. Who was she, now? Instead of celebrating the return to her comfortable bubble, she was swearing in an Italian regional accent and missing a great chunk of her heart. She hugged a cushion and snorted a sob. Couldn't she go back?

To what?

Her phone rang and she jumped. She fumbled in her handbag and grimaced to see it was her mother calling with video. She swiped at her face and fanned herself in a futile attempt to calm the blotchiness. It only reminded her of Tiziano describing how she looked when she drank wine.

'Hi, Umma,' she said as brightly as she could.

'What's wrong?'

Oh, no. 'What would be wrong?'

'Why does your face look like that? Have you been using that cream I sent you? Have you come out in freckles?'

'It was very sunny in Italy.'

'I hope you covered up.'

Jenn covered her choke with a cough. If only Umma knew about that day by the Piave. She caught movement in the back of the shot behind her mother. 'Who's that?'

'Nobody,' her mother said decisively. 'Why are you looking at me like that? What is that weird expression?'

Jenn stifled a flummoxed smile. Not only did it appear that she'd picked up some weird facial expres-

sions from Tiziano, but her mother had a 'guest' in her apartment. 'Do you have a boyfriend, Umma?'

'No!' she said defensively, sending a furtive glance over her shoulder.

'Good for you.'

'I said I don't—'

'It's all right. It's not like I'm going to tell anyone and I won't judge you. Maybe I'm happy for you.'

'Your happiness is a little premature, Eun-jin-a. How was your trip? Was your boss satisfied? You were away such a long time I was worried.'

'You know, wine isn't an exact science,' Jenn explained thoughtfully.

'Even with your sense of smell?'

Jenn nodded ruefully. 'It's more like art or... *life*. It's unpredictable and not always in our control. I've always been able to pick out aromatic compounds and analyse flavours, but I was missing the point.' She paused to take a breath, listening to her own words back.

'What point? You are a highly-trained master of wine. Has your boss been questioning your expertise? I always tell you we have to fight for every bit of success as women in our fields – as *Asian* women.'

Jenn's eyes unexpectedly filled with tears all of a sudden. Dear Umma. She was such a strong woman –

cut from the same cloth as Halmoni, even if they had spent half their lives estranged. Jenn might be feeling mixed up about what she wanted from life, but she could only imagine how adrift she would be if she hadn't had her mother's firm voice behind her.

'Eun-jin-a! Mu-seun il?'

'I'm okay, Umma,' she muttered. Hearing her mother slip back into Korean had an oddly calming effect, as though Jenn were seeing the real woman underneath, instead of the straight-backed financial genius who spoke perfect English. 'You're amazing, do you know that?'

'What?'

'I've been doing a lot of thinking, that's all.'

'I suppose if you have no reliable internet, that's what you do. I can't believe there was no Wi-Fi. Practically the entire city of Seoul is covered by public Wi-Fi these days. Thank God you're back in civilisation.'

Jenn gave a pained smile. The city was civilisation? In the city, she was productive and supported the economy and contributed to services like reliable public transport.

But a bus couldn't hug you.

'What have you been thinking about? If you don't want to wait around for this Filippo Baretti to promote you, then look around for something else. I have contacts in Hong Kong and I know they're desperate for wine buyers over there. Your trip must have been great experience.'

'That's just it,' she said faintly. 'It wasn't what I expected and now I... I'm not sure I want to be a wine buyer at all.' The expected silence was heavy, but Jenn breathed again after she'd got the words out. 'I don't want to disappoint you, but it's not where my strengths are.'

'But you're a marvel with wine tasting.'

She shook her head. 'Do you know, my damn nose has been more trouble than it's worth. Yes, it's helpful to be able to pick up on the nuances of flavour, but do you have any idea how stressful it is to be in a group of people and smell *everything*? I can't think straight and then I say peculiar things. I get so tired.'

'Where is this coming from? Who has stolen your confidence? Didn't the trip go well?'

'The trip was wonderful,' Jenn said softly. 'I haven't lost confidence. I've gained some. I'm not perfect. There are some parts of my job that I'm not good at. But that's okay.'

'I didn't raise you to accept failure! I know how hard we have to work to get what we want.'

Her mother wasn't wrong, but it made Jenn see how important it was to make sure she was working for the most important things. 'It's not failure. It's being human. What if I want something different to what you wanted?'

'And what's that?'

Jenn hesitated. How had she talked herself into this corner? She and her mother didn't talk honestly like this. Their conversations were more like strategy meetings, but Jenn had no strategy for this – for the complexities of life she'd only begun to appreciate.

'I want to be part of something, not *a*part from everything.' *I want family...* She kept that one to herself. She didn't doubt her mother had enough guilt to carry around, without realising how much loneliness Jenn had swallowed down over the years.

She didn't necessarily mean she wanted children. That dream had come from a deep vulnerability she hadn't understood. Now she knew that family meant a lot more than people connected by birth. If she had Tiziano's family around her – Maryam and Nonna and all the others – that would be enough. She suspected Tiziano would teach her to love Dinah and Alessandro as much as she'd ever love her own children.

'Jenn, you are different. I tried to help you accept that, find a way to follow your own path with your own special talents—'

'I do understand,' Jenn insisted. 'We had something to prove. Halmoni never let me forget it. But it doesn't matter as much as you think.' She sounded like Tiziano. Did she truly think she could belong there, with his family, among the little hills of golden vines? Apparently, she did, because the words kept tumbling out. 'As long as your heart is open to others, as long as you can be willing to make mistakes and be honest and forgive – that's community. It's family. And it's... beautiful.'

It's love.

The argument she'd had with Tiziano rushed back to her with a stab of regret. Why had they given up? He'd told her to embrace her mistakes and move past them. He'd demanded honesty from her and shown her the depths of intimacy between two people who accepted each other's faults.

He should have seen how much she loved him. She'd tried to tell him last night, but he'd still walked away this morning.

The fear that he didn't love her in return throbbed in the back of her mind, but it wasn't necessarily the reason he'd left. He had a big heart and a sensitive soul, held together by the love of others – that soul had seeped into the community, the very land. He would do anything for the people he loved – including letting them go, if he thought it was what they wanted.

She'd never told him she didn't want him to let her go.

'It's like wine,' she said with a baffled laugh. 'There are quality distinctions, flavour notes, scientific – and less scientific – production methods and individual tastes. But the most important thing is who you drink it with. The best wine in the world is the one you drink with the people you love.'

That was point she'd always missed. Her tasting notes, her recommendations, the wine supplies in every Brampton hotel across the world, existed only to create a memorable meal, a sociable drink – to connect people. Filippo wanted the finest, the most select, the wine people drank because they thought they *should,* and Jenn had learned at his knee.

But the prosecco producers didn't work like that. Wine was for the table and the table sat at the heart of the family. Jenn had always been an outsider at the table with Filippo, unable to drink more than a glass and worrying about saying the wrong thing, but she'd always been welcome at every table in Valdobbiadene.

'You... there *is* someone,' her mother said softly.

Jenn nodded vigorously. 'There is definitely someone.'

'In Italy?'

Jenn nodded again, her expression caught between

a smile and a grimace. 'I fell in love with a Veneto country boy and I don't know what to do.'

Her mother took a deep breath and blew it out on a huff. 'All right. This is a little more complicated than I'm accustomed to, but we can work this out. Does he love you?'

'Maybe.'

'I see we have quite a way to go. He will love you, if he knows what's good for him.'

Jenn grinned, wishing she could give her mother a hug.

'I love you, Umma.'

'Well, miracles do happen,' her mother muttered. 'I love you, too, Eun-jin-a. Now, what do you need to do?'

'Don't freak out,' she began, making her mother's eyes pop. 'I'm going to quit my job.'

'Whaaat?'

'I said don't freak out. It's not entirely because of Tiziano. I enjoy doing guided tastings and I could offer those remotely, go into business for myself. If all else fails, I'll come to Chicago and move in with you – and your boyfriend.' Her mother coughed and spluttered, giving Jenn a surprising feeling of satisfaction. 'Or I'll take a job in Hong Kong. No matter what happens, I'm making a change. I don't want to work with Filippo any more.'

'He does sound like a *ba-bo*.'

Jenn chuckled. 'Actually, he's a bit of a geh-se-kki, Umma.' Her mother's gasp at her bad language was another source of satisfaction.

'Who taught you to swear in Korean?'

'Netflix,' she explained with a grin. 'Do you think Halmoni just turned in her grave? I know women aren't supposed to swear.'

'She turned in her urn – absolutely.'

'She would have hated Tiziano.'

'That's his name, is it? Strange name.'

Jenn snorted. 'He told me to call him Tits.'

'Strange man,' her mother said with a frown. 'Are you sure you know what you're doing?'

'I have no idea what I'm doing and Tiziano *is* a very strange man. But I'm definitely in love with him.'

38

Jenn's resignation didn't go down well. Filippo blustered about her squandering her opportunities and not being cut out for the next step in her career. Those comments would have crippled her confidence two months ago, but now she saw them for what they were: Filippo being defensive and refusing to examine his own values. Jenn almost wished Tiziano had appeared for that meeting at the distillery and made Filippo swallow his own hand-crafted leather shoe in embarrassment.

He made her work her notice, which meant launching the new wines at the VIP tasting event as planned. It would be a fitting end to this stage of her career and, once it was done, she hoped Tiziano would be ready to hear what she had to say – if she could just work out how, where and when to say it.

She presented her tasting notes to Filippo the day before the launch with some trepidation. She was leaving Brampton, so it shouldn't have mattered if he wanted her to reword some of her more flowery expressions. But she'd drawn her descriptions straight from the silty earth of the hills and the hearts of the people who tended the vines – straight from her own heart, on occasion. It was a small legacy that was important to her.

Filippo glanced at her curiously, as they clicked through the slides together, but he was satisfied enough not to request any significant changes.

'You captured a mood here, Jenn,' he said with approval. 'I can tell you've been in Italy. I'm looking forward to seeing you present them.'

Her throat was thick with nerves at the thought of standing in front of the guests and pouring out her thoughts, but she could pretend Tiziano was there, grinning at her, and she'd get through it.

In that unexpectedly civil moment, she couldn't hold in the question she'd been wanting to ask for three weeks. 'I didn't... I don't see the Big V on the new menu.'

Filippo's inarticulate grumble made her glad she

hadn't asked earlier. 'That company is impossible to work with. Did you know the man we met, the CEO, can't actually sign the contracts?'

Jenn bit her lip. She hoped Filippo's question was rhetorical and not genuine. Yes, she had known. 'What are you going to do?'

'I have to meet the owner, apparently, and he's busy. I managed to arrange a phone call with him and the only thing that got his attention was the promise of a free trip to London! Unbelievable!'

That sounded like Tiziano.

'You don't usually shy away from wining and dining clients,' Jenn pointed out.

'I don't know who he thinks he is, but he's coming tomorrow and we can get everything signed quickly,' Filippo said with a humph.

Jenn stilled. 'He's coming? Tomorrow?'

Filippo grunted a reluctant affirmative. 'I had to invite him to the party for the new wine list, as our meeting is the next day.'

A flood of tingles shot over Jenn's skin. Knowing she'd see him, talk to him and not only that, he would hear her tasting notes, emptied the room of all oxygen. Would he understand everything she'd poured into her notes? Would he be listening for hints of how he'd changed her life?

After weeks of fretting over how she would prove to Tiziano that she loved him, he'd placed the solution in her lap and solved her problem without even knowing she had one.

'I only hope he respects the dress code,' Filippo muttered, oblivious to the way Jenn's heart was floating on the ceiling. 'His name is Tiziano, like that lover boy of yours, and he sounds just as much a country bumpkin. I hope he doesn't arrive on a tractor!'

'Imagine that,' she said with a snort of laughter that she had to hide behind her hand. The old Lamborghini would certainly make an impression on the streets of Mayfair.

Tomorrow... She didn't have much time. As soon as she left Filippo's office, she pulled out her phone to call in reinforcements. Maryam replied immediately, her enthusiasm obvious. Tomorrow, she would reach out for what she wanted with everything she had. She only hoped he would be ready to reach out in return.

* * *

Tiziano gazed grimly around him. Sure, these brick buildings with the white detailing were impressive, if you liked that sort of thing. The shops were all glitzy and minimalist; no plastic people in the window in strange poses, like the shops he frequented in Monte-belluna when his flannel shirts wore out. A black-and-white pub with leaded windows stood on the corner, looking cosy and inviting in the waning light of early evening.

Probably overpriced with warm beer, he assured himself.

A black cab pootled past, unable to get up any speed on the narrow road. The street was busy and grey and crowded and... quite nice, actually, damn it! Up until he'd arrived in Mayfair, he'd kept his nerves at bay, noting the grime, the noise and the smells – God, the smells! How did Jenn torture herself every day on the Underground? – of the city she called home. Surely she'd been miserable since she left. He was banking on her missing the little paradise he called home.

But she worked in Mayfair, in a historic hotel with fine stonework and seven elegant storeys – he'd counted them. He tugged on the collar of his stiff white shirt. What was he doing here? Maryam's order to bring her back had seemed simple until he'd arrived here and seen everything she'd have to give up. Per-haps Matteo was right and he should take things slowly. He'd ask her to dinner – no pressure, no expec-tations. He should have told her he was coming, instead of this stupid idea to surprise her and sweep her off her feet.

As if wearing a suit would be enough for that.

His phone buzzed with a call from Matteo. 'Va bene?' Tiziano asked with concern.

'Sì, sì, calma, fradel. I'm looking out for you this time. Are you wearing a tie?'

'Yes, for fuck's sake.'

'Did you take your piercings out?'

He thought about lying, but he hesitated too long to pull it off. 'She likes the piercings,' he insisted instead.

'But you're supposed to make an impression, like at the end of *Grease*.'

'I'm the girl?'

'In this case, yes. You want to show her you can be serious.'

'Unfortunately, she already knows me. Varda, I'm at the hotel. I need to go.' He swallowed, wanting to wimp out. How would she react? If he found her all sleek and proud and frowning, like the day they met, he wasn't sure how he'd deal with the disappointment.

'Wait, what? Hold on, Maryam wants to talk to you.'

'Remember what you have to do!' she said without even muttering a greeting. 'I'm relying on you, Tiziano.

Bring her home!' He heard Matteo grumbling in the background. 'What? It's too important to leave it up to you two! She'll love the suit, but don't forget it's *you* that will bring her back. Whatever you do, Tiziano, don't leave without telling her you love her.'

'Capito. As soon as I see her – bam – I love you.' He was joking, but he'd come this far – both physically and in himself. He could make her happy. And he looked damn good in this suit.

The doors of the hotel swished open and another man in a suit with a phone to his ear nearly collided with Tiziano.

'Cazzo!'

'Casso!' they said at the same moment, then jerked their heads up in surprise. 'I have to go, Maryam,' Tiziano murmured. 'Filippo Baretti is here.' The last thing he heard before he disconnected the call was Dinah repeating the foul curse her mother had muttered into the phone. They certainly were raising another proud child of Veneto.

'Sei tu!' Filippo exclaimed.

'Siete voi,' Tiziano replied in the polite form with a tight smile. Dealing with this stronzo was not what he wanted to be doing.

'Did Jenn invite you? I almost didn't recognise you outside of your... natural habitat.'

'No, Jenn didn't invite me. *You* did.'

'What?'

'Perhaps we should start again.' He held out his hand. 'Tiziano Lucchetta,' he said, waiting for the lightbulb to turn on.

Filippo's face drained of colour. 'Tiziano... *Lucchetta.*'

39

Jenn was holding herself together with adrenaline and anticipation. The launch party was about to start; her presentation and guided tasting were prepared. Seven types of prosecco waited in the wine fridge for the arrival of the VIP loyalty members, along with platters of cheese, grapes and salami.

How many of these evenings had Jenn led in her career? Dozens, by now, and yet this one was entirely different. The fondness she felt for those wine bottles, the way she could almost taste the fruity, fresh notes without even pulling a cork, the vivid memories that struck her from the smell of the sopressa the chef had sourced – everything about the evening was intense. And that was before she contemplated Tiziano's reaction to her tasting notes – and her reaction to seeing him again.

She was nervous. She had this one chance to convince Tiziano he was everything she wanted in a family – even without kids. That was difficult enough, but then she needed him to invite her to stay. She could only hope he would love the surprise she'd prepared for the end of the night as much as she thought he would.

Life would definitely have been easier if she hadn't fallen for him. But who needed an easy life when she could have family?

Her phone beeped with a message from her co-conspirator Maryam and she froze when she read it. *Crap*. Rushing to the foyer of the hotel, she hoped she would be in time to avert disaster. In all of her worrying, she'd almost forgotten this confrontation had to happen tonight too.

Go away, Filippo, she thought with a groan.

Raised voices speaking in Italian reached her ears as she approached the doors and, when they swished open, the sight that greeted her made her stop short. Filippo was chuckling and shaking Tiziano's hand enthusiastically. And Tiziano... was wearing a stylish, tailored black suit.

The jacket fitted his lanky frame to perfection. He

looked tall and confident and nothing short of dashing. His hair was slicked to the side in a neat wave. His shoulders were back and his smile wide; he was charm personified, and not because the suit rendered him presentable. *He* gave the suit its spark. Filippo had impeccable taste and an expert tailor, but Tiziano wore his suit with character and she couldn't tear her eyes from him.

She was happy to see he wasn't entirely presentable. He had a small gold hoop in each ear and were they skulls on his tie? She was so distracted, at first she didn't question why Filippo wasn't angry.

Then Tiziano looked over and saw her. She could have blurted out that she loved him right then and there, in front of Filippo – in front of everyone.

'She's just as shocked as I was!' Filippo said, still grinning. He clapped Jenn on the shoulder and she stumbled. 'I have to congratulate you on your taste, after all. Your little summer fling has landed me exactly the contact I needed and you didn't even know.'

'My... what?'

'If you want me to sign, watch your language, vecio,' Tiziano said, his tone casual, but firm enough that Filippo eyed him. 'I'm not here for you.' Jenn's hair stood on end and her skin tingled. He wasn't here for Filippo?

'Who are you calling "old man"? And it's *vecchio*, unless you'll insist on speaking dialect to me every time.'

Tiziano lifted his hands in a gesture of surrender. 'I didn't think you'd be so delicate. *Allora*, where's the party?'

Jenn cleared her throat. 'Uh, this way,' she said, her tone entirely too formal. She'd built this up too much. She should have just jumped on a plane and spoken to him at the top of Nonna's vineyard. And she could do with a shot of grappa right now to put some hair on her chest.

She took off for the function room, now filling with guests who were admiring the photos she'd framed and inspecting the sample bottles. Just inside the door, Tiziano snagged her arm.

'Everything okay?' he asked softly, ducking to study her face. His thumb stroked her arm. He wasn't here for Filippo. He looked at her as though she could be his world and it was everything she wanted.

She wasn't quite sure how it happened, but suddenly she was kissing him for all she was worth, wrapping one arm around his neck. He recovered quickly and leaned into the kiss, one hand in her hair.

Grasping the lapels of his jacket to steady herself, she wrenched away with some difficulty. 'Wait!' she rasped, pushing at his chest. 'I have... stuff to tell you, to show you. I have a presentation to make. And I can't talk with... your mouth...'

He snorted with laughter and she nearly kissed him again, that grin was such a welcome sight after three long weeks.

'Make your presentation, and then we'll talk, okay?' He brushed a finger under her chin.

'Okay,' she said, her chest still heaving. Filippo cleared his throat pointedly and Jenn peeked over Tiziano's shoulder to catch numerous furtive glances in their direction. 'The presentation,' she began, catching Tiziano's sleeve before he could pull away. 'It's for... everyone.' *It's for you.* 'I, um, I quit my job.' *For you.*

'What?'

'Just listen when I present my tasting notes, okay?'

'Okay. Do you want me to film the presentation? Show everyone back home?'

Jenn was kicking herself for deciding to do this in public, when what she really wanted was to lock herself into a small room with him until the words came out. He'd better believe she was crazy about him after this. 'Thanks,' she agreed with a sigh.

He squeezed her elbow. 'You'll do great. I know how much the growers mean to you.'

No, you don't – not yet.

'And we'll… talk, afterwards.' She studied his face for reassurance and what she got was a familiar smile. It was enough for now.

* * *

Tiziano ambled around the function room, studying the photos with a deep ache inside him. Lorenzo and his moustache, Valentina laughing with her father in front of their steel tanks. She'd caught a beautiful shot of Nonna, her wizened hands wielding secateurs on her old vines. She'd also selected photos of a gnarled old apple tree, a hedge of flowering jasmine and the spreading hazelnut at the top of the hill behind the farmhouse.

But it was the shots of the many glasses of prosecco that struck him. There was his own hand steadying a glass of tranquillo. She'd used depth of field for a shot from Alessandro's baptism meal, so the figures of his family were indistinct behind three glasses of bubbles, raised in a toast. The photo of the sunset over the Piave, with a plastic cup of col fondo prosecco in the foreground, brought back so many tender memories.

Jenn had been brave that day. Might she be brave enough to take a chance on him after all?

Before Tiziano had finished looking and feeling and enjoying Jenn's display, Filippo strode on stage and invited the guests to take their seats. Tiziano pulled out his phone, ready to capture the moment for Jenn and send her message to the prosecco producers. He'd sent a quick text to Valentina and organised to stream the presentation live on the social media accounts of the consortium. He'd already posted a few photos from the event. Filippo began his introduction and Tiziano started the stream.

'Our wine expert, Jenn Park, will take you through the tasting this evening and, as you'll see, prosecco has a very *special* place in her heart. She spent five weeks getting to know the terroir and I think you'll all agree that there is a lot more to prosecco than a cheap and cheerful tipple.'

'What more could you want than a cheerful tipple?' Tiziano muttered.

'We are proud to have seven carefully selected wines to taste tonight, which will soon be available at all Brampton hotels,' Filippo continued.

'*You're* proud,' Tiziano snorted in disdain. 'Ca... volo,' he whispered, just managing to censor himself when he realised his asides had been caught on the livestream and comments were starting to appear. 'Off you go,' he murmured as Filippo kept talking. 'We want Jenn.' He stifled a chuckle when more comments appeared, echoing his thoughts.

She strode on stage with a nervous smile, shaking Filippo's hand far too graciously with her usual unconscious bow, and Tiziano's grip on the phone wavered. He had to bring her back. He would make her happy, no matter what it took.

'Dio, te vojo tantissimo ben.' Those words slipped out much more easily in dialect, when she couldn't hear them. *I love you so much.* Celebratory emojis appeared in the comments on the video: confetti and party blowers and clinking champagne flutes that were obviously supposed to be filled with prosecco tonight. 'Isn't she gorgeous?' he murmured.

When she took her position to the side of the stage and the title slide of her presentation appeared, Tiziano fell silent in anticipation.

'The world of DOCG Prosecco is both very small and incredibly varied. I think there is a favourite prosecco out there for everyone – every taste. One day you'll taste a prosecco and know that's the one for you. Tonight, I want to share my notes on flavour, but I also want to share the way of life of a small place where family and community come first – and wine a very close second – where time is taken to grow food and where there is always an extra seat at the table for guests.' A spontaneous round of applause greeted her words and, before Tiziano realised what he was doing, he was knocking the phone from side to side as he clapped as well.

'I must admit at this point,' Jenn said with a self-deprecating smile, 'that I arrived in the Colline del Prosecco, the Prosecco Hills, looking only for fine wine that we could offer our hotel guests with exclusive marketing. But, as you'll see, drinking prosecco is not an exclusive wine experience. It's an *inclusive* one. And that's why tonight will be a little different and I hope you all enjoy the journey with me.'

40

A fleet of waiters fanned out through the room, filling glasses. Tiziano made sure to hold the label on the bottle in shot, and the little seal bearing the DOCG certification. It was one of Lorenzo's.

'We'd normally start at one end of the sweetness scale and move to the other, but it's a measure I find very rudimentary in judging wine, so we're starting in the middle of the scale, with a Prosecco Conegliano-Valdobbiadene Superiore DOCG Extra Dry from the Quattro Brezze winery in Premaor. Now I'd like you all to say *that* ten times fast and you'll have an idea of how I felt when I arrived in prosecco country.'

'You were gorgeous, when you arrived,' Tiziano mumbled.

The slide changed to a picture of the bottle and the tasting notes from the wine list – Jenn's tasting notes. 'I must admit that I find sparkling wines the most difficult to taste, because the bubbles overwhelm my nose.' She glanced at Tiziano as she said it and he lifted his glass in support. Prompting the guests to take a sip, she described the feel, the flavours and the aftertaste.

'Not really sure how a wine can be "confident", but you're the expert,' Tiziano commented.

But she wasn't finished. 'The point with this wine is to confront your prejudices.' Tiziano waited for her to look at him again, but she glanced down at her toes. 'In the English-speaking world, sweet wine has traditionally been a synonym for bad wine, but in Italy, and many other places around the world, it's simply a matter of taste. There's a lot to love about this wine, even though it has a little more residual sugar than most of the proseccos available in the UK. Don't focus on the sweetness, which your palate has been trained to identify. Look instead for the fruit notes, the texture of the wine – because that smooth texture is partly the result of the sugar. The sweetness here isn't from additives masking poor ingredients, it's the perfect counterbalance to the acidity of the grapes and it gives a wonderful complexity, when you open your heart to it.'

Tiziano chuckled, beginning to see what she was trying to do. Goosebumps sneaked up his arms at the prospect of reliving her five weeks in his life, one glass of wine at a time.

'Don't feel you need to drink it all,' she continued. 'These are small tasting glasses, but, even so, I'm led to believe that seven glasses of wine are enough to make even the heartiest of farmers keel over.'

'And two glasses of grappa,' Tiziano added under his breath.

'As the next glass is poured, take a moment to try the salami or the cheese. These rugged flavours show the versatility of a prosecco, especially the next one we'll taste, the tranquillo.' She lifted the next glass and swirled it. 'When pairing prosecco with food, you can go two ways: pair with mild flavours for a light, refreshing palate, or pair with strong flavours, to balance the palate. Either way, prosecco is particularly tasty with many Asian dishes, seafood or otherwise.'

'The second one, definitely,' Tiziano murmured. 'The way you balance me.'

After describing the tranquillo, she glanced at Tiziano and added, 'This is wine for the family, for those precious everyday moments that you never realised were so special.' She cleared her throat and he stared at her, wondering how soon they could have their talk so he could give her a hug.

Next was Lorenzo's rosé. Jenn said something about the creamy perlage, although she said pinot noir instead of pinot nero for the red grape in the blend. 'Need to teach you better Italian, amore.'

'This rosé is a lazy summer evening,' she continued, 'which is something I wasn't always very good at enjoying. In this day and age, there's so much to do and we can put so much pressure on ourselves to succeed. But how do we even know what success looks like unless we stop and think, feel the sunshine on our skin and watch the tip of the fishing rod twitch with the nibble of a fish that will never bite.

'Most importantly, stopping to smell the rosé with a friend enables us to see outside our own world of responsibilities, and discover what others need, or allow them to help us. A true friend is someone who has time for you.'

There was nothing at all he could say to that, he felt so proud. Only after two whole minutes and about ten comments, did he finally realise he was livestreaming the white jacquard tablecloth and nothing else. He whipped the phone back up, blinking at the image of her on the little screen, because he felt too much when he looked at her in person.

'The next wine,' she said with a small smile, 'is something very special. It has traditionally been called a col fondo, a prosecco fermented in the bottle by the traditional method without disgorging the lees, the yeast.' She went on to describe the flavour profile and the extremely low residual sugar content, her enthusiasm clearly spreading to the guests as they exclaimed about the pronounced note of pear and the complex minerality.

'It's... volatile,' she went on. 'Lunatico, you might call it in Italian – which doesn't really mean lunatic, by the way. It means moody and emotional.'

Tiziano snorted his wine, coughing and spluttering and making the livestream judder.

'But this is an honest wine. We all have... faces we show to the world.' Her smile was delicate and heartbreaking. 'But have you ever had a time where you were safe enough and brave enough to show someone who you truly are? Those people who *see* you – don't let them go.'

She lifted her gaze slowly until her eyes locked with his. The phone clattered to the table in front of him and he didn't care. He saw what she was doing. Yes, her presentation was for the prosecco producers, to honour them with her respect and enthusiasm. But it was also for *him*.

He went to stand up, but she gave a slight shake of her head. 'I'm not finished,' she murmured, covering the microphone on her lapel.

'You don't need to finish,' he said softly, even though she couldn't hear. 'I love you more than you even realise.'

'The next wine is from the heart of the Prosecco Hills, an area so special, most of the tiny plots have been passed down through generations and the stories are still told of how the region struggled after the devastation of the First World War, when the Piave river was the front. This is Rive di Cartizze, from a vineyard with a 39 per cent gradient, where one-hundred-year-old vines hang onto the clay-limestone soil for dear life. Every winemaker knows that the hardest years produce the best wines. This is a real hardship wine to remind us that the best things in life aren't easy, but they are worthwhile.' Tiziano could only stare as she met his gaze again. 'This is a wine to celebrate the things that are truly important in life.'

She swiped at her face and he nearly leapt to his feet again.

'Just a moment,' she said, striding to the side of the stage where a glass of water and a tulip glass of another clear liquid stood on a side table. After a moment's hesitation, she reached for the tulip glass and took a sip.

'Brava la mia tósa,' he said with a smile. 'She's my woman.'

She cleared her throat and turned back to the audience with a smile. 'Excuse me. I just needed a little grappa to clear my chest. We have only two wines left.'

'And then I can kiss you again,' Tiziano added with a groan.

'Next is the Conegliano-Valdobbiadene Superiore DOCG Brut, the fruity, dry prosecco you have been waiting for all evening.'

Tiziano realised he'd dropped the phone and snapped it up again. 'Me spiase,' he apologised to the audience back in Veneto. 'I forgot you all want to see her, too. Isn't she lovely?'

After reading her tasting notes, she paused to look around the room. 'This is the wine you want at your wedding,' she declared, to a chorus of approval and raised glasses around the room. 'It's the wine I want at *my* wedding.' She had the audacity to give him a wink. 'You drink a new vintage again at your tenth anniversary and it brings everything back. It's great for your grandmother's birthday, too, and your nephew's baptism.' Another little moment of eye contact that sent shivers of awareness through him. 'Because celebrating the good times is also a way of honouring the bad times. Sometimes you're high up on the hill in the sunshine and sometimes down in the dark valley – and sometimes both at the same time. Making memories is what connects us. And once you've made a memory and shared it with someone you love, it's always with you. You won't lose it.'

Tiziano remembered the way she'd studied the photos of Rico in the middle of the night on his crappy old sofa. She didn't want him to give up the memories, to 'move on', whatever that meant. She wanted to share them.

This was her solution. He'd wasted so much time worrying about scaring her off, about not being enough for her, when the problem had been *him* all along. It made his head spin to think that he could simply ask her to come home and she'd come. She'd already quit her job. She was standing in front of a room full of strangers telling their love story using prosecco.

She'd accomplished the hard part. He only had to tell the ending and he didn't think he could wait another minute.

CASA MARIA ROSA VALDOBBIADENE SUPERIORE DOCG DRY:

In this light prosecco from the hills of Colbertaldo, a kick of sweetness complements the natural acidity of the finest glera grapes in a balanced wine that is superbly enjoyable. The bubbles are light and persistent and the finish honeyed and creamy. A dry prosecco is a good accompaniment for dessert, but also for cheese platters, particularly aromatic cheeses such as pecorino or matured Piave DOP.

41

Jenn's blood rushed in her ears and her throat was dry and if she'd had any scrap of doubt about her feelings, she would never have got through this. One more tasting and then she could whisk him away for his reaction and her final surprise.

She'd just about pulled herself together when Tiziano leapt to his feet, scattering startled waiters in all directions. He rushed forward, making her heart pound, but he didn't approach her immediately. He went to the side of the stage and downed the rest of the grappa in one gulp.

Tugging at his tie and running his hands through his hair until nothing remained of the neat wave, he stalked along the front of the stage and came to a stop where she stood. He stared up at her, breathing hard, his hands on his hips.

'I love you, Jenn Park!' He seemed to jump at the strength in his own voice. Certainly, he'd spoken loudly enough that the entire room had heard and cheers broke out in all corners. 'I know it's too soon, but I'm so crazy for you. I want everything.'

Jenn's carefully maintained composure took a nosedive and she felt rather crazy herself as she gazed down at him, her unlikely Romeo, and her vision blurred with tears.

'I want a baby – if you still do.' She sucked in a startled breath, but she couldn't doubt him when his jaw was so fiercely set and his expressive face was curled up tight with emotion. 'I mean it. You were right, I won't lose Rico. If it happens, I... want to experience that again – with you.'

She took a step forward, but her legs were jelly and she only got far enough to steady herself against his shoulder. He still wasn't finished.

'I want to watch you sneeze when you drink that prosecco at our wedding. And I want to wear this fucking suit again – but just once.'

'It's a really nice suit,' she murmured, catching her lip between her teeth and curling her fingers into the fine wool.

He blinked. 'I could... wear it a few more times, maybe.'

'I think we both might be crazy,' she said, reaching for his face with her other hand. 'Because I love you, too.'

He tugged her to the edge of the stage, where he stood looking up at her. 'Te vojo tantissimo ben,' he mumbled in his rural dialect. He lifted his face to hers. 'Come home, Jenn. Wherever you want to live, I'll be there, but you'll always belong at home with us.'

She wasn't sure how hard he was trying to give her a serious look, but his lips were twitching and she couldn't quite believe how happy she was to be looking with certainty into the face of the person she would peacefully grow old with.

'I'll come home,' she assured him. 'You're my favourite person in the world, Tiziano, and the only bad thing is that I didn't meet you until two months ago.'

His big hands came up to cup her face and her breath hitched as she met his mouth with her own. It was a kiss for the future.

The room erupted in cheers and, with the clink of many glasses, the audience went on with their wine tasting without her. Tiziano pressed one last hard, quick kiss to her lips and then swung her into his arms, making her squeal. The sound echoed in the function room and she realised the microphone on her lapel had picked up every word of their declarations. A glance at his table revealed an older woman holding Tiziano's phone high, still streaming the scene.

It appeared the world had witnessed her putting her pride on the line for Tiziano and she didn't regret a moment of it. She waved to the camera and blew a kiss, thinking of Valentina and Maryam and the many others that might have been watching – back home.

'We have one more wine to taste!' she said, digging her fingers into his jacket.

Jenn looked back desperately at the guests as Tiziano strode purposefully across the room. 'This last one is labelled "dry", but it's actually the sweetest level of prosecco commonly available. It's not a – oof! – dessert wine, but it pairs very well with sweets or c-cake!' Tiziano was bumping her on purpose, she was certain. 'Anyway, don't be afraid of a prosecco that's a little sweeter!'

'Nothing wrong with sweet wine!' Tiziano agreed, ducking his head to speak into the microphone. 'Prosecco is Italian, after all, and we know la vita è dolce!'

To the sound of applause, he whisked her through the doors and into the foyer of the hotel, setting her on her feet and leaning in for another kiss. She stared up at him, her brow knit. 'Did you mean it – you want children? Because it doesn't matter—'

'I mean it,' he assured her. 'I was holding Alessandro and then I knew.'

'We won't forget Rico. He's part of you and I love you and—'

His hands closed over hers and brought them to his chest. 'I want to dream again, Jenn – with you. I want to sit on the terrace with you when we're ninety, surrounded by our grandchildren.'

'I think I *am* dreaming,' she murmured, drawing his head down for another kiss. 'Wait,' she said. 'I have a surprise for you. I wasn't sure how much convincing you'd need so... well, you'll see.' She tugged him through the sliding doors of the hotel and out onto the footpath. 'Wait here.'

He grasped after her. 'I don't need any more convincing!'

'I didn't know that and I've organised it, now!' she grumbled.

'Don't take too long. I've already waited three weeks to see you!'

* * *

Tiziano took the opportunity to retrieve his phone from the woman at his table and headed back outside to wait for Jenn's mysterious surprise. He grinned as he scrolled through the comments on the video. Maryam had sent her approval which was only fair, since she had ordered him to bring her back.

He had no idea what more Jenn could have planned that would top what he'd just experienced, but she was taking longer than he liked. He heard a faint rumble that he at first thought was thunder, but the sound was consistent – and getting closer. He peered in the direction the sound came from, wondering why it sounded familiar.

He kicked himself a moment later when she came bouncing around the corner, her eyes wide and her hands panicked on the controls of a sweet John Deere 6E.

Passers-by stopped and stared. Traffic was backed up behind her. He was so proud he was bursting.

The tractor decelerated jerkily and she overcompensated for the turn. The enormous front wheels jumped the kerb and he had to leap out of the way. She cursed and stamped on the brake, cursing again when she took her foot off and the big machine lurched forward.

'Put it in neutral!' he called, laughing as she frantically groped for the shuttle on the dashboard. When she finally brought the beast to a full stop, she gave an enormous sigh and flopped back against the seat. He sauntered to the steps of the cab and opened the glass door, grinning up at her. 'You got your licence back?'

She turned to him, her eyes wild. 'Is that all you can say? Do you have any idea what a monster this thing is to drive?'

'I have an idea,' he quipped. He leaned closer, loving the way her gaze softened as he approached. 'This is the sexiest thing I've ever seen. But I'll need to give you some lessons.'

'Maybe we could buy a reliable car?'

'We had fun in all of my vehicles, didn't we?' He hopped up the steps and tapped her hip. 'Dismount!' Settling into the driver's seat, he pulled her onto his lap. He started the engine again, waving to the woman capturing everything on her phone as he manoeuvred the big vehicle back onto the street and executed a sharp turn with one hand on the steering wheel. 'Al-lora, where's the sunset?'

ACKNOWLEDGMENTS

As readers will imagine, this book was a joy to research, but not only because of the many wine tastings that went into it. I had a very memorable trip to the Colline del Prosecco and so many special encounters.

My kids deserve a particular mention for this book, because I dragged them with me, down on the train, on all the buses, and they joined in the adventures among the vines – often on foot. We had lots of fun together and I was happy to reward all of us with Pizza Pepe and Giangelato (Giangelato probably deserves its own mention: 'This book was brought to you by the delicious mascarpone ice cream and generous slushies of Giangelato in Bigolino, TV – enjoyed every day during a June trip in a heat wave.' Haha.)

Having my kids with me also had a profound impact on the way the story grew, so I am so grateful that they came with me, despite the various inconveniences of travelling with a ten-year-old, an eight-year-old and a five-year-old! So many friendly and interested people stopped us to chat and there was always someone willing to help us.

An extra special thanks goes to Giulia at the Col del Lupo winery in Vidor, whose inventive children's programme gave my husband and me a wine tasting to remember and an insight into the workings of a small, family-run winery. Also thanks to the staff at Al Canevon and Dea Rivalta for their time.

This book was also made possible by Mobilità di Marca, the public transport enterprise of the province of Treviso. We spent a lot of time on buses and I'm so thankful these services exist for people like me who prefer not to drive (and the many who can't drive).

I am also incredibly thankful to the wonderful author Alessia Saint and her patient husband for putting up with my dialect questions during the editing process and for their enthusiasm for this project, which really motivated me. As always, thanks to my writing community, especially Lucy Keeling, Lucy Morris, Anita Faulkner, Katie Ginger, Emma Jackson, Jaimie Admans, Kate Smith and Jenna Lo Bianco for your support through the whole process. And special thanks to my editor Sarah Ritherdon – working together is just so easy – and my amazing publisher

Boldwood Books, which is doing great things for British publishing.

I also can't complete these acknowledgements without mentioning the boys from Rumatera and Giorgio Gozzo in particular, who have created a wealth of text sources of Veneto dialect (and great music, of course) with their songs. It was a huge highlight to catch a gig from Giorgio Gozzo while I was in Veneto and many of his songs ended up woven into this book, too.

I hope I've done justice to a beautiful and welcoming part of the world and I'm truly grateful that this book gave us an opportunity to explore it.

MORE FROM LEONIE MACK

We hope you enjoyed reading *A Taste of Italian Sunshine*. If you did, please leave a review.

If you'd like to gift a copy, this book is also available as an ebook, paperback, hardback, digital audio download and audiobook CD.

Sign up to Leonie Mack's mailing list for news, competitions and updates on future books.

https://bit.ly/LeonieMackNewsletter

Explore more wonderful escapist romance from Leonie Mack...

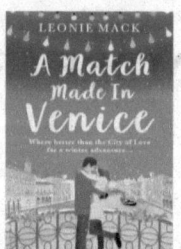

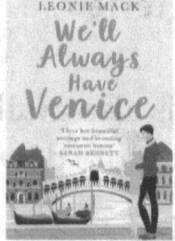

ABOUT THE AUTHOR

Leonie Mack is a bestselling romantic novelist. Having lived in London for many years her home is now in Germany with her husband and three children. Leonie loves train travel, medieval towns, hiking and happy endings!

Visit Leonie's website: https://leoniemack.com/

Follow Leonie on social media:

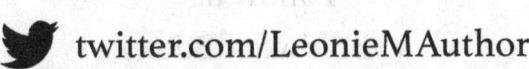 twitter.com/LeonieMAuthor

 instagram.com/leoniejmack

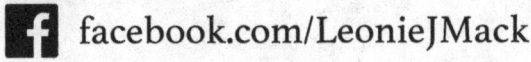 facebook.com/LeonieJMack

Boldwood

Boldwood Books is an award-winning fiction publishing company seeking out the best stories from around the world.

Find out more at www.boldwoodbooks.com

Join our reader community for brilliant books, competitions and offers!

Follow us
@BoldwoodBooks
@BookandTonic

Sign up to our weekly deals newsletter

https://bit.ly/BoldwoodBNewsletter

www.ingramcontent.com/pod-product-compliance
Lightning Source LLC
Chambersburg PA
CBHW010657100726
47900CB00010B/2694